I'm a Little Teapot!

Presenting Preschool Storytime

Compiled by Jane Cobb
Illustrated by Magda Lazicka

BLACK SHEEP PRESS
Vancouver, British Columbia

For all my little friends, large and small, especially Jake. –J.C.

Cover design by James Glen
Photography by Donna Hagerman
Hand Tinting by Nancy Bryant
Cover Model: Rachel Tetrault

Printed in Canada
on recycled paper by Hignell Printing Ltd.

Published by Black Sheep Press

Black Sheep Press
6–2626 Granville Street
Vancouver, BC Canada
V6H 3H8

Black Sheep Press
P.O. Box 2217
Point Roberts, WA USA
98281-2217

on the web: www.blacksheeppress.com
e-mail: info@blacksheeppress.com
tel/fax: (604) 731-2653

Canadian Cataloguing in Publication Data

Cobb, Jane
  I'm a little teapot

  First ed. has title: I don't want to be a teapot.
  Includes bibliographical references and index.
  ISBN 0-9698666-0-7

  1. Storytelling--Handbooks, manuals, etc. 2. Children's
libraries--Activity programs. I. Lazicka, Magda. II. Title.
III. Title: I don't want to be a teapot.
Z718.3.C622 1996   027.62'51   C94-910720-4

Table of Contents

Acknowledgements

Every effort has been made to trace the ownership of all copyrighted material and to secure the necessary permissions to reprint material. The publisher would like to express apologies for any inadvertent omissions.

Grateful acknowledgement is made to the following for permission to reprint the copyrighted material listed below.

A & C Black (Publishers) Ltd. in association with Inter-Action Inprint for the first verse of "The Monster Stomp" by John Perry from *Game-Songs With Prof Dogg's Troupe*. Used by permission.

Amadeo-Brio Music for "Morningtown Ride" by Malvina Reynolds © 1967 Amadeo-Brio Music, International Copyright Secured. Used by permission.

Bernice Wells Carlson for "Five Birthday Candles," "Jack-in-the-Box," "The Little Fish," and "Mr. Tall and Mr. Small," from *Listen! and Help Tell the Story* © 1965 Abingdon Press, renewed 1983 by the author. Used by permission.

Egos Anonymous for "Spider on the Floor" (The Spider Song), © 1977 Egos Anonymous. All rights reserved. Used by permission.

Ell-Bern Publishing Co. for "You'll Sing a Song and I'll Sing a Song," words and music by Ella Jenkins © 1966 Ell-Bern Publiching Co. Used by permission.

Ann Elliott for "Little Arabella Miller" © 1933. Reproduced by permission of Stainer & Bell, London, England.

Robert B. Luce, Inc. for "Clap Your Hands" by Marion Grayson, from *Let's Do Fingerplays* © Robert B. Luce, 1962. Used by permission.

MGA Agency for "Alligator Pie," "Lying on Things," and "Willoughby, Wallaby Woo" from *Alligator Pie* © 1974 Dennis Lee; "Jelly Belly", "Little Miss Dimble," "Lazy Lousy Liza Briggs," and "Thumbelina" from *Jelly Belly* © 1983 Dennis Lee. Used by permission.

Partner Press for "The Brown Kangaroo," "The Elephant's Trunk," "Five Gray Elephants," "Fuzzy Little Caterpillar," "Robbie the Rabbit," "Roly Poly Caterpillar," and "The Yellow Giraffe," from *Finger Frolics*, compiled by Liz Cromwell et al., © Partner Press 1976. Used by permission.

TRO for "Mail Myself To You," words and music by Woody Guthrie, TRO - © 1962 (renewed), 1963 (renewed) Ludlow Music, Inc., New York, NY; "Mary Wore Her Red Dress" (Mary Was a Red Bird), collected, adapted and arranged by Alan Lomax and John A. Lomax, TRO - © 1941 (renewed) Ludlow Music, Inc., New York, NY; "Must Be Santa," words and music by Hal Moore and Bill Fredricks, 1960

Hollis Music Inc., renewed; "Pick a Bale O' Cotton," words and music by Huddie Ledbetter, collected and adapted by John A. Lomax and Alan Lomax, TRO - © 1936 (renewed) Folkways Music Publishers, Inc., New York, NY; "Put Your Finger in the Air," words and music by Woody Guthrie, TRO - © 1954 (renewed) 1963, Folkways Music Publishers, Inc., New York, NY. Used by permission.

Troubadour Records for "Brush Your Teeth," traditional, adapted by Raffi & Louise Dain Cullen, © 1976; "I'm in the Mood," words and music by Raffi, © 1980; "Shake My Sillies Out," music by Raffi, words by Raffi & B. & B. Simpson, © 1977; "Thanks a Lot," words and music by Raffi, © 1980; "Time to Sing," words and music by Raffi, D. Pike, and B. & B. Simpson, © 1985; Homeland Publishing, a division of Troubadour Records Ltd. All rights reserved. Used by permission.

Warner Bros. Publications Inc. for "Frosty the Snowman" by Steve Nelson and Walter E. Rollins © 1950 (renewed); "Here Comes Santa Claus" by Oakley Haldeman and Gene Autry © 1947 (renewed); "Peter Cottontail" by Steve Nelson and Walter E. Rollins © 1949 (renewed). All rights reserved. Used by permission.

The publisher would like to acknowledge Elizabeth Matterson, compiler of *This Little Puffin*, Penguin Books, 1969, and the children's staff of the Flint Public Library, compilers of *Ring a Ring O' Roses* for many of the fingerplays reprinted herein.

The publisher would also like to acknowledge the authors of the following rhymes:

Mary Louise Allen for "The Mitten Song," and "My Zipper Suit;" Maude Burnham for "The Finger Band;" Mrs. Wyn Daniel Evans for "Five Little Ducks," and "Ten Galloping Horses Came Through Town;" Vachel Lindsay for "There Was a Little Turtle;" Mary Britton Miller for "Cat;" Emilie Poulson for "Here Is the Beehive," and "Here's a Ball for Baby;" and Christina Rossetti for "The Pancake" and "Who Has Seen the Wind."

And thanks to all the Children's Librarians and Early Childhood Educators who keep these verses alive by passing them on through the oral tradition.

Introduction

THIS BOOK IS FOR YOU

I'm a Little Teapot is a selection of the best picture books, nursery rhymes, fingerplays, songs, games, and simple craft ideas to use with groups of preschool children at storytime, whether it's in a library, a daycare, a preschool, or at home. It's for preschool teachers planning circle time activities as part of the early childhood education curriculum, for primary teachers developing language arts programs, for librarians planning storytime programs, and it's for parents who are looking for the best books and rhymes to share with their children. It's for everybody who knows how important stories are in children's lives and wants to find their way to the best.

What I sought in the beginning of my career as a children's librarian was a practical handbook for storytime planning with everything I needed in one place. I couldn't find one, so I created my own. And here it is, in a second edition.

NEW, EXPANDED EDITION

I'm a Little Teapot was originally compiled and published in 1986 as a planning handbook for the storytellers at Vancouver Island Regional Library. The title was, *I Don't Want to Be a Teapot! a Handbook for Planning Preschool Storytime*. This book proved to be so popular that an updated and expanded edition was called for.

As a children's librarian I read hundreds of books, thousands of books, millions and billions and trillions of books, and I keep an index of the ones that are most appropriate for preschool storytime. That's how this book was compiled.

The new edition includes: updated lists of more than five hundred STORIES TO READ ALOUD, and the addition of more than five hundred books in new sections, which are MORE STORIES for one-to-one sharing, and NONFICTION. It includes more than five hundred fingerplays and songs, and many more ideas for storytelling and craft activities. It has a new section of RECOMMENDED RESOURCES for further research, a BIBLIOGRAPHY of the books listed within each theme, and an INDEX for easier access to the nursery rhymes, finger-plays and songs.

THEMATIC ARRANGEMENT

I'm a Little Teapot is arranged alphabetically by theme for quick and easy reference. There are sixty-three themes, each of which contains a list of STORIES TO READ ALOUD, MORE STORIES, NONFICTION, NURSERY RHYMES, FINGERPLAYS, SONGS, and MORE IDEAS.

While many storytellers plan programs on a single theme, particularly for special occasions like Halloween, many of us find planning a more rewarding experience when we let the stories themselves suggest alternate thematic directions.

I like to use the themes as a way of finding relevant fingerplays and songs. Then I let the needs of my particular audience, the availability of books, and the mood of the moment be my guide, rather than letting myself be constrained by the choice of a particular theme.

STORIES TO READ ALOUD is a selection of the very best stories, new and old, that are just the right length to hold the attention of a preschool audience, which is about five minutes. They also have pictures that are large enough for an audience of about twenty-five children to see. They were chosen for their poetic language (sound and imagery), clear plot structures, captivating illustrations, balance between pictures and text on each page, as well as for their charm and child appeal.

MORE STORIES is a selection of more wonderful stories that are ideal for situations other than group storytime, such as one-to-one sharing. They are either too long for the preschool group experience, wordless, too simple or too sophisticated for a typical preschool group, or they may have tiny illustrations. Some are adaptable to alternate forms of presentation, through puppetry or on the felt board. I display these at storytime, sometimes giving a brief book talk, so the children can check them out after a library program.

NONFICTION is a selection of informational books related to the themes that are designed specifically for young children. There has been a publishing explosion in the field of nonfiction for young children in recent years, which is cause for celebration. These books satisfy inquisitive preschoolers who are bursting with curiosity about the real world, and they satisfy parents who often want books about real people, places, and things to read to their children. These usually lack the language and literature qualities I'm looking for in a group read-aloud, but they are great for one-to-one sharing and discussion. I also display these at storytime. A story about a dog leads to a comment about "my dog," and then a nonfiction book like *A Puppy Is Born* becomes relevant.

The **NURSERY RHYMES, FINGERPLAYS,** and **SONGS** that follow the books have been culled from various sources, most of which can be found in RECOMMENDED RESOURCES at the back of this book. These participation activities add an element of fun to a storytime program, and help children listen and enjoy. The song title comments throughout this new edition and the index to SONGS ON SOUND RECORDINGS will be useful to those who want to add the spice of music to their storytime programs.

MORE IDEAS is the section reserved for comments such as which stories in that particular theme work best for presentation on the felt board, references to other storytelling resources, such as draw-and-tell, as well as participation stories, and some ideas for simple crafts and games.

WHERE TO FIND THE BOOKS

The bibliographies in the back of this book are meant to be a selection guide for those who want to develop their own storytime collections. All of these books should be available at your public library.

Most of the books listed in STORIES TO READ ALOUD and MORE STORIES will be found in the library's picture book collection, filed on the shelf by the first letter in the author's last name. Folk and fairy tales, like the *Three Billy Goats Gruff* and *The Three Bears* will be found in the children's nonfiction section in 398.2, and nursery rhymes, like *The Three Little Kittens,* will be in 398.8. Song books, like *Hush Little Baby,* will be in 784, and poetry, like Dennis Lee's *Alligator Pie,* will be in 821.

Librarians have different ways of classifying NONFICTION for young children. Sometimes you will find concept books, such as alphabet and counting books, in the fiction section under the authors' last names, and sometimes you will find them in the nonfiction section classified by Dewey decimal number. When in doubt about how things work in your own library, ask your children's librarian!

GOOD LUCK

I hope this book will be an inspiration to you as you pick and choose and plan storytime programs that are right for you and your own groups of children. I hope it will make planning easier. When you are well prepared, then you will be ready to enjoy the other half of the story-time experience — the pleasure of your children's responses. Have fun!

Program Planning

If you are planning a storytime program that will take place in a public library, you will want to have made some decisions about your program before you begin to choose the books and rhymes you will present at each storytime. You will want to have made decisions about: the time and day of the week you will present the program, the duration of the session, the location for the program, the age range of the children you will invite, and the desired size of your audience. You will want to have decided whether it will be a drop-in affair, or whether you will take registrations and make name tags for the children. You might have decided to make name tags for the caregivers too, as this is a nice way for parents and caregivers in the community to get to know one another. After all of these issues have been settled, and you've advertised your session, you will want to start planning the contents for your weekly programs. That is where this book begins.

This section briefly describes the goals, the format of storytime, and the planning process. The next section describes some presentation techniques. The third section offers some tried and true examples of opening and closing songs and fingerplays, and some all-time anytime favourites.

PURPOSE

I often remind myself of the purpose of story-time: to introduce the pleasure of stories, to inspire excitement about learning to read, and to provide access to the world of books and ideas. What children gain is what we all gain from reading stories: entertainment and diversion, vicarious experience, and information. On a deeper level they gain a greater understanding of themselves and the world around them, new ways of seeing themselves and their experiences, new ways of describing their thoughts and feelings, and reassurance that someone else has thought and felt the way they do. Ultimately they are learning the language that they need to express themselves and to communicate with other people. What the attending adults gain is a way of interpreting and using books with children, and a repertoire of songs and rhymes to use in educational play with children at home.

PROGRAM STRUCTURE

A typical storytime program in the public library takes about thirty minutes to perform, and looks like this:

Opening Rituals (five minutes), Daily Program (twenty minutes), and Closing Rituals (five minutes). Each read-aloud story takes about five minutes, and each fingerplay or song takes two to three minutes. Here's a map.

OPENING RITUALS

-Opening song.

-Opening fingerplay.

-Greeting from puppet. (optional)

DAILY PROGRAM

-Read-aloud story #1.

-Fingerplay or song.

-Read-aloud story #2.

-Fingerplay or song.

-Read-aloud or told story #3.

CLOSING RITUALS

-Closing song.

-Goodbye from puppet. (optional)

-Rubber hand stamp. (optional)

When time permits, especially in preschool and classroom situations, crafts and games based on the day's stories can be added successfully at the end of a storytime program. You will find ideas for this in MORE IDEAS at the end of each theme in this book.

OPENING & CLOSING RITUALS

Opening and closing rituals envelop the body of the program and are repeated each week. The rituals signal the beginning and end of the program each day, and make the children feel secure and comfortable within a familiar framework. Many storytellers play recorded music to welcome children as they gather before the program. The opening ritual then includes a greeting song and an opening fingerplay. Often a puppet mascot is then used to welcome the children and introduce the theme for the day or the first read-aloud story. Playing a musical instrument such as a guitar, a recorder, or a kazoo is a nice way to gather everyone together.

Close the program the way you began, with a song or with your puppet saying goodbye. Rubber stamps based on characters from the day's stories applied to little hands at the very end are a great expectation in most libraries. It's a nice way to have a moment's close contact with individual children, and the smudged little image that remains later in the day will help them remember the storytime experience.

My favourite rubber stamps are designed by children's book illustrators, and come from Kidstamps. Send for a catalogue and price list to Kidstamps, P.O. Box 18699, Cleveland Heights, Ohio, 44118 U.S.A.

PREPARING DAILY PROGRAMS

Once you have chosen the opening and closing rituals you will use each week, you will be ready to plan the contents of each program. Follow these steps, and you won't go wrong.

1. CHOOSE THE THEME FOR EACH DAY.

Start with a calendar and identify all the holidays and special days in the season that you want to celebrate. Think about what will be going on in the children's lives at that particular time of year. In the autumn, plan for back to school, Thanksgiving and the harvest, Halloween and monsters, the departure of the ducks and geese, the changing seasons, and hibernation. In the spring, plan for Valentine's Day, Easter, birthdays, Mother's Day, gardening and so on. Let yourself be inspired by a new book or by favourite stories. Have a variety of materials to choose from, and remain flexible enough to respond to the children's interests. If someone has a new baby at home, for example, celebrate babies the next time you meet.

2. CHOOSE STORIES TO READ ALOUD.

When you have found a theme or idea you like, choose three or four stories you like from the read-aloud lists in this book. When choosing the stories, try to vary the mood and pace, and choose at least one story that invites participation. There is only one unbreakable rule here: never choose to share a story that you don't love yourself. It's a good idea to read the longest story first while the children's attention is sharp. The last story of the program is usually presented with felts or puppets.

Further notes on book selection. Keep in mind the preschool child's experience of the world, and your group's experience in particular. Be sensitive to the children's need to see themselves reflected in the stories you read to them. Lots of city children live in apartment buildings, not in houses. Lots of children have one parent, not two. Not all children have white skin, not all children come from middle-class homes, not all children are boys. And so on. In choosing stories and rhymes to tell, aim for a balance that includes difference and diversity.

3. CHOOSE STORIES FOR BOOKTALK AND DISPLAY.

Make your selections for booktalks and displays from the STORIES TO READ ALOUD, MORE STORIES and NONFICTION lists in each theme. Add audio and video cassettes as you like. This is a way to introduce children and caregivers to all the great books and materials they can share at home. Children will want to look at these before storytime and check them out after a library program.

4. CHOOSE NURSERY RHYMES.

The rhythm and rhyme of nursery rhymes makes them eminently suitable for preschool storytime. Children love the sound and enjoy the nonsense. Like traditional folktales, they contain stock characters that should be a part of every child's early language experience. Use liberally and repeat often. Read picture book versions aloud, sing, or clap to the rhythm of the beat. Present them with finger puppets or on the felt board. There is a core list of single editions and collections of poetry and nursery rhymes just right for this age group in RECOMMENDED RESOURCES.

5. CHOOSE FINGERPLAYS & ACTION RHYMES.

Fingerplays and action rhymes are an essential component of every storytime program. They provide a graceful transition between the read-aloud stories, and an opportunity for the children to participate in a playful activity that involves language and physical movement. They also provide a short release from quiet listening. When these are acted out, they become action rhymes which provide an opportunity for dramatic interpretation. Many of these, too, can be presented with finger puppets or on the felt board. The ones that are most adaptable to these purposes are noted throughout this book.

As it is with the picture books you choose to read aloud, it is important to select only the best fingerplay verses to recite. And it is more important to choose a good rhyme than it is to choose a rhyme that matches the theme of the book you've just read. The best have a memorable rhythm and rhyme and are often lovely little stories in themselves.

6. CHOOSE SONGS TO SING

Music is used in a variety of ways at storytime: to sing hello, to say goodbye, to instill a quiet wistful mood, or to entice excited involvement in a participation game. An easy way to learn good songs, even if you have inherited the old family piano and you can read music, is to listen to children's audio cassettes. Canada has a vast array of talented children's musicians to choose from. My favourites for learning songs for storytime are Raffi, Pat Carfra, Bob McGrath, Katharine Smithrim, and Sharon, Lois & Bram. Ella Jenkins has a lovely style with preschoolers, and her material is available on CD and video cassette. References to sound and music where these are available have been included in notes after the song titles throughout this book. You will also find an index to selected cassettes in SONGS ON SOUND RECORDINGS in RECOMMENDED RESOURCES at the back of the book.

7. CHOOSE STORIES TO TELL

It's a good idea to include at least one story with strong visual representation at every program for young children, and one of the easiest mediums for this is the felt board. Most story-tellers in the public library save this for the last story in the program when attention may be waning for some. I like to tell participation stories.

You will find suggestions for puppetry, draw-and-tell, and participation stories in MORE IDEAS at the end of each theme, and even more ideas in the STORYTELLING section in RECOMMENDED RESOURCES.

8. PRACTISE!

Once you have made your selection of material, read the stories you will be presenting enough times to know them well, and memorize all the little rhymes and activities that go between. Some storytellers use index cards for new rhymes, but storytime is a much more rewarding experience for you and the children if you know the rhymes by heart.

FELT STORIES

Felt stories, also called flannelgraphs, are a popular choice for preschool storytime for many reasons. They provide a visual focus to a told story, they are especially appropriate for presentation to large audiences, and they are essential for ESL and special needs children who require lots of visual stimulation to understand and stay involved with a story.

Telling rather than reading a story also provides you, the storyteller, with an opportunity to look at your audience, which is a most satisfying experience for all concerned. Although you should know the story well enough to tell by heart, the felt pieces act at prompts, so you can hardly miss if the pieces are in order. Always check this before your program.

Read-aloud stories can also be repeated as felt participation stories in later programs. Hand out pieces to the children and invite them to add the pieces to the felt board in turn as you tell the story. It's a good idea to have lots of clouds or pieces of chocolate cake in reserve so that every child has something to add. My children have always found this a thrilling experience, and if they are not too shy, they will even repeat their characters' lines.

Here are some criteria to use when selecting stories to make in felt. Choose stories with clear and simple plot structures, cumulative story lines, and repetitive language. Reduce the numbers for stories with too many little pieces, stories like *The Snake that Sneezed* and *Caps for Sale*, for example.

Three books on the STORYTELLING list include patterns for felt stories. They are Anderson's *Storytelling with the Flannel Board*, and Judy Sierra's two books, *Flannel Board Storytelling Book* and *Multicultural Folktales: Stories to Tell Young Children*.

For a list of felt stories made for the Vancouver Public Library, and available for purchase at reasonable prices, contact: The 3H Society, 2112 West 4th Avenue, Vancouver, B.C. V6K 1N6 (604) 736-2113.

A CORE LIST OF FELT STORIES

Here is a list of tried and true stories that work in felt – stories that come in many illustrated versions, and some notable picture books:

Goldilocks and the Three Bears.

The House That Jack Built.

Old Mother Hubbard and Her Dog.

"Strange Company," (From Judy Sierra's *Flannel Board Storytelling Book.)*

The Three Billy Goats Gruff.

The Three Little Kittens.

The Three Little Pigs.

Aliki. *Hush Little Baby.*

Asch, Frank. *Monkey Face.*

Balian, Lorna. *Humbug Witch.*

Bright, Robert. *My Red Umbrella.*

Brown, Margaret Wise. *Runaway Bunny.*

Burningham, John. *Mr. Gumpy's Motor Car.*

Burningham, John. *Mr. Gumpy's Outing.*

Carle, Eric. *The Very Hungry Caterpillar.*

De Paola, Tomie. *I Love You Mouse.*

Ets, Marie Hall. *Elephant in a Well.*

Flack, Marjorie. *Ask Mr. Bear.*

Galdone, Paul. *Henny Penny.*

Galdone, Paul. *Over in the Meadow.*

Galdone, Paul. *The Three Billy Goats Gruff.*

Ginsburg, Mirra. *Mushroom in the Rain.*

Harper, Wilhelmina. *The Gunniwolf.*

Hewitt, Anita. *Mrs. Mopple's Washing Line.*

Kalan, Robert. *Jump, Frog, Jump.*

Kent, Jack. *Fat Cat.*

Lotteridge, Celia. *The Name of the Tree.*

McGovern, Ann. *Too Much Noise.*

Martin, Bill. *Brown Bear, Brown Bear.*

Leydenfrost, Robert. *The Snake That Sneezed.*

Nicol, B.P. *Once, a Lullaby.*

Preston, Edna. *One Dark Night.*

Rees, Mary. *Ten in a Bed.*

Rockwell, Anne. "The Gingerbread Man" from *The Three Bears and Other Stories.*

Rockwell, Anne. *Poor Goose.*

Shaw, Charles. *It Looked Like Spilt Milk.*

Slobodkina, Esphyr. *Caps for Sale.* (six monkeys and seven caps will do.)

Tolstoy, Alexei. *The Great Big Enormous Turnip.*

Tresselt, Alvin. *The Mitten.*

Van Laan, Nancy. The *Big Fat Worm.*

Watanabe, Shigeo. *How Do I Put It On?*

Zolotow, Charlotte. *Mr. Rabbit and the Lovely Present.*

USING FOLK & FAIRY TALES

Traditional folk and fairy tales for young audiences that have short strong plots and plenty of dramatic action are good for preschool storytime too. There are many illustrated versions of these to enjoy.

Some notable picture book versions are listed in FOLK & FAIRY TALES in RECOMMENDED RESOURCES at the back of this book.

Judy Sierra's *Multicultural Folktales* is a great resource to use for stories that include children from different cultures and to introduce different cultural traditions at storytime.

Save fairy tales like *Beauty and the Beast* and *Sleeping Beauty* for school-aged children. These are far too sophisticated for the average preschool child and are too long and complex for preschool storytime.

Here is a core list for young audiences.

The Three Little Pigs

Goldilocks and the Three Bears

The Three Billy Goats Gruff

Jack and the Beanstalk

The Princess and the Pea

Henny Penny

Little Red Riding Hood

Presentation Tips

There are many books on the lists of RECOMMENDED RESOURCES that describe storytelling techniques, including the use of puppets and felt (or flannel) board stories. These can help with your presentation. You can also visit a public library at storytime and watch a children's librarian, who's probably been telling stories for years. Have confidence. With experience you will soon develop an inimitable style of your own.

INTRODUCING A STORY

Introduce the author, title, and illustrator by name so that children and their attending caregivers can become familiar with them. This will help them find the books they like on their own, another time.

Tell the audience where the story or song comes from if it's from a folk tradition. This stretches children's awareness of the world, and makes those with different cultural backgrounds feel proud of their heritage.

You might also comment on the age of a book or story. This might be why the illustrations are black and white. This contributes to an awareness of the history of children's books.

Mention something about the illustrator's technique –that all of the pictures were created out of plasticine, for example, when introducing Barbara Reid. Plasticine is a children's medium after all, so children are enthralled by that idea.

Mention the award winners, especially if there is a medal on the front cover of the book, so that the audience can become aware of these and what they mean.

All of this takes only a few seconds, and your comments will stimulate the children's curiosity about and involvement with books.

Explain unusual words and concepts before you begin a story. Say, "Does everybody know what a python is?" before you read *Why Mosquitoes Buzz in People's Ears*, for example. "Right, it's a snake. And the big snake in this story is referred to as a python."

Similarly, if you want the children to participate by singing along with you at the appropriate places in the story, as you would with *The Gunniwolf*, for example, it's a good idea to teach them the song first. Listening is heightened by the anticipation of joining in at the right moment.

I usually introduce a story like this. I'll say, "This is a story about a grumpy old sheep named Amos. Have you ever felt grumpy? Me too. Let's find out why Amos is so grumpy." Then title, author, illustrator, and away we go. "Grumpy" is a concept children can relate to, so I focus on that.

Some stories are best introduced with a question. "Does anyone here have a baby at home? You do? And do you help take care of her? That's good. Well this is a story about a little girl named Robin who finds a baby in her sand box one day. Imagine! Let's find out what she does with it." I don't usually give away the surprise, but in this case it doesn't ruin the suspense.

The point of the introduction is to draw the children into the story, and to help them find the story's connection to their own lives so they can relate to it in a personal way.

READING ALOUD

Here are some tips on physical handling. Hold the book so that the whole audience can see the illustrations. Hold it up for people in the back, and down for people in the front. Pan to the right and to the left. Vary right and left hand delivery. Tip the book slightly forward to avoid glare from overhead lighting, and to compensate for your slightly elevated position when reading to children seated on the floor. Be careful not to obstruct the view with your hand while turning pages. Make sure the illustrations on each page match the text you are reading aloud.

Speak clearly, enunciating each word, and project your voice so that the children in the back row can hear you. Use volume, speed, pitch, tone, and inflection to read with expression! Make sure you can sustain character voices if you choose to use them. Keep an even pace overall, and slow down for younger audiences, and for children whose first language is other than English.

Respect the author's carefully chosen words, and each story's integrity, and do not interrupt the flow with your own personal comments. Do not paraphrase or skip read. If these comments are necessary, you've got a book that is more appropriate for a different group or for one-to-one sharing.

DISCUSSING A STORY

At the end of a story, close the book showing the front cover again, and repeat the title, author, and illustrator. Then pause to give the children time to respond. Some child-directed discussion may ensue. Encourage children to talk about characters, surprises, and what they thought was interesting about a story. These responses will give you insights into the way your children think, and will help you select more material that they will like. This is also an important time to include as it provides a sense of closure, and brings the children's awareness out of the story and back to storytime in preparation for the next activity. If discussion gets out of control, a song or fingerplay will usually grab everyone's attention again.

INTRODUCING FINGERPLAYS

Memorize the verses to songs and fingerplays, and repeat them often so children and their caregivers can learn them and repeat them at home. When new verses are introduced, they should always be repeated on the spot.

Play with these! You can get a lot of mileage out of a short verse by repeating it. Speed it up and turn up the volume to build excitement, then slow it down and whisper to quiet the group at the end.

You can count on some distraction during storytime, and you can count on songs, finger-plays and action rhymes to bring the children's attention back to you. Your group will let you know what their favourties are.

ARTS, CRAFTS & GAMES

Follow-up activities, in the form of arts, crafts, or games, reinforce and extend a story's content and meaning for children. How much more memorable is "Alligator Pie" with a real (egg carton) alligator to chant with! Or a real (spinach) alligator pie to munch on for lunch!

Songs and rhymes from the story program can be sung or chanted with great pleasure during the activity. If you break up for arts and crafts, be sure to bring everyone together again for a song to close the program.

For a bibliography of useful resources on this topic, see ARTS, CRAFTS, & ACTIVITIES in RECOMMENDED RESOURCES at the back of this book.

IN CLOSING

The time for hand stamps at the end of the program is the time for individual attention and discussion. This is the time for hugs and thank yous and the little intimacies that make story-time such a rewarding experience. As you get to know the children, they will tell you about thoughts and incidents in their world that were triggered by the stories. Usually it's of this variety: "You know what?" "What?" "Our cat had kittens and . . . " And it's important for you to listen to these comments, not just to be polite, not just because children need to be listened to, but because they can give you free ideas for future storytime programs!

Songs & Fingerplays
for Opening, Closing, & Anytime In Between

OPENING SONGS

Hello Everybody

Hello everybody, how d'ya do,
How d'ya do, how d'ya do?
Hello everybody, how d'ya do,
How are you today?

Hello everybody, clap your hands,
Clap your hands, clap your hands,
Hello everybody, clap your hands,
How are you today?
Hello everybody, . . .

> *Repeat as above.*

. . . stamp your feet,
. . . touch your nose,
. . . touch your toes,
. . . how d'ya do.

Let's Clap Our Hands Together

> *Suit actions to words. Make up your own verses.*
> *Sing to the tune of "If I Could Have a Windmill."*
> *You can listen to that song on Sharon, Lois &*
> *Bram's cassette* Great Big Hits. *See music in*
> Sharon, Lois & Bram's Mother Goose.

Let's clap our hands together,
Let's clap our hands together,
Let's clap our hands together,
Because it's fun to do.

Let's tap our legs together . . .
Let's stomp our feet together . . .
Let's blink our eyes together . . .
Let's hit the ground together . . .

The More We Get Together

> *Listen to the tune on Bob McGrath's* Sing Along
> with Bob, Vol. One. *Words and music are in Tom*
> *Glazer's* Eye Winker, Tom Tinker, Chin
> Chopper.

The more we get together, together, together,
The more we get together, the happier we'll be.
For your friends are my friends,
And my friends are your friends.
The more we get together, the happier we'll be.

The more we read together . . .
The more we sing together . . .

> *Repeat first verse.*

Hello, My Friends, Hello

> *This is a lovely multicultural opener. Add any other*
> *languages, as you like.*

Hello, my friends, hello,
Hello, my friends, hello,
Hello, my friends, hello, my friends,
Hello, my friends.

in Coast Salish:
Ee ch aw' y al,' my friends, ee ch aw' y al' . . .

in Cantonese:
Nay ho ma, my friends, nay ho ma . . .

in French:
Bonjour, mes amies, bonjour,

in German:
Guten tag, my friends, guten tag . . .

in Hindi:
Na mustay, meri dost, na mustay . . .

in Japanese:
Kanishiwa, my friends, kanishiwa . . .

in Korean:
Yo bo say yo, my friends, yo bo say yo . . .

in Punjabi:
Sat sri akal, meri dost, sat sri akal . . .

in Spanish:
Ola, mis amigos, Ola . . .

in Swahili:
Jambo, my friends, jambo . . .

in Tagalog:
Komasta, my friends, komasta . . .

in Ukrainian:
Yukshamia, my friends, yukshamia . . .

You'll Sing a Song and I'll Sing a Song

> *Listen to the sound of Ella Jenkins as she sings tunes*
> *perfect for preschoolers on her CD* You'll Sing a
> Song and I'll Sing a Song.

You'll sing a song, and I'll sing a song,
And we'll sing a song together.
You'll sing a song, and I'll sing a song,
In warm or wintry weather.

You'll play a tune, and I'll play a tune . . .
You'll whistle a tune, and I'll whistle a tune . . .

Time to Sing

Listen to the tune on Raffi's cassette, One Light, One Sun. *Words and music are in* The Second Raffi Songbook.

It's time to sing a song or two,
You with me and me with you.
Time for us to sing a-while,
Hey, hey, hey.

It's time for us to clap our hands,
In rhythm to the beat.
Time for hands to clap a-while,
Hey, hey, hey.

And it's time for saying, 'Hi' and 'Hello'
Let's all sing a song that we know.

It's time to tap our toes,
Together with our feet.
Time for toes to tap a-while,
Hey, hey, hey.

It's time to make a sound you like,

Whistle or hum the verse.

It's time to sing a song or two,
You with me and me with you.
Time for us to sing a-while,
Hey, hey, hey.

I'm in the Mood for Stories

This is an adaptation of Raffi's "I'm in The Mood . . ." for storytime. The tune is on Raffi's Rise and Shine *cassette. Words and music to Raffi's song are in* The Second Raffi Songbook.

I'm in the mood for stories.
Hey, how about you?
I'm in the mood for stories.
Hey, how about you?
I'm in the mood for stories,
Stories to share with you.
Hey, hey, what do you say?
I'm in the mood for that today.
Hey, hey, what do you say?
I'm in the mood for that.

I'm in the mood for listening . . .
I'm in the mood for singing . . .
I'm in the mood for clapping . . .

OPENING FINGERPLAYS

Open Them, Shut Them

Hold up ten fingers.

Open them, shut them,
Open and clench fists.
Open them, shut them,
Open and close again.
Give them a great big clap.
Clap.
Open them, shut them,
Open them, shut them,
Repeat as above.
Fold them together,
And put them in your lap.
Fold together and place in lap.
Now creep them, creep them,
Right up to your little mouth,
Creep like spiders up to your mouth.
But don't put them in!
Shake head.
Now set them on your shoulders,
Set hands on shoulders.
And like little birds let them fly up into the sky,
Flutter fingers up high.
Way up high.
Stretch.
Then falling, falling, almost to the ground,
Flutter almost to the ground.
Quickly pick them up again
Sweep hands up and roll round and round.
And turn them round and round,
Roll hands.
Faster and faster and faster,
Roll quickly.
Then slower and slower and slower,
Roll slowly.
And fold them together,
And put them in your lap.

Sometimes

Sometimes my hands are at my side,
Then behind my back they hide.
Sometimes I wiggle my fingers so,
Shake them fast, shake them slow.
Sometimes my hands go clap, clap, clap,
Then I rest them in my lap.
Now they're quiet as can be
Because it's listening time, you see.

I Have Ten Little Fingers

I have ten little fingers,
> *Hold up ten fingers.*

And they all belong to me.
I can make them do things,
Would you like to see?
> *Wiggle fingers.*

I can shut them up tight,
> *Clench fists.*

Or open them all wide.
> *Open wide.*

I can put them all together,
> *Interlock fingers.*

Or make them all hide.
> *Hide them behind your back.*

I can make them jump high;
> *Fingers jump to the sky.*

I can make them jump low.
> *Fingers jump to the floor.*

I can fold them quietly,
> *Fold hands together.*

And hold them just so.
> *Place in lap.*

CLOSING SONGS

So Long
> *Children join hands and sway to the music.*

So long, it's been good to see you,
So long, it's been good to see you,
So long, it's been good to see you,
So long, and I'll see you next week.

Now It's Time to Say Goodbye
> *Sing to the tune of "London Bridge."*

Now it's time to say goodbye,
Say goodbye, say goodbye,
Now it's time to say goodbye,
I'll see you all next week.
> *Say goodbye to all the children by name,
> then repeat the song.*

Goodbye, My Friends, Goodbye
> *Here is a closing song to go with "Hello, My Friends." Ask your audience for more ways to say goodbye.*

Goodbye, my friends, goodbye,
Goodbye, my friends, goodbye,
Goodbye, my friends, goodbye, my friends,
Goodbye, my friends.

in Coast Salish:
Ee tsun, my friends, ee tsun . . .

in Cantonese:
Joy-guin, my friends, joy-guin . . .

in French:
Au revoir, mes amies, au revoir,

in German:
Auf wiedersehn, my friends, auf wiedersehn . . .

in Hindi:
Namustay, meri dost, namustay . . .

in Japanese:
Sayonora, my friends, Sayonora . . .

in Korean:
An yiung, my friends, an yiung . . .

in Punjabi:
Sat siri akal, meri dost, sat siri akal . . .

in Swahili:
Kwahiri, my friends, kwahiri . . .

in Spanish:
Adios, mis amigos, adios . . .

in Tagalog:
Pa-a-lam, my friends, pa-a-lam . . .

in Ukranian:
Yukshamia, my friends, yukshamia . . .

SONGS & FINGERPLAYS FOR ANYTIME IN-BETWEEN

Shake My Sillies Out

Thank you Raffi! Listen to the tune on Raffi's cassette, More Singable Songs. *Words and music are in* The Raffi Singable Songbook.

Everybody stand up and suit actions to words.

Gotta shake, shake, shake my sillies out
Shake, shake, shake my sillies out
Shake, shake, shake my sillies out
And wiggle my waggles away.

Gotta clap, clap, clap my crazies out . . .
Gotta jump, jump, jump my jiggles out . . .
Gotta yawn, yawn, yawn my sleepies out . . .
Gotta shake, shake, shake my sillies out . . .

This Little Light of Mine

Listen to the tune of this popular classic on Raffi's Rise and Shine *cassette. See music in* The Second Raffi Songbook. *A song to keep for a lifetime!*

Chorus:
This little light of mine,
I'm gonna let it shine.
This little light of mine,
I'm gonna let it shine.
This little light of mine,
I'm gonna let it shine.
Let it shine, let it shine, let it shine.
    Hold up one finger throughout.

I'm gonna take this light around the world,
And I'm gonna let it shine.
I'm gonna take this light around the world,
And I'm gonna let it shine.
I'm gonna take this light around the world,
And I'm gonna let it shine.
Let it shine, let it shine, let it shine.
    Describe a big circle with that finger, three times.
    Repeat chorus.

I won't let anyone blow it out,
I'm gonna let it shine.
I won't let anyone blow it out,
I'm gonna let it shine.
I won't let anyone blow it out,
I'm gonna let it shine.
    Blow on finger three times.

    Repeat chorus.

Put Your Finger in the Air

Thank you Woody Guthrie! Same tune as Raffi's "Spider on the Floor." Bob McGrath sings it on his cassette Sing Along with Bob, Vol. Two. *Words and music are in Tom Glazer's* Eye Winker Tom Tinker Chin Chopper. *Suit actions to words.*

Put your finger in the air, in the air,
Put your finger in the air, in the air,
Put your finger in the air,
And leave it about a year,
Put your finger in the air, in the air.

Put your finger on your head, on your head,
Put your finger on your head, on your head,
Put your finger on your head,
Tell me is it green or red?
Put your finger on your head, on your head.

Put your finger on your nose, on your nose,
Put your finger on your nose, on your nose,
Put your finger on your nose,
And let the cold wind blow,
Put your finger on your nose, on your nose.

Put your finger on your shoe, on your shoe,
Put your finger on your shoe, on your shoe,
Put your finger on your shoe,
And leave it a week or two,
Put your finger on your shoe, on your shoe.

Put your finger on your chin, on your chin,
Put your finger on your chin, on your chin,
Put your finger on your chin,
That's where the food slips in,
Put your finger on your chin, on your chin.

Put your finger on your cheek, on your cheek,
Put your finger on your cheek, on your cheek,
Put your finger on your cheek,
And leave it about a week,
Put your finger on your cheek, on your cheek.

Put your finger on your belly, on your belly,
Put your finger on your belly, on your belly,
Put your finger on your belly,
And shake it like apple jelly,
Put your finger on your belly, on your belly.

Put your fingers all together, all together,
Put your fingers all together, all together,
Put your fingers all together,
And we'll clap for better weather,
Put your fingers all together, all together.

I Wiggle My Fingers

Hold up ten fingers and act it out!

I wiggle my fingers,
I wiggle my toes,
I wiggle my shoulders,
I wiggle my nose.
Now all the wiggles
Are out of me
And I'm just as quiet
As I can be.

Not Say a Single Word

Act this out standing up, or leave it as a fingerplay.

Can you hop, hop, hop like a bunny,
Hopping motion with hand.

And run, run, run like a dog?
Running motion with fingers.

Can you walk, walk, walk like an elephant,
Walking motion with arms.

And jump, jump, jump like a frog?
Jumping motions with arms.

Can you swim, swim, swim like a goldfish,
Swimming motion with hands.

And fly, fly, fly like a bird?
Flying motion with arms.

Can you sit right down and fold your hands,
Fold hands in lap.

And not say a single word?
Hush finger to lips.

Teddy Bear, Teddy Bear

Everybody stand up!

Teddy bear, teddy bear, turn around;
Turn around.

Teddy bear, teddy bear, touch the ground.
Touch the ground.

Teddy bear, teddy bear, show your shoe;
Hold out foot.

Teddy bear, teddy bear, I love you.
Give yourself a big hug.

Teddy bear, teddy bear, climb upstairs;
Climb up stairs.

Teddy bear, teddy bear, say your prayers.
Hands in prayer.

Teddy bear, teddy bear, turn out the light;
Switch out the light.

Teddy bear, teddy bear, say, "good night!"
Head on hands folded together.

Tommy Thumbs

Tommy Thumbs up and
Thumbs up, both hands.

Tommy Thumbs down,
Thumbs down.

Tommy Thumbs dancing
Thumbs up and bounce to the right.

All around the town.
Bounce to the left in front of you.

Dance 'em on your shoulders,
Bounce them on your shoulders.

Dance 'em on your head,
Bounce them on your head.

Dance 'em on your knees and
Bounce them on your knees.

Tuck them into bed.
Fold arms hiding hands.

Peter Pointer up and Peter Pointer down . . .
Repeat using index finger.

Toby Tall up and Toby Tall down . . .
Repeat using tall finger, and so on.

Ring Man up and Ring Man down . . .
Baby Finger up and Baby Finger down . . .
Finger Family up and Finger Family down . . .

Head and Shoulders

Sing to the tune of "London Bridge Is Falling Down." This is a nice stretch, anytime, especially for younger children.

Head and shoulders,
Place hands on head, then shoulders.

Knees and toes,
Knees and toes.

Knees and toes,
Repeat knees and toes.

Knees and toes,
Repeat knees and toes.

Head and shoulders,
Place hands on head, shoulders,

Knees and toes,
Repeat knees and toes.

Eyes, ears, mouth and nose.
Point to eyes, ears, mouth and nose.

Tête, Epaule

"Head and Shoulders" in French.

Tête, épaules, genoux et pieds
Genoux et pieds, genoux et pieds
Tête, épaule, genoux et pieds
Yeux, oreilles, bouche et nez.

Head and Shoulders, Baby

*Here is a jazzier version for older children. Listen
to the tune on Sharon, Lois & Bram's cassette* Car
Tunes for Schooldays *or* Smorgasbord. *See
music in* Elephant Jam. *Make up your own
verses.*

Head and shoulders, baby; one, two, three.
Head and shoulders, baby; one, two, three.
Head and shoulders,
Head and shoulders,
Head and shoulders, baby; one, two, three.
*Touch head and shoulders and clap on one, two
three.*

Hips and thighs, baby . . .
Knees and ankles, baby . . .
Do the twist, baby . . .

Clap Your Hands

Clap your hands, clap your hands,
Clap them just like me.
Touch your shoulders, touch your shoulders,
Touch them just like me.
Tap your knees, tap your knees,
Tap them just like me.
Clap your hands, clap your hands,
Now let them quiet be.

Wiggle Fingers

Wiggle fingers, wiggle so,
Wiggle high, wiggle low,
Wiggle left, wiggle right,
Wiggle fingers out of sight.

Two little feet go tap, tap, tap,

Two little feet go tap, tap, tap,
Two little hands go clap, clap, clap,
Two little fists go thump, thump, thump,
Two little legs go jump, jump, jump,
One little child turns slowly around,
One little child sits quietly down.

We All Clap Hands Together

*Sing to the tune of "If I Could Have a Windmill."
You can listen to that song on Sharon, Lois &
Bram's cassette* Great Big Hits. *See music in
Sharon, Lois & Bram's* Mother Goose.

We all clap hands together, together, together,
We all clap hands together because it's fun to do.

We all stand up together, together, together,
We all stand up together because it's fun to do.

We all turn round together . . .
We all sit down together . . .
We all fall down together . . .

Fun With Hands

*Suit actions to words. Sing to the tune of "Row,
Row, Row Your Boat" if you like.*

Roll, roll, roll your hands,
As slowly as can be.
Roll, roll, roll your hands,
Do it now with me.
Roll, roll, roll your hands,
As fast, as fast can be.
Roll, roll, roll your hands,
Do it now with me.

Clap, clap, clap your hands . . .
Shake, shake, shake your hands . . .
Stamp, stamp, stamp your feet . . .

A Ram Sam Sam

*This one is nice as a chant or a song. Watch the
way Katharine Smithrim does it with toddlers on
her video* Songs and Games for Toddlers, *or
listen to the tune on the cassette of the same name.
Speed it up with volume, and slow it down with a
whisper.*

A ram sam sam, a ram sam sam,
Clap three times on ram sam sam.

Guli, guli, guli, guli, guli ram sam sam.
Roll hands on guli, and clap three times.

A ram sam sam, a ram sam sam,
Guli, guli, guli, guli, guli ram sam sam.
Repeat actions.

Arafi, arafi,
Throw hands in the air.

Guli, guli, guli, guli, guli ram sam sam.
Repeat as above.

Arafi, arafi,
Guli, guli, guli, guli, guli ram sam sam.

Repeat the first verse.

Alphabet Books

STORIES TO READ ALOUD

The Most Amazing Hide and Seek Alphabet Book
CROWTHER, ROBERT

Bill and Pete
DE PAOLA, TOMIE

I Unpacked My Grandmother's Trunk
HOGUET, SUSAN RAMSAY

Chicka, Chicka Boom Boom
MARTIN, BILL

Crictor
UNGERER, TOMI

MORE ALPHABET BOOKS

A Prairie Alphabet
BANNATYNE-CUGNET, JO

By The Sea
BLADES, ANN

ABC
CLEAVER, ELIZABETH

Babar's ABC
DE BRUNHOFF, LAURENT

Eating the Alphabet: Fruits and Vegetables from A to Z
EHLERT, LOIS

Jambo Means Hello: A Swahili Alphabet Book
FEELINGS, MURIEL

The Alphabet in Nature
FELDMAN, JUDY

A Northern Alphabet
HARRISON, TED

26 Letters and 99 Cents
HOBAN, TANA

C Is for Curious: An ABC of Feelings
HUBBARD, WOODLEIGH

Lucy & Tom's ABC
HUGHES, SHIRLEY

Apples, Alligators and also Alphabets
JOHNSON, ODETTE

Animal Alphabet
KITCHEN, BERT

Alison's Zinnia
LOBEL, ANITA

On Market Street
LOBEL, ARNOLD

Alphabatics
MACDONALD, SUSE

The Great B.C. Alphabet Book
MORGAN, NICOLA

Curious George Learns the Alphabet
REY, H. A.

Dr. Seuss's ABC
SEUSS, DR.

The Wildlife ABC
THORNHILL, JAN

An Alphabet of Animals
WORMELL, CHRISTOPHER

SONGS

A B C D E F G

Sing to the tune of "Twinkle Twinkle Little Star."

A B C D E F G,
H I J K L M N O P,
Q R S and T U V,
W and X Y Z.
Now I've learned my A B Cs,
Next time won't you sing with me.

BINGO

There was a farmer who had a dog
And Bingo was him name-o
B-I-N-G-O, B-I-N-G-O, B-I-N-G-O,
And Bingo was his name-o.

Sing out the letters B-I-N-G-O on the first verse, clap once for B on the second verse, twice for B-I on the third verse, and so on, substituting claps for letters until you clap out Bingo's whole name, keeping the rhythm of the song as you go. This is also effective with a glove puppet with big red letters on each finger and a little puppy puppet stuck in the centre. You can also use letters and a little dog on the felt board.

A B C D E F G H I J K L M

This is a marching rhyme with lots of rhythm. Sharon Lois and Bram sing it as a quick tempo nursery rhyme medley to the tune of "The Grand Old Duke of York" on their Sing A to Z cassette. Celebrate the alphabet by putting letters on the felt board and adding felt characters with the nursery rhymes.

A B C-D E F G-H I J K L M
N O P-Q R S T U- V W X Y Z.

Mary had a little lamb
Whose fleece was white as snow.
And everywhere that Mary went,
The lamb was sure to go.
Oh, A B C-D E F G-H I J K L M
N O P-Q R S T U-V W X Y Z.

Little Miss Muffet sat on her tuffet,
Eating her curds and whey,
Along came a spider and sat down beside her,
And frightened Miss Muffet away,
Oh, A B C-D E F G-H I J K L M
N O P-Q R S T U-V W X Y Z.

Jack be nimble, Jack be quick,
Jack jump over the candle stick,
Oh, A B C-D E F G-H I J K L M
N O P-Q R S T U-V W X Y Z.

The grand old Duke of York,
He had ten thousand men.
He marched them up to the top of the hill
And he marched them down again.
And when they were up they were up.
And when they were down they were down.
But when they were only half way up,
They were neither up nor down.
Oh, A B C-D E F G-H I J K L M
N O P-Q R S T U-V W X Y Z.

MORE IDEAS

1. This is a fun theme to use in connection with starting school. *The Most Amazing Hide and Seek Alphabet Book*, a pop-up, is an intriguing book to use to create excitement about learning the alphabet, and *Crictor* is an old favourite to tell using a snake puppet. Let the children suggest letters for Crictor to act out.

2. After reading *Apples, Alligators and Also Alphabets*, help children spell their names, or first letters, with plasticine.

3. If storytime is in the library, draw attention to the letters of the alphabet in the picture book area. This encourages awareness of the ways in which the alphabet is used to establish order in the world, and teaches children and parents how to find books in the library. Many people do not realize that fiction is shelved in the library by the first letter in the author's last name.

4. Look for more spelling songs on the *Sharon, Lois & Bram Sing A to Z* cassette.

Animals of the Wild

STORIES TO READ ALOUD

Why Mosquitoes Buzz in People's Ears
AARDEMA, VERNA

Annie and the Wild Animals
BRETT, JAN

Salt Hands
CHELSEA, JANE

May I Bring a Friend?
DE REGNIERS, BEATRICE

Nuts to You!
EHLERT, LOIS

The Monkey and the Crocodile
GALDONE, PAUL

Crafty Chameleon
HADITHI, MWENYE

Greedy Zebra
HADITHI, MWENYE

Lazy Lion
HADITHI, MWENYE

The Snake That Sneezed
LEYDENFROST, ROBERT

The Name of the Tree
LOTTERIDGE, CELIA

Polar Bear, Polar Bear, What Do You Hear?
MARTIN, BILL

White Bear, Ice Bear
RYDER, JOANNE

The Wide Mouthed Frog
SCHNEIDER, REX

MORE STORIES

Who's in Rabbit's House?
AARDEMA, VERNA

Deer at the Brook
ARNOSKY, JIM

Otters Under Water
ARNOSKY, JIM

Raccoons and Ripe Corn
ARNOSKY, JIM

Watching Foxes
ARNOSKY, JIM

Beaver at Long Pond
GEORGE, WILLIAM T.

The Camel Who Took a Walk
TWORKOV, JACK

I Can't Have Bannock, but the Beaver Has a Dam
WHEELER, BERNELDA

NONFICTION

Tigress
COWCHER, HELEN

Whistling Thorn
COWCHER, HELEN

Wolf Island
GODKIN, CELIA

A Children's Zoo
HOBAN, TANA

Zebra (also *Giraffe, Hippo, Elephant*)
(*Animals in the Wild* series)
HOFFMAN, MARY

Two by Two
REID, BARBARA

Joey: The Story of a Baby Kangaroo
RYDEN, HOPE

The Wildlife ABC (and *The Wildlife 123*)
THORNHILL, JAN

NURSERY RHYMES

The Lion and the Unicorn

This one is fun to use after Lazy Lion.
Clap hands in rhythm to the beat.

The lion and the unicorn
Were fighting for the crown;
The lion beat the unicorn
All round about the town.
Some gave them white bread,
And some gave them brown;
And some gave them plum cake
And drummed them out of town.

FINGERPLAYS

Gray Squirrel

Suit actions to words.

Gray squirrel, gray squirrel,
Swish your bushy tail.
Gray squirrel, gray squirrel,
Swish your bushy tail.
Wrinkle up your little nose.
Hold a nut between your toes.
Gray squirrel, gray squirrel,
Swish your bushy tail.

The Crocodile

She sailed away on a lovely summer's day,
On the back of a crocodile.
Place right hand on back of left.

"You see," said she,
"It's as plain as plain can be,
I'll go sailing down the Nile."
Move in swaying motion.

The croc winked his eye,
Wink.

As she waved them all good-bye,
Wave.

Wearing a happy smile.
Smile.

At the end of the ride,
The lady was inside,
Rub tummy.

And the smile on the crocodile.
Open and shut palms.

Five Little Monkeys

Use fingers, or monkey finger puppets.

Five little monkeys swinging from a tree,
*Hold up five fingers on right hand. Swing
rhythmically.*

Teasing Mister Crocodile, "Can't catch me!"
Wave fingers at left hand.

Along came Mister Crocodile, slowly as could be,
Make mouth with fingers and thumb of left hand.

SNAP!
Bite off a finger!

Four little monkeys . . .
Three little monkeys . . .
Two little monkeys . . .
One little monkey . . .
No little monkeys swinging from a tree,
I'd better watch out or he might catch me!
Point to self.

MORE IDEAS

1. Here is an opportunity to introduce children to wild animals in their natural habitats without referring to zoos. For appropriate rhymes and stretches to complement the books you choose, see: BEARS, BIRDS, DUCKS & GEESE, ELEPHANTS, and other related themes.

2. Felt Stories: *May I Bring a Friend, The Snake That Sneezed, The Name of the Tree,* and *The Camel Who Took a Walk.*

3. Dramatize *Who's in Rabbit's House* with simple animal masks.

4. Tell *The Wide-Mouthed Frog* with a frog puppet. Pattern and instructions are in *Storytelling Made Easy with Puppets* by Jan VanSchuyver.

5. Introduce children to First Nations legends, with picture books such as Elizabeth Cleaver's *The Loon's Necklace, The Mountain Goats of Temlaham,* and *The Enchanted Caribou. The Enchanted Caribou* makes a lovely shadow puppet play. Patterns are included in the book.

6. *White Bear, Ice Bear; Lizard in the Sun;* and *Snail's Spell,* all by Joanne Ryder in the *Just for a Day* series, invite children to imagine life in the natural world in a unique way.

7. Introduce children and parents to the many good magazines on wildlife available at the library: *Ranger Rick, Owl, Chickadee,* and *National Geographic World.*

Babies

STORIES TO READ ALOUD

Hush Little Baby
ALIKI

Avocado Baby
BURNINGHAM, JOHN

Simply Ridiculous
DAVIS, VIRGINIA

Where's the Baby?
HUTCHINS, PAT

Peter's Chair
KEATS, EZRA JACK

Another Mouse to Feed
KRAUS, ROBERT

Whose Mouse Are You?
KRAUS, ROBERT

The Wild Baby
LINDGREN, BARBRO

Murmel, Murmel, Murmel
MUNSCH, ROBERT

On Mother's Lap
SCOTT, ANN HERBERT

The Elephant and the Bad Baby
VIPONT, ELFRIDA

Owl Babies
WADDELL, MARTIN

Noisy Nora (big book format)
WELLS, ROSEMARY

Oonga Boonga
WISHINSKY, FRIEDA

Do You Know What I'll Do?
ZOLOTOW, CHARLOTTE

MORE STORIES

Nobody Asked Me If I Wanted a Baby Sister
ALEXANDER, MARTHA

Here Come the Babies
ANHOLT, CATHERINE & LAURENCE

Daniel's Dog
BOGART, JO ELLEN

Darcy and Gran Don't Like Babies
CUTLER, JANE

Julius, the Baby of the World
HENKES, KEVIN

The New Baby
McCULLY, EMILY ARNOLD

Deep Thinker and the Stars
MURDOCH, PATRICIA

101 Things to Do with a Baby
ORMEROD, JAN

Plain Noodles
WATERTON, BETTY

More, More, More, Said the Baby
WILLIAMS, VERA B.

But Not Billy
ZOLOTOW, CHARLOTTE

William's Doll
ZOLOTOW, CHARLOTTE

NONFICTION

How You Were Born
COLE, JOANNA

Being Born (adult)
KITZINGER, SHEILA

The New Baby
ROGERS, FRED

NURSERY RHYMES

Pat-A-Cake

Pat-a-cake, pat-a-cake, baker's man,
Clap four times in rhythm.

Bake me a cake as fast as you can.
Cup hands.

Pat it, and dot it, and mark it with a B,
Mime actions.

And put it in the oven
Extend both hands.

For Baby and me.
Point to a child, then yourself.

Rock-A-Bye Baby
Pretend to rock baby in arms.

Rock-a-bye baby on the tree top;
When the wind blows, the cradle will rock;
When the bough breaks, the cradle will fall;
And down will come baby, cradle and all.

Bye Baby Bunting

Bye, baby bunting,
Daddy's gone a hunting,
He's gone to get a rabbit skin
To put the baby bunting in.

FINGERPLAYS

This Is a Baby Ready for a Nap

This is a baby ready for a nap.
Hold up one finger.

Lay him down in his mother's lap.
Place in palm of other hand.

Cover him up so he won't peep.
Wrap fingers around it.

Rock him till he's fast asleep.
Rock finger back and forth.

Here's a Ball for Baby

Here's a ball for Baby
Big and soft and round.
*Hold up two hands touching fingertips
to form ball.*

Here is baby's hammer
Make a fist.

See how he can pound.
Pound fist on palm of other hand.

Here is baby's music
Clapping, clapping so.
Clap hands.

Here are baby's soldiers
Standing in a row.
Hold ten fingers erect.

Here is baby's trumpet
Toot, too, too, too, too.
Hold one fist in front of other at mouth.

Here's the way that baby
Plays at peek-a-boo.
Spread fingers in front of eyes.

Here's a big umbrella
To keep the baby dry.
*Hold index finger of right hand erect.
Place palm of left hand on top of finger.*

And here is baby's cradle
*Make cradle of interlocked fingers, knuckles up,
erect index and smallest fingers.*

To rock-a-baby bye.
Rock hands.

Baby's Bath

Baby's ready for her bath.
Here's the baby's tub,
Make circle with arms.

Here's the baby's washcloth,
Hold hand up, palm flat.

See how she can scrub.
Pretend to rub face.

Here's the baby's cake of soap,
Make a fist.

And here's the towel dry,
Hold hands flat, thumbs touching.

And here's the baby's cradle
Make imaginary cradle and rock back and forth.

Rock-a-baby bye.

Knives and Forks

Here are the lady's knives and forks,
Interlock fingers, palms up.

Here is the lady's table.
Keep fingers interlocked, and turn palms down.

Here is the lady's looking glass,
As before, elbows together.

And here is the baby's cradle.
Make peak of two pointers and peak of little fingers and rock.

This Is My Family

Hold up one hand, or finger family, fingers extended, and point to fingers with other hand.

This is my mother.
Point to thumb.

This is my father.
Point to index finger.

This is my brother tall.
Point to middle finger.

This is my sister.
Point to ring finger.

This is the baby.
Point to baby finger.

Oh, how I love them all!
Clap left hand over all fingers and hug to chest!

Thumbkin

Sing to the tune of "Frère Jacques." Hide your hands behind your back to start.

Where is thumbkin ?
Where is thumbkin?
Here I am!
Bring out one hand, thumb up.

Here I am!
Bring out the other hand, thumb up.

How are you today, sir?
Nod one thumb.

Very well, I thank you.
Nod the other thumb.

Run away, run away,
Hide one hand behind back.

Run away and hide.
Hide other hand behind back.

Repeat using "Pointer," "Tall Man," "Ring Man," and "the Baby."

Come A' Look A' See

Sing with a calypso rhythm.

Come a'look a'see,
Here's my mama.
Point to thumb.

Come a'look a'see,
Here's my papa.
Point to index finger.

Come a'look a'see,
My brother tall,
Point to tall finger.

Sister, baby,
Point to ring then baby fingers.

I love them all.
Cover fingers with other hand and hug.

One Little Baby

One little baby
Hold up one finger.

Rocking in a tree.
Rock in palm of other hand.

Two little babies
Hold up two fingers.

Splashing in the sea.
Splash hands.

Three little babies
Hold up three fingers.

Crawling on the floor.
Crawl fingers along floor or knee.

Four little babies
Hold up four fingers.

Banging on the door.
Pound fists on imaginary door.

Five little babies
Hold up five fingers.

Playing hide and seek.
Cover up you eyes.

Keep your eyes closed tight now
Until I say . . . peek!
Throw hands away from eyes on "peek!"

SONGS

Hush, Little Baby

Sing this one with the book or use a felt board.

Hush, little baby, don't say a word,
Mama's gonna buy you a mocking bird;
If that mocking bird don't sing,
Mama's gonna buy you a diamond ring;
If that diamond ring is brass,
Mama's gonna buy you a lookin' glass;
If that looking glass gets broke,
Mama's gonna buy you a billy goat;
If that billy goat don't pull,
Mama's gonna buy you a cart and bull;
If that cart and bull turn over,
Mama's gonna buy you a dog named Rover;
If that dog named Rover don't bark,
Mama's gonna buy you a horse and cart;
If that horse and cart break down,
You'll still be the sweetest little baby in town.

Over In the Meadow

See MOTHER'S DAY, page 136.

MORE IDEAS

1. Start storytime on this theme by asking the children if they have babies in their families. Suggest that they might want to try some of the rhymes you'll teach them on their own baby siblings. Then teach them "This Little Piggy," "Round and Round the Garden," and other simple rhymes.

2. Felt story: *Hush Little Baby.*

3. Tell *Murmel, Murmel, Murmel* without the book. Tell *Whose Mouse Are You?* with a mouse puppet.

4. For an alternative action song, see "What Will We Do with the Baby-O?" in Tom Glazer's *Eye Winker, Tom Tinker, Chin Chopper.*

5. Tell the story of "The Wide-Mouthed Frog," about a mother frog who goes searching for the perfect food for her little frog babies, with a frog puppet. There is a pattern with instructions in *Storytelling Made Easy with Puppets* by Jan VanSchuyver.

6. You can buy or make a little baby puppet with a nylon head on a flannel nightgown, wrapped up in a flannel blanket, that is extremely life-like when you move the head and arms. Mine never fails to mesmerize the audience. Let the children take turns holding her as you tell stories. What love and tenderness they will show this baby!

7. *Noisy Nora*, by Rosemary Wells, is a wonderful story, although the book is a little small for reading aloud to large audiences. Thankfully, it is available in big book format for all to see.

8. For the words to "Miss Polly Had a Dolly Who Was Sick, Sick, Sick" see SICKNESS & HEALTH. This one is nice to use after *The Lady with the Alligator Purse.* See other doll rhymes in TOYS.

9. Here's a great video to promote on coping with sibling rivalry: *Hey, What About Me?: A Video Guide for Brothers and Sisters of New Babies.* It's written by Jane Murphy and Karen Tucker (Newton, MA: Kidvidz, 1987).

10. For more ideas, see FAMILIES.

Bathtime

STORIES TO READ ALOUD

Mr. Archimedes' Bath
ALLEN, PAMELA

No More Baths
COLE, BROCK

Andrew's Bath
McPHAIL, DAVID

The Mud Puddle
MUNSCH, ROBERT

Five Minutes Peace
MURPHY, JILL

Nobody Knows I Have Delicate Toes
PATZ, NANCY

Piggy in the Puddle
POMERANTZ, CHARLOTTE

King Bidgood's in the Bathtub
WOOD, AUDREY

Harry the Dirty Dog
ZION, GENE

MORE STORIES

Malcolm's Runaway Soap
BOGART, JO ELLEN

Time to Get Out of the Bath, Shirley
BURNINGHAM, JOHN

A Whale of a Bath
BRUNEEL, ETIENNE

Kyle's Bath
EYVINDSON, PETER

The Bear in the Bathtub
JACKSON, ELLEN B.

Moonlight
ORMEROD, JAN

I Can Take a Bath!
WATANABE, SHIGEO

Let's Go Swimming!
WATANABE, SHIGEO

No Bath Tonight
YOLEN, JANE

NONFICTION

Splash! All About Baths
BUXBAUM, SUSAN KOVAES

NURSERY RHYMES

Rub-A-Dub-Dub

Rub-a-dub-dub, three men in a tub,
And who do you think they be?
The butcher, the baker, the candlestick maker
And all of them gone to sea.
       or an alternate last line:
Turn 'em out, knaves all three!

FINGERPLAYS

After a Bath
       Suit actions to words.

After my bath, I try, try, try,
To wipe myself 'till I 'm dry, dry, dry.
Hands to wipe, and fingers and toes,
And two wet legs and a shiny nose.
Just think, how much less time I'd take,
If I were a dog, and could shake, shake, shake.

This Is the Way We Wash Our Hands

Sing to the tune of "Here We Go 'Round the Mulberry Bush."

This is the way we wash our hands,
Wash our hands, wash our hands,
This is the way we wash our hands,
So early in the evening.

This is the way we scrub our face . . .
This is the way we swish out our ears . . .
This is the way we comb our hair . . .
This is the way we brush our teeth . . .

MORE IDEAS

1. Ask the children if they like taking baths. Stories about kids and a dog who hate to take a bath are: *No More Baths, No Bath Tonight, Kyle's Bath, I Hate to Take a Bath,* and *Harry the Dirty Dog.* After *No Bath Tonight,* ask children if they can think of any more ingenious ways to avoid bathing.

2. *The Mud Puddle* is easy to learn and fun to tell, especially with sound effects à la Robert Munsch. You can hear his technique on his *Munsch Favourite Stories* cassette.

3. For lovely short poems to recite together, see *Read-Aloud Rhymes for the Very Young* selected by Jack Prelutsky, pages 26 - 27.

4. For more bathtime songs, see: "Bathtime" on Raffi's *Everything Grows* cassette; and "There's a Hippo in My Tub" on Anne Murray's cassette of the same name.

5. Use water songs and rhymes from SEASONS – RAINY DAY such as "Five Little Ducks," "Row Row Row Your Boat," "I Love to Row in My Big Blue Boat," and "Eeensy Weensy Spider." Sing "There's a Little White Duck," (page 70), which is also nice in felt. For fishy themes, see SEA & SEASHORE.

6. Link this theme with getting ready for bed – see BEDTIME & MOON STORIES.

7. Sing Raffi's song, "Brush Your Teeth", on his *Singable Songs for the Very Young* cassette. Find the words and music in *The Raffi Singable Songbook.*

8. Look for washing clothes and getting dressed ideas in CLOTHING.

9. Go for a swim, instead of a bath, with *Pig in a Pond* by Martin Waddell, *Maisy Goes Swimming* (a pop-up) by Lucy Cousins, *Who Sank the Boat* by Pamela Allen, *Froggy Learns to Swim* by Jonathan London, and *Mr. Gumpy's Outing* by John Burningham.

Bears & Teddy Bears

STORIES TO READ ALOUD

Moonbear
ASCH, FRANK

Jesse Bear, What Will You Wear?
CARLSTROM, NANCY WHITE

Goldilocks and the Three Bears
CAULEY, LORINDA

Ask Mr. Bear
FLACK, MARJORIE

Beady Bear
FREEMAN, DON

Corduroy
FREEMAN, DON

Cully Cully and the Bear
GAGE, WILSON

Two Greedy Bears
GINSBURG, MIRRA

Mr. Bear's Chair
GRAHAM, THOMAS

This Is the Bear and the Scary Night
HAYES, SARAH

Teddy Bears' Picnic
KENNEDY, JIMMY

Milton the Early Riser
KRAUS, ROBERT

Oh A-Hunting We Will Go
LANGSTAFF, JOHN

What's That Noise?
LEMIEUX, MICHELLE

Ten Bears in My Bed
MACK, STAN

Brown Bear, Brown Bear
MARTIN, BILL

Bear's Toothache
McPHAIL, DAVID

Emma's Pet
McPHAIL, DAVID

First Flight
McPHAIL, DAVID

Peace at Last
MURPHY, JILL

Bear's Picture
PINKWATER, DANIEL

We're Going on a Bear Hunt
ROSEN, MICHAEL

Mumble Bear
RUCK-PAUQUET, GINA

White Bear, Ice Bear
RYDER, JOANNE

Lizard's Song
SHANNON, GEORGE

Ira Sleeps Over
WABER, BERNARD

How Do I Put It On?
WATANABE, SHIGEO

MORE STORIES

Angel and the Polar Bear
GAY, MARIE-LOUISE

Brown Bear in a Brown Chair
HALE, TRINA

Blueberries for Sal
McCLOSKEY, ROBERT

Somebody and the Three Blairs
TOLHURT, MARILYN

NONFICTION

Alphabears: An ABC Book
HAGUE, KATHLEEN

Bear
HOFFMAN, MARY

FINGERPLAYS

Little Brown Bear

This one is nice with a little bear finger puppet.

A little brown bear went in search of some
 honey,
Isn't it funny, a bear wanting honey?
He sniffed at the breeze,
Sniff air.

And he listened for bees,
Cup hand to ear and listen.

And would you believe it?
He even climbed trees!
Fingers of one hand climb the opposite arm.

Bears Everywhere

Bears, bears, bears, everywhere!
Point in all directions.

Bears climbing stairs,
Pretend to climb.

Bears sitting on chairs,
Pretend to sit.

Bears collecting fares,
Reach out for fares. Place hands in pockets.

Bears giving stares,
Stare at group.

Bears washing hairs,
Pretend to wash hair.

Bears, bears, bears, everywhere!

Teddy Bear, Teddy Bear

Everybody stand up!

Teddy bear, teddy bear, turn around;
Turn around.

Teddy bear, teddy bear, touch the ground.
Touch the ground.

Teddy bear, teddy bear, show your shoe;
Hold out foot.

Teddy bear, teddy bear, I love you.
Give yourself a big hug.

Teddy bear, teddy bear, climb upstairs;
Climb up stairs.

Teddy bear, teddy bear, say your prayers.
Hands in prayer.

Teddy bear, teddy bear, turn out the light;
Switch out the light.

Teddy bear, teddy bear, say, "good night!"
Head on hands folded together.

SONGS

Five Brown Teddies

Sing to the tune of "Ten Green Bottles."

Five brown teddies sitting on a wall,
Five brown teddies sitting on a wall,
And if one brown teddy should accidentally fall,
There'd be four brown teddies sitting on the wall.

Four brown teddies . . .
Three brown teddies . . .
Two brown teddies . . .

One brown teddy sitting on a wall,
One brown teddy sitting on a wall,
And if one brown teddy should accidentally fall,
There'd be no brown teddy sitting there at all!

Teddy Bears' Picnic

If you go down to the woods today,
You'd better go in disguise.
If you go down to the woods today,
You're in for a big surprise.
For every bear that ever there was
Is gathered there for certain because,
Today's the day the teddy bears have their picnic.

Bear Went Over the Mountain

*Walk fingers up arm to shoulder,
then back down again.*

The bear went over the mountain,
The bear went over the mountain,
The bear went over the mountain,
To see what he could see.
And all that he could see,
And all that he could see,
Was the other side of the mountain,
The other side of the mountain,
The other side of the mountain,
Was all that he could see.

GAME

Let's Go on a Bear Hunt

*This is a call and response chant. Children
repeat each line after the leader.*

Let's go on a bear hunt.
All right.
Let's go.
Slap hands on thighs to walk.

Oh look,
I see a wheat field!
Can't go around it,
Can't go under it.
Let's go through it.
All right.
Let's go .
Swish, swish, swish.
Brush hands together to swish through the wheat.

Oh look,
I see a tree!
Can't go over it,
Can't go under it,
Let's go up it.
All right.
Let's go.
*Pretend to climb a tree. When top is reached, place
hand to forehead and look around. Climb down.*

Oh look,
I see a swamp !
Can't go around it,
Can't go under it.
Let's swim through it.
All right.
Let's go.
Pretend to swim.

Oh look,
I see a bridge!

Can't go around it,
Can't go under it.
Let's cross over it.
All right.
Let 's go.
Make clicking sound with tongue and stamp feet.

Oh look,
I see a cave !
Can't go around it,
Can't go under it.
Let's go in it.
All right.
Let's go.
*Cup hands and clap together to make a hollow
sound.*

Golly, it's dark in here.
Better use my flashlight.
Doesn't work.
I think . . . I see something.
It's big!
It's furry!
I think . . . it's a bear.
Say this with suspense in voice.

IT IS A BEAR!
LET'S GO!
*Repeat everything backwards quickly, wipe brow,
heave a big sigh of relief.*

"WHEW! WE MADE IT!"

MORE IDEAS

1. Felt stories: *Brown Bear, Brown Bear; Ask Mr.
Bear;* and *Goldilocks and the Three Bears.*

2. *How Do I Put It On?* is fun to perform with a
stuffed teddy bear and clothes props as an
opener for this theme.

3. Two of my favourite books to sing are here:
Oh A-Hunting We Will Go, which preschool
children find hilarious, and can be made into
felts if you're ambitious, and *Lizard's Song* by
George Shannon. Make up a tune for the
lizard's little song, teach it to the children before
you start, and ask them to join you when he
sings. *Lizard's Song* is a good story for
unobtrusively introducing concepts of mutual
respect and self-esteem.

4. Plan your own teddy bears' picnic. Ask the
children to bring along their favourite stuffed
animals. Play "The Teddy Bears Picnic" cassette
as they come in to storytime.

5. There are two good participation stories about bears in *Look Back And See: Twenty Lively Tales for Gentle Tellers* by Margaret Read MacDonald. "Grandfather Bear Is Hungry" is a lovely story about sharing. Children will join in on Grandfather Bear's refrain "I am so hungry!" moaning and holding their stomachs. It's especially fun to use just before lunch. In "Why Koala Has No Tail," children join in with Tree Kangaroo as he digs and digs a well so the thirsty animals can drink.

6. For a draw-and-tell story see "How Bear Lost His Tail" in *More Tell and Draw Stories* by Margaret Oldfield.

7. Tell *Goldilocks and the Three Bears* with finger puppets or felts. You'll find easy-to-make felt patterns in Judy Sierra's *Multicultural Folktales.*

8. After the children are familiar with the story of *Goldilocks and the Three Bears,* read *Somebody and the Three Blairs* by Marilyn Tolhurt.

9. For bears and hibernation, see SEASONS – WINTER.

Bedtime & Moon Stories

STORIES TO READ ALOUD

Hush Little Baby
ALIKI

The Princess and the Pea
ANDERSEN, H. C.

Moonbear
ASCH, FRANK

Happy Birthday, Moon
ASCH, FRANK

Ten, Nine, Eight
BANG, MOLLY

Goodnight Moon
BROWN, MARGARET WISE

Dorothy's Dream
DENTON, KADY MACDONALD

Granny Is a Darling
DENTON, KADY MACDONALD

Time for Bed
FOX, MEM

Moonbeam on a Cat's Ear
GAY, MARIE-LOUISE

Four Brave Sailors
GINSBURG, MIRRA

Where Does the Sun Go at Night?
GINSBURG, MIRRA

Goodnight, Owl
HUTCHINS, PAT

Jeremiah and Mrs. Ming
JENNINGS, SHARON

Midnight Farm
LINDBERGH, REEVE

There's a Nightmare in My Closet
MAYER, MERCER

There's an Alligator Under My Bed
MAYER, MERCER

What Do You Do with a Kangaroo?
MAYER, MERCER

Close Your Eyes
MARZOLLO, JEAN

Penguin Moon
MITRA, ANNIE

Louis and the Night Sky
MORGAN, NICOLA

The Dark
MUNSCH, ROBERT

Mortimer
MUNSCH, ROBERT

Peace at Last
MURPHY, JILL

Mother, Mother I Want Another
POLUSHKIN, MARIA

Squawk to the Moon, Little Goose
PRESTON, EDNA MITCHELL

Night in the Country
RYLANT, CYNTHIA

In the Night Kitchen
SENDAK, MAURICE

The Thing that Bothered Farmer Brown
SLOAT, TERI

We Can't Sleep
STEVENSON, JAMES

Bedtime Mouse
STODDARD, SANDOL

Ira Sleeps Over
WABER, BERNARD

Midnight Moon
WATSON, CLYDE

What the Moon Saw
WILDSMITH, BRIAN

The Napping House
WOOD, AUDREY

Hush Little Baby
ZEMACH, MARGOT

MORE STORIES

I Can't Sleep
FARMER, PATTI

The Sun's Asleep Behind the Hill
GINSBURG, MIRRA

Bedtime for Frances
HOBAN, RUSSELL

Sleepers
KHALSA, DAYAL KAUR

Nicole's Boat
MORGAN, ALLEN

The Story Book Prince
OPPENHEIM, JOANNE

Moonlight
ORMEROD, JAN

The Moon Jumpers
UDRY, JANICE

NONFICTION

The Baby's Catalogue
AHLBERG, JANET & ALLAN

The Baby's Bedtime Book (poetry & lullabies)
CHORAO, KAY

When the Dark Comes Dancing (poetry)
LARRICK, NANCY

NURSERY RHYMES

Twinkle, Twinkle, Little Star

Twinkle, twinkle, little star,
How I wonder what you are.
> *Hold hands up high and rotate wrist in time to the music.*

Up above the world so high,
Like a diamond in the sky.
> *Make a diamond shape with index fingers and thumbs.*

Twinkle, twinkle, little star,
How I wonder what you are.
> *Hold hands up high and rotate wrists again.*

Star Light, Star Bright

Star light, star bright,
First star I see tonight,
I wish I may,
I wish I might,
Have this wish,
I wish tonight.

Rock-A-Bye Baby

Rock-a-bye baby, on the tree top;
When the wind blows, the cradle will rock;
When the bough breaks, the cradle will fall;
And down will come baby, cradle and all.

Wee Willie Winkie

Wee Willie Winkie runs through the town,
Upstairs and downstairs, in his nightgown,
Rapping at the window,
Crying through the lock,
"Are the children in their beds?
For now it's eight o'clock."

Diddle, Diddle Dumpling

Diddle, diddle dumpling, my son John,
Went to bed with his trousers on;
One shoe off and one shoe on,
Diddle, diddle dumpling, my son John.

Jack Be Nimble

Jack be nimble,
Jack be quick,
Jack jump over
The candlestick.

The Man in the Moon

The man in the moon
Looked out of the moon,
Looked out of the moon and said,
It's time, I think, for all good children
To think about going to bed.

There Was an Old Woman

> *For felt pieces you will need: an old woman with a broom, a basket, and stringy stars for the sky.*

There was an old woman tossed up in a basket,
Seventeen times as high as the moon.
Where she was going I couldn't but ask it,
For in her hand she carried a broom.
Old woman, old woman, old woman, quoth I,
Where are you going to up so high?
To brush the cobwebs off the sky!
May I go with you? Aye, by and by.

FINGERPLAYS

Before I Jump into My Bed

Before I jump into bed at night,
Jump.

Before I dim the light,
Switch out the light.

I put my shoes together,
Hands together.

So they can talk at night.
Hands talk.

I'm sure they would be lonesome
If I tossed them here and there,
Toss hands left and right.

So I put them close together,
Place hands together.

For they're a friendly pair.

Going to Bed

Use fingers or finger puppets. Repeat for a little girl.

Here's a bed
Hold out palm of one hand.

And here's a little boy.
Hold up finger of other hand.

Down on the pillow he lays his head.
Lay finger on palm of other hand/bed.

He wraps himself in the covers tight,
Cover with fingers of other hand.

And this is the way he sleeps all night.
Morning comes, he opens his eyes.
Off with a toss the covers fly.
Open fingers.

Soon he is up and dressed and away,
Hold up finger.

Ready for fun and play all day.

This Is a Baby Ready for a Nap

This is a baby ready for a nap.
Hold up one finger.

Lay her down in her mother's lap.
Place in palm of other hand.

Cover her up so she won't peep.
Wrap fingers around it.

Rock her till she's fast asleep.
Rock finger back and forth.

I'm Sleepy, Very Sleepy

Suit actions to words.

I'm sleepy, very sleepy.
I want to stretch and yawn.
I'll close my eyes and just pretend
That daylight time has gone.
I'll breathe so softly and be so still
A little mouse might creep
Across the floor, because he thought
That I was fast asleep.

At Night I See the Twinkling Stars

This is a good lead-in to "Hush Little Baby."

At night I see the twinkling stars
And a great big smiling moon,
My mommy tucks me into bed
And sings a goodnight tune.

Five Little Monkeys

jumping on the bed . . . See MONKEYS, page 130.

Teddy Bear, Teddy Bear

See BEARS & TEDDY BEARS, page 24.

SONGS

Frère Jacques

Sing softly at first, then add volume when the morning bells start ringing. Sing it first in French, then in English.

Frère Jacques, Frère Jacques,
Dormez-vous? Dormez-vous?
Sonnez les matines,
Sonnez les matines,
Ding, dang, dong!
Ding, dang, dong!

Are you sleeping, are you sleeping
Brother John? Brother John?
Morning bells are ringing,
Morning bells are ringing,
Ding, dang, dong!
Ding, dang, dong!

Morningtown Ride

Listen to the tune of this lovely Malvina Reynolds song on Raffi's Baby Beluga *cassette. Words and music in* The Second Raffi Song Book. *Substitute names with names of your own storytime children.*

Train whistle blowin' makes a sleepy noise,
Underneath their blankets go all the girls and boys.
  Chorus:
    Rockin', rollin', ridin', out along the bay
    All bound for Morningtown many miles away.

Jill is at the engine, Laura rings the bell,
Neil swings a lantern to show that all is well.
  Sing Chorus

Maybe it is raining where our train will ride,
All the little travellers are warm and snug inside.
  Sing Chorus

Somewhere sun is shining, somewhere it is day,
Somewhere there is Morningtown,
  many miles away.

Hush, Little Baby

Listen to the tune on Bob McGrath's cassette, Sing Along with Bob, Vol. Two. *Words and music are in* Eye Winker, Tom Tinker, Chin Chopper *by Tom Glazer. Sing it with the book or with the felt board.*

Hush, little baby, don't say a word,
Mama's gonna buy you a mocking bird;
If that mocking bird don't sing,
Mama's gonna buy you a diamond ring;
If that diamond ring is brass,
Mama's gonna buy you a lookin' glass;
If that looking glass gets broke,
Mama's gonna buy you a billy goat;
If that billy goat don't pull,
Mama's gonna buy you a cart and bull;
If that cart and bull turn over,
Mama's gonna buy you a dog named Rover;
If that dog named Rover don't bark,
Mama's gonna buy you a horse and cart;
If that horse and cart break down,
You'll still be the sweetest little baby in town.

Aikendrum

Sing to the tune of "Here We Go Round the Mulberry Bush." Words and music are in The Raffi Singable Songbook. *For variation, sing beating different household instruments, such as spoons, saucepans, lids, chopsticks, and repeat the second verse substituting words for ladle. Also works in felt.*

There was a man lived in the moon,
In the moon, in the moon,
There was a man lived in the moon
And his name was Aikendrum.

And he played upon a ladle,
A ladle, a ladle,
He played upon a ladle
And his name was Aikendrum.

And his hat was made of cream cheese . . .
And his coat was made of roast beef . . .
And his pants were made of haggis . . .
There was a man lived in the moon . . .

Roll Over

This is great fun to sing with the felt board. You will need a bed, nine little animal characters, one child, and a blanket to cover them all up. Roll hands on "Roll over."

Ten in the bed, and the little one said,
"Roll over! Roll over!"
So they all rolled over and one fell out.

Nine in the bed, and the little one said,
"Roll over! Roll over!"
They all rolled over and one fell out.

Eight in the bed . . .
Seven in the bed . . .
Six in the bed . . .
Five in the bed . . .
Four in the bed . . .
Three in the bed . . .
Two in the bed . . .

One in the bed, and the little one said,
"Alone at last!"

MORE IDEAS

1. Have a pajama storytime early in the evening and tell bedtime stories. Ask children to come in pajamas and bring their teddy bears.

2. Craft: Using black construction paper, make night scenes using pre-pasted stars and other cut shapes. Try glue and silver sparkle dust.

3. *A Bed Just So* by Hardendorff is a wonderful bedtime story to tell with just a walnut shell.

Birds

STORIES TO READ ALOUD

The Lighthouse Keeper's Lunch
ARMITAGE, RONDA

Feathers for Lunch
EHLERT, LOIS

The Short Tree and the Bird That Could Not Sing
FOON, DENNIS

Goodnight, Owl
HUTCHINS, PAT

Jennie's Hat
KEATS, EZRA JACK

Round Robin
KENT, JACK

Owliver
KRAUS, ROBERT

The Owl and the Pussy Cat
LEAR, EDWARD

Tacky the Penguin
LESTER, HELEN

I Wish I Could Fly
MARIS, RON

Penguin Moon
MITRA, ANNIE

Mr. Monkey and the Gotcha Bird
MYERS, WALTER DEAN

Who Took the Farmer's Hat?
NODSET, JOAN

Have You Seen Birds?
OPPENHEIM, JOANNE

Sing a Song of Sixpence
PEARSON, TRACEY

Owl Lake
TEJIMA

Owly
THALER, MIKE

The Big Fat Worm
VAN LAAN, NANCY

FARMYARD BIRDS

Henny Penny
GALDONE, PAUL

Little Red Hen
GALDONE, PAUL

The Chick and the Duckling
GINSBURG, MIRRA

Rosie's Walk
HUTCHINS, PAT

Wings: A Tale of Two Chickens
MARSHALL, JAMES

Squawk to the Moon, Little Goose
PRESTON, EDNA MITCHELL

The Chicken Book
WILLIAMS, GARTH

NONFICTION

Chickens Aren't the Only Ones
HELLER, RUTH

What Is a Bird?
HIRSCHI, RON

Where Do Birds Live?
HIRSCHI, RON

The Penguin
ROYSTON, ANGELA

Owl
TAYLOR, KIM

NURSERY RHYMES

Sing a Song of Sixpence

This one calls for a pie plate and some little felt blackbirds.

Sing a song of sixpence,
A pocket full of rye;
Four-and-twenty blackbirds,
Baked in a pie!

When the pie was opened,
The birds began to sing;
Wasn't that a dainty dish,
To set before the king?

The king was in his counting-house,
Counting out his money.
The queen was in the parlor,
Eating bread and honey.

The maid was in the garden,
Hanging out the clothes;
When down came a blackbird,
And snapped off her nose!

Hickety, Pickety, My Black Hen

Hickety, Pickety, my black hen,
She lays eggs for gentlemen.
Gentlemen come every day,
To see what my black hen doth lay.
Sometimes nine and sometimes ten,
Hickety, Pickety, my black hen.

A Wise Old Owl

A wise old owl sat in an oak,
The more he heard the less he spoke;
The less he spoke the more he heard.
Why aren't we all like that wise old bird?

FINGERPLAYS

This Little Bird

Sing to the tune of "Here We Go Round the Mulberry Bush." Hook thumbs together and flap hands. Fly away up on the last line.

This little bird flaps its wings,
Flaps its wings, flaps its wings,
This little bird flaps its wings,
And flies away in the morning.

Chook, Chook

Chook, chook, chook, chook, chook,
Good morning, Mrs. Hen.
     Interlock fingers, knuckles up, thumbs and baby fingers point up to make a hen.

How many chickens have you got?
Madam, I've got ten.
     Hold up ten fingers.

Four of them are yellow,
     Four fingers.

And four of them are brown,
     Four fingers.

And two of them are speckled red,
     Two thumbs.

The nicest in the town.

Ten Little Chickadees

Hold up ten fingers. Throw hands up in the air when one bird flies away and return hands with one more finger tucked away each time.

Ten little chickadees sitting on a line,
One flew away and then there were nine.
Nine little chickadees on a farmer's gate,
One flew away and then there were eight.
Eight little chickadees looking up to heaven,
One flew away and then there were seven.
Seven little chickadees gathering up sticks,
One flew away and then there were six.
Six little chickadees learning how to dive,
One flew away and then there were five.
Five little chickadees sitting at a door,
One flew away and then there were four.
Four little chickadees could not agree,
One flew away and then there were three.
Three little chickadees looking very blue,
One flew away and then there were two.
Two little chickadees sitting in the sun,
One flew away and then there was one.
One little chickadee living all alone,
He flew away and then there was none!

Little Robin Redbreast

Little Robin Redbreast
     Thumb and little finger make head and tail.

Sat upon a rail;
Niddle noodle went his head,
     Wiggle thumb.

Wiggle waggle went his tail.
     Wiggle little finger.

Two Little Dicky Birds

Use finger puppets or just fingers.

Two little dicky birds sitting on a wall,
Two hands closed, thumbs up resemble bird.

One named Peter, one named Paul.
Slightly raise one hand, then the other.

Fly away, Peter; fly away, Paul;
Fly away behind your back, one at a time.

Come back, Peter; come back, Paul.
Bring back one, and then the other.

Once I Saw a Little Bird

Once I saw a little bird
Come hop, hop, hop.
Hop two fingers of one hand.

I cried, "Little bird,
Will you stop, stop, stop!"
Stop hopping on last stop.

I went to the window,
Walk two fingers of other hand.

Saying, "How do you do?"
Wag finger of other hand.

But he shook his little tail,
And away he flew.
Flutter fingers of first hand up over head.

Pretty Nest

For a lovely tune see This Little Puffin,
1969 edition.

I have made a pretty nest,
Look inside, look inside.
Interlock fingers, palms upwards.

Hungry birdies with their beaks,
Open wide, open wide.
*Place index fingers and thumbs of each hand
together and 'open and close' them.*

See my little birdies grow,
Day by day, day by day,
Gradually spread hands apart to indicate growth.

Till they spread their little wings,
And then they fly away.
Cross arms at wrist and flap hands.

My Pigeon House

My pigeon house I open wide
*Interlock fingers, palms down. Then turn upside
down.*

And I set all my pigeons free.
Wiggle fingers.

They fly around on every side
Interlock thumbs and flap hands (wings).

And perch on the highest tree.
Flap up high.

And when they return
From their merry flight,
Fly back home.

They close their eyes
Close eyes.

And say, 'Good night.'
Rest head on hands.

Coo-oo coo, coo-oo coo,
Coo-oo coo, coo-oo coo,
Coo-oo coo, coo-oo coo, coo-oo.

The Ostrich

Here is the ostrich straight and tall,
Raise one arm straight up for the ostrich.

Nodding his head above us all.
Bob hand.

Here is the hedgehog prickly and small,
Clasp hands with fingers sticking up.

Rolling himself into a ball.
Flatten hands into a ball.

Here is the spider scuttling around,
Make a spider hand.

Treading so lightly on the ground.
Skitter along.

Here are the birds that fly so high,
Interlock thumbs and flap hands for birds.

Spreading their wings across the sky.
Let them fly away.

Here are the children fast asleep,
Pretend to sleep.

While in the night the owls do peep,
Ring eyes for owls.

Tuit tuwhoo, tuit tuwhoo.

Bird Story

A father and mother bird
Lived in a tree.
> *Hold up first two fingers of right hand.*

In their nest were babies,
One, two, and three.
> *Hold up three fingers of left hand.*

The parent birds fed them
All day long .
> *Hold up two fingers of right hand.*

And soon the babies
Were big and strong.
> *Hold up three fingers of left hand.*

They fluttered down
From the nest one day,
> *Move three fingers as if fluttering.*

And hid in some bushes
Not far away.
> *Move three fingers as if running along the ground.*

The father bird saw
A cat creep by.
> *Move thumb of right hand slowly.*

He cried: "My children,
You'll have to fly !
You needn't be fearful,
Just follow me!"
> *Three baby birds follow parents upward.*

And off they flew
To their nest in the tree.

SONGS

Kookaburra

Kookaburra sits in the old gum tree,
Merry, merry king of the bush is he,
Laugh, Kookaburra, laugh
Kookaburra, gay your life must be.

Kookaburra sits in the old gum tree,
Counting all the monkeys he can see,
Stop Kookaburra, stop, Kookaburra
That's not a monkey, that's me.

Kookaburra sits in the old gum tree,
Eating all the gumdrops he can see,
Sing, Kookaburra, sing
Kookaburra, gay your life must be.

CIRCLE GAME

Bluebird, Bluebird

> *Listen to this lovely tune on Sharon, Lois & Bram's cassette* Mainly Mother Goose.

Bluebird, bluebird, through my window,
Bluebird, bluebird, through my window,
Bluebird, bluebird, through my window,
Oh, Johnnie, I am tired!

Find a little friend and tap him on the shoulder,
Find a little friend and tap him on the shoulder,
Find a little friend and tap him on the shoulder,
Oh, Johnnie, I am tired!

Children stand in a circle with hands raised to form arches. One child, the bluebird, skips in and out of the arches, and chooses another child to be the bluebird in the second verse. This is repeated until all the children are bluebirds. In the end, they all fall down to rest.

MORE IDEAS

1. For songs, "Six Little Ducks" and "There's a Little White Duck," see DUCKS & GEESE.

2. Felt stories: *The Little Red Hen; The Owl and the Pussy Cat; Who Took the Farmer's Hat?; The Big Fat Worm; Squawk to the Moon, Little Goose;* and *Jenny's Hat.*

3. Have a storytime about owls with *Goodnight, Owl; Owl Lake;* and *Owliver.* Don't miss the wonderful owl in *Have You Seen Birds?.*

4. Tell *Jenny's Hat* as you decorate a plain hat with all the props. It is especially nice to celebrate this way with the return of the birds in spring.

5. Art activity after *Owl Lake*: Have the children paint any colours they like, completely covering a sheet of paper. Use poster paint or water colour. When it's dry, cover all over in black crayon. With a fairly sharp object, scratch out pictures that imitate the style of the illustrations in the book.

6. For "Sing a Song of Six Pence," make a simple pie out of pie plates stapled together. Remove a pie shaped piece and pull out twenty-four little blackbirds strung together with thread. Act it out with a paper nose and blackbird finger puppet while children play the king and queen. For dramatization ideas and puppet patterns, see *Pocketful of Puppets: Mother Goose* by Tamara Hunt and Nancy Renfro. Give away little blackbird finger puppets for each child at the end of the program.

Birthdays

STORIES TO READ ALOUD

Happy Birthday, Moon
ASCH, FRANK

Little Gorilla
BORNSTEIN, RUTH

Aunt Nina and Her Nephews and Nieces
BRANDENBERG, FRANZ

The Secret Birthday Message
CARLE, ERIC

Paul's Christmas Birthday
CARRICK, CAROL

Fortunately
CHARLIP, REMY

Ask Mr. Bear
FLACK, MARJORIE

Night Noises
FOX, MEM

Spot's Birthday Party
HILL, ERIC

The Doorbell Rang
HUTCHINS, PAT

Happy Birthday, Sam
HUTCHINS, PAT

The Surprise Party
HUTCHINS, PAT

Letter to Amy
KEATS, EZRA JACK

The Mysterious Tadpole
KELLOG, STEVEN

The Birthday Thing
KISER, SUANN & KEVIN

Ice Cream Soup
MODELL, FRANK

Moira's Birthday
MUNSCH, ROBERT

Elephant's Wish
MUNARI, BRUNO

Love from Uncle Clyde
PARKER, NANCY WINSLOW

Mary Wore Her Red Dress and Henry Wore His Green Sneakers
PEEK, MERLE

Benny Bakes a Cake
RICE, EVA

The Surprise
SHANNON, GEORGE

Mouse's Birthday
YOLEN, JANE

The Three Wishes
ZEMACH, MARGOT

No Roses for Harry
ZION, GENE

Mr. Rabbit and the Lovely Present
ZOLOTOW, CHARLOTTE

MORE STORIES

10 for Dinner
BOGART, JO ELLEN

Babar's Birthday Surprise
DE BRUNHOFF, LAURENT

A Birthday for Frances
HOBAN, RUSSELL

Alfie Gives a Hand
HUGHES, SHIRLEY

"Birthday Soup" in *Little Bear*
MINARIK, ELSE

Happy Birthday to You!
SEUSS, DR.

Sylvester and the Magic Pebble (wishes)
STEIG, WILLIAM

NONFICTION

A Piece of Cake: Fun and Easy Theme Parties for Children (adult)
BOECHLER, GWEN

Party Rhymes
BROWN, MARC

Things to Make and Do for Your Birthday
GIBBONS, GAIL

Mr. Dressup's Birthday Party Book (adult)
TANAKA, SHELLEY

NURSERY RHYMES

Star Light, Star Bright

Star light, star bright,
First star I see tonight,
I wish I may,
I wish I might,
Have this wish,
I wish tonight.

Jack Be Nimble

> *Hold up thumb for candlestick, two fingers for Jack. Jump over!*

Jack be nimble,
Jack be quick,
Jack jump over
The candlestick!

Pat-A-Cake

Pat-a-cake, pat-a-cake, baker's man,
> *Clap four times in rhythm.*

Bake me a cake as fast as you can.
> *Cup hands.*

Pat it, and dot it, and mark it with B.
> *Pantomime this action.*

And put it in the oven
> *Extend both hands.*

For Baby and me.
> *Point to member of audience then to self.*

FINGERPLAYS

Five Birthday Candles

> *This is effective with five little fingers. Raise one hand with fingers extended. Starting with thumb, lower one finger each time you blow out a candle. It's also nice with five large candles on the felt board, especially for younger children.*

Five birthday candles;
Wish there were more.
Blow out one
> *Blow quickly.*

Then there are four.
Four birthday candles;
Pretty as can be.
Blow out one
> *Blow quickly.*

Then there are three.
Three birthday candles;
Mother bought them new.
Blow out one
> *Blow quickly.*

Then there are two.
Two birthday candles;
Birthday cakes are fun.
Blow out one
> *Blow quickly.*

Then there is one.
One birthday candle;
> *Pause.*

A birthday wish is fun.
Blow out one
> *Blow slowly.*

Then there is none.

I'm a Little Teapot

> *Have a cup of tea with your birthday cake!*
> *See FOOD, page 96.*

Here's a Cup

> *See FOOD, page 95.*

Ten Little Candles

Ten little candles on a chocolate cake.
> *Hold up ten fingers, palms toward you.*

Wh! Wh! Now there are eight.
> *Blow and drop two fingers.*

Eight little candles on candlesticks.
> *Eight fingers left.*

Wh! Wh! Now there are six.
> *Blow and drop two fingers.*

Six birthday candles and not one more.
> *Six fingers left.*

Wh! Wh! Now there are four.
> *Blow and drop two fingers.*

Four birthday candles, red, white and blue.
> *Four candles left.*

Wh! Wh! Now there are two.
> *Blow and drop two fingers.*

Two little candles standing in the sun.
> *Two candles left.*

Wh! Wh!
> *Blow and drop two fingers.*

Now there are none!
> *No fingers left, just fists.*

A Birthday

Today is _____'s birthday.
> *Insert child's name.*

Let's make her (him) a cake.
> *Form cake with hands.*

Mix and stir, stir and mix,
> *Action of stirring.*

Then into the oven to bake.
> *Pretend to place cake in oven.*

Here's our cake so nice and round.
> *Make a circle with arms.*

We frost it pink and white.
> *Action of spreading frosting.*

We put four candles on it,
> *Hold up four fingers.*

To make a birthday light.

Birthday Candles

Today I have a birthday
I'm four years old, you see.
> *Hold up four fingers.*

And here I have a birthday cake
Which you may share with me.
> *Make circle with arms.*

First we count the candles,
Count them every one.
One, two, three, four,
> *Hold up fingers one by one.*

The counting now is done.
Let's blow out the candles.
Out each flame will go.
"Wh . . . , wh . . . , wh . . . , wh . . . , "
> *Pretend to blow out candles.*

As one by one we blow.
> *Bend down fingers one at a time as you blow.*

ACTION SONGS

If You're Happy and You Know It
> *Everybody stand up!*

If you're happy and you know it, clap your hands.
If you're happy and you know it, clap your hands.
If you're happy and you know it,
Then your face is gonna show it,
If you're happy and you know it, clap your hands.

If you're sad and you know it, wipe your eyes,
If you're sad and you know it, wipe your eyes,
If you're sad and you know it,
Then your face is gonna show it,
If you're sad and you know it, wipe your eyes.

If you're mad and you know it, stamp your feet,
If you're mad and you know it, stamp your feet,
If you're mad and you know it,
Then your face will surely show it,
If you're mad and you know it, stamp your feet.

> *Repeat first verse.*

MORE IDEAS

1. Felt stories: *Ask Mr. Bear, Mr. Rabbit and the Lovely Present, The Surprise,* and "Five Birthday Candles."

2. "The Chinese Fan" (page 187) is a lively action song to sing for birthdays.

3. Celebrate all the year's birthdays at once. Give everyone party hats to wear. Sing "Happy Birthday to Me." Give out small gifts of stickers, balloons, bookmarks, or cupcakes at the end of the program. These could arrive in one big wrapped present for everybody.

4. Have a storytime about wishes using *The Three Wishes; The Elephant's Wish;* and *Wiggles, the Little Wishing Pig.* Recommend *Sylvester and the Magic Pebble* for reading at home.

5. Have a storytime about strange or unusual gifts with *The Mysterious Tadpole* (a dinosaur), *Crictor* (a snake), and *Love from Uncle Clyde* (a hippo). Ask children about the strangest or most wonderful gifts they have received.

6. Have a storytime about parties with *The Surprise Party, Letter to Amy,* and *The Doorbell Rang.*

7. Show the children how easy it is to misinterpret a message. After *The Surprise Party,* play the listening whispering game. Whisper something in one child's ear and let it travel around the circle. Say, "Let's play pin the tale on the donkey," for example. When it gets back to you, say whatever it has become out loud and hoot. See "A Wise Old Owl" in BIRDS for an owl that is wiser than the one in this story.

8. For ideas about growing and becoming more self-sufficient, see TEENY TINY THINGS. For a lovely poem about growing and birthdays, see Jack Prelutsky's *Read-Aloud Rhymes for the Very Young,* page 29.

9. Game: If children like the memory game, play it here with various toys they might receive for a birthday: a top, a toy car, a book, a cake, candles, a puppy, and so on, all made of felt. (Use felt pieces from stories you have.) Let children memorize the objects on the felt board for a few minutes, then cover with a sheet. Ask children to name the items they remember. Little presents could be given out as awards for good memories.

10. Party Game: Play "Pin the Tail on the Donkey." Make a big donkey for the felt board. Make felt tails, one for each child, with their names written on. Blindfold children one at a time and let them take turns "pinning" the tale on the donkey. Wind up by singing "Tingalayo!" See words in FARMS. Listen to the tune on Sharon, Lois & Bram's *One Elephant* cassette, or on Raffi's *One Light, One Sun* cassette.

Cats & Kittens

STORIES TO READ ALOUD

Annie and the Wild Animals
BRETT, JAN

A Dark, Dark Tale
BROWN, RUTH

Our Cat Flossie
BROWN, RUTH

It Does Not Say Meow
DE REGNIERS, BEATRICE

Four Fierce Kittens
DUNBAR, JOYCE

Feathers for Lunch
EHLERT, LOIS

Angus and the Cat
FLACK, MARJORIE

Millions of Cats
GAG, WANDA

Three Little Kittens
GALDONE, PAUL

Pet Show
KEATS, EZRA JACK

Fat Cat
KENT, JACK

The Owl and the Pussy Cat
LEAR, EDWARD

Seen Any Cats?
MODELL, FRANK

The Cat Came Back
SLAVIN, BILL

The Mitten
TRESSELT, ALVIN

Do Not Open
TURKLE, BRINTON

John Brown, Rose, and the Midnight Cat
WAGNER, JENNY

Nine-In-One, Grr! Grr!
XIONG, BLIA

LION STORIES TO READ ALOUD

Why Mosquitoes Buzz in People's Ears
AARDEMA, VERNA

Dandelion
FREEMAN, DON

Lazy Lion
HADITHI, MWENYE

Crocodile Beat
JORGENSEN, GAIL

Leo the Late Bloomer
KRAUS, ROBERT

Lizzy's Lion
LEE, DENNIS

The Name of the Tree
LOTTERIDGE, CELIA

Foolish Rabbit's Big Mistake
MARTIN, RAFE

A Lion for Lewis
WELLS, ROSEMARY

MORE STORIES

Puss in Boots
GALDONE, PAUL

Can You Catch Josephine? (and other *Josephine* titles)
POULIN, STEPHAN

Pierre
SENDAK, MAURICE

The Very Best of Friends
WILD, MARGARET

NONFICTION

Kitten
BURTON, JANE

Birth of a Kitten
FISCHER-NAGEL, ANDREAS

Count the Cats
WEIHS, ERIKA

NURSERY RHYMES

Three Little Kittens

*This is effective with finger puppets or as a felt
story. For puppets, put a face on front and back, and
put mittens on back only.*

Three little kittens lost their mittens
And they began to cry.
Oh Mother, dear, see here, see here,
Our mittens we have lost.
What! Lost your mittens you naughty kittens
Now you shall have no pie.
Meow, meow, meow, now you shall have no pie.

Three little kittens found their mittens
And they began to sigh.
Oh Mother, dear, see here, see here,
Our mittens we have found.
What! Found your mittens you darling kittens.
Now you shall have some pie.
Meow, meow, meow, now you shall have some pie.

Three little kittens soiled their mittens
And they began to cry,
Oh Mother, dear, we greatly fear,
Our mittens we have soiled.
What! Soiled your mittens you naughty kittens
Then they began to sigh,
Meow, meow, meow, then they began to sigh.

Three little kittens washed their mittens
And hung them out to dry.
Oh Mother, dear, see here, see here,
Our mittens we have washed.
What! Washed your mittens, then you're good
    little kittens,
But I smell a rat close by.
Meow, meow, meow, we smell a rat close by.

Hey Diddle, Diddle

Hey diddle diddle,
The cat and the fiddle,
The cow jumped over the moon.
The little dog laughed to see such sport,
And the dish ran away with the spoon.

Pussy Cat, Pussy Cat

Pussy cat, pussy cat, where have you been ?
I've been to London to visit the Queen.
Pussy cat, pussy cat, what did you there?
I frightened a little mouse under a chair.

Ding, Dong, Bell

Ding, dong, bell,
Pussy's in the well!
Who put her in?
Little Johnny Green.
Who pulled her out?
Little Tommy Stout.
What a naughty boy was that
To try to drown poor pussycat,
Who never did him any harm,
And killed the mice in his father's barn.

There Once Were Two Cats of Kilkenny

There once were two cats of Kilkenny.
Each thought there was one cat too many;
So they fought and they fit,
And they scratched and they bit,
'Til, excepting their nails,
And the tips of their tails,
Instead of two cats, there weren't any!

I Love Little Pussy

I love little pussy,
Her coat is so warm,
And if I don't hurt her
She'll do me no harm.
So I'll not pull her tail,
Nor drive her away,
But pussy and I
Very gently will play.
She shall sit by my side,
And I'll give her some food;
And pussy will love me
Because I am good.

Dame Trot and Her Cat

Dame Trot and her cat,
Sat down for a chat;
The Dame sat on this side,
And puss sat on that.

Puss, says the Dame,
Can you catch a rat,
Or a mouse in the dark?
Purr, says the cat.

Pussy Cat Mole

Pussy Cat Mole jumped over a coal,
And in her best petticoat burnt a great hole.
Poor pussy's weeping, she'll have no more milk,
Until her best petticoat's mended with silk.

The Lion and the Unicorn

The lion and the unicorn
Were fighting for the crown;
The lion beat the unicorn
All round about the town.
Some gave them white bread,
And some gave them brown;
And some gave them plum cake
And drummed them out of town.

FINGERPLAYS

Little Cat

One little cat and two little cats
Went for a romp one day.
One little cat and two little cats
Make how many cats at play?
Three little cats had lots of fun
Till growing tired, away ran one.
I really think he was most unkind
To the two little cats
That were left behind.

Soft Kitty

Soft kitty, warm kitty
Little ball of fur.
    Make fist of left hand for kitty.
Lazy kitty, pretty kitty,
"Purr, purr, purr."
    Pet kitty with right hand.

A Kitten

A kitten is fast asleep under the chair,
    Hide thumb under one hand.
And Donald can't find her.
He's looked everywhere.
    Fingers circle eyes to look.
Under the table,
    Peek under one hand.
And under the bed.
    Peek under other hand.
He looked in the corner,
And then Donald said:
"Come Kitty, come Kitty,
This milk is for you."
    Cup hands for dish.
And out came the kitty,
Calling, "Meow, meow."
    Thumb walks across lap.

Little Puppies and Kittens

One little, two little, three little kittens,
    Hold up three fingers of one hand.
Were napping in the sun.
    Bend fingers down.
One little, two little, three little puppies said,
    Hold up three finger of other hand.
"Come, let us all have fun."
Up to the kittens the puppies went creeping,
    Move puppy fingers slowly toward kitten fingers.
As quiet, as quiet could be.
One little, two little, three little kittens
Went scampering up a tall tree.
    Move kitten fingers quickly into the air.

Can You Walk on Tiptoe
    Act this out in a circle for freedom of movement.

Can you walk on tiptoe
As softly as a cat?
And can you stamp along the road,
Stamp, stamp, just like that?
Can you take some great big strides
The way a giant can?
Or walk along so slowly
Like a poor bent old man?

Mrs. Pussy

Mrs. Pussy, nice and fat,
With her kittens four,
> *Pussy is the thumb, and the four fingers are kittens.*

Went to sleep upon the mat,
Beside the kitchen door.
> *Fingers relax upon palm of hand.*

Mrs. Pussy heard a noise,
And up she jumped in glee
> *Thumb jumps up, then four fingers.*

"Kittens, maybe that's a mouse!
Let us go and see."
Creeping, creeping, creeping on
Silently they stole
> *Hand creeps rapidly.*

Back the little mouse had gone,
Back into its hole.
> *Left thumb is mouse. Conceal in palm of left hand.*

Cat

> *A lovely poem to act out, by Mary Britton Miller.*

The black cat yawns,
Opens her jaws,
Stretches her legs,
And shows her claws.

Then she gets up
And stands on four
Long stiff legs
And yawns some more.

She shows her sharp teeth,
She stretches her lip,
Her slice of a tongue
Turns up at the tip.

Lifting herself
On her delicate toes,
She arches her back
As high as it goes.

She lets herself down
With particular care
And pads away
With her tail in the air.

My Kitty Cat

I have a kitty cat named Puff.
> *Hold up one thumb.*

He's round and soft as a ball of fluff.
> *Make a fist, thumb sticking out.*

Each day he laps up all his milk,
> *Wiggle thumb.*

And his fur is soft as silk.
> *Stroke with other hand.*

When he's happy you will know,
For his fluffy tail swings to and fro.
> *Wiggle little finger.*

MORE IDEAS

1. Felt stories: *Fat Cat, The Owl and the Pussy Cat,* and *Three Little Kittens.*

2. Tell and Draw "The Tale of a Black Cat" by Carl Withers. You will find this in *When the Lights Go Out: Scary Stories to Tell* by Margaret Read MacDonald.

3. Words and music to "The Cat Came Back" are in *Fred Penner's Sing Along Play Along Song & Activity Book.*

4. *Nine-In-One, Grr! Grr!* is a folktale from Laos, and makes a good story to tell. Ask the children to join in on the chant.

5. Maurice Sendak's story about *Pierre,* the little boy who didn't care, is great to use in a lion program. I have also used it in programs celebrating exceptional characters. Unfortunately, the book is a little small for group presentation. Present it instead with puppets. Find an easy presentation idea in *Storytelling Made Easy with Puppets* by Jan VanSchryver.

Christmas

STORIES TO READ ALOUD

Harvey Slumfenburger's Christmas Present
BURNINGHAM, JOHN

Jingle Bugs (pop-up)
CARTER, DAVID

The Christmas Boot
DENTON, KADY MacDONALD

Claude the Dog
GACKENBACH, DICK

Spot's First Christmas
HILL, ERIC

Jingle Bells
KOVALSKI, MARYANN

Silent Night
MOHR, JOSEPH

The Night Before Christmas
MOORE, CLEMENT

Max's Christmas
WELLS, ROSEMARY

Morris's Disappearing Bag (big book)
WELLS, ROSEMARY

MORE STORIES

Christmas in the Barn
BROWN, MARGARET WISE

On Christmas Eve
BROWN, MARGARET WISE

Paul's Christmas Birthday
CARRICK, CAROL

Babar and Father Christmas
DE BRUNHOFF, JEAN

The Friendly Beasts: An Old English Christmas Carol
DE PAOLA, TOMIE

Petunia's Christmas
DUVOISIN, ROGER

Lucy & Tom's Christmas
HUGHES, SHIRLEY

The Silver Christmas Tree
HUTCHINS, PAT

The Little Drummer Boy
KEATS, EZRA JACK

The Christmas Gift
McCULLY, EMILY ARNOLD

The Christmas Stockings
PRICE, MATTHEW

How the Grinch Stole Christmas
SEUSS, DR.

Twinkle, Twinkle, Little Star
TAYLOR, JANE

Polar Express
VAN ALLSBURG, CHRIS

Merry Christmas Ernest and Celestine
VINCENT, GABRIELLE

NONFICTION

The Family Christmas Tree Book
DE PAOLA, TOMIE

Christmas Time
GIBBONS, GAIL

The Raffi Christmas Treasury (song book)
RAFFI

Things to Make and Do for Christmas
WEISS, ELLEN

NURSERY RHYMES

Little Jack Horner

Little Jack Horner sat in a corner
Eating his Christmas pie.
He stuck in his thumb
And pulled out a plum
And said, "What a good boy am I!"

Christmas Is Coming

Christmas is coming.
The geese are getting fat,
Pat tummy.

Please to put a penny
In the old man's hat.
Pretend to put a penny in one palm.

If you haven't got a penny,
A ha'penny will do;
Pat palm.

If you haven't got a ha'penny,
Then God bless you!
Point to a child.

FINGERPLAYS

Here Is the Chimney
A little Santa finger puppet makes a delightful surprise here.

Here is the chimney,
Make fist enclosing thumb.

Here is the top.
Palm of other hand on top of fist.

Open the lid,
Remove top hand quickly.

And out Santa will pop.
Pop up thumb.

Santa's Spectacles

These are Santa's spectacles,
Circle eyes with fingers.

And this is Santa's hat.
Make pointed shape on head.

This is the way he folds his hands,
And puts them in his lap!
Place hands in lap.

Shy Santa
This is perfect with Max's Christmas.

Isn't it the strangest thing
That Santa is so shy?
Hide face with hands.

We can never, never catch him,
Catching motion.

No matter how we try.
Running motion with arms.

It isn't any use to watch,
Hold hand over eyes and look around.

Because my mother said,
"Santa Claus will only come
When children are in bed."
Lay head on hands.

Santa Is Back

Two merry blue eyes,
Point to eyes.

A cute little nose,
Point to nose.

A long snowy beard,
Make motion as if stroking beard.

Two cheeks like a rose,
Point to cheeks.

A round, chubby form,
Rub tummy.

A big bulging sack.
Shoulders bent, hands holding sack.

Hurrah for old Santa!
Clap hands.

We're glad that he's back.

Santa Claus and His Reindeer

Here is old Santa.
Left thumb.

Here is his sleigh.
Right thumb.

These are his reindeer which he drives away.
Hold up eight fingers.

Dasher, Dancer, Prancer, Vixen,
Comet, Cupid, Donner, Blitzen,
Point to each finger in turn.

Away they all go!
Hands move to side, fingers fluttering.

Elves in the Workshop

Hold up ten fingers and wiggle one at a time.
It's also nice with ten little elves on the felt board.

At the North Pole, far away,
Ten little elves work night and day.
This little elf dips chocolate drops,
This little elf makes lollipops,
This little elf colours candy canes,
This little elf builds choo-choo trains.
This little elf tests planes that fly,
This little elf dresses dolls that cry,
This little elf paints horns that toot,
This little elf fills stockings with fruit.
This little elf wraps all the toys,
This little elf checks on the girls and boys.
Then, on Christmas Eve, they fill the sleigh,
With gifts for you on Christmas Day!

Five Little Brownies

All stand up. Hold up five fingers.
Suit actions to words.

Five little brownies standing in a row,
The first one twirled and pointed to his toe,
The second one nodded and winked his eye,
The third one clapped and gave a big sigh.
The fourth one smiled and bowed his head,
The fifth one whispered, "I hope they're in bed."
It was Christmas Eve, you see,
And they'd finished the gifts for you and me.

Santa Claus

Down the chimney dear Santa crept,
*Hold up left arm and creep fingers of right hand
down it.*

Into the room where the children slept.
Close eyes and put head on hands.

He saw their stockings hung in a row,
Suspend three fingers of left hand.

And he filled them with goodies from top to toe.
Make motion of filling stockings.

Although he counted them, one, two, three,
Count three fingers.

The baby's stocking he couldn't see.
"Ho, ho," said Santa, "that won't do."
Hold tummy and laugh.

So he popped her present right into her shoe!
Cup left hand and pop in fingers of right hand.

The Christmas Tree

I am a Christmas tree growing up tall,
Stretch up tall.

But when I first started, I was this small.
Crouch down.

Then I grew bigger and had branches this wide,
Stand slowly, arms out.

And I made pine cones with seeds hiding inside.
Hands for pine cones.

The wind shakes my branches,
Shake arms.

And down those seeds fall,
Flutter fingers downward.

To make new little pine trees for tinsel and balls.
*Point hands together for tree, opening slowly to form
ball shape.*

Christmas Presents

*This is lovely in felt. You'll need a big tree and
presents shaped as indicated. Then act it out.*

See all the presents by the Christmas tree.
Hands in sweeping motion.

Some for you
Point to children.

And some for me.
Point to self.

Long ones,
Hands spread wide apart.

Tall ones,
Measure from the floor.

Short ones, too.
Hands close together.

And here is a round one
Make circle with arms.

Wrapped in blue.
Isn't it fun to look and see
All the presents by the Christmas tree?
Nod.

Here Is the Chimney

Here is the chimney,
Away up high.
Hold fist in the air.

Watch just a moment,
Old Santa you'll spy!
Pop thumb up.

Make a Plum Pudding

Into a big bowl put the plums;
Drop imaginary plums in bowl.

Stir-about, stir-about, stir-about, stir!
Stir, as if with a big wodden spoon.

Next the good white flour comes;
Add flour.

Stir-about, stir-about, stir-about, stir!
Stir.

Add sugar, and peel, eggs, and spice;
Add new ingredients.

Stir-about, stir-about, stir-about, stir!
Stir.

Mix them, and fix them, and cook them twice.
Stir. Place bowl in oven.

Then eat it up! Eat it up! Eat it up!
Eat.

YUMMMMMMMM!
Rub stomach.

Christmas Cake

Bake a cake for Christmas,
Arms in circle form a bowl.

Stir it with a spoon,
Stir with one hand.

Pop it in the oven, and,
Push cake in oven.

Pull it out at noon.
Pull it out again.

Spread the frosting on it,
Hold cake with one hand and spread frosting with the other.

What a pretty sight!
Hold out both hands.

For you and me and Santa Claus
Point to friend, then self, then form Santa's beard with hands.

To see on Christmas night.

Santa's Elves

Santa's elves worked with one hammer, one hammer, one hammer, all day long.
Make fist. Pound on palm of other hand.

Santa's elves worked with two hammers, two hammers, two hammers, all day long.
Pound two fists in the air.

Santa's elves worked with three hammers, three hammers, three hammers, all day long.
Pound with two fists and one foot.

Santa's elves worked with four hammers, four hammers, four hammers, all day long.
Pound with two fists, and two feet.

And then they stopped!

Let's Go on a Santa Hunt!

Let's go on a Santa Hunt!
Ready? Let's go.
Slap hands on thighs.

I can hardly wait to see if I can find him before it's too late.
Oh, oh, what do I see? A big icy lake.
Can't go under it, can't go around it, gotta go over it.
Stop slapping rhythm, and make skating motion.

Oh, oh, what do I see? A snow storm.
Can't go over it, can't go around it, gotta go through it.
Dress up in hats scarves, etc., shiver in the wind.

Oh, oh, what do I see? A herd of reindeer.
Can't go over it, can't go through it, gotta go around it.
Stamp feet.

Oh, oh, what do I see? A big cave. Let's go inside.
I see two bright eyes, a big black nose,
And yikes! Sharp white teeth.
It's a polar bear!
Run all the way back the way you came.

Whew! We made it.
Maybe we'll find Santa the next time we go on a Santa hunt.

Five Little Bells

Use five fingers, or five little bells. Follow with "Ring Ring Ring the Bells."

Five little bells hanging in a row,
The first one said, "Ring me slow."
The second one said, "Ring me fast."
The third one said, "Ring me last."
The fourth one said, "I'm like a chime."
The fifth one said, "Ring us all at Christmas time."

SONGS

Must Be Santa

Sing it plain, sing it with a musical instrument, act it out, or sing it as you dress up a Santa on the felt board. Felt pieces you will need: Santa, beard, a star for the special night, boots, red jacket, cap, cherry nose, eight reindeer, and a sleigh. Listen to Raffi's version on Raffi's Christmas Album.

Who's got a beard that's long and white?
Santa's got a beard that's long and white.
Who comes around on a special night?
Santa comes around on a special night.
Special night, beard that's white,

Must be Santa, must be Santa,
Must be Santa, Santa Claus.

Who's got boots and a suit of red?
Santa's got boots and a suit of red.
Who wears a long cap on his head?
Santa wears a long cap on his head.
Cap on head, suit that's red,
Special night, beard that's white,

Must be Santa, must be Santa,
Must be Santa, Santa Claus.

Who's got a great big cherry nose?
Santa's got a great big cherry nose.
Who laughs this way, "Ho, ho, ho?"
Santa laughs this way, "Ho, ho, ho."
Cap on head, suit that's red,
Special night, beard that's white,

Must be Santa, must be Santa,
Must be Santa, Santa Claus.

Who very soon will come our way?
Santa very soon will come our way.
Eight little reindeer pull his sleigh,
Santa's little reindeer pull his sleigh.
Reindeer sleigh, come our way,
Ho, ho, ho, cherry nose,
Cap on head, suit that's red,
Special night, beard that's white,

Must be Santa, must be Santa,
Must be Santa, Santa Claus.

Jingle Bells

Jingle Bells, Jingle Bells, Jingle all the way,
Oh, what fun it is to ride in a one-horse open sleigh!
Jingle Bells, Jingle Bells, Jingle all the way,
Oh, what fun it is to ride in a one-horse open sleigh!

Dashing through the snow, in a one-horse open sleigh,
O'er the fields we go, laughing all the way.
Bells on bobtails ring, making spirits bright.
What fun it is to ride and sing a sleighing song tonight!

Repeat first verse.

Rudolph the Red-Nosed Reindeer

Rudolph the red-nosed reindeer
Had a very shiny nose.
And if you ever saw him
You would even say it glows.
All of the other reindeer
Used to laugh and call him names.
They never let poor Rudolph
Play in any reindeer games.
Then one foggy Christmas Eve,
Santa came to say,
"Rudolph with your nose so bright
Won't you guide my sleigh tonight."
Then how the reindeer loved him
As they shouted out with glee,
"Rudolph the red-nosed reindeer,
You'll go down in history."

S-A-N-T-A

Sing to the tune of "BINGO." Use a glove puppet with big red letters on fingers, and a tiny Santa in the palm.

I know a man with a long white beard
And Santa is his name-o.
S-A-N-T-A, S-A-N-T-A, S-A-N-T-A,
And Santa is his name-o.

He slides down the chimney with a pack on his back,
And Santa is his name-o.
S-A-N-T-A, S-A-N-T-A, S-A-N-T-A,
And Santa is his name-o.

Eight little reindeer pull his sleigh,
And Santa is his name-o.
S-A-N-T-A, S-A-N-T-A, S-A-N-T-A,
And Santa is his name-o.

Ring, Ring, Ring the Bells

Sing to the tune of "Row, Row Row Your Boat."
Use fingers or bells.

Ring, ring, ring, the bells
Ring them loud and clear,
To tell the children everywhere
That Christmas time is here.

Here Comes Santa Claus

Here comes Santa Claus,
Here comes Santa Claus,
Right down Santa Claus lane.
Vixen and Blitzen and all his reindeer
Are pulling on the rein.
Bells are ringing, children singing,
All is merry and bright.
So hang your stockings, and say your prayers,
'Cause Santa Claus comes tonight.

We Wish You a Merry Christmas

We wish you a merry Christmas,
We wish you a merry Christmas,
We wish you a merry Christmas,
And a Happy New Year.

Let's all do a little clapping . . .
Let's all do a little stamping . . .
Let's all do a little twirling . . .
To spread Christmas cheer!

Good tidings to you, wherever you are,
Good tidings for Christmas and a Happy New Year!

He'll Be Comin' Down the Chimney

This is an adaptation of "She'll Be Comin' Round the Mountain." Add your own verses.

He'll be comin' down the chimney when he
    comes . . . (squish, squeeze).
He'll be driving nine brown reindeer when he
    comes . . . (whoa back).
We will all be sound asleep when he comes . . .
    (snore).
But we'll leave him milk and cookies when he
    comes . . . (nibble, nibble).
We will all hear him laughing when he goes . . .
    (ho, ho, ho).

MORE IDEAS

1. Felt Stories: *The Elves and the Shoemaker* (simplified), *Merry Christmas Harry* by Mary Chalmers, *Christmas Present for a Friend* by Mary Blakely, and *Christmas in the Chicken Coop* by Felecia Bond.

2. For snowmen rhymes, see WEATHER – SNOWY DAY.

3. Tell the story of *The Gingerbread Man*, then serve gingerbread cookies and have a Christmas party.

4. Puppetry: "Cookies" from *Frog and Toad All Year* by Arnold Lobel is an easily adapted story about the irresistibility of Christmas cookies.

5. Puppetry: "The Forgetful Santa." This can be made into an elaborate full-scale production for two puppeteers, or it can be scaled down for a simpler one-person show. Ask for the script at the public library.

6. Talk about how children celebrate Christmas in Mexico. A smashing celebration can be had with a real home-made pinata with candies inside. See Ernie Coombs' *Mr. Dressup's 50 More Things to Make & Do* for an easy pattern.

7. Tell-and-Draw "Santa Claus" from *Lots More Tell and Draw Stories* by Margaret Oldfield.

8. Tell the story "Sensible, Quiet Clifford Jones," who is the first to shake Santa's hand at a Christmas party from *Listen! And Help Tell the Story* by Bernice Wells Carlson.

9. See "The Singing Dreidle," "Gloria's Christmas Angel," and "The Spirit of Christmas" in *"Cut & Tell" Scissor Stories for Winter* by Jean Warren.

CRAFTS

1. Take a Christmas present wrapped in blue paper to storytime. Then after the "Christmas Presents" fingerplay, give out simple tree ornament shapes: bells, diamonds, circles, rectangles, cut from coloured construction paper. Decorate using crayons, glue, and sparkle dust.

2. Make paper chains out of strips of coloured construction paper glued together.

3. Make Rudolph paper bag puppets. Trace hands on brown construction paper. These are the antlers. Cut out and glue onto a small paper bag. Draw on eyes. Glue on a red pompom nose.

4. Dip palms in green paint and make handprint wreaths or a giant Christmas tree with fingers pointing down.

5. See WEATHER – SNOWY DAY for snowmen craft ideas. Popcorn snowmen are especially nice at Christmas time.

Circus

STORIES TO READ ALOUD

Lottie's Circus
BLOS, JOAH W.

Circus
EHLERT, LOIS

Bearymore
FREEMAN, DON

Fat Charlie's Circus
GAY, MARIE-LOUISE

Harriet Goes to the Circus
MAESTRO, BETSY

Circus Baby
PETERSHAM, MAUD

MORE STORIES

Cannonball Simp
BURNINGHAM, JOHN

Carousel
CREWS, DONALD

Parade
CREWS, DONALD

Mirette on the High Wire
McCULLY, EMILY ARNOLD

Randy's Dandy Lions
PEET, BILL

Circus Numbers
PEPPE, RODNEY

Curious George Rides a Bike
REY, H. A.

The Clown's Smile
THALER, MIKE

Ernest and Celestine at the Circus
VINCENT, GABRIELLE

Morgan the Magnificent
WALLACE, IAN

Brian Wildsmith's Circus
WILDSMITH, BRIAN

NONFICTION

Face Painting
(KLUTZ PRESS)

Painting Faces
HALDANE, SUZANNE

Circus! Circus! (poetry)
HOPKINS, LEE BENNET

Clowns
SOBOL, HARRIET LANGSAM

Paper Circus: How to Create You Own Circus
WEST, ROBIN

FINGERPLAYS

Who Is It? Mr. Clown!

Who is it that wears a happy smile,
Use index fingers to pull corners of mouth up.

That almost stretches half a mile?
Who is it that turns it up side down,
Pull corners of mouth down.

And changes his smile into a frown?
Who is it that turns his face all around,
Why, who could it be but Mr. Clown?

I Wish I Were a Circus Clown

I wish I were a circus clown,
  Point to self.

With smile so wide and eyes so round,
  Draw wide smile. Make rings around eyes.

With pointed hat and funny nose,
  Make a tent of hands, and place on head.
  Point to nose.

And polka dots upon my clothes.
  Point to clothes.

To hospitals and homes I'd go,
Where children cried when they felt low,
  Rub eyes with fists.

I'd make them dry their salty tears
  Dab your eyes.

By wiggling my floppy ears.
  Place hands on ears and wiggle.

Tightrope Walker

  Pretend you're a tightrope walker.

While the band is playing,
Back and forth I go.
High above the people,
Sitting far below.
While the crowd is cheering,
I sway from side to side.
Now my act is over,
Down the pole I slide.

Stand up Tall

Stand up tall, hands in the air;
  All stand and raise hands in the air.

Now sit down, in your chair.
  Sit down.

Clap your hands;
  Clap three times.

Make a frown.
  Frown.

Smile and smile,
  Smile.

And flop like a clown!
  Relax with arms dangling.

This Little Clown

  Hold up five fingers one at a time.

This little clown is fat and gay;
This little clown does tricks all day;
This little clown is tall and strong;
This little clown sings a funny song;
This little clown is wee and small,
But he can do anything at all!

Riding the Merry-Go-Round

Ride with me on the merry-go-round,
Around and around and around.
  Move one hand in circles.

Up the horses go, up!
  Raise arms in the air.

Down the horses go, down!
  Lower arms.

You ride a horse that is white.
  Point to neighbor.

I ride a horse that is brown.
  Point to self.

Up and down on the merry-go-round.
  Raise and lower arms.

Our horses go round and round.
  Move one hand in circles.

MORE IDEAS

1. Felts: *Harriet Goes to the Circus*, which is a simple concept book.

2. Tell-and-Draw "The Circus," from *Tell and Draw Stories* by Margaret Oldfield.

3. Art activity: Paint clown faces on paper plates. Paint a happy face on one side and a sad face on the other.

4. Art and drama activity: Let the children choose the kinds of animals (or clowns) they would like to be. Paint animal or clown masks on paper plates, and attach to sticks to hold up, or tie with string to hang around the neck. Then have a circus parade.

5. Face painting is a favourite activity. Look for ideas in *Painting Faces* and *Make-up Magic*.

6. For more ideas see: ELEPHANTS, MONKEYS, and ANIMALS OF THE WILD.

Clothing

STORIES TO READ ALOUD

Animals Should Definitely Not Wear Clothing
BARRETT, JUDITH

Mister Magnolia
BLAKE, QUENTIN

Big Sarah's Little Boots
BOURGEOIS, PAULETTE

The Mitten
BRETT, JAN

Jesse Bear, What Will You Wear?
CARLSTROM, NANCY WHITE

Maisy Goes Swimming
COUSINS, LUCY

Charlie Needs a Cloak
DE PAOLA, TOMIE

Shoes from Grandpa
FOX, MEM

Three Little Kittens
GALDONE, PAUL

Something from Nothing
GILMAN, PHOEBE

Mrs. Mopple's Washing Line
HEWETT, ANITA

You'll Soon Grow into Them, Titch
HUTCHINS, PAT

The Pigs' Picnic
KASZA, KEIKO

Jennie's Hat
KEATS, EZRA JACK

Socks for Supper
KENT, JACK

The Quangle Wangle's Hat
LEAR, EDWARD

Froggy Gets Dressed
LONDON, JONATHAN

Amos's Sweater
LUNN, JANET

Mrs. McDockerty's Knitting
MARTINEZ, RUTH

The Paper Bag Princess
MUNSCH, ROBERT

Thomas's Snowsuit
MUNSCH, ROBERT

Who Took the Farmer's Hat?
NODSET, JOAN

Mary Wore Her Red Dress and Henry Wore His Green Sneakers
PEEK, MERLE

Caps for Sale
SLOBODKINA, ESPHYR

Red Is Best
STINSON, KATHY

The Mitten
TRESSELT, ALVIN

Pig in a Pond
WADDELL, MARTIN

How Do I Put It On?
WATANABE, SHIGEO

Max's Dragon Shirt
WELLS, ROSEMARY

MORE STORIES

The Emperor's New Clothes
ANDERSEN, H. C.

Pelle's New Suit
BESKOW, ELSA

Not So Fast Songololo
DALY, NIKI

Brown Bear in a Brown Chair
HALE, IRINA

NONFICTION

NURSERY RHYMES

One Misty, Moisty Morning

One misty, moisty morning,
When cloudy was the weather,
I chanced to meet an old man,
Clothed all in leather.
He began to compliment
And I began to grin,
How do you do, and how do you do,
And how do you do again?

Gregory Griggs

Gregory Griggs, Gregory Griggs
Had twenty-seven different wigs.
He wore them up, he wore them down,
To please the people of the town.
He wore them east, he wore them west,
But never could tell which he loved best.

Hector Protector Dressed All in Green

Hector Protector was dressed all in green;
Hector Protector was sent to the Queen.
The Queen did not like him,
No more did the King,
So Hector Protector was sent back again.

Three Young Rats with Black Felt Hats

Three young rats with black felt hats,
Three young ducks with white straw flats,
Three young dogs with curling tails,
Three young cats with demi-veils,
Went out to walk with three young pigs
In satin vests and sorrel wigs.
But suddenly it chanced to rain,
And so they all went home again.

Cock-a-doodle-doo!

Cock-a-doodle-doo!
My dame has lost her shoe,
My master's lost his fiddling stick
And doesn't know what to do.

Cock-a-doodle-doo!
What is my dame to do?
Till master finds his fiddling stick
She'll dance without her shoe.

Cock-a-doodle-doo!
My dame has found her shoe,
And master's found his fiddling stick,
Sing doodle-doodle-doo.

Cock-a-doodle-doo!
My dame will dance with you,
While master fiddles his fiddling stick
For dame and doodle-doo.

Round and Round the Cobbler's Bench

See more verses in MONKEYS, page 129.

Round and round the cobbler's bench,
Two fingers run around palm of other hand.

The monkey chased the weasel.
The monkey thought 'twas all in fun,
Pop! Goes the weasel.
Clap on pop.

Cobbler, Cobbler

Join two rhymes together for a longer verse.

Cobbler, cobbler, mend my shoe,
Pound fists together in rhythm.

Get it done by half past two.
Let arms indicate half past two on the clock.

'Cos my toe is peeping through,
Push your thumb up through left hand and wiggle.

Cobbler, cobbler, mend my shoe.
Pound fists together again.

Cobbler, Cobbler

Cobbler, cobbler, mend my shoe,
Pound fists together in rhythm.

Get it done by half past two.
Let arms indicate half past two on the clock.

Stitch it up and stitch it down,
Hands up, hands down.

Then I'll give you half a crown.
Pretend to give away money.

There Was a Maid on Scrabble Hill

There was a maid on Scrabble Hill,
And if not dead, she lives there still.
She grew so tall, she reached the sky,
And on the moon hung clothes to dry.

Three Little Kittens

See CATS & KITTENS, page 40.

FINGERPLAYS

My Snowsuit

Perfect after Thomas's Snowsuit!

My zipper suit is bunny brown.
Point to chest.

The top zips up,
Draw fingers up from tummy to chin.

The legs zip down.
Draw fingers down leg to ankle.

I wear it every day.
My daddy brought it out from town.
Zip it up and zip it down,
Repeat zipper motion.

And hurry out to play!

Tying My Shoe

Suit actions to words.

I know how to tie my shoe.
I take the loop and poke it through.
It's very hard to make it stay,
Because my thumb gets in the way.

All by Myself, Just Me!

Suit actions to words.

Hat on head, chin strap here,
Snap just so, you see ;
I can put my cap on
All by myself - just me!

One arm in, two arms in,
Buttons one, two, three;
I can put my coat on
All by myself - just me!

Toes in first, heels push down,
Pull, pull, pull and "whee!"
I can put my boots on
All by myself - just me!

Fingers here, thumbs right here,
Hands are warm as can be;
I can put my mittens on
All by myself - just me!

The Mitten Song

"Thumb in the thumb place
Fingers all together!"
Hold up one hand, fingers together, thumb apart.

This is the song we sing in mitten weather.
When it's cold,
Rub hands together.

It doesn't matter whether,
Mittens are wool,
Or made of finest leather.
Hold up two hands, fingers together, thumb apart.

This is the song we sing in mitten weather,
"Thumb in thumb place
Fingers all together!"
Repeat action.

My Hat

My hat, it has three corners.
*Join thumbs and index fingers in a triangle shape,
and place on top of head.*

Three corners has my hat.
Raise three fingers.

If it did not have three corners,
Raise three fingers and shake head.

It would not be my hat!
*Join thumbs and index fingers in a triangle shape,
and place on top of head again.*

I Can

Act it out!

I can tie my shoe lace.
I can comb my hair.
I can wash my hands and face,
And dry myself with care.

I can brush my teeth, too,
And button up my frocks;
I can say, "How do you do?"
And put on both my socks.

Shiny Shoes

First I loosen mud and dirt.
Hold up one hand for shoe. Brush off with other.

My shoes I then rub clean.
Rub shoe with palm of other hand.

For shoes in such a dreadful sight
Never should be seen.
Hide shoe behind back for a moment.

Next I spread the polish on,
*Join thumb and index finger of one hand to make
polish spreader, and pretend to coat shoe.*

And then I let it dry.
I brush and brush, and brush and brush.
Make fist and brush shoe vigorously.

How those shoes shine! Oh, my!
Extend hand and admire.

Before I Jump into Bed

Before I jump into bed at night,
Jump.

Before I dim the light,
Switch out the light.

I put my shoes together,
Hands together.

So they can talk at night.
Hands talk.

I'm sure they would be lonesome
If I tossed them here and there,
Toss hands left and right.

So I put them close together,
Place hands together.

For they're a friendly pair.

The Washing Machine

Roll hands and move, rolling, up and down.

Washing in the washing machine,
Going round and round.
Washing in the washing machine,
Moving up and down.
Round and round and up and down,
It makes a noisy sound.
Faster, faster, faster,
Round and round and round.
Then stop!

Washing Clothes

Here's a little washtub,
Cup hands to make tub.

And here's a cake of soap.
Clench one fist.

Here's a little washboard,
Use back of hand turned sideways.

And this is how we scrub.
Rub across fingers.

Here's a clothes line way up high,
Form high imaginary line with hands.

Now the clothes are drying.
Wooooo the wind comes by.
Sweeping motion with hand.

Now the clothes are dry.

This Is the Way We All Get Dressed

*Sing to the tune of the "Mulberry Bush" and act it
out. Ham it up by putting your socks on your ears,
and so on!*

This is the way we all get dressed,
All get dressed, all get dressed,
This is the way we all get dressed,
So early in the morning.

This is the way we put on our socks . . .
. . . our pants
. . . our tights
. . . our shirts
. . . our shoes
. . . our coats
. . . our mitts
. . . our hats

Here We Go Round the Mulberry Bush

Mime the actions suggested by the words. Make up specific verses for caring for clothes, or add the Mulberry Bush verse and play the song as a circle game.

Here we go round the mulberry bush,
The mulberry bush, the mulberry bush,
Here we go round the mulberry bush,
On a cold and frosty morning.

This is the way we wash our clothes,
Wash our clothes, wash our clothes,
This is the way we wash our clothes,
On a cold and frosty morning.

This is the way we iron our clothes . . .
This is the way we sweep our rooms . . .
This is the way we mend our shoes . . .
This is the way we wash our hands . . .
This is the way we brush our teeth . . .
This is the way we comb our hair . . .
Here we go round the mulberry bush . . .

This Is the Way We Wash Our Clothes

This is another variation of "Here We Go 'Round the Mulberry Bush." Suit actions to words.

This is the way we wash our clothes,
Rub-a-dub-dub, rub-a-dub-dub.
This is the way we wash our clothes,
So early in the morning.

Watch them getting clean and white,
Rub-a-dub-dub, rub-a-dub-dub!
Watch them getting clean and white,
So early in the morning.

This is the way we mangle them,
Rumble-de-dee, rumble-de-dee.
This is the way we mangle them,
So early in the morning.

Round and round the handle goes,
Rumble-de-dee, rumble-de-dee!
Round and round the handle goes,
So early in the morning.

This is the way we hang them out,
Flippity-flap, flippity-flap.
This is the way we hang them out,
So early in the morning.

See them blowing in the wind.
Flippity-flap, flippity-flap!
See them blowing in the wind.
So early in the morning.

This is the way we iron them,
Smooth as can be, smooth as can be.
This is the way we iron them,
So early in the morning.

Soon our wash day will be done,
Yippie ai ay, yippie ai ay,
Soon our wash day will be done,
Then we'll have our tea.

If You're Wearing Red Today

Sing to the tune of "Mary Had a Little Lamb." When all are standing up, form a circle and play another game like "The Grand Old Duke of York."

If you're wearing red today,
Red today, red today,
If you're wearing red today,
Please stand up.

If you're wearing green today,
Green today, green today,

. . . and so on.

Mary Wore Her Red Dress

This is very nice after Red Is Best. Hear the tune of this lovely simple song on Raffi's Everything Grows cassette. Words and music in The Raffi Everything Grows Songbook.

Mary wore her red dress, red dress, red dress,
Mary wore her red dress all day long.

Mary wore her red hat . . . all day long.
Mary wore her red shoes . . . all day long.
Mary wore her red gloves . . . all day long.
Mary was a red bird . . . all day long.
Mary wore her red dress . . . all day long.

Whistle or hum the last verse.

Jenny Jenkins

Get dressed in the morning with Jenny Jenkins.
See COLOUR, page 59.

MORE IDEAS

1. Felt Stories: *Caps for Sale, How Do I Put It On?, The Mitten, Who Took The Farmer's Hat?, Jennie's Hat, The Three Little Kittens, Mrs. Mopple's Washing Line,* and *My Shirt is White* by Dick Bruna, a very simple story for toddlers.

2. Stories good for toddlers: *Animals Should Definitely Not Wear Clothing; Jesse Bear, What Will You Wear?; Maisy Goes Swimming; You'll Soon Grow into Them, Titch; Who Took The Farmers Hat?; Caps for Sale; Red Is Best; How Do I Put It On?; Three Little Kittens;* and *My Shirt Is White.*

3. *How Do I Put It On?* is fun to perform with a teddy bear and clothes props. It's also fun to perform with your own clothes props.

4. Make an Amos sheep puppet, get a wool sweater that almost fits, and tell *Amos's Sweater.*

5. Have a Hat Day with: *The Quangle Wangle's Hat, Caps for Sale, Who Took the Farmer's Hat?,* and *Jennie's Hat.*

6. When you tell *Caps for Sale,* (six little monkeys and six little caps will do), encourage the children to imitate the monkeys while you play the peddler. Follow up with "Five Little Monkeys," "The Cobbler's Bench" and other verses from MONKEYS.

7. *Jenny's Hat* is a wonderful story to perform with props. Get yourself a plain hat and decorate with dried flowers, coloured eggs, and pictures as you tell. Ask one of the storytime children to sit for you if you like. This is an especially lovely story to tell in spring time.

8. Have a Shoe Day with: *Mr. Magnolia, Shoes from Grandpa,* and *Big Sarah's Little Boots.*

9. Have a Mitten day with: *The Mitten, The Three Little Kittens,* and "Baa Baa Black Sheep."

10. Get dressed in winter with any of these: *Amos's Sweater, Thomas's Snowsuit, The Mitten, Mrs. McDockerty's Knitting, Froggy Gets Dressed,* and "Baa Baa Black Sheep."

11. Get dressed for rainy weather with *Big Sarah's Little Boots* and "The Rainhat." Add more stories from WEATHER – RAINY DAY.

12. Tell the story of "The Rainhat" from *Just Enough to Make a Story* by Nancy Schimmel. Then help children fold their own rainhats out of newsprint.

13. Get undressed to go swimming with *Pig in a Pond, Maisy Goes Swimming,* and *Froggy Goes for a Swim* by Jonathan London. Wind up with an accidental swim with *Mr. Gumpy's Outing.* Sing "Row Row Row Your Boat," and other boating songs from SEA & SEASHORE.

14. Get dressed in the morning with "Frère Jacques," "This is the way we all get dressed," "Lazy Lousy Liza Briggs," "Lazy Mary," *Froggy Gets Dressed, Thomas's Snowsuit, How Do I Put It On?,* or *Red Is Best.*

15. Make props out of scraps of fabric for telling *Something from Nothing.* Or, tell "The Tailor" from Nancy Schimmel's *Just Enough to Tell a Story,* a slightly different version of the same story.

16. Use a travel clothesline (with tiny clothes-pins) strung between two chairs, and sing "The Farmer in the Dell" or "Old MacDonald," hanging up paper animal masks as you go. Clotheslines also appear in *Mrs. Mopple's Washing Line, Three Little Kittens,* and in "Sing a Song of Sixpence."

17. *Timothy Goes to School* makes a tale for two tellers using giant (adult sized) clothes cut-outs as props. Great for a back-to-school performance!

18. There's a whole book on this theme! *Glad Rags: Stories and Activities Featuring Clothes for Children* by Jan Irving.

Colour & Art

STORIES TO READ ALOUD

Monkey Face
ASCH, FRANK

Big Sarah's Little Boots
BOURGEOIS, PAULETTE

Planting a Rainbow
EHLERT, LOIS

Rainbow of My Own
FREEMAN, DON

A Colour of His Own
LIONNI, LEO

Frederick
LIONNI, LEO

Let's Make Rabbits
LIONNI, LEO

Little Blue and Little Yellow
LIONNI, LEO

The Great Blueness and Other Predicaments
LOBEL, ARNOLD

Brown Bear, Brown Bear
MARTIN, BILL

Mary Wore Her Red Dress and Henry Wore His Green Sneakers
PEEK, MERLE

Bear's Picture
PINKWATER, DANIEL

The Big Orange Splot
PINKWATER, MANUS

Who Said Red?
SERFOZO, MARY

Oh! Were They Ever Happy
SPIER, PETER

Red Is Best
STINSON, KATHY

I Went Walking
WILLIAMS, SUE

Mr. Rabbit and the Lovely Present
ZOLOTOW, CHARLOTTE

MORE STORIES

Carousel
CREWS, DONALD

Freight Train
CREWS, DONALD

The Wing on a Flea: A Book About Shapes
EMBERLY, ED

White Is the Moon
GREELEY, VALERIE

Colours
HUGHES, SHIRLEY

Emma
KESSELMAN, WENDY

Samuel Todd's Book of Great Colours
KONIGSBURG, E.L.

Green Eggs and Ham
SEUSS, DR.

Mouse Paint
WALSH, ELLEN STOLL

The Bears' Book of Colours
WILD, JOCELYN

A Million Chameleons
YOUNG, JAMES

NONFICTION

Color Farm
EHLERT, LOIS

Color Zoo
EHLERT, LOIS

Is It Red? Is It Yellow? Is It Blue?
HOBAN, TANA

Color Dance
JONAS, ANN

Growing Colors
McMILLAN, BRUCE

Colours
REISS, JOHN

Colors
YENAWINE, PHILIP

Shapes
YENAWINE, PHILIP

ABOUT ART & ARTISTS

Monkey Face
ASCH, FRANK

Visiting the Art Museum (nonfiction)
BROWN, LAURENE KRASNY

Morgan and the Artist
CARRICK, DONALD

No Good in Art
COHEN, MIRIAM

Liang and the Magic Paintbrush
DEMI

The Art Lesson
DE PAOLA, TOMIE

Legend of the Indian Paintbrush
DE PAOLA, TOMIE

Speak Up, Blanche!
McCULLY, EMILY ARNOLD

NURSERY RHYMES

Hector Protector

Hector Protector was dressed all in green;
Hector Protector was sent to the Queen.
The Queen did not like him,
No more did the King,
So Hector Protector was sent back again.

Baa Baa Black Sheep

*Sing this twice. Once for the little girl who lives
down the lane.*

Baa, Baa, Black Sheep,
Have you any wool?
Yes, sir, yes, sir,
Three bags full.
One for my master,
One for my dame,
And one for the little boy
Who lives down the lane.
Baa, Baa, Black Sheep,
Have you any wool?
Yes, sir, yes, sir,
Three bags full.

Little Boy Blue

Little Boy Blue,
Come Blow your horn!
The sheep's in the meadow,
The cow's in the corn.
Where is the boy
Who looks after the sheep?
He's under a haystack, fast asleep.
Will you wake him?
No, not I,
For if I do,
He's sure to cry.

Little Blue Ben

Little Blue Ben, who lives in the glen,
Keeps a blue cat and one blue hen,
Which lays of blue eggs a score and ten;
Where shall I find the little Blue Ben?

FINGERPLAYS

Two Little Blackbirds

Two little blackbirds sitting on a hill,
Hold up two thumbs.

One named Jack and one named Jill,
Lift one, then the other.

Fly away Jack,
Hide one behind your back.

Fly away Jill,
Hide the other behind your back.

Come back Jack,
Then bring them back home again, one at a time.

Come back Jill.

What Color Are You Wearing?

Suit actions to words. Repeat until most of the common colours are used.

Leader says:
Red, red, red, red,
Who is wearing red today?
Red, red, red, red,
Who is wearing red?

All children with red showing say:

I am wearing red today.
Look at me and you will say
Red, red, red, red,
I am wearing red today.

SONGS

If You're Wearing Red Today

Sing to the tune of "Mary Had a Little Lamb." When all are standing up, form a circle and play another game like "The Grand Old Duke of York."

If you're wearing red today,
Red today, red today,
If you're wearing red today,
Please stand up.

If you're wearing green today,
Green today, green today,

. . . and so on.

Mary Wore Her Red Dress

This is very nice after Red Is Best. *Hear the tune of this lovely simple song on Raffi's* Everything Grows *cassette. Words and music are in* The Raffi Everything Grows Songbook.

Mary wore her red dress, red dress, red dress,
Mary wore her red dress all day long.

Mary wore her red hat . . . all day long.
Mary wore her red shoes . . . all day long.
Mary wore her red gloves . . . all day long.
Mary was a red bird . . . all day long.
Mary wore her red dress . . . all day long.

Whistle or hum the last verse.

Jenny Jenkins

Listen to the tune of this funky crazy song on Sharon, Lois & Bram's Great Big Hits. *Music is in* Elephant Jam. *Roll hands toegether on "Roll, Jenny Jenkins, roll." Make up your own verses.*

Will you wear white
Oh my dear, oh my dear?
Will you wear white, Jenny Jenkins?
No-o-o-o I won't wear white
For the colour's too bright.

Chorus:
I'll buy me a foldy, roldy,
Tiddly toldy, rufty, tufty,
Girlie whirlie,
Roll, Jenny Jenkins, roll.

Will you wear red
Oh my dear, oh my dear?
Will you wear red, Jenny Jenkins?
No-o-o-o I won't wear red
I'd rather soak my head.

Repeat chorus.

Will you wear green
Oh my dear, oh my dear?
Will you wear green, Jenny Jenkins?
No-o-o-o I won't wear green
I would look like a bean.

Repeat chorus.

Will you wear blue
Oh my dear, oh my dear?
Will you wear blue, Jenny Jenkins?
No-o-o-o I won't wear blue
I'd rather eat my shoe.

Repeat chorus.

Then what will you wear
Oh my dear, oh my dear?
What will you wear, Jenny Jenkins?
Well then, I'll just go bare
With a ribbon in my hair.

Repeat chorus.

Stop Says the Red Light

*Singing tune is an upbeat version of
"Twinkle Twinkle Little Star."*

Stop says the red light
Go says the green.
Slow says the yellow light in between.
Stop says the red light,
Go says the green,
We must obey them, even the queen!

MORE IDEAS

1. Felt Stories: *Brown Bear, Brown Bear*; *I Went Walking*; *Monkey Face*; *Mr. Rabbit and the Lovely Present*; and "There's a Little White Duck" (page 70).

2. *Mr. Rabbit and the Lovely Present* also makes a lovely and simple puppet show.

3. Give children little pieces of blue and yellow transparencies so they can understand about green before reading *Little Blue and Little Yellow*. Or demonstrate with drops of food colouring in a jar of water and follow up by mixing all kinds of colours.

4. Have children draw rainbows with crayons or paints.

5. Drama: Act out the story of *The Great Blueness* by Arnold Lobel. Make pictures that are only blue, only yellow, only red. Use this story as the basis for experimenting with colour mixing.

6. For a circle game with "Bluebird, Bluebird" see BIRDS, page 34.

7. Play "I Spy." The storyteller says, "I spy, with my little eye, something that is red." And the children guess what in the room is red. And so on. This could lead to a surprise in the end such as a basket full of grapes for everybody to eat, or all the fruit from *Mr. Rabbit and the Lovely Present*.

8. Have a special storytime celebrating the art work of Tomie De Paola with *The Art Lesson*, a child's biography, and more of De Paola's stories. Focus on any illustrator and follow up with art activities inspired by the illustrator's technique. Ezra Jack Keats could be followed up with collage, Barbara Reid and Odette Johnson with plasticine, Tejima with wax resist, and so on.

9. *Monkey Face* is my favourite story to draw-and-tell using coloured markers on a big pad of paper. Unfortunately this book is out of print, but ask your children's librarian. There may be copies about.

10. Art: Have a special storytime on art and artists. *Liang and the Magic Paint Brush* is easy to learn, fun to tell, and full of expression. Add *Monkey Face. The Art Lesson, Emma,* and *Bear's Picture* are good stories to read aloud. The best book I have found for adults helping little artists develop their talent is *Scribble Cookies.* (See the ARTS, CRAFTS, & ACTIVITIES in RECOMMENDED RESOURCES at the back of this book for publishing details.) The books by Yenawine are useful for introducing children to classical art and artists.

Counting

STORIES TO READ ALOUD

Ten, Nine, Eight
BANG, MOLLY

The Rooster Who Set Out to See the World
CARLE, ERIC

The Very Hungry Caterpillar
CARLE, ERIC

One Red Rooster
CARROLL, KATHLEEN

The Most Amazing Hide and Seek Counting Book
CROWTHER, ROBERT

Over in the Meadow
GALDONE, PAUL

1 Hunter
HUTCHINS, PAT

The Doorbell Rang
HUTCHINS, PAT

Over in the Meadow
LANGSTAFF, JOHN

The Balancing Act: A Counting Song
PEEK, MERLE

Roll Over: A Counting Song
PEEK, MERLE

Crictor
UNGERER, TOMI

MORE COUNTING BOOKS

Byron and His Balloon: An English-Chipewyan Counting Book
(BY THE CHILDREN OF LA LOCHE)

Anno's Counting House
ANNO, MITSUMASA

Anno's Mysterious Multiplying Jar
ANNO, MITSUMASA

10 for Dinner
BOGART, JO ELLEN

1, 2, 3 to the Zoo: A Counting Book
CARLE, ERIC

Up to Ten and Down Again
ERNST, LISA CAMPBELL

Moja Means One
FEELINGS, MURIEL

One White Sail: A Caribbean Counting Song
GARNE, S. T.

Teddy Bears One to Ten
GETZ, SUSANNA

Count Your Way Through Japan
(and other countries)
HASKINS, KIM

Count and See
HOBAN, TANA

26 Letters and 99 Cents
HOBAN, TANA

Lucy and Tom's 1 2 3
HUGHES, SHIRLEY

Cat Count
LEWIN, BETSY

One Gorilla
MOROZUMI, ATSUKO

One Was Johnny
SENDAK, MAURICE

How Much Is a Million?
SCHWARTZ, DAVID

Who's Counting?
TAFURI, NANCY

NURSERY RHYMES

Hickory Dickory Dock

Hickory dickory dock,
Swing arms like a pendulum.

The mouse ran up the clock.
Run two fingers up your arm.

The clock struck one,
Hold up one finger.

And down he run,
Run two fingers back down your arm.

Hickory, dickory, dock.
Swing arm like a pendulum again.

One, Two, Buckle My Shoe

Clap hands in time. Put "a big fat hen" on the felt board and jump into "Hickety Pickety."

One, two, buckle my shoe;
Three, four, open the door;
Five, six, pick up sticks;
Seven, eight, lay them straight;
Nine, ten, a big fat hen;

Eleven, twelve, dig and delve;
Thirteen, fourteen, maids a-courting;
Fifteen, sixteen, maids in the kitchen;
Seventeen, eighteen, maids a-waiting;
Nineteen, twenty, my plate's empty.

Hickety, Pickety, My Black Hen

This then leads into "Ten Fluffy Chickens," page 88.

Hickety, Pickety, my black hen.
She lays eggs for gentlemen.
Gentlemen come every day
To see what my black hen doth lay.
Sometimes nine, and sometimes ten,
Hickety, Pickety, my black hen.

Thirty Days Hath September

Thirty days hath September
April, June, and November;
All the rest have thirty-one,
Excepting leap year, that's the time
When February's days are twenty-nine.

One for the Money

One for the money,
Two for the show,
Three to get ready,
And four to go!

FINGERPLAYS

Five Little Monkeys

Use with fingers or finger puppets or act it out with as many little monkeys as you have at story-time! Turn up the volume as you go.

Five little monkeys
Five fingers up.

Jumping on the bed,
Bouncing up and down.

One fell out
One finger down.

And hurt his head.
Hold your head.

Mother called the doctor
Pretend to use the telephone.

And the doctor said,
"No more monkeys jumping on the bed."
Shake "doctor" finger at "monkeys."

Four little monkeys . . .

. . . *and so on.*
For the last line, sing:
"Put those monkeys straight to bed!"

Once I Caught a Fish Alive

One, two, three, four, five
Count on fingers

Once I caught a fish alive.
Wriggle hand like a fish

Six, seven, eight, nine, ten,
Count fingers

Then I let him go again.
Pretend to throw fish back

Why did you let him go?
Because he bit my finger so.
Shake hand violently

Which one did he bite?
This little finger on the right.
Hold up little finger on right hand

La Mariposa

It's fun to count in other languages. Here is one in Spanish. Play on fingers as in the previous verse.

Uno, dos, tres, cuatro, cinco,
One, two, three, four, five

Cogi una mariposa de un brinco.
Once I caught a butterfly

Seis, siete, ocho, nueve, diez,
Six, seven, eight, nine, ten

La solte brincando otra vez.
Then I let him go again.

SONGS

This Old Man

Teach children the actions to the refrain first.

This old man, he played one,
Hold up one finger.

He played knick-knack on my thumb,
Touch thumbs.

With a knick-knack paddy wack,
Give the dog a bone,
This old man came rolling home.

On each knick-knack, tap knees.
On each paddy-wack, clap hands twice.
On each bone, extend hand.
On each last line, roll hands.

This old man, he played two,
Hold up two fingers.

He played knick-knack on my shoe,
Tap shoes.

With a knick-knack paddy wack,
Give the dog a bone,
This old man came rolling home.

This old man, he played three,
Hold up three fingers.

He played knick-knack on my knee,
Tap knees.

With a knick-knack paddy wack,
Give the dog a bone,
This old man came rolling home.

This old man, he played four,
Hold up four fingers.

He played knick-knack on my door,
Pretend to knock at the door.

With a knick-knack paddy wack,
Give the dog a bone,
This old man came rolling home.

This old man, he played five,
Hold up five fingers.

He played knick-knack on my hive,
Make a beehive with fists together.

With a knick-knack paddy wack,
Give the dog a bone,
This old man came rolling home.

This old man, he played six,
He played knick-knack on my sticks,
Wiggle fingers for sticks.

With a knick-knack paddy wack,
Give the dog a bone,
This old man came rolling home.

This old man, he played seven,
He played knick-knack up in heaven,
Point up to heaven.

With a knick-knack paddy wack,
Give the dog a bone,
This old man came rolling home.

This old man, he played eight,
He played knick-knack on my gate,
Pretend to open a gate.

With a knick-knack paddy wack,
Give the dog a bone,
This old man came rolling home.

This old man, he played nine,
He played knick-knack on my spine,
Point to your spine.

With a knick-knack paddy wack,
Give the dog a bone,
This old man came rolling home.

This old man, he played ten,
He played knick-knack all over again,
Throw arms up.

With a knick-knack paddy wack,
Give the dog a bone,
This old man came rolling home.

One Elephant

Count as high as you care to. Bounce hands on knees in rhythm. Hold one finger up, then two and so on. The tune is on Pat Carfra's cassette, Lullabies and Laughter, and on Sharon, Lois & Bram's cassette, One Elephant. Music is in Sharon, Lois & Bram's Elephant Jam.

One elephant went out to play
On a spider's web one day;
She had such enormous fun
That she called on another elephant to come.

Two elephants went out to play
On a spider's web one day;
They had such enormous fun
That they called on another elephant to come.

Three elephants went out to play . . .

And that can go on forever!

Roll Over

Sing it with felt pieces! Start out with ten characters in a bed and count backwards as they fall out one by one. Roll hands on "roll over."

Ten in the bed, and the little one said,
"Roll over! Roll over!"
So they all rolled over and one fell out.

Nine in the bed, and the little one said:
"Roll over! Roll over!"
They all rolled over and one fell out.

Eight in the bed, and the little one said:
"Roll over! Roll over!"
They all rolled over and one fell out.

Seven in the bed, and the little one said:
"Roll over! Roll over!"
They all rolled over and one fell out.

Six in the bed, and the little one said:
"Roll over! Roll over!"
They all rolled over and one fell out.

Five in the bed . . .
Four in the bed . . .
Three in the bed . . .
Two in the bed . . .

One in the bed, and the little one said,
"Alone at last!"

The Ants Came Marching

See INSECTS, page 126.

Over in the Meadow

See MOTHER'S DAY, page 136.

MORE IDEAS

1. Felt stories: *The Very Hungry Caterpillar, Roll Over*, and *Over in the Meadow*.

2. Here is an opportunity to introduce all the amazing counting books in the library. Invite children who speak languages other than English to count to five or ten so all the children can learn.

3. Tie this theme to telling time or counting money.

4. For a Counting Money theme, tell "The Drake's Tale," from Judy Sierra's *Multicultural Folktales*. The refrain is so much fun: "Quack, quack, quack, when will I get my money back!"

5. *Ten, Nine, Eight* is lovely in a big book format.

6. Sing "Let's Do the Numbers Rhumba" from Raffi's *Rise and Shine* cassette. Words and music are in *The Second Raffi Songbook*.

7. Art: Make decorative coin rubbings after *26 Letters and 99 Cents*.

8. Note: Some libraries keep counting books with children's picture book nonfiction in the 500s, while others put them on the picture book shelves by author. You'll have to find out where they are in your own library.

Dogs

STORIES TO READ ALOUD

The Last Puppy
ASCH, FRANK

Our Puppy's Holiday
BROWN, RUTH

The Comic Adventures of Old Mother Hubbard
DE PAOLA, TOMIE

Hunky Dory Ate It
EVANS, KATIE

Angus and the Cat
FLACK, MARJORIE

Angus and the Ducks
FLACK, MARJORIE

Angus Lost
FLACK, MARJORIE

A Bag Full of Pups
GACKENBACH, DICK

Where's Spot?
HILL, ERIC

Whistle for Willie
KEATS, EZRA JACK

Brenda and Edward
KOVALSKI, MARYANN

What Faust Saw
OTTLEY, MATT

Buster's Echo
SCAMELL, RAGNHILD

Harry the Dirty Dog
ZION, GENE

John Brown, Rose, and the Midnight Cat
WAGNER, JENNY

MORE STORIES

Carl's Masquerade
DAY, ALEXANDRA

David and Dog
HUGHES, SHIRLEY

I Want a Dog
KHALSA, DAYAL KAUR

Julian
KHALSA, DAYAL KAUR

Henry and Mudge (readers series)
RYLANT, CYNTHIA

Tiffky Doofky
STEIG, WILLIAM

NONFICTION

Puppy
BURTON, JANE

A Puppy Is Born
FISCHER-NAGEL, HEIDEROSE

NURSERY RHYMES

Higglety, Pigglety, Pop!

Higglety, pigglety, pop!
The dog has eaten the mop;
The pig's in a hurry,
The cat's in a flurry,
Higglety, pigglety, pop!

Hark, Hark, the Dogs Do Bark

Hark, Hark,
The dogs do bark,
The beggars are coming to town;
Some in rags,
And some in jags,
And one in a velvet gown.

Hey Diddle, Diddle

Hey diddle diddle,
The cat and the fiddle,
The cow jumped over the moon;
The little dog laughed
To see such sport,
And the dish ran away with the spoon.

FINGERPLAYS

The Puppy

Call the puppy
Beckon with hand or finger.

And give him some milk.
Pretend to pour milk into bowl.

Brush his coat
Pretend to brush dog.

Till it shines like silk.
Call the dog
Beckon with hand or finger.

And give him a bone
Hold two fingers as if holding a bone.

Take him for a walk,
Pretend to hold leash of dog.

Then put him in his home.
Form shape of a dog house.

Little Puppies and Kittens

One little, two little, three little kittens
Hold up three fingers of one hand.

Were napping in the sun.
Bend fingers down.

One little, two little, three little puppies
Hold up three fingers of other hand.

Said, "Come, let's have some fun!"
Up to the kittens the puppies went creeping
As quiet, as quiet could be.
Move puppy fingers slowly toward kitten fingers.

One little, two little, three little kittens
Went scampering up a tall tree.
Move kitten fingers quickly into the air.

Five Little Puppies

Five little puppies were playing in the sun.
This one saw a rabbit and he began to run.
This one saw a butterfly and he began to race.
This one saw a pussycat and he began to chase.
This one tried to catch his tail, and he went
    round and round.
This one was so quiet, he never made a sound.

Puppy's Dog House

This is puppy's dog house.
Put tips of fingers together.

This is puppy's bed.
Hands flat, palms upward.

This is puppy's pan of milk,
Cup hands together for bowl.

So that he can be fed.
This puppy has a collar,
Encircle neck with fingers.

With his name upon it, too.
Take a stick and throw it,
Make throwing motion.

And he'll bring it back to you!
Clap.

Five Little Puppy Dogs

*Hold up five fingers and bend down one at a time
as the verse progresses. This is also nice with finger
puppets or five little puppies on the felt board.*

Five little puppy dogs
Sitting by the door,
Mommy called one puppy home,
Then there were four.

Four little puppy dogs
Running 'round a tree,
One stopped to dig a bone,
Then there were three.

Three little puppy dogs
Playing with a shoe,
One went to chase a cat
Then there were two.

Two little puppy dogs
Having so much fun.
One went to have a nap
Then there was one.

One little puppy dog
Sitting in the sun,
He went inside the house
Then there were none.

SONGS

BINGO

There was a farmer who had a dog
And Bingo was him name-o
B-I-N-G-O, B-I-N-G-O, B-I-N-G-O,
And Bingo was his name-o.

*Sing out the letters B-I-N-G-O on the first verse, clap
once for B on the second verse, twice for B-I on the third
verse, and so on, substituting claps for letters until you
clap out Bingo's whole name, keeping the rhythm of the
song as you go. May be used very effectively with a
younger audience using a glove puppet with big red
letters on each finger and a little puppy stuck in the
centre. In this case children clap when you remove the
letters from the glove puppet.*

My Dog Rags

*Listen to Bob McGrath's version of this song on
his cassette* Sing Along with Bob: Volume One.
See words and music in Sharon, Lois & Bram's
Elephant Jam.

I have a dog and his name is Rags.
Hang hands by your ears.

He eats so much that his tummy sags.
Hold hands in front of tummy.

His ears flip flop, and his tail wig wags.
Flop hands by ears, and wag your tail!

And when he walks he goes zig zag.
Cross arms in front to zig, open up to zag.

Chorus:
He goes flip flop, wig wag, zig zag.
Put it all together now, and repeat.

He goes flip flop, wig wag, zig zag.
He goes flip flop, wig wag, zig zag.
I love Rags, and he loves me.

My dog Rags, he loves to play.
Hang hands by your ears.

He rolls around in the mud all day.
Roll hands.

I whistle and I whistle but be won't obey.
Whistle.

He always runs the other way.

Repeat chorus.

Do Your Ears Hang Low?

*Act it out, increasing speed each time verse is
repeated. Listen to the tune on Bob McGrath's
cassette* Sing Along with Bob, Vol. Two.

Do your ears hang low
Do they wobble to and fro?
Can you tie them in a knot,
Can you tie them in a bow?
Can you throw them over your shoulder,
Like a Continental soldier,
Do your ears hang low?

Where, Oh Where Has My Little Dog Gone?

Where, oh where has my little dog gone?
Place hands, palms up, near shoulders.

Oh where, oh where can he be?
Swivel head, searching.

With his tail cut short,
Wag hands behind back.

And his ears cut long,
Flop hands at ears.

Oh where, oh where can he be?
Place hands, palms up, near shoulders.

How Much Is That Doggie?

Listen to the tune on Sharon, Lois & Bram's
Great Big Hits *cassette.*

How much is that doggie in the window?
The one with the waggly tail.
How much is that doggie in the window?
I do hope that doggie's for sale.

I must take a trip to California
And leave my poor sweetheart alone.
If he has a dog he won't be lonesome.
And that doggie would have a good home.

Repeat first verse.

CIRCLE GAME

A Tisket, a Tasket

A tisket, a tasket, a green and yellow basket;
I wrote a letter to my love
And on the way I dropped it.
A little puppy picked it up
And put it in his pocket.
I won't bite you and I won't bite you
But I will bite you!

Children form a circle holding hands. One child, chosen to be the puppy, walks around the outside of the circle holding a handkerchief as all the children sing and the circle moves in the opposite direction. After "pocket" the circle stops moving and the puppy goes from child to child saying, "I won't bite you." When she reaches the child she chooses to be the puppy next, she says, "I will bite you," and drops the handkerchief behind him. She then runs one way around the circle while the chosen friend picks up the handkerchief and runs in the opposite direction. The last to make it to the gap in the circle is the new puppy.

MORE IDEAS

1. Eric Hill's simple *Spot* books are always a hit, especially with younger audiences.

2. Make puppy puppets out of paper bags small enough to fit over the children's hands, or use paper plates. Adorn with pre-cut ears, tongues, etc., and draw on faces.

Ducks & Geese

STORIES TO READ ALOUD

Go Tell Aunt Rhody
ALIKI

Angus and the Ducks
FLACK, MARJORIE

The Story About Ping
FLACK, MARJORIE

Gertrude the Goose Who Forgot
GALDONE, PAUL

Henny Penny
GALDONE, PAUL

The Story of Little Quack
GIBSON, BETTY

The Chick and the Duckling
GINSBURG, MIRRA

Silly Goose
KENT, JACK

The Day the Goose Got Loose
LINDBERGH, REEVE

Duck Cakes for Sale
LUNN, JANET

Squawk to the Moon, Little Goose
PRESTON, EDNA MITCHELL

Poor Goose
ROCKWELL, ANNE

Three Ducks Went Wandering
ROY, RON

Dibble and Dabble
SAUNDERS, DAVIE & JULIE

Farmer Duck
WADDELL, MARTIN

MORE STORIES

Peeping Beauty
AUCH, MARY JANE

Dawn
BANG, MOLLY

Petunia
DUVOISIN, ROGER

Make Way for Ducklings
McCLOSKEY, ROBERT

The Little Wood Duck
WILDSMITH, BRIAN

NONFICTION

The Life Cycle of a Duck
BAILEY, JILL

A Duckling Is Born
ISENBART, HANS-HEINRICH

Duck
ROYSTON, ANGELA

NURSERY RHYMES

Goosey, Goosey Gander

Goosey, goosey gander,
Whither shall I wander?
Upstairs and downstairs,
And in my lady's chamber.
There I met an old man,
Who would not say his prayers,
I took him by the left leg
And threw him down the stairs!

FINGERPLAYS

Stretch Up High

Stretch, stretch, away up high;
Reach arms up high.

On your tiptoes, reach the sky.
Stand on tiptoes and reach.

See the bluebirds flying high.
Wave hands.

Now bend down and touch your toes;
Bend to touch toes.

Now sway as the North Wind blows;
Sway body back and forth.

And waddle as the gander goes!
Walk in waddling motion.

SONGS

Five Little Ducks

Use finger puppets, or five little fingers on one hand. Mother duck quacks with the other. Listen to Raffi's version on his Rise and Shine *cassette. Words and music are in* The Second Raffi Songbook.

Five little ducks went swimming one day
Hold up five fingers.

Over the hills and far away.
Swim them behind your back.

Mama Duck said, "Quack, Quack, Quack, Quack."
Make quacking motion with thumb and four fingers.

And four little ducks came swimming back.
Leave one finger puppet behind, or drop one finger.

Four little ducks went swimming one day . . .
Three little ducks went swimming one day . . .
Two little ducks went swimming one day . . .
One little duck went swimming one day . . .

Repeat actions until . . .

No little ducks came swimming back.
Shake head, no.

No little ducks went swimming one day
They were over the hill and far away.
Sing this verse while you're madly attaching finger puppets behind your back.

Mama Duck said, "Quack, Quack, Quack, Quack!"
Repeat if you need more time.

And five little ducks came swimming back.

There's a Little White Duck

Sing with felts. All you'll need is a white duck, a lily pad, a green frog, a black bug, and a red snake. Listen to the tune on Raffi's Everything Grows *cassette. Words and music in the* Everything Grows Songbook.

There's a little white duck sitting in the water.
A little white duck doing what he oughter.
He took a bite of a lily pad
Flapped his wings, and said, "I'm glad
I'm a little white duck, sitting in the water,
Quack, quack, quack."

There's a little green frog swimming in the water.
A little green frog doing what he oughter.
He jumped right off of the lily pad
That the little duck bit and he said, "I'm glad
I'm a little green frog, swimming in the water,
Croak, croak, croak."

There's a little black bug floating on the water.
A little back bug doing what he oughter.
He tickled the frog on the lily pad
That the little duck bit and he said, "I'm glad
I'm a little black bug, floating in the water,
Chirp, chirp, chirp."

There's a little red snake lying on the water
A little red snake doing what he oughter.
He frightened the duck and the frog so bad
He ate the little bug and he said, "I'm glad
I'm a little red snake, lying on the water,
SSSS! SSSS! SSSS!"

Now there's nobody left sitting in the water.
Nobody left doing what he oughter.
There's nothing left but the lily pad.
The duck and the frog ran away, I'm sad.
Now there's nobody left, sitting in the water,
Boo! Hoo! Hoo!

If I Could Have a Windmill

Listen to the tune of this delightful old English folk song on Sharon, Lois & Bram's cassette, Great Big Hits. *Music is in* Sharon, Lois & Bram's Mother Goose.

If I could have a windmill, a windmill, a windmill,
If I could have a windmill, I know what I would do.

I'd have it pump some water, some water, some water,
I'd have it pump some water all up from the river below.

And then I'd have a duckpond, a duckpond, a duckpond,
And then I'd have a duckpond, for ducks and geese to swim.

The ducks would make their wings flap, their wings flap, their wings flap,
The ducks would make their wings flap, and then they would say "Quack, quack."

The geese would stretch their long necks, their long necks, their long necks,
The geese would stretch their long necks, and then they would answer "s-s-s-s!"

1st verse: Stretch out both arms and swing them round.
2nd verse: Put clenched fists together and raise them up and down.
3rd verse: Pretend to scoop a hole in the ground.
4th verse: Put hands on hips and waggle elbows.
5th verse: Lower and raise heads stretching necks as far as possible.

Six Little Ducks

Act it out! Hear the tune on Raffi's More Singable Songs *cassette. Music is in* The Raffi Singable Songbook.

Six little ducks that I once knew.
Fat ones, skinny ones, fair ones too.
But the one little duck with the feather on his back.
He led the others with his quack, quack, quack,
Quack, quack, quack.
He led the others with his quack, quack, quack.

Down to the river they would go,
Wibble, wobble, wibble, wobble to and fro.
But the one little duck with the feather on his back,
He led the others with his quack, quack, quack.
Quack, quack, quack.
He led the others with his quack, quack, quack.

Home from the river they would come.
Wibble, wobble, wibble wobble, ho ho hum.
But the one little duck with the feather on his back,
He led the others with his quack, quack, quack.
Quack, quack, quack.
He led the others with his quack, quack, quack.

Go Tell Aunt Rhody

Go tell Aunt Rhody,
Go tell Aunt Rhody,
Go tell Aunt Rhody,
The old gray goose is dead.

The one she's been saving,
The one she's been saving,
The one she's been saving,
To make a feather bed.

The old gander's weeping,
The old gander's weeping,
The old gander's weeping,
Because his wife is dead.

The goslings are mourning,
The goslings are mourning,
The goslings are mourning,
Because their mother's dead.

She died in the millpond,
She died in the millpond,
She died in the millpond,
Standing on her head.

Go tell Aunt Rhody,
Go tell Aunt Rhody,
Go tell Aunt Rhody,
The old gray goose is dead.

MORE IDEAS

1. Felt Stories: *Poor Goose* and "There's a Little White Duck."

2. Talk about geese when you hear them honking overhead, saying hello in the spring and good-bye in the fall, and tie to these seasonal themes.

3. Tell "The Drake's Tail," from Judy Sierra's *Multicultural Folktales*. It's a good participation story about a delightful little quacker.

4. Have a Mother Goose Medley with rhymes that connect gracefully. Here are two examples.

Jack and Jill; Ding Dong Bell Pussy's in the Well; Pussy Cat Mole; Pussy Cat, Pussy Cat Where Have You Been; Hickory Dickory Dock; and Three Little Kittens.

Jack and Jill; Jack be Nimble; Little Miss Muffet; Eensy Weensy Spider; It's Raining, It's Pouring; Doctor Foster; Lazy Mary; Lazy Lousy Liza Briggs; Five Little Pigs.

Move the characters you have along the felt board into new settings as you move into new rhymes.

5. Sing "The Grand Old Duke of York" as "The Grand old Duck of York," and waddle up to the top of the hill!

Easter

STORIES TO READ ALOUD

The Big Fat Hen
BAKER, KEITH

The Golden Egg Book
BROWN, MARGARET WISE

Goodnight Moon Room (pop-up)
BROWN, MARGARET WISE

Home for a Bunny
BROWN, MARGARET WISE

The Runaway Bunny
BROWN, MARGARET WISE

Yes
GOFFIN, JOSSE

The Most Wonderful Egg in the World
HEINE, HELME

Jennie's Hat
KEATS, EZRA JACK

Hatch, Egg, Hatch: A Touch-and Feel Action Flap Book
RODDIE, SHEN

The Great Big Especially Beautiful Easter Egg
STEVENSON, JAMES

Max's Chocolate Chicken
WELLS, ROSEMARY

Mr. Rabbit and the Lovely Present
ZOLOTOW, CHARLOTTE

MORE STORIES

The Easter Egg Artists
ADAMS, ADRIENNE

Humbug Rabbit
BALIAN, LORNA

A Rabbit for Easter
CARRICK, CAROL

The Easter Bunny That Overslept
FRIEDRICH, PRISCILLA

World in the Candy Egg
TRESSELT, ALVIN

The Bunny Who Found Easter
ZOLOTOW, CHARLOTTE

NONFICTION

Things to Make and Do for Easter
COLE, MARION

Easter
GIBBONS, GAIL

Chickens Aren't the Only Ones
HELLER, RUTH

NURSERY RHYMES

Humpty Dumpty

Humpty Dumpty sat on a wall.
Humpty Dumpty had a great fall;
All the King's horses, and all the King's men,
Couldn't put Humpty together again.

FINGERPLAYS

Ears So Funny

Here's a bunny with ears so funny,
Right fist with two fingers bent.

And here's his home in the ground.
Form circle with left hand.

When a sound he hears, he pricks up his ears,
Straighten fingers.

And pop! He jumps into the ground.
Right two fingers dive into circle.

Easter Bunny

All stand up to start.

Easter bunny's ears are floppy.
Place hands by ears and flop.

Easter bunny's feet are hoppy.
Feet hop.

His fur is soft,
Stroke arm.

And nose is fluffy,
Touch nose.

Tail is short and powder-puffy.
Wiggle hands behind back.

Easter Eggs

Use with fingers, finger puppets or felts. Slurp the first four easter eggs and gulp the last. Hold up five fingers to start, and bend down one at a time.

Five little Easter eggs lovely colours wore;
Mother ate the blue one, then there were four.
Four little Easter eggs, two and two you see;
Daddy ate the red one, then there were three.
Three little Easter eggs, before I knew,
Sister ate the yellow one, then there were two.
Two little Easter eggs, oh, what fun!
Brother ate the purple one then there was one.
One little Easter egg, see me run!
I ate the very last one, and then there was none.

Ten Fluffy Chickens

Five eggs,
Hold up five fingers.

And five eggs,
Hold up other five fingers.

That makes ten.
Sitting on top is the Mother Hen.
Lock fingers togethe, knuckles up.

Crackle, crackle, crackle, what do I see?
Clap hands.

Ten fluffy chickens as yellow as can be.
Hold up ten fingers.

Not Say a Single Word

A fingerplay or stand up stretch.

I can hop, hop, hop like a bunny,
Hopping motion with hands.

And run, run, run like a dog;
Running motion.

I can walk, walk, walk like an elephant,
Walking motion.

And jump, jump, jump like a frog.
Jumping motion.

I can swim, swim, swim like a fish,
Swimming motion.

And fly, fly, fly like a bird;
Flying motion.

I can sit right down and fold my hands,
Fold hands in lap.

And not say a single word!

Little Rabbit

I saw a little rabbit go hop, hop, hop.
Hold up two fingers and go hop, hop, hop.

I saw his long ears go flop, flop, flop.
Place hands above head and flop at wrists.

I saw his little eyes go wink, wink, wink.
Wink.

I saw his little nose go twink, twink, twink.
Wiggle nose.

I said, "Little Rabbit, won't you stay?"
Make beckoning motion.

But he just looked at me and hopped away.
Make two fingers hop away.

Let's Go on an Egg Hunt

Actions are the same as for "The Bear Hunt."
Have children repeat each line after you. Pat
hands on thighs rhythmically.

Let's go on an egg hunt.
Hope we find some.
I'm kind of hungry,
And Easter eggs are nice.
All right, let's go.
> *Slap hands on thighs.*

Oh, oh, what do I see?
I see some tall grass!
Can't look over it,
Can't look under it,
Better look through it.
Swish, swish, swish, swish.
> *Brush hands together to swish through the grass.*

Oh, wow, look what I've found!
I've found a nice blue egg.
Better look for more.
Hope we find some.

Oh look,
I see a tree!
Can't go over it,
Can't go under it,
Let's climb it.
All right.
Let's go.
> *Pretend to climb a tree. When top is reached, place*
> *hand on forehead and look around. Climb down.*

Look what I've found!
I've found a nice red egg.
Better look for more.
Hope we find some.

Oh look,
I see a swamp!
Can't go around it,
Can't go under it.
Let's swim through it.
All right.
Let's go.
> *Pretend to swim.*

Look what I've found!
I've found a nice purple egg.
Better look for more.
Hope we find some.

Oh look,
I see a bridge!

Can't go around it,
Can't go under it.
Let's cross over it.
All right.
Let's go.
> *Make clicking sound with tongue and stamp feet.*

Look what I've found!
I've found a nice green egg.
Better look for more.
Hope we find some.

Oh look,
I see a cave !
Can't go around it,
Can't go under it.
Let's go in it.
All right.
Let's go.
> *Cup hands and clap together to make a hollow*
> *sound.*

Golly, it's dark in here.
Better use my flashlight.
Doesn't work.
Oh, oh . . . where am I?
Where are the other kids?
I think I'm lost!
BOOO HOOO!
But wait! I think I'll just go back the way I came.

Through the cave,
> *Cup hands and clap together.*

Over the bridge,
> *Make clicking sound with tongue and stamp feet.*

Through the swamp,
> *Pretend to swim.*

Up the tree,
> *Pretend to climb a tree. When top is reached, place*
> *hand on forehead and look around. Climb down.*

Through the tall grass,
> *Brush hands together to swish.*

WHEW! We're back! Let's eat!

A Poem in Praise of Rabbits

From Marshmallow *by Clare Newberry.*
This is nice to tell with a stuffed rabbit.

A bunny is a quiet pet,
A bunny is the best thing yet,
A bunny never makes a sound,
A bunny's nice to have around.

Puppies whimper, bark, and growl;
Kittens mew, and tom cats yowl;
Birdies twitter, chirp, and tweet;
Moo-cows moo, and lambkins bleat;

Some creatures bellow, others bray;
Some hoot, or honk, or yap, or neigh;
Most creatures make annoying noises,
Even little girls and boyses.

A bunny, though is never heard,
He simply never says a word.
A bunny's a delightful habit,
No home's complete without a rabbit.

How Would You Like a Rabbit?

This poem can be mounted on the back of a rabbit
picture, or told using a puppet or a stuffed rabbit.
Let the children pat.

How would you like a rabbit?
A great big chocolate rabbit?
A rabbit full of jelly beans
All sugary and sweet?

I'd rather have a real one
A kind of furry-feel one.
I'd give him lots of lettuce greens
And carrots for a treat.

SONG

Peter Cottontail

Here comes Peter Cottontail,
Hopping down the bunny trail,
Hippity-hoppity, Easter's on its way.
Bringing all the girls and boys,
Baskets full of Easter joys,
Things to make their Easter bright and gay.
He's got jelly beans for Tommy,
Coloured eggs for sister Sue.
There's an orchid for your Mother,
And an Easter bonnet too.
Oh, here comes Peter Cottontail,
Hopping down the bunny trail,
Hippity-hoppity, happy Easter Day.

MORE IDEAS

1. Felt Stories: *Jennie's Hat, The Egg Book,* and *The Runaway Bunny.*

2. *Jenny's Hat* is fun to tell with props too. This story naturally leads to more stories about birds in spring. It also leads to a craft idea. Have various bits of feathers, old greeting cards, dried flowers, etc. on hand and make Easter bonnets. Decorate a paper pie plate, punch two holes in the rim at either side and tie on with ribbon. Put on some music and have an Easter parade where children get to show off their new hats.

3. Cut and tell "The Chocolate Easter Egg" or "Lost and Found" from *Paper Stories* by Jean Stangle.

4. Tell "The Easter Basket" from *Tell and Draw Stories* by Margaret Oldfield.

5. Craft: Decorate hard boiled eggs. For lots of ideas see *A Pumpkin in a Pear Tree: Creative Ideas for Twelve Months of Holiday Fun* by Ann Cole. Celebrate with egg salad sandwiches for lunch.

6. Have an easter egg hunt!

7. *Mr. Rabbit and the Lovely Present* makes a lovely one-person puppet show for a special occasion.

8. Take real bunnies to storytime for show and tell.

9. See RABBITS, SEASONS – SPRING, or chick stories in FARMS for more ideas.

Elephants

STORIES TO READ ALOUD

Effie
ALLINSON, BEVERLY

Elephant in a Well
ETS, MARIE H.

Little Elephant
FORD, MIELA

The Name of the Tree
LOTTERIDGE, CELIA

Where Can an Elephant Hide?
McPHAIL, DAVID

The Elephant's Wish
MUNARI, BRUNO

Nobody Knows I Have Delicate Toes
PATZ, NANCY

Circus Baby
PETERSHAM, MAUD

Rose and Dorothy
SCHWARTZ, ROSLYN

The Elephant and the Bad Baby
VIPONT, ELFRIDA

Seven Blind Mice
YOUNG, ED

MORE STORIES

The Story of Babar (and others)
DE BRUNHOFF, JEAN

The Elephant's Child
KIPLING, RUDYARD

Jacques' Jungle Ballet
LAVUT, KAREN

Uncle Elephant (reader)
LOBEL, ARNOLD

17 Kings and 42 Elephants
MAHY, MARGARET

Doctor De Soto Goes to Africa
STEIG, WILLIAM

NONFICTION

Elephant
HOFFMAN, MARY

Elephant Crossing
YOSHIDA, TOSHI

FINGERPLAYS

Willoughby Wallaby Woo

A poem to chant, from Dennis Lee's Alligator Pie. *Listen to Raffi's version on his* Singable Songs for the Very Young *cassette. Words and music are in* The Raffi Singable Songbook. *Make up verses using the names of your own children.*

Willoughby, wallaby woo.
I don't know what to do.
Willoughby, wallaby, wee.
An elephant sat on me.
Willoughby, wallaby wash.
I'm feeling kind of squash.
Willoughby, wallaby, woo.
And I don't know what to do.

Elephant

Right foot, left foot, see me go.
> *Put weight on one foot, then the other, swaying from side to side.*

I am gray and big and very slow.
When I come walking down the street
I bring my trunk and four big feet.
> *Extend arms together in front and swing like a trunk.*

An Elephant

An elephant goes like this and that.
> *Pat knees.*

He's terrible big,
> *Hands up high.*

And he's terrible fat.
> *Hand out wide.*

He has no fingers
> *Wriggle fingers.*

And he has no toes,
> *Touch toes.*

But goodness gracious, what a nose!
> *Make curling motion away from nose.*

Five Gray Elephants

Five gray elephants marching through a glade
> *March fingers of right hand.*

Decide to stop and play; they're having a parade.
The first swings his trunk and announces he'll lead,
> *Swing arm like trunk.*

The next waves a flag which of course they need.
> *Wave hand over head.*

The third gray elephant trumpets a song,
> *Blow through hand.*

The fourth beats a drum as he marches along.
> *Beat a drum.*

While the fifth makes believe he's the whole show,
And nods and smiles to the crowd as they go.
> *Nod head to left and right, and smile.*

Five gray elephants marching through the glade
Having a lot of fun during their parade.

The Elephant's Trunk

The elephant has a great big trunk
> *Pretend an arm is the trunk.*

That goes swinging, swinging so.
> *Swing trunk.*

He has tiny, tiny eyes that show him where to go.
> *Point to eyes.*

His huge, long ears go flapping up and down,
> *Pretend hands are ears.*

His great feet go stomping, stomping on the
ground.
> *Stomp around.*

The Elephant

> *Walk around very slowly, swing from side to side; head bent down and one arm hanging down as the trunk.*

The elephant is big and strong;
His ears are large, his trunk is long.
He walks around with heavy tread,
His keeper walking at his head.

SONG

One Elephant

> *Count as high as you care to. Bounce hands on knees in rhythm. Hold one finger up, then two and so on. The tune is on Pat Carfra's cassette, Lullabies and Laughter, and on Sharon, Lois & Bram's cassette, One Elephant. Music is in Sharon, Lois & Bram's Elephant Jam.*

One elephant went out to play
On a spider's web one day;
She had such enormous fun
That she called on another elephant to come.

Two elephants went out to play
On a spider's web one day;
They had such enormous fun
That they called on another elephant to come.

Three elephants went out to play . . .

And that can go on forever after five!

MORE IDEAS

1. Felt Stories: *Elephant in a Well* and *The Elephant's Wish.*

2. Promote Jack Nicholson's reading of *The Elephant's Child* on cassette. The reading is wonderfully expressive and so is the musical accompaniment.

3. Somehow huge always goes well with small and this theme mixes nicely with ants and other INSECTS after *Effie*, or MICE after *Elephant in a Well* or *Seven Blind Mice*. See also ANIMALS OF THE WILD.

Emotions

STORIES TO READ ALOUD

Two Greedy Bears
GINSBURG, MIRRA

The Gunniwolf
HARPER, WILHELMINA

Peter's Chair
KEATS, EZRA JACK

It Wasn't My Fault
LESTER, HELEN

Prince Bertram the Bad
LOBEL, ARNOLD

There's a Nightmare in My Closet
MAYER, MERCER

David's Father
MUNSCH, ROBERT

The Boy in the Drawer
MUNSCH, ROBERT

Where the Wild Things Are
SENDAK, MAURICE

Big Fat Enormous Lie
SHARMAT, MARJORIE W.

Alexander and the Terrible, Horrible . . .
VIORST, JUDITH

Ira Sleeps Over
WABER, BERNARD

Noisy Nora (big book format)
WELLS, ROSEMARY

MORE STORIES

Franklin in the Dark
(and other *Franklin* titles)
BOURGEOIS, PAULETTE

Willy the Wimp
BROWNE, ANTONY

Pierre
SENDAK, MAURICE

My Mama Says . . .
VIORST, JUDITH

NONFICTION

Feelings
ALIKI

C Is for Curious: An A B C of Feelings
HUBBARD, WOODLEIGH

NURSERY RHYMES

Two Cats of Kilkenny

There once were two cats of Kilkenny.
Each thought there was one cat too many;
So they fought and they fit,
And they scratched and they bit,
Till, excepting their nails,
And the tips of their tails,
Instead of two cats, there weren't any!

FINGERPLAY

A Great Big Happy Smile

I have something in my pocket
It belongs across my face.
I keep it very close to me
In a most convenient place.
You'll never never guess it
If you guess a long long while
So I'll take it out and put it on,
It's a great big happy smile.

SONGS

If You're Happy and You Know It

Suit actions to words. Listen to the tune on Bob McGrath's Sing Along with Bob, Vol. Two.

If you're happy and you know it, clap your hands.
If you're happy and you know it, clap your hands.
If you're happy and you know it,
Then your face will surely show it,
If you're happy and you know it, clap your hands.

If you're sad and you know it, wipe your eyes,
If you're sad and you know it, wipe your eyes,
If you're sad and you know it,
Then your face is gonna show it,
If you're sad and you know it, wipe your eyes.

If you're mad and you know it, stamp your feet, . . .

Repeat first verse.

Shake My Sillies Out

Listen to the tune on Raffi's More Singable Songs *cassette. Words and music are in* The Raffi Singable Songbook. *Everybody stand up and suit actions to words.*

Gotta shake, shake, shake my sillies out
Shake, shake, shake my sillies out
Shake, shake, shake my sillies out
And wiggle my waggles away.

Gotta clap, clap, clap my crazies out . . .
Gotta jump, jump, jump my jiggles out . . .
Gotta yawn, yawn, yawn my sleepies out . . .
Gotta shake, shake, shake my sillies out . . .

Kumbaya

Listen to this lovely sad song on Raffi's Baby Beluga *cassette. Words and music are in* The Second Raffi Songbook.

Chorus:
Kumbaya, my Lord, kumbaya,
Kumbaya, my Lord, kumbaya,
Kumbaya, my Lord, kumbaya,
Oh, Lord, kumbaya.

Additional verses:
Someone's crying, Lord, kumbaya . . .
Someone's praying, Lord, kumbaya . . .
Someone's singing, Lord, kumbaya . . .
Someone's dreaming, Lord, kumbaya . . .
Someone's laughing, Lord, kumbaya . . .

Repeat chorus.

Arabella Miller

See INSECTS, *page 124.*

CIRCLE GAME

Little Sally Waters

For music see Singing Bee. *Sally sits in the middle of the circle crying then flying to the east and to the west. The person she picks to love the best then becomes Sally Waters until everyone has had a turn.*

Little Sally Waters, sitting in the sun,
Crying and weeping, lonesome little one.
Rise, Sally, rise; wipe off your eyes;
Fly to the East, Sally,
Fly to the West, Sally,
Fly to the one you love the very best.

MORE IDEAS

1. *The Gunniwolf* is a wonderful participation story to tell preschoolers. Ask them to join in on the wolf's chant and the little girl's song. It's also great with lap puppets. See Margaret Read MacDonald's *Twenty Tellable Tales* for storytelling tips.

2. Present the story of *Pierre*, the boy who didn't care, with a puppet. Find an easy presentation idea in *Storytelling Made Easy with Puppets* by Jan VanSchryver.

3. Talk about the feelings evoked by the stories. Talk about feeling scared after *The Gunniwolf* or *The Three Billy Goats Gruff*, for example. Ask children how they think characters feel and how they feel themselves after the stories. Talk about feeling sad, feeling angry, feeling happy, feeling proud, feeling sorry, feeling jealous, and so on whenever these feelings come up. Children need to learn how to describe their emotions the same way they need to learn how to describe colours, and storytime provides a wonderful opportunity for this.

4. Talk about what it would feel like to be very small, and tell "One Inch Tall" from *Where the Sidewalk Ends* by Shel Silverstein, using a tiny person finger puppet.

5. *Noisy Nora* is available in big book format for all to see.

Families

STORIES TO READ ALOUD

Just Like Daddy
ASCH, FRANK

Aunt Nina and Her Nephews and Nieces
BRANDENBERG, FRANZ

The Runaway Bunny
BROWN, MARGARET WISE

Avocado Baby
BURNINGHAM, JOHN

Baby-O
CARLSTROM, NANCY WHITE

Granny Is a Darling
DENTON, KADY MacDONALD

Tidy Titch
HUTCHINS, PAT

Titch
HUTCHINS, PAT

A Mother for Choco
KASZA, KEIKO

Peter's Chair
KEATS, EZRA JACK

Horace
KELLER, HOLLY

Leo the Late Bloomer
KRAUS, ROBERT

Whose Mouse Are You?
KRAUS, ROBERT

Just for You
MAYER, MERCER

Me Too!
MAYER, MERCER

David's Father
MUNSCH, ROBERT

Murmel, Murmel, Murmel
MUNSCH, ROBERT

Five Minutes Peace
MURPHY, JILL

The Mice Who Lived in a Shoe
PEPPE, RODNEY

Mother, Mother, I Want Another
POLUSHKIN, MARIA

Mrs. Pig's Bulk Buy
RAYNER, MARY

The Relatives Came
RYLANT, CYNTHIA

Oh! Were They Ever Happy
SPIER, PETER

Sam Vole and His Brothers
WADDELL, MARTIN

Hazel's Amazing Mother
WELLS, ROSEMARY

Noisy Nora (big book format)
WELLS, ROSEMARY

Our Granny
WILD, MARGARET

Do You Know What I'll Do?
ZOLOTOW, CHARLOTTE

MORE STORIES

The Piggybook
BROWNE, ANTHONY

Miss Rumphius
COONEY, BARBARA

Katie Morag and Her Two Grandmothers
HEDDERWICK, MAIRI

Sheila Rae, the Brave
HENKES, KEVIN

A Baby Sister for Frances
HOBAN, RUSSELL

My Family Vacation
KHALSA, DAYAL KAUR

Tales of a Gambling Grandma
KHALSA, DAYAL KAUR

My Kokum Called Today
LOEWEN, IRIS

The New Baby
McCULLY, EMILY ARNOLD

Picnic
McCULLY, EMILY ARNOLD

Sunshine
ORMEROD, JAN

Pierre
SENDAK, MAURICE

Sylvester and the Magic Pebble
STEIG, WILLIAM

A Chair for My Mother
WILLIAMS, VERA

My Daddy Takes Care of Me
QUINLAN, PATRICIA

NONFICTION

Dinosaurs Divorce: A Guide for Changing Families
BROWN, LAURENE KRASNY

NURSERY RHYMES

The Old Woman Who Lived in a Shoe

There was an old woman who lived in a shoe.
She had so many children she didn't know what
  to do.
She gave them some broth
And a big slice of bread,
Kissed them all soundly
And tucked them into bed.

Jack and Jill

Jack and Jill went up the hill
To fetch a pail of water
Jack fell down, and broke his crown,
And Jill came tumbling after.

Ride-Away, Ride-Away

Ride away, ride away,
Johnny shall ride,
He shall have a pussy cat
Tied to his side;
He shall have a little dog
Tied to the other,
And Johnny shall ride
To see his grandmother.

FINGERPLAYS

How Many People

> *For alternate families, change, for example, to
> "One, my mother, Two my mother." Or change
> for two fathers.*

How many people live at your house?
One, my mother,
> *One finger.*

Two, my father,
> *Two fingers, etc.*

Three, my sister,
Four, my brother.
There's one more, now let me see
> *Scratch head.*

Oh yes, of course. It must be me!
> *Point to yourself.*

This Is My Family

This is my mother.
> *Thumb.*

This is my father.
> *Pointer finger.*

This is my brother tall.
> *Middle finger.*

This is my sister.
> *Ring finger.*

This is the baby.
> *Little finger.*

Oh, how I love them all!
> *Clap left hand over all fingers and hug!*

Come A' Look A' See

Sing with a calypso rhythm.

Come a'look a'see,
Here's my mama.
Point to thumb.

Come a'look a'see,
Here's my papa.
Point to index finger.

Come a'look a see,
My brother tall,
Point to tall finger.

Sister, baby,
Point to ring then baby fingers.

I love them all.
Cover fingers with other hand and hug.

Thumbkin

The finger family! Sing to the tune of "Frère Jacques." Hide hands behind back to start.

Where is thumbkin?
Where is thumbkin?
Here I am!
Bring out one hand, thumb up.

Here I am!
Bring out the other hand, thumb up.

How are you today, sir?
Nod one thumb.

Very well, I thank you.
Nod the other thumb.

Run away, run away,
Hide hands behind back again, one at a time.

Run away and hide.

Repeat using "Pointer," "Tall Man," "Ring Man," and "the Baby" in place of Thumbkin.

Five Little Pigs

Play this game on five fingers. It's also nice with five little pig finger puppets.

Five little pigs went out to play.
The first little pig said,
"Let's go to the woods today."
The second little pig said,
"What will we do there?"
The third little pig said,
"We'll look for our mother."
The fourth little pig said,
"What will we do when we find her?"
"We'll hug her and kiss her and kiss her!"
Said the fifth little pig.

Tommy Thumbs

Tommy Thumbs up and
Thumbs up, both hands.

Tommy Thumbs down,
Thumbs down.

Tommy Thumbs dancing
Dance them to the right.

All around the town.
Then dance them to the left.

Dance 'em on your shoulders,
Bounce them on your shoulders.

Dance 'em on your head,
Bounce them on your head.

Dance 'em on your knees and
Bounce them on your knees.

Tuck them into bed.
Fold arms, hiding hands.

Peter Pointed up . . .
Repeat using index fingers, and so on.

Toby Tall up . . .
Ring Man up . . .
Baby Fingers up . . .
Finger Family up . . .
Repeat using all fingers.

Grandma's Glasses

These are Grandma's glasses,
Make circles around eyes with pointer finger and thumb.

This is Grandma's hat,
Place hands in triangle shape on head.

This the way she folds her hands,
Fold hands.

And lays them in her lap.
Lay in lap.

Here are Grandpa's glasses,
As above.

And here is Grandpa's hat,
As above.

And here's the way he folds his arms,
Fold arms.

And sits like that.
Lean back and put your feet up.

SONGS

He's Got the Whole World in His Hands

Chorus:
> *On words, "the whole world", describe a great globe with both arms in front. Repeat throughout chorus.*

He's got the whole world in His hands,
He's got the whole world in His hands,
He's got the whole world in His hands,
He's got the whole world in His hands.

Verse 1:
> *Rock a little baby in your arms.*

He's got the little bitty baby in His hands,
He's got the little bitty baby in His hands,
He's got the little bitty baby in His hands,
He's got the whole world in His hands.

> *Repeat chorus.*

Verse 2:
> *Point to boys on "brother."*

He's got you and me, brother, in His hands,
He's got you and me, brother, in His hands,
He's got you and me, brother, in His hands,
He's got the whole world in His hands.

> *Repeat chorus.*

Verse 3:
> *Point to girls on "sister."*

He's got you and me, sister, in His hands,
He's got you and me, sister, in His hands,
He's got you and me, sister, in His hands,
He's got the whole world in His hands.

> *Repeat chorus.*

MORE IDEAS

1. It's a good idea to include stories about alternate family lifestyles here in recognition of the many children who live in single parent families, gay parent families, adopted families, and so on. Adapt the fingerplays to suit families with two mothers and two fathers.

2. Sing "The Farmer in the Dell" using clothesline puppets, or play it as a circle game. It's also nice on the felt board, or with finger puppets.

3. Raffi has a lovely song about families, "All I Really Need" . . . is love in my family. Listen to the tune on Raffi's *Baby Beluga* cassette. Words and music are in *The Second Raffi Songbook*.

4. Sing "She'll Be Comin' 'Round the Mountain" an action song with lots of sound effects. Words are on page 156. Hear the tune on Sharon, Lois & Bram's *One Elephant* cassette. Words and music are in *Elephant Jam*. This is fun to use after *The Relatives Came*.

5. Focus on grandmothers with: *Our Granny, Granny Is a Darling, Albert's Toothache, The Very Worst Monster,* and *David's Father*.

6. Focus on brothers and sisters with: *Titch, Whose Mouse Are You?, Sam Vole and His Brothers,* and *Do You Know What I'll Do?* Recommend Hoban's *Francis* books, which are a bit long for storytime, but wonderful for reading at home.

7. This theme ties in nicely with new babies too. See BABIES for more ideas.

8. Celebrate adoption with: *David's Father, Horace,* and *A Mother for Choco*.

9. Tell the story "Olga's Rescue" with Matrioshka dolls (Russian nesting dolls), or with felts. See *Globalchild: Multicultural Resources for Young Children* by Maureen Cech.

10. Tell *Whose Mouse Are You?* with a mouse puppet.

11. Tell *Pierre* with a lion puppet. For a simple pattern and telling technique, see Jan VanSchryver's *Storytelling Made Easy with Puppets*.

12. For more ideas, see: MOTHER'S DAY and FATHER'S DAY.

Farms

STORIES TO READ ALOUD

Tractor
BROWN, CRAIG

Old MacDonald Had a Farm
CAULEY, LORINDA BRYAN

The New Baby Calf
CHASE, EDITH NEWLIN

Cat Goes Fiddle-i-Fee
GALDONE, PAUL

Henny Penny
GALDONE, PAUL

Little Red Hen
GALDONE, PAUL

Old Woman and Her Pig
GALDONE, PAUL

The Three Billy Goats Gruff
GALDONE, PAUL

The Story of Little Quack
GIBSON, BETTY

Good Morning, Chick
GINSBURG, MIRRA

The Man Who Kept House
HAGUE, KATHLEEN

Mrs. Mopple's Washing Line
HEWETT, ANITA

Something to Crow About
LANE, MEGAN HALSEY

Going to Sleep on the Farm
LEWISON, WENDY CHEYETTE

Treeful of Pigs
LOBEL, ARNOLD

Mrs. McDockerty's Knitting
MARTINEZ, RUTH

Too Much Noise
McGOVERN, ANN

Who Took the Farmer's Hat?
NODSET, JOAN

The Box with Red Wheels
PETERSHAM, MAUD

Piggy in the Puddle
POMERANTZ, CHARLOTTE

The Farmer in the Dell
RAE, MARY MAKI

Emily's House
SCHARER, NIKO

The Thing that Bothered Farmer Brown
SLOAT, TERI

Farmer Duck
WADDELL, MARTIN

Pig in the Pond
WADDELL, MARTIN

I Know an Old Lady Who Swallowed a Fly
WESTCOTT, NADINE

The Chicken Book
WILLIAMS, GARTH

The Little Red Hen
ZEMACH, MARGOT

MORE STORIES

The Auction
ANDREWS, JAN

A Prairie Alphabet
BANNATYNE-CUGNET, JO

If You're Not From the Prairies
BOUCHARD, DAVE

Rosie's Walk
HUTCHINS, PAT

Crocus
DUVOISIN, ROGER

Petunia
DUVOISIN, ROGER

Cowboy Dreams
KHALSA, DAYAL KAUR

Old MacDonald Had a Farm
PEARSON, TRACEY CAMPBELL

Our Animal Friends on Maple Hill Farm
PROVENSEN, ALICE

The Year at Maple Hill Farm
PROVENSEN, ALICE

Belle's Journey
REYNOLDS, MARILYNN

Farmer Palmer's Wagon Ride
STEIG, WILLIAM

NONFICTION

Chicken and Egg
BACK, CHRISTINE

Milk
CARRICK, DONALD

Calf
CLAYTON, GORDON

Foal
CLAYTON, GORDON

Farm Animals (and other titles)
(EYE OPENERS SERIES)

Farming
GIBBONS, GAIL

Milk Makers
GIBBONS, GAIL

Chickens Aren't the Only Ones
HELLER, RUTH

What Is a Horse?
HIRSCHI, RON

Where Do Horses Live?
HIRSCHI, RON

Baby Animals on the Farm
ISENBART, HANS-HEINRICH

A Calf Is Born
KAIZUKI, KIYONORI

What Do You Do at a Petting Zoo?
MACHOTKA, HANA

The Chicken and the Egg
OXFORD SCIENTIFIC FILMS

Chick
ROYSTON, ANGELA

Baby Farm Animals
WINDSOR, MERRILL

NURSERY RHYMES

Hickety, Pickety, My Black Hen

Hickety, Pickety, my black hen.
She lays eggs for gentlemen.
Gentlemen come every day
To see what my black hen doth lay.
Sometimes nine, and sometimes ten,
Hickety, Pickety, my black hen.

To Market, to Market
Clap your hands in rhythm.

To market, to market, to buy a fat pig.
Home again, home again, jiggity jig.
To market, to market, to buy a fat hog.
Home again, home again, jiggity jog.
To market, to market, to buy a plum bun,
Home again, home again, market is done.

Little Boy Blue

Little Boy Blue
Come blow your horn!
The sheep's in the meadow,
The cow's in the corn.
Where is the boy
Who looks after the sheep?
He's under the haystack,
Fast asleep.
Will you wake him?
No, not I
For if I do,
He's sure to cry.

Baa Baa Black Sheep
See page 167.

Little Bo-Peep
See page 168.

Mary Had a Little Lamb
See page 168.

FINGERPLAYS

This Is the Way the Ladies Ride

Children pretend they're riding horses.

This is the way the ladies ride,
Hold reins up and ride delicately .

Nim, nim, nim,
Bounce on toes.

This is the way the gentlemen ride,
A little firmer now.

Trim, trim, trim,
Bounce on heels and toes.

This is the way the farmers ride,
Use a lumbering trot.

T-rot, t-rot, t-rot,
One foot at a time.

This is the way the hunters ride,
Huge strides.

Gallop, a-gallop, a-gallop, a-gallop, a-gallop!
Bounce on toes in a fast galloping motion.

Piggie Wig and Piggie Wee

Piggie Wig and Piggie Wee
Hold up two thumbs.

Hungry pigs as pigs could be,
For their dinner had to wait
Down behind the garden gate.
Gate made of fingers.

Piggie Wig and Piggie Wee
Wiggle thumbs as named.

Climbed the barnyard gate to see,
Thumbs through fingers.

Peeking through the gate so high
But no dinner could they spy.
Wiggle thumbs.

Piggie Wig and Piggie Wee got down,
Back thumbs out of "gate."

Sad as pigs could be,
But the gate soon opened wide,
Hands swing apart.

And they scampered forth outside.
Thumbs run out.

Piggie Wig and Piggie Wee
Greedy pigs as pigs could be,
For their dinner ran pell mell
And into the trough both piggies fell.
Make trough with hands, thumbs fall in.

Two Mother Pigs

Two mother pigs lived in a pen,
Two thumbs up.

Each had four babies and that made ten.
Wiggle four fingers on each hand.

These four babies were black and white.
Wiggle four fingers of one hand.

These four babies were black as night.
Wiggle four fingers of other hand.

All eight babies loved to play.
Wiggle eight fingers.

And they rolled and they rolled in the mud all day.
Roll hands.

At night, with their mother,
They curled up in a heap,
Make fists, palms up.

And squealed and squealed
'Til they went to sleep.
Tuck thumbs under fingers.

The Farm Yard

In the farm yard at the end of the day,
All the animals politely say,
"Thank you for my food today."
The cow says, "Moo."
Point to thumb.

The pigeon, "Coo."
Point to index finger.

The sheep says, "Baa."
Point to middle finger.

The lamb says, "Maaa."
Point to fourth finger.

The hen, "Cluck, cluck, cluck."
Point to little finger.

Point to fingers of the opposite hand for remaining animals.

"Quack," says the duck.
The dog, "Bow wow."
The cat, "Meow."
The horse, "Neigh."
The pig grunts, "Oink."
Then the barn is locked up tight,
And the farmer says, "Goodnight."
Hands together against cheek.

Ten Fluffy Chicks

Five eggs and five eggs
Hold up five fingers and five fingers.

That makes ten.
Wiggle ten fingers.

Sitting on top is the Mother Hen
Lock fingers together, knuckles up.

Crackle, crackle, crackle, what do I see?
Clap hands.

Ten fluffy chickens as yellow as can be.
Hold up ten fingers.

Five Little Chicks

This one works very nicely on the felt board.

Said the first little chick with a queer little squirm,
"I wish I could find a fat little worm."

Said the next little chick with an odd little shrug,
"I wish I could find a fat little slug."

Said the third little chick with a sharp little squeal,
"I wish I could find some nice yellow meal."

Said the fourth little chick with a sigh of grief,
"I wish I could find a little green leaf."

Said the fifth little chick with a faint little moan,
"I wish I could find a wee gravel stone."

"Now, see here," said the mother from the green
  garden patch,
"If you want any breakfast, just come here and
  scratch!"

Five Little Pigs

Play this game on five fingers.

Five little pigs went out to play.
The first little pig said,
"Let's go to the woods today."
The second little pig said,
"What will we do there?"
The third little pig said,
"We'll look for our mother."
The fourth little pig said,
"What will we do when we find her?"
"We'll hug her and kiss her and kiss her!"
Said the fifth little pig.

Ten Galloping Horses

Ten galloping horses came through the town.
Hold up ten fingers and pretend to gallop.

Five were white and five were brown.
Hold up five and five.

They galloped up and galloped down;
Gallop them up and down.

Ten galloping horses came through town.

This Little Cow

Point to each finger in turn.

This little cow eats grass,
This little cow eats hay,
This little cow looks over the hedge,
This little cow runs away,
And this BIG cow does nothing at all
But lie in the fields all day!
Lay thumb on palm.

We'll chase her and chase her and chase her!
Draw circles around that lazy thumb!

Five Little Farmers

Five little farmers,
Fingers of one hand are closed over thumb.

Woke up with the sun.
Open hand.

For it was early morning
When chores must be done.
The first little farmer
Point to first finger.

Went to milk the cow.
Make milking motion.

The second little farmer
Point to second finger, and so on . . .

Thought he'd better plow.
Hold plow; move hand to right and left.

The third little farmer
Fed the hungry hens.
Hold feed in left hand, toss with right.

The fourth little farmer
Mended broken pens.
Make hammer of fist and pound.

The fifth little farmer
Took his vegetables to town.
Riding motion.

Baskets filled with cabbages
Make fists.

And sweet potatoes, brown.
Straighten out fingers.

SONGS

Old MacDonald

Old MacDonald had a farm, E-I-E-I-O.
And on his farm he had a cow, E-l-E-I-O.
With a moo-moo here and a moo-moo there,
Here a moo, there a moo, everywhere a moo-moo,
Old MacDonald had a farm, E-l-E-I-O.

Old MacDonald had a farm, E-I-E-I-O.
And on his farm he had a pig, E-I-E-I-O . . .

. . . and so on with a duck, a horse, a donkey, and some chickens, running through all the sounds backwards with the addition of each new animal. This one can be sung alone, with a book, with felts, or it can be acted out. Look for complete verses and ideas for actions in Tom Glazer's Tom Tinker, Eye Winker, Chin Chopper.

Tingalayo

Sing to a calypso rhythm. Hear the tune on Sharon Lois and Bram's One Elephant *cassette. Words and music in* Elephant Jam. *Hear Raffi's version on his cassette* One Light, One Sun. *Words and music are in* The Second Raffi Songbook. *The verses are sung in echo fashion, and the chorus is sung in unison. This is fun to play with sticks, drums and shakers as accompaniment.*

Chorus:
Tingalayo, run my little donkey run!
Tingalayo, run my little donkey run!

M' donkey hee, m' donkey haw,
M' donkey sleep in a bed of straw.
> *Repeat both lines.*
> *Chorus.*
M' donkey short, m' donkey wide,
Don't get too close to his backside.
> *Repeat both lines.*
> *Chorus.*
M' donkey walk, m' donkey talk,
M' donkey eat with a knife and fork.
> *Repeat both lines.*
> *Chorus.*
M' donkey laugh, m'donkey cry,
M' donkey love peanut butter pie.
> *Repeat both lines.*
> *Chorus.*
You can sing this slow, you can sing this fast,
You can sing this sittin' on the grass.
> *Repeat both lines.*
> *Chorus.*

Down on Grandpa's Farm

This song is fun to sing using all kinds of animal puppets. Hear the tune on Raffi's One Light, One Sun *cassette. Words and music are in* The Second Raffi Songbook. *Improvise! Add your own animals!*

Chorus:
Oh, we're on our way, we're on our way,
On our way to Grandpa's farm,
We're on our way, we're on our way,
On our way to Grandpa's farm.

Verses:
Down on Grandpa's farm there is a big brown cow,
Down on Grandpa's farm there is a big brown cow,
The cow, she makes a sound like this: Moo! Moo!
The cow, she makes a sound like this: Moo! Moo!

. . . there is a little red hen,
. . . there is a little white sheep,
. . . there is a big black dog,
. . . there is a big pink pig,
. . . there is a big brown horse,

The Farmer in the Dell

This classic song can be sung using felts, finger puppets, or clothesline puppets. It's also fun to sing as a circle game with children holding masks or props. If the children like playing this game, use it to wrap up each session in a storytime series.

The farmer in the dell,
The farmer in the dell,
Heigh-ho the derry-o
The farmer in the dell.

The farmer takes a wife . . .
The wife takes a child . . .
The child takes a nurse . . .
The nurse takes a dog . . .
The dog takes a cat . . .
The cat takes a rat . . .
The rat takes the cheese . . .
The cheese stands alone . . .

The Farmer and His Seeds

Sing to the tune of "Farmer in the Dell."

The farmer plants the seeds,
The farmer plants the seeds,
Heigh-ho the derry-o,
The farmer plants the seeds.
Stoop and pretend to plant seeds.

The sun comes out to shine . . .
Make large circle with arms.

The rain begins to fall . . .
Flutter fingers down to the ground.

The seeds begin to grow . . .
Children stand up, then reach up.

The farmer cuts them down . . .
Move arms to imitate a mower.

He binds them into sheaves . . .
Encircle sheeves in arms.

And now we'll have some bread . . .
Pretend to eat.

The Farmyard Song

I had a cat and my cat pleased me.
I fed my cat under yonder tree.
Cat goes fiddle-i-fee.

I had a hen and my hen pleased me.
I fed my hen under yonder tree.
Hen goes chimmy-chuck, chimmy-chuck,
Cat goes fiddle-i-fee.

I had a duck and my duck pleased me.
I fed my duck under yonder tree.
Duck goes quack, quack,
Hen goes chimmy-chuck, chimmy-chuck,
Cat goes fiddle-i-fee.

I had a goose and my goose pleased me.
I fed my goose under yonder tree.
Goose goes swishy, swashy,
Duck goes quack, quack,
Hen goes chimmy-chuck, chimmy chuck,
Cat goes fiddle-i-fee.

And so on with a sheep, a cow, a pig, a horse, and a dog.

MORE IDEAS

1. Felts or finger puppets: *The Farmer in the Dell, Old MacDonald, The Farm Yard Song, I Know an Old Lady Who Swallowed a Fly,* and *Henny Penny.*

2. Find wonderful felt stories that are just right for this theme in Judy Sierra's *Multicultural Folktales: Stories to Tell Young Children,* especially: "The Elegant Rooster," and "The Goat in the Chile Patch."

3. Instructions for animal clothesline puppets can be found in *Puppetry in Early Childhood Education* by Tamara Hunt and Nancy Renfro. It's fun to let the children make their own animal puppets and act out the stories.

4. *Too Much Noise,* by Margot Zemach, is a great story to act out. Use a table for the farmer's house, or a blanket will do. Take the role of the farmer, and ask the children to come in as the various animals making the animal sounds. If you have props available, you could give the children animal noses, or masks to wear. Warning: There may be too much noise!

5. Have a storytime about chickens! For lap puppet ideas to use with *Something to Crow About* and *The Little Red Hen,* see *Storytelling Made Easy with Puppets* by Jan VanSchuyver.

6. "The Five Little Chicks" counting rhyme, upon which Garth Williams' *The Chicken Book* is based, makes a lovely little piece for the felt board. For a pattern see Judy Sierra's *Flannel Board Storytelling Book.*

7. For the words to *I Know an Old Lady Who Swallowed a Fly,* which has lots of farmyard characters, see page 97.

8. For the words to "If I Could Have a Windmill, " and "Go Tell Aunt Rhody," more good farmyard songs, see DUCKS & GEESE.

9. Follow "Tingalayo" with a game of "Pin the Tail on the Donkey." Make a big felt donkey and place it on the felt board. Blindfold each child in turn and let them stick on felt tails with their names on.

10. Sing "She'll Be Comin' 'Round the Mountain" (page 162), an action song with lots of sound effects.

11. Recommend books representing farm life on the Canadian prairies: *The Auction, A Prairie Alphabet,* and *If You're Not From the Prairies.*

12. For more ideas on related themes see: GARDENING, DUCKS & GEESE, PETS, PIGS, and SHEEP.

Father's Day

STORIES TO READ ALOUD

Just Like Daddy
ASCH, FRANK

The Man Who Kept House
HAGUE, KATHLEEN

The Man Who Took the Inside Out
LOBEL, ARNOLD

Close Your Eyes
MARZOLLO, JEAN

Just Me and My Dad
MAYER, MERCER

Guess How Much I Love You
McBRATNEY, SAM

David's Father
MUNSCH, ROBERT

Murmel, Murmel, Murmel
MUNSCH, ROBERT

Peace at Last
MURPHY, JILL

The Piney Woods Peddler
SHANNON, GEORGE

Only the Best
ZOLA, MEGUIDO

MORE STORIES

Old Enough
EYVINDSON, PETER

I'll See You When the Moon Is Full
FOWLER, SUSI GREGG

At the Crossroads
ISADORA, RACHEL

This Old Man
JONES, CAROL

Else-Marie and her Seven Little Daddies
LINDENBAUM, PIJA

Farm Morning
McPHAIL, DAVID

Moonlight
ORMEROD, JAN

My Dad Takes Care of Me
QUINLAN, PATRICIA

My Daddy's Mustache
SALUS, NAOMI

William's Doll
ZOLOTOW, CHARLOTTE

NURSERY RHYMES

The Man in the Moon

The man in the moon
Looked out of the moon,
Looked out of the moon and said,
It's time, I think, for all good children
To think about going to bed.

Peter Peter Pumpkin Eater

Peter Peter pumpkin eater,
Had a wife and couldn't keep her,
So he kept her in a pumpkin shell,
And there he kept her very well.

Michael Finnegan

There was a man named Michael Finnegan.
He grew long whiskers on his chin-igan.
A wind came up and blew them in again.
Poor old Michael Finnegan. Begin again.

FINGERPLAYS

Funny Little Man

There's a funny little man
Thumb.

In a funny little house
Wrap fingers around thumb.

And right across the way, there's another
Funny little man in another funny little house
Do the same with the other hand.

And they play hide and seek all day.
One funny little man through his window peeps
Thumb peeks out between fingers.

Sees no one looking, then softly creeps
Out his door. He comes so slow
Thumb crawls out of fist.

Looks up and down and high and low
Thumb looks up and down.

Then back into his house he goes.
Thumb back in fist.

Then the other little man through his window peeps
Thumb peeks out between fingers.

Sees no one looking, then softly creeps
Out his door. He comes so slow
Thumb crawls out of fist.

Looks up and down and high and low
Thumbs looks up and down.

Then back into his house he goes.
Thumb back in fist.

Sometimes these little men forget to peep
And out of their doors they softly creep
Both thumbs creep out.

Look up and down, high and low
See each other and laugh, "Ho ho!"
Then back into their houses they go.

The Bent-Over Man

I'm a bent over, bent over, bent over man,
I try to stand just as straight as I can,
But all I can do is bend and bend,
Because I'm a bent over, bent over, bent over man.

The Bent-Over Man

I'm a wiggly, wiggly, wiggly man.

- . . . bouncy
- . . . swaying
- . . . stooping
- . . . twirling
- . . . jumping
- . . . hopping

SONGS

This Old Man

See COUNTING, page 63.

Hush Little Baby

*Change "Mama" to "Papa", see BABIES,
page 20.*

MORE IDEAS

1. Use the "Five Little Ducks" fingerplay and change the last line to "Papa duck said." See page 70.

2. Tell the short story of "Mr. Tall and Mr. Small," page 179.

3. See FAMILIES for more ideas.

Food

STORIES TO READ ALOUD

Each Peach Pear Plum (big book format)
AHLBERG, JANET

The Lighthouse Keeper's Lunch
ARMITAGE, RONDA

The Runaway Pancake
ASBJORNSEN, P.C.

Sand Cake
ASCH, FRANK

Stone Soup
BROWN, MARCIA

Avocado Baby
BURNINGHAM, JOHN

The Shopping Basket
BURNINGHAM, JOHN

Pancakes, Pancakes!
CARLE, ERIC

Today Is Monday
CARLE, ERIC

The Very Hungry Caterpillar
CARLE, ERIC

Mother, Mother, I Feel Sick
CHARLIP, REMY

The Comic Adventures of Old Mother Hubbard and Her Dog
DE PAOLA, TOMIE

A Cake for Barney
DUNBAR, JOYCE

The Gingerbread Boy
GALDONE, PAUL

The Magic Porridge Pot
GALDONE, PAUL

Greedy Greeny
GANTOS, JACK

Two Greedy Bears
GINSBURG, MIRRA

The Doorbell Rang
HUTCHINS, PAT

The Pigs' Picnic
KASZA, KEIKO

Fat Cat
KENT, JACK

Socks for Supper
KENT, JACK

"Alligator Pie" in *Alligator Pie* (poetry)
LEE, DENNIS

The Giant Jam Sandwich
LORD, JOHN

Yummers
MARSHALL, JAMES.

Here Comes Henny
POMERANTZ, CHARLOTTE

One Potato
PORTER, SUE

But No Cheese!
PIROTTA, SAVIOUR

Mrs. Pig's Bulk Buy
RAYNER, MARY

Benny Bakes a Cake
RICE, EVA

In the Night Kitchen
SENDAK, MAURICE

Gregory, the Terrible Eater
SHARMAT, MITCHELL

I Know an Old Lady Who Swallowed a Fly
WESTCOTT, NADINE

Peanut Butter and Jelly: A Play Rhyme
WESTCOTT, NADINE

The Little Red Hen
ZEMACH, MARGOT

The Three Wishes
ZEMACH, MARGOT

MORE STORIES

Medieval Feast
ALIKI

Strega Nona
DE PAOLA, TOMIE

Bread and Jam for Frances
HOBAN, LILLIAN

How Pizza Came to Our Town
KHALSA, DAYAL KAUR

Picnic (wordless)
McCULLY, EMILY ARNOLD

Chicken Soup with Rice
SENDAK, MAURICE

Green Eggs and Ham
SEUSS, DR.

Ernest and Celestine's Picnic
VINCENT, GABRIELLE

Plain Noodles
WATERTON, BETTY

I Can't Have Bannock But the Beaver Has a Dam
WHEELER, BERNELDA

Twenty-Four Robbers
WOOD, AUDREY

NONFICTION

The Popcorn Book
DE PAOLA, TOMIE

Eating the Alphabet: Fruits and Vegetables from A to Z
EHLERT, LOIS

Growing Colors
McMILLAN, BRUCE

NURSERY RHYMES

Old Mother Hubbard

Old Mother Hubbard went to the cupboard
To fetch her poor doggie a bone.
But when she got there
The cupboard was bare
And so the poor doggie had none.

Jack Spratt

Jack Spratt could eat no fat
His wife could eat no lean.
And so between the two of them
They licked the platter clean.

Little Jack Horner

Little Jack Horner sat in a corner
Eating his Christmas pie.
He put in his thumb
And pulled out a plum
And said, "What a good boy am I."

Little Miss Muffet

> *Children love to act this out.*

Little Miss Muffet
Sat on a tuffet
Eating her curds and whey.
Along came a spider
And sat down beside her
And frightened Miss Muffet away.

Pat-A-Cake

Pat-a-cake, pat-a-cake, baker's man.
> *Clap hands in rhythm.*

Bake me a cake as fast as you can.
Pat it, and roll it, and mark it with "B,"
> *Pat palm of left hand, roll hands, draw a B on palm of left hand.*

And put it in the oven for baby and me.
> *Lay hands flat and pretend to put in oven.*

Pease Porridge Hot

Clap it out alone, or clap it out with partners.

Pease porridge hot,
Pease porridge cold,
Pease porridge in the pot,
Nine days old.
Some like it hot,
Some like it cold,
Some like it in the pot,
Nine days old!

The Cat and the Fiddle

This is fun to represent in felt.

Hey diddle diddle, the cat and the fiddle,
The cow jumped over the moon.
The little dog laughed to see such sport,
And the dish ran away with the spoon.

Hippety-Hop

Stand up and skip!

Hippety-hop to the baker's shop,
To buy three sticks of candy.
One for you, and one for me,
And one for uncle Sandy.

Sing, Sing, What Shall I Sing?

Sing, sing, what shall I sing?
The cat's run away with the pudding string!
Do, do, what shall I do?
The cat's run away with the pudding too!

FINGERPLAYS

Cup of Tea

Here's a cup,
Form cup with one hand.

And here's a cup,
Form cup with other hand.

And here's a pot of tea.
Form tea pot with both hands.

Pour a cup,
Pouring motion.

And pour a cup,
Repeat.

And have a drink with me.
Pretend to drink.

Alligator Pie

Use an alligator puppet and ask children to chant along. From Dennis Lee's Alligator Pie.

Alligator pie, alligator pie,
If I don't get some I think I'm going to die.
Give away the green grass, give away the sky,
But don't give away my alligator pie.

Alligator stew, alligator stew,
If I don't get some I don't know what I'll do.
Give away my furry hat, give away my shoe,
But don't give away my alligator stew.

Alligator soup, alligator soup,
If I don't get some I think I'm gonna droop.
Give away my hockey-stick, give away my hoop,
But don't give away my alligator soup.

A Delicious Cake

Mix the batter, stir the batter,
Make stirring motion.

Shake some flour in.
Make shaking motion with one hand.

Mix the batter, stir the batter,
Repeat stirring motion.

Place it in a tin.
Make pouring motion.

Sprinkle little raisins on,
Make motion of sprinkling raisins onto batter.

Pop it in to bake.
Make motion of placing cake in oven.

Open wide the oven door,
Bend down and make motion as if opening oven door.

And out comes a cake!
Extend open palms.

Pancake

Suit actions to words.

Mix a pancake, stir a pancake,
Pop it in a pan.
Fry a pancake, toss a pancake,
Catch it if you can!

I'm a Little Teapot

I'm a little teapot short and stout.
Here is my handle, here is my spout.
Right hand on hip, left hand bent at elbow,
pointing away from body.
When I get all steamed up hear me shout.
Tip me over and pour me out.

I'm a special teapot, yes it's true.
Here let me show you what I can do.
I can change my handle and my spout.
Change hands.
Tip me over and pour me out!

Making Cookies
Suit actions to words.

I am making cookie dough,
Round and round the beaters go.
Add some flour from a cup,
Stir and stir the batter up.
Roll them, cut them, nice and neat,
Put them on a cookie sheet.
Bake them, count them, 1, 2, 3,
Serve them to my friends for tea.

Popcorn

You put the oil in the pot
And you let it get hot.
You put the popcorn in
And you start to grin.
Sizzle, sizzle, sizzle, sizzle
Sizzle, sizzle, sizzle, sizzle
Sizzle, sizzle, sizzle, sizzle
POP!

I Eat My Peas with Honey
Clap hands in rhythm.

I eat my peas with honey.
I've done it all my life.
I know it may seem funny,
But it keeps them on my knife.

Five Fat Sausages
This is especially fun after The Three Wishes.

Five fat sausages frying in a pan,
Hold up five fingers.
All of a sudden one went 'BANG!'
Clap hands loudly.
Four fat sausages frying in a pan,
Hold up four fingers.
All of a sudden one went 'BANG!'
Clap hands loudly again.
Three fat sausages . . .
Two fat sausages . . .
One fat sausage frying in a pan
All of a sudden it went 'BANG!'
Then there were NO sausages left!
Hold up a fist. Fingers all gone.

Five Fat Peas

Five fat peas in a pea-pod pressed,
Clasp one hand over the other to make a ball.
One grew, two grew,
Extend thumbs together then index fingers.
And so did all the rest.
Raise middle, ring, and little fingers in turn.
They grew, and they grew,
Pull hands apart slowly as pod grows.
And they grew, and they grew,
They grew so fat and portly
That the pea-pod POPPED!
Finish with a loud clap.

Jelly in the Bowl
Stand up and act it out. Do a wobbly walk for the
first verse. Do it fast, then do it slow.

Jelly in the bowl,
Jelly in the bowl,
Wibble wobble, wibble wobble,
Jelly in the bowl.

Cookies in the tin,
Cookies in the tin,
Shake 'em up, shake 'em up,
Cookies in the tin.

Candles on the cake,
Candles on the cake,
Blow 'em out, blow 'em out,
Candles on the cake.

SONGS

I Know an Old Lady Who Swallowed a Fly

*This works nicely with felts or a paper bag puppet.
Wiggle and jiggle each time you get to the spider.*

I know an old lady who swallowed a fly
I don't know why she swallowed a fly
Perhaps she'll die.

I know an old lady who swallowed a spider
That wriggled and jiggled and tickled inside her.
She swallowed the spider to catch the fly.
I don't know why she swallowed the fly.
Perhaps she'll die.

I know an old lady who swallowed a bird.
Now, how absurd to swallow a bird.
She swallowed the bird
To catch the spider
That wriggled and jiggled and tickled inside her.
She swallowed the spider to catch the fly.
I don't know why she swallowed the fly,
Perhaps she'll die.

I know an old lady who swallowed a cat.
Imagine that! She swallowed a cat.
She swallowed the cat to catch the bird.
She swallowed the bird to catch the spider
That wriggled and jiggled and tickled inside her.
She swallowed the spider to catch the fly.
I don't know why she swallowed the fly.
Perhaps she'll die.

I know an old lady who swallowed a dog.
What a hog to swallow a dog!
She swallowed the dog to catch the cat.
She swallowed the cat to catch the bird.
She swallowed the bird to catch the spider
That wriggled and jiggled and tickled inside her.
She swallowed the spider to catch the fly.
I don't know why she swallowed the fly.
Perhaps she'll die.

I know an old lady who swallowed a cow.
I don't know how she swallowed a cow.
She swallowed the cow to catch the dog.
She swallowed the dog to catch the cat.
She swallowed the cat to catch the bird.
She swallowed the bird to catch the spider.
That wriggled and jiggled and tickled inside her.
She swallowed the spider to catch the fly.
I don't know why she swallowed the fly.
Perhaps she'll die.

I know an old lady who swallowed a horse.
She died of course!

The Muffin Man

Listen to the tune on Bob McGrath's cassette, Sing
Along with Bob, Vol. One. *Words and music are
in* Sharon, Lois & Bram's Elephant Jam.

Oh, do you know the muffin man,
The muffin man, the muffin man,
Oh, do you know the muffin man,
Who lives on Drury Lane?

Oh, yes, I know the muffin man,
The muffin man the muffin man,
Oh, yes, I know the muffin man,
Who lives on Drury Lane?

Now we all know the muffin man,
The muffin man, the muffin man,
Now we all know the muffin man,
Who lives on Drury Lane.

On Top of Spaghetti

This is especially nice after Cloudy with a
Chance of Meatballs. *Sing in echo fashion,
swaying gently side to side. The children
follow your lead.*

On top of spaghetti,
All covered with cheese,
I lost my poor meatball,
When somebody sneezed.
It rolled off the table
And onto the floor,
And then my poor meatball
Rolled out of the door.
It rolled in the garden
And under a bush,
And then my poor meatball
Was nothing but mush.
The mush was as tasty
As tasty could be,
And early next summer,
It grew into a tree.
The tree was all covered,
With beautiful moss,
It grew lovely meatballs,
And tomato sauce.
So if you eat spaghetti,
All covered with cheese,
Hold on to your meatballs,
And don't ever sneeze!

Apples and Bananas

Listen to the tune on Raffi's One Light, One Sun *cassette. Words and music are in* The Second Raffi Songbook.

I like to eat, eat, eat, apples and bananas.
I like to eat, eat, eat, apples and bananas.

I like to ate . . . aypuls and banaynays.
I like to eet . . . eeples and baneenees.
I like to ite . . . iples and baninis.
I like to ote . . . oples and banonos.
I like to ute . . . uples and banunus.

Hambone

See page 187.

MORE IDEAS

1. Felt Stories: *The Very Hungry Caterpillar, The Great Big Enormous Turnip, I Know an Old Lady Who Swallowed a Fly,* and *Fat Cat.*

2. Tell *The Gingerbread Man* with finger puppets and invite children to join you in the Gingerbread Man's chant. Elaborate by getting children to help you make the imaginary dough: Reach for the big bowl way up high in the cupboard, add flour, milk, eggs, ginger and mix before you start the story.

3. *I Know an Old Lady Who Swallowed a Fly* can be dramatized in various ways. For construction of an old lady paper bag puppet, see *Storytelling with Puppets* by Connie Champlin & Nancy Renfro.

4. Chant and act out *Peanut Butter and Jelly: A Play Rhyme*. See page 162.

5. Make some alligator (spinach) pie for lunch and chant as you go about it. Ask the children what they would put in. Make some green eggs and ham with food colouring!

6. Sing "Going on a Picnic" or "The Corner Grocery Store." The tunes are on Raffi's *Singable Songs for the Very Young* cassette. The words and music to both are in *The Raffi Singable Songbook*.

7. Sing "Day-O", the "Banana Boat Song" from Trinidad and ask the children to join on the refrain, "daylight come and me wan' go home." Tell the children about how men and women worked all night to load the banana boats and how much they must have wanted to go home in the morning to rest, and so they invented this beautiful song. The tallyman counted the banana bunches and paid the workers in the morning. The tune is on Raffi's *Baby Beluga* cassette. Words and music are in *The Second Raffi Songbook*.

8. For "Sing a Song of Six Pence," make a simple pie out of pie plates stapled together. Remove a pie shaped piece and pull out 24 little blackbirds strung together. The kids might be interested to know that dishes like this were actually served to royal families in the Middle Ages. See Aliki's *Medieval Feast* for more details and sumptuous illustrations.

9. Focus on one particular aspect of this theme. Focus on cooking pots, for example, with *Stone Soup, The Magic Cooking Pot,* and *Strega Nona*. Focus on fussy eaters with *Mrs. Pig's Bulk Buy, Gregory the Terrible Eater,* and *Bread and Jam for Frances*.

10. Focus on where food comes from with *The Little Red Hen, The Giant Vegetable Garden,* and other stories in FARMS and GARDENING.

11. Focus on foods that are good for growing little bodies with: *The Very Hungry Caterpillar, Gregory the Terrible Eater, Avocado Baby,* and *Eating the Alphabet*.

12. Veer off in a silly direction with *Fat Cat, The Old Lady Who Swallowed a Fly,* and *The Lady with the Alligator Purse* (in SICKNESS & HEALTH). Add *The Three Wishes* by Margot Zemach in which a man ends up with sausages growing from his nose.

13. Memory Game: Use laminated pictures of food with felt strips on the back or felt pieces to apply to the felt board. Some of your requirements may be fulfilled using pieces from *The Very Hungry Caterpillar*. Ask children to name foods that are good for them to eat and put these on the felt board. Then cover the board with a special memory blanket or sheet and ask children to try to remember all the items on the board. Play the game again with items like pie and lollipops and chips and all those things that are so tasty to eat, but not so good for little bodies to grow on.

14. There's a whole book on this subject: *Mudluscious: Stories and Activities Featuring Food for Preschool Children* by Jan Irving and Robin Currie.

Foxes & Wolves

STORIES TO READ ALOUD

Borreguita and the Coyote
AARDEMA, VERNA

Hattie and the Fox
FOX, MEM

Red Hen and Sly Fox
FRENCH, VIVIAN

The Gingerbread Boy
GALDONE, PAUL

What's in Fox's Sack?
GALDONE, PAUL

The Three Little Pigs
GALDONE, PAUL

Henny Penny
GALDONE, PAUL

Mushroom in the Rain
GINSBURG, MIRRA

The Gunniwolf
HARPER, WILHELMENA

One Fine Day
HOGROGIAN, NONNY

The Wolf's Chicken Stew
KASZA, KEIKO

The Gingerbread Man
KIMMEL, ERIC

The Tomten and the Fox
LINDGREN, ASTRID

Wings: A Tale of Two Chickens
MARSHALL, JAMES

Little Wolf and the Giant
PORTER, SUE

Dance Away
SHANNON, GEORGE

Fox's Dream
TEJIMA

Going to Squintum's: A Foxy Folktale
WESTWOOD, JENNIFER

MORE STORIES

Watching Foxes
ARNOSKY, JIM

Rosie's Walk
HUTCHINS, PAT

Little Red Riding Hood (folk tale)
HYMAN, TRINA SCHART
(AND MANY OTHER ILLUSTRATORS)

Flossie and the Fox
McKISSACK, PATRICIA

"The Gingerbread Man" in *The Three Bears & Other Stories*
ROCKWELL, ANNE

The True Story of the Three Little Pigs
SCIESZKA, JON

The Fox Went Out on a Chilly Night
SPIER, PETER

The Amazing Bone
STEIG, WILLIAM

Doctor De Soto
STEIG, WILLIAM

The Three Little Wolves and the Big Bad Pig
TRIVIZAS, EUGENE

NONFICTION

Wolf Island
GODKIN, CELIA

Foxes
BURTON, JANE

SONGS

Fox Went Out on a Chilly Night

Fox went out on a chilly night,
And he prayed for the moon to give him light,
For he'd many a mile to go that night,
Before he reached the town-o, town-o, town-o,
He'd many a mile to go that night,
Before he reached the town-o.

He ran till he came to the farmer's bin,
Where the ducks and the geese were kept penned in.
"A couple of you will grease my chin
Before I leave this town-o, town-o, town-o,
A couple of you will grease my chin
Before I leave this town-o."

First he caught the grey goose by the neck,
Then he swing a duck across his back,
And he didn't mind the quack, quack, quack,
Or their legs all dangling down-o, down-o, down-o,
And he didn't mind the quack, quack, quack,
Or their legs all dangling down-o.

Then old mother Giggle-Gaggle jumped out of bed,
And out of the window she popped her head,
Crying, "John! John! Our grey goose is gone,
And the fox is in the town-o, town-o, town-o,"
Crying, "John! John! Our grey goose is gone,
And the fox is in the town-o."

Then John, he ran to the top of the hill,
Blew his horn both loud and shrill,
The fox, he said, "I better go with my kill
Or they'll soon be on my tail-o, tail-o, tail-o,"
The fox, he said, "I better go with my kill
Or they'll soon be on my tail-o."

He ran till he came to his nice warm den,
There were the little ones, eight, nine, ten,
They said, "Daddy, better go back again,
Because it must be a wonderful town-o, town-o,
  town-o,"
They said, "Daddy, better go back again,
Because it must be a wonderful town-o."

Then the fox and his wife, without any strife,
Cut up the goose with a fork and a knife,
They never ate such a dinner in their life,
And the little ones chewed on the bones-o.

MORE IDEAS

1. Celebrate knowing sly little foxes and big bad wolves, the better to know them by!

2. Felt stories: *The Gunniwolf, The Gingerbread Man, Chicken Little,* and *The Three Little Pigs.* Ask children to join in on the chants.

3. Tell *The Gingerbread Man* with finger puppets. The version I like best for telling is in Anne Rockwell's *The Three Bears and Other Stories.*

4. Tell *The Gunniwolf* with or without lap puppets. It's wildly popular simply as a participation story, and you can see Margaret Read MacDonald's *Twenty Tellable Tales* for inspiration. It's fun to split the audience into two groups. One half can sing the little girl's song with you (make up a simple tune for this), and the other half can be the wolf and run "hunkercha" after her with you. My children usually want to join in on both parts.

5. More mature audiences will enjoy *The True Story of the Three Little Pigs* when they are familiar with the old fairytale.

6. Use rhymes suggested by characters in the stories and all purpose rhymes and songs, such as "Shake My Sillies Out," and "If You're Happy," etc.

Friends

STORIES TO READ ALOUD

Effie
ALLINSON, BEVERLY

Mr. Gumpy's Outing
BURNINGHAM, JOHN

The Grouchy Ladybug
CARLE, ERIC

Bill and Pete
DE PAOLA, TOMIE

May I Bring a Friend?
DE REGNIERS, BEATRICE

Play with Me
ETS, MARIE H.

Wilfrid Gordon MacDonald Partridge
FOX, MEM

Corduroy
FREEMAN, DON

My Best Friend
HUTCHINS, PAT

Something to Crow About
LANE, MEGAN HALSEY

A Porcupine Named Fluffy
LESTER, HELEN

The Wizard, the Fairy, and the Magic Chicken
LESTER, HELEN

David's Father
MUNSCH, ROBERT

Millicent and the Wind
MUNSCH, ROBERT

Yo! Yes?
RASCHKA, CHRIS

Rose and Dorothy
SCHWARTZ, ROSLYN

The Lamb and the Butterfly
SUNDGAARD, ARNOLD

Ira Sleeps Over
WABER, BERNARD

The Bunyip of Berkely Creek
WAGNER, JENNY

Mr. Nick's Knitting
WILD, MARGARET

MORE STORIES

We Are Best Friends (losing a friend)
ALIKI

Best Friends
COHEN, MIRIAM

Miss Tizzy
GRAY, LIBBA MOORE

Friends
HEINE, HELME

Chester's Way
HENKES, KEVIN

Jessica
HENKES, KEVIN

Best Friends for Frances
HOBAN, RUSSELL

David and Dog
HUGHES, SHIRLEY

Frog and Toad Are Friends (reader series)
LOBEL, ARNOLD

George and Martha One Fine Day (reader series)
MARSHALL, JAMES

Hug Me
STREN, PATTI

NONFICTION

Making Friends
ROGERS, FRED

NURSERY RHYMES

Jack and Jill

Jack and Jill went up the hill
To fetch a pail of water.
Jack fell down
And broke his crown.
And Jill came tumbling after.

Up Jack got and home did trot
As fast as he could caper.
He jumped into bed
And plastered his head
With vinegar and brown paper.

The Cat and the Fiddle

Hey diddle diddle, the cat and the fiddle,
The cow jumped over the moon.
The little dog laughed to see such sport,
And the dish ran away with the spoon.

Polly Put the Kettle On

Polly put the kettle on
Polly put the kettle on
Polly put the kettle on
We'll all have tea!

Sukie take it off again
Sukie take it off again
Sukie take it off again
They've all gone home!

Tweedledum and Tweedledee

Tweedledum and Tweedledee
Agreed to have a battle,
For Tweedledum said Tweedledee
Had spoiled his nice new rattle.
Just then flew by a monstrous crow
As black as a tar-barrel,
Which frightened both the heroes so,
They quite forgot their quarrel.

Mary Had a Little Lamb

See page 168.

FINGERPLAYS

New Friends

Suit actions to words.

See this finger? It is Sue,
To storytime she came.
She looked and looked around the room
She didn't know a name.
Four children looked right up and smiled
And then they waved at Sue!
So she smiled back and then she waved
And took a step or two.
Soon she was clapping with them all
And when 'twas time to play,
She said, "I'm glad we're friends
At storyime today."

Four Friends

Two little friends are better than one
Hold up two fingers on left hand and one finger on right hand.
Three are better than two
Three fingers on left hand, two on right hand.
And four are much better still
Four fingers on left hand.
Just think what four friends can do!

SONGS

The More We Get Together

Listen to the tune on Bob McGrath's Sing Along with Bob, Vol. One. *Words and music are in Tom Glazer's* Eye Winker, Tom Tinker, Chin Chopper.

The more we get together, together, together,
The more we get together, the happier we'll be.
For your friends are my friends,
And my friends are your friends.
The more we get together, the happier we'll be.

The more we read together, together, together,
The more we read together, the happier we'll be.
For your friends are my friends,
And my friends are your friends.
The more we read together, the happier we'll be.

1st verse: Hug yourself and sway rhythmically, side to side, point to "your friends," then to yourself on "my friends," then back to hugging.

Rig-A-Jig-Jig

Listen to this tune on Bob McGrath's Sing Along with Bob, Vol. Two. *Stand in a circle to sing the middle verse. Skip in a circle with partners to rig-a-jig-jig.*

Rig-a-jig-jig and away we go,
'way we go, 'way we go;
Rig-a-jig-jig and away we go,
Heigh-ho, heigh-ho, heigh-ho!

As I was walking down the street,
Down the street, down the street,
A pretty girl (boy) I chanced to meet,
Heigh-ho, heigh-ho, heigh-ho!

Rig-a-jig-jig and away we go,
'way we go, 'way we go;
Rig-a-jig-jig and away we go,
Heigh-ho, heigh-ho, heigh-ho!

Skinnamarink

Listen to this tune on Sharon, Lois & Bram's One Elephant *cassette. Words and music are in* Elephant Jam.

Skinnamarinky dinky dink,
Place right elbow in left hand and wave fingers of right hand.

Skinnamarinky doo,
Switch to left elbow in right hand.

I love you!
Point to eye, place both hands over heart and flutter, then point to the audience.

Skinnamarinky dinky dink,
Repeat actions.

Skinnamarinky doo,
I . . . love . . . you!
I love you in the morning,
Put hands together at knee level for the sun in the morning.

And in the afternoon,
Raise hands together to waist level.

I love you in the evening
Raise hands together over your head.

Underneath the moon.
Open arms for a big round moon.

Skinnamarinky dinky dink,
Repeat actions of first verse.

Skinnamarinky doo,
I . . . love . . . you!

For "I love you" in sign: hold up baby finger for "I," cross arms across your chest for "love," and point to someone for "you."

CIRCLE GAMES

Did You Ever See a Lassie

Just sing this, or, form a circle and let children make up movements for others to follow in the verses. All take turns.

Did you ever see a lassie, a lassie, a lassie?
Did you ever see a lassie go this way and that?
Go this way and that way and this way and that way.
Did you ever see a lassie go this way and that?

Did you ever see a laddie, a laddie, a laddie?
Did you ever see a laddie go this way and that?
Go this way and that way and this way and that way.
Did you ever see a laddie go this way and that?

Little Sally Waters

For music see Singing Bee. *One child, "Sally," sits in the middle of the ring pretending to weep while others circle around and sing. She rises, flies to the east and then to the west, and then to her very best friend. The person she picks to "love the best" then becomes Sally Waters until everyone has had a turn.*

Little Sally Waters, sitting in the sun,
Crying and weeping, lonesome little one.
Rise, Sally, rise; wipe off your eyes;
Fly to the East, Sally
Fly to the West, Sally,
Fly to the one you love the very best.

Little Sally Walker

This version is from the African-American tradition. Listen to the tune on the cassette that goes with Shake It to the One That You Love the Best *by Cheryl Warren-Mattox.*

Little Sally Walker sittin' in a saucer,
Rise, Sally, rise.
Wipe your weeping eyes.
Put your hands on your hips,
And let your backbone slip.
Ah, shake it to the east,
Ah, shake it to the west,
Ah, shake it to the one that you love the best!

There's a Brown Girl in the Ring

This song comes from the West Indies. Listen to the tune on the cassette that goes with Shake It to the One That You Love the Best *by Cheryl Warren-Mattox, or on Raffi's cassette* Everything Grows. *Raffi's words and music are in the* Raffi Everything Grows Songbook.

There's a brown girl in the ring,
Tra-la-la-la-la,
There's a brown girl in the ring,
Tra-la-la-la-la,
Brown girl in the ring,
Tra-la-la-la-la,
And she looks like the sugar in a plum, plum, plum.

Now show me your motion,
Tra-la-la-la-la,
Now show me your motion,
Tra-la-la-la-la,
Show me your motion,
Tra-la-la-la-la,
And she looks like the sugar in a plum, plum, plum.

Let's skip across the ocean,
Tra-la-la-la-la,
Let's skip across the ocean,
Tra-la-la-la-la,
Skip across the ocean,
Tra-la-la-la-la,
And she looks like the sugar in a plum, plum, plum.

On first verse, the child in the middle dances around while the rest join hands and dance in a ring around her. In the next two verses, players follow the lead of the brown girl in the ring who makes up different motions. Take turns being the one in the ring.

MORE IDEAS

1. Felt stories: *Mr. Gumpy's Outing* and *May I Bring a Friend.*

2. Tell one of Arnold Lobel's *Frog and Toad* stories with finger, hand, or table-top puppets.

3. *Hug Me* by Patti Stren is a great friendship story. Unfortunately, the illustrations are rather small for a large audience. Best to tell it using porcupine puppets, or on the felt board.

4. Invite all your little friends to get on board the train and sing "Morningtown Ride." See BEDTIME & MOON STORIES, page 30.

5. Pick up the tempo with "*If You're Happy and You Know It*" (page 80).

6. See also: DOGS, CATS and PETS for animal friends.

Frogs

STORIES TO READ ALOUD

Jump, Frog, Jump
KALAN, ROBERT

The Mysterious Tadpole
KELLOG, STEVEN

The Caterpillar and the Polliwog
KENT, JACK

Frog Went A-Courtin'
LANGSTAFF, JOHN

Over in the Meadow
LANGSTAFF, JOHN

Froggy Gets Dressed
LONDON, JONATHAN

Froggy Learns to Swim
LONDON, JONATHAN

The Wide-Mouthed Frog
SCHNEIDER, REX

April Showers
SHANNON, GEORGE

Foolish Frog
SEEGER, PETE

The Hour of the Frog
WYNNE-JONES, TIM

MORE STORIES

Frog and Toad (reader series)
LOBEL, ARNOLD

Friend or Frog
PRICEMAN, MARJORIE

NONFICTION

Tadpole and Frog
BACK, CHRISTINE

A Frog's Body
COLE, JOANNA

Frogs
GIBBONS, GAIL

The Common Frog
OXFORD SCIENTIFIC FILMS

Frog
ROYSTON, ANGELA

The Life Cycle of a Frog
WILLIAMS, JOHN

FINGERPLAYS

Five Green and Speckled Frogs

This is fun with green frog finger puppets or on the felt board. The tune is on Raffi's Singable Songs *cassette.*

Five green and speckled frogs
Sat on a speckled log
Eating some most delicious bugs - yum yum!
One jumped into the pool
Where it was nice and cool
Then there were four green speckled frogs.
Repeat for four, three, two and one, removing froggies, or bending fingers down, as you go.

Froggies

Hold up five fingers or five froggy finger puppets.

This little froggie broke his toe.
Point to one finger at a time.
This little froggie said, "Oh, oh, oh."
This little froggie laughed and was glad.
This little froggie cried and was sad.
This little froggie did just what he should.
Hopped straight to his mother as fast as he could.
Hop fingers away.

Five Little Froggies

Use fingers or finger puppets, and reduce the numbers as you go.

Five little froggies sitting on a well;
One looked up and down he fell;
Point up, then point down.

Froggies jumped high
Reach up high.

Froggies jumped low;
Reach down low.

Four little froggies dancing to and fro.
Dance four fingers back and forth.

Four little froggies . . .

Repeat until there are no little froggies left.

Little Toad

I am a little toad.
Hold up two hands.

Hopping down the road.
Hop hands.

Just listen to my song.
I sleep all winter long.
Palms together on cheek.

When spring comes, I peep out,
Peep behind hands.

And then I jump about.
Make arms jump.

And now I catch a fly.
Clap hands.

And now I wink my eye.
Wink one eye.

And now and then I hop.
Make hands hop.

And now and then I stop.
Fold hands.

Can You Jump Like a Frog?

Suit actions to words.

Can you hop, hop, hop like a bunny?
Can you jump, jump, jump like a frog?
Can you walk, walk, walk like a duck?
Can you run, run, run like a dog?
Can you fly, fly, fly like a bird?
Can you swim, swim, swim like a fish?
But can you still be a quiet little child?
And sit as still as this?

MORE IDEAS

1. Tell "The Frog Trap," from *Just Enough to Tell a Story* by Nancy Schimmel.

2. Tell a slightly different version of *The Wide-Mouthed Frog* with a frog puppet. Pattern and instructions are in *Storytelling Made Easy with Puppets* by Jan VanSchuyver.

3. Arnold Lobel's *Frog and Toad* stories make marvellous puppet scripts for short puppet plays, either on your lap, on a tabletop, or in a puppet theatre.

4. Songs featuring frogs: "There's a Little White Duck" (page 70), "There's a Hole in the Bottom of the Sea" (page 158), "Over in the Meadow" (page 136), *Frog Went A-Courtin'* (page 197), and "A Frog He Would A-Wooing Go," in *The Golden Songbook* by Katherine Wessels.

5. With *Jump, Frog, Jump*, ask children to crouch like frogs, and jump each time the frog jumps.

6. Put on a Frog Prince puppet show.

Gardening

STORIES TO READ ALOUD

Flower Garden
BUNTING, EVE

Jasper's Beanstalk
BUTTERWORTH, NICK

Growing Vegetable Soup
EHLERT, LOIS

Mole's Hill
EHLERT, LOIS

Planting a Rainbow
EHLERT, LOIS

Mushroom in the Rain
GINSBURG, MIRRA

Two of Everything (folktale)
HONG, LILY TOY

Titch
HUTCHINS, PAT

Bear and Bunny Grow Tomatoes
KOSCIELNIAK, BRUCE

The Carrot Seed (big book format)
KRAUSS, RUTH

Inch by Inch
LIONNI, LEO

The Rose in My Garden
LOBEL, ARNOLD

One Watermelon Seed
LOTTERIDGE, CELIA

Snail's Spell
RYDER, JOANNE

The Great Big Enormous Turnip
TOLSTOY

The Big Fat Worm
VAN LAAN, NANCY

The Giant Vegetable Garden
WESTCOTT, NADINE

The Little Red Hen (folktale)
ZEMACH, MARGOT

MORE STORIES

Jim and the Beanstalk
BRIGGS, RAYMOND

Miss Rumphius
COONEY, BARBARA

The Tiny Seed
CARLE, ERIC

Mr. Mead and His Garden
LORD, JOHN

This Year's Garden
RYLANT, CYNTHIA

NONFICTION

Your First Garden Book
BROWN, MARC

From Seed to Plant
GIBBONS, GAIL

The Reason for a Flower
HELLER, RUTH

Earthworms As Pets
HENWOOD, CHRIS

Snails as Pets
HENWOOD, CHRIS

All About Seeds
KUCHALLA, SUSAN

Alison's Zinnia
LOBEL, ANITA

Snail
OLESEN, JENS

Apple Tree
PARNALL, PETER

NURSERY RHYMES

Mistress Mary

Mistress Mary, quite contrary
How does your garden grow?
With silver bells and cockle shells,
And pretty maids all in a row.

I Had a Little Nut Tree

I had a little nut tree, and nothing would it bear
But a silver nutmeg, and a golden pear.
The King of Spain's daughter, came to visit me,
And all for the sake of my little nut tree.

There Was a Young Gardener of Leeds

There was a young farmer of Leeds,
Who swallowed six packets of seeds.
It soon came to pass
He was covered with grass,
And he couldn't sit down for the weeds.

Moses Supposes

*Felt pieces: make Moses a baby, sitting under a
rose bush with his toeses showing.*

Moses supposes his toeses are roses,
But Moses supposes erroneously,
For nobody's toeses are posies of roses,
As Moses supposes his toeses to be.

Sing a Song of Sixpence

Sing a song of sixpence,
A pocket full of rye;
Four-and-twenty blackbirds,
Baked in a pie!

When the pie was opened,
The birds began to sing;
Wasn't that a dainty dish,
To set before the king?

The king was in his counting-house,
Counting out his money.
The queen was in the parlor,
Eating bread and honey.

The maid was in the garden,
Hanging out the clothes;
When down came a blackbird,
And snapped off her nose!

FINGERPLAYS

My Garden

This is my garden;
    Extend one hand, palm up.
I'll rake it with card,
    *Make raking motion on palm with three fingers
    of other hand.*
And then some flower seeds
I'll plant in there.
    *Make planting motion with thumb and index
    finger.*
The sun will shine,
    Make circle with arms overhead.
And the rain will fall,
    Flutter fingers down to lap.
And my garden will blossom,
    Cup hands together
And grow straight and tall.
    Extend hands upward slowly.

The Flower

Here's a green leaf,
    Show hand.
And here's a green leaf;
    Show other hand.
That, you see, makes two.
    Hold up two fingers.
Here is a bud,
    Cup hands together.
That makes a flower;
    Open cupped hands gradually.
Watch it bloom for you!

What's in a Seed?

*This is nice on the felt board. It's also nice to act
out. To start, children lay sleeping.*

In the heart of a seed
Buried deep so deep
A dear little plant lay fast asleep.
Wake! said the sunshine
And creep to the light
Wake! said the voice of the raindrops bright.
The little plant heard
And it rose to see
What the wonderful outside world could be.

Relaxing Flowers

Five little flowers
> *Hold up five fingers.*

Standing in the sun;
See their heads nodding,
> *Make fingers nod.*

Bowing, one by one.
> *Make fingers bow.*

Down, down, down
Falls the gentle rain,
> *Flutter fingers downward.*

And the five little flowers
Lift up their heads again!
> *Hold up five fingers.*

Flower Play

If I were a little flower
> *Stoop down close to floor.*

Sleeping underneath the ground,
> *Pretend to cover head.*

I'd raise my head and grow and grow,
> *Slowly raise up from floor.*

And stretch my arms and grow and grow,
> *Raise arms to the sky.*

And nod my head and say:
> *Nod and smile at one another.*

"I'm glad to see you all to-day."

Dig a Little Hole

Dig a little hole,
> *Dig.*

Plant a little seed.
> *Drop seed.*

Pour a little water,
> *Pour.*

Pull a little weed,
> *Pull up and throw away.*

Chase a little bug,
> *Chasing motion with hands.*

Heigh-ho, there he goes!
> *Shade eyes.*

Give a little sunshine,
> *Cup hands, lift to the sun.*

Grow a little rose.
> *Smell flower, eyes closed, smiling.*

Little Seed in the Ground
> *A variant of "Jack in the Box."*

Little seed in the ground
> *Crouch down on the floor, hands covering heads.*

Sitting so still.
> *Stay crouching.*

Little seed, will you sprout?
Yes, I will!
> *Jump up.*

The Tree

I am a tall tree.
> *Both hands reach up.*

I reach toward the sky.
> *Arms stretch toward sky.*

Where bright stars twinkle,
> *Look up, flutter fingers.*

And clouds float by.
> *Arms swaying slowly.*

My branches toss high
> *Arms wave wildly.*

As the wild winds blow,
And they bend forward,
> *Arms hang heavily at sides.*

Laden with snow.
When they sway gently
> *Arms out in front, swaying gently.*

I like it best.
Then I rock birdies to sleep
In their nest.
> *Continue swaying, form nest with hands, place head against hands, and close eyes.*

Way Up High in the Apple Tree

Way up high in the apple tree,
> *Hold arms up high.*

Two red apples looked down at me.
> *Make fists for apples.*

I shook that tree as hard as I could,
> *Shake the tree.*

And down fell the apples
> *Hands fall to the ground.*

Mmmm were they good!
> *Take a bite, and rub your tummy.*

Five Red Apples

Use five red apples on a glove puppet or on the felt board. Sing to the tune of "Ten Green Bottles."

Farmer Brown had five red apples
Hanging on the tree.
Farmer Brown had five red apples
Hanging on the tree.
Then he plucked one apple
And he ate it hungrily,
Leaving four red apples
Hanging on the tree.

. . . and so on, until . . .

Farmer Brown had one red apple
Hanging on the tree.
Farmer Brown had one red apple
Hanging on the tree.
Then he plucked one apple,
And he gave it all to me.
Now there are no red apples
Hanging on the tree.

The Apple Tree

Sing to the tune of "Rock-a-bye Baby."

Here is a tree with leaves so green.
Forearms together, elbows to wrists, hands spread.

Here are the apples that hang in between.
Clench fists for apples.

When the wind blows the apples will fall.
Wave arms in the wind and let apples fall suddenly.

Here is a basket to gather them all.
Make a basket with both hands, fingers interlocked.

What Do You Suppose?

What do you suppose?
A bee sat on my nose!
Place finger on nose.

Then what do you think?
He gave me a great big wink,
Wink.

And said, "I beg your pardon,
I thought you were a garden!"

The Apple Pip

Once I found an apple pip
And stuck it in the ground,
When I came to look at it
A tiny shoot I found.
The shoot grew up and up each day;
It soon became a tree.
I picked the rosy apples then
And ate them for my tea.

Pretending

I like to pretend that I am a rose
Cup hands.

That grows and grows and grows.
Open hands gradually.

My hands are a rosebud closed up tight.
Close hands.

With not a tiny speck of light.
Then slowly the petals open for me,
Let hands open gradually.

And here is a full-blown rose, you see!

Creatures in the Garden

This is really a tickling rhyme, but it's also a nice fingerplay. The first time through, creep and run fingers along the floor to the children's legs. This is usually pretty thrilling. The second time through, children join you like this:

Slowly, slowly, very slowly
Creeps the garden snail
Slowly, slowly, very slowly
Up the garden rail.
With two fingers, slowly creep up one leg.

Quickly, quickly, very quickly
Quickly runs the little mouse
Quickly, quickly, very quickly
All around the house.
Quickly run fingers around your knees.

Slowly, slowly, very slowly
Creeps the garden turtle
Slowly, slowly, very slowly
Through the garden myrtle.
Slowly creep up other leg with other two fingers.

Quickly, quickly, very quickly
Quickly runs the little rabbit
Quickly, quickly, very quickly
That's his everyday habit.
Quickly run fingers around your knees.

Five Fat Peas

Five fat peas in a pea-pod pressed,
Clasp one hand over the other to make a ball.

One grew, two grew,
Extend thumbs together then index fingers.

And so did all the rest.
Raise middle, ring, and little fingers in turn.

They grew, and they grew,
Pull hands apart slowly as pod grows.

And they grew, and they grew,
They grew so fat and portly
That the pea-pod POPPED!
Finish with a loud clap.

SONGS

The Farmer and His Seeds

Sing to the tune of "Farmer in the Dell."

The farmer plants the seeds,
Children stoop and pretend to plant seeds.

The farmer plants the seeds,
Heigh-ho the derry-o,
The farmer plants the seeds.

The sun comes out to shine . . .
Make large circle with arms.

The rain begins to fall . . .
Hands flutter up and down.

The seeds begin to grow . . .
Children stand up.

The farmer cuts them down . . .
Move arms to imitate a mower.

He binds them into sheaves . . .
Hold arms in a circle.

And now we'll have some bread . . .
Pretend to eat.

Pick a Bale of Cotton

This one requires an irresistibly lively rhythm.

Gonna jump down, turn around, pick a bale of cotton,
Gonna jump down, turn around, pick a bale a day.
Jump, turn around and make picking motion.

Oh Lawdy, pick a bale of cotton,
Oh Lawdy, pick a bale a day.
Clap in rhythm.

Me and my brother, we can pick a bale of cotton,
Me and my brother, we can pick a bale a day.
Picking motion in rhythm.

Oh Lawdy, pick a bale of cotton,
Oh Lawdy, pick a bale a day.
Clap hands in rhythm

Me and my sister, we can pick a bale of cotton,
Me and my sister, we can pick a bale a day.
Picking motion in rhythm.

Oh Lawdy, pick a bale of cotton,
Oh Lawdy, pick a bale a day.
Clap hands in rhythm

I can pick a pick a pick a pick a bale of cotton,
I can pick a pick a pick a pick a bale a day.
Picking motion in rhythm.

Oh Lawdy, pick a bale of cotton,
Oh Lawdy, pick a bale a day.
Clap hands in rhythm

Oats and Beans and Barley Grow

Hear this tune on Raffi's Baby Beluga *cassette.*
Music is in The Second Raffi Songbook.

Chorus:
Oats and beans and barley grow,
Oats and beans and barley grow,
Do you or I or anyone know
How oats and beans and barley grow?

First the farmer plants the seeds,
Stands up tall and takes his ease,
Stamps his feet and claps his hands
And turns around to view his land.

Repeat chorus

Then the farmer waters the ground,
Watches the sun shine all around,
Stamps his feet and claps his hands
And turns around to view his land.

Repeat chorus

MORE IDEAS

1. Felt stories: *Mushroom in the Rain, A Big Fat Worm, The Great Big Enormous Turnip, Little Red Hen,* and *The Very Hungry Caterpillar.*

2. Puppetry ideas: *Jack and the Beanstalk* (the folktale), and "The Garden" in *Frog and Toad Together* by Arnold Lobel.

3. Emphasize flowers or vegetables that grow in gardens, using Anita Lobel's *Alison's Zinnia* to identify different kinds of flowers, and Lois Ehlert's *Growing Vegetable Soup* and *Planting a Rainbow* to identify different kinds of vegetables. Take pictures to storytime and make a collage of different types of plants. Take a trip to a garden. Learn to identify garden insects, snails, seeds. The possibilities are endless.

4. Plant a bean, which germinates quickly, and watch it grow from week to week. Plant different kinds of seeds to see which ones grow fastest. For lots of beginners' gardening ideas see *Your First Garden Book* by Marc Brown. I particularly like the idea of planting alyssum in the cracks of sidewalks.

5. *Earthworms As Pets* and others in the very original *Keeping Minibeasts Series* have lots of ideas on trapping and keeping garden creatures long enough to study them. Then you let them go!

6. Raffi's song "In My Garden" makes a nice activity rhyme. Hear the tune on his *One Light, One Sun* cassette. Words and music are in *The Second Raffi Song Book.*

7. Related themes: See INSECTS or SNAKES for more ideas on what goes on in a garden. See FOOD for "I Eat My Peas with Honey." For planting themes, see SEASONS – SPRING and for harvest themes see SEASONS – AUTUMN.

8. If you are telling *The Little Red Hen,* show parents Margaret Atwood's version in *Good Bones.* It's a wonderfully amusing interpretation of the folktale .

Giants

STORIES TO READ ALOUD

Effie
ALLINSON, BEVERLY

Jack and the Beanstalk
BIRO, VAL

Jack and the Beanstalk
CAULEY, LORINDA

The History of Mother Twaddle and Her Son Jack
GALDONE, PAUL

Shhh! Lift the Flaps But Don't Wake Up the Giant!
GRINDLEY, SALLY

Jack and the Beanstalk
HOWE, JOHN

Jelly Belly (poetry)
LEE, DENNIS

Giant John
LOBEL, ARNOLD

The Giant Jam Sandwich
LORD, JOHN

David's Father
MUNSCH, ROBERT

Little Wolf and the Giant
PORTER, SUE

Abiyoyo
SEEGER, PETE

The Giant Vegetable Garden
WESTCOTT, NADINE

Rude Giants
WOOD, AUDREY

MORE STORIES

Jim and the Beanstalk
BRIGGS, RAYMOND

The Giant's Toe
COLE, BROCK

Molly Whuppie
DE LA MARE, WALTER

Fin M'Coul: The Giant of Knockmany Hill
DE PAOLA, TOMIE

The Terrible Fin MacCoul
HARPUR, TOM

The Selfish Giant
WILDE, OSCAR

I'll Make You Small
WYNNE-JONES, TIM

NURSERY RHYMES

The Dreadful Doings of Jelly Belly

From Jelly Belly *by Dennis Lee. Ask children to recite this with you the second time around building to a crescendo.*

Jelly Belly bit
With a big fat bite.
   Show your teeth and take a big bite.

Jelly Belly fought
With a big fat fight.
   Throw your fists up in the air.

Jelly Belly scowled
With a big fat frown.
   Put on your biggest scowl.

Jelly Belly yelled
Till his house fell down!
   Throw fists in the air and growl!

Fee, Fi, Fo, Fum

Fee, fi, fo, fum,
I smell the blood of an Englishman;
Be he alive or be he dead,
I'll grind his bones to make my bread.

FINGERPLAYS

Fee, Fie, Foe, Fum

Fee, fie, foe, fum,
Extend each finger in turn.

See my fingers?
Wiggle fingers.

See my thumb?
Wiggle thumb.

Fee, fie, foe, fum
Fold down one finger at a time.

Fingers gone,
Hide fingers in hand.

So is thumb.
Hide thumb.

Suppose

Do you suppose a giant
Who is tall, tall, tall,
Reach toward ceiling and stand on tiptoe.

Could ever be a brownie
Who is small, small, small?
Crouch down on floor.

But the brownie who is tiny
Will try, try, try
To reach up to the giant
Who is high, high, high.
Reach toward ceiling.

One Is a Giant
Get your giant face on and use a giant voice.

One is a giant who stomps his feet,
Stomp like a giant.

Two is a fairy so light and neat,
Twirl on tiptoe like a fairy.

Three is a mouse who crouches small,
Crouch down on the floor.

And four is a great big bouncing ball.
Jump up and bounce, arms swinging.

MORE IDEAS

1. If you're musically inclined, get out the guitar and sing "Abiyoyo." You'll find it on Pete Seeger's cassette *Stories & Songs for Little Children.*

2. Tell Shel Silverstein's wonderful poem "Me And My Giant" in *Where the Sidewalk Ends.*

3. Tell Dennis Lee's wonderful poem "Like a Giant in a Towel" in *Alligator Pie.*

4. See "Mr. Tall and Mr. Small," and other ideas in TEENY TINY THINGS.

Halloween

STORIES TO READ ALOUD

Popcorn
ASCH, FRANK

Humbug Witch
BALIAN, LORNA

A Dark Dark Tale
BROWN, RUTH

In the Haunted House
BUNTING, EVE

Scary, Scary Halloween
BUNTING, EVE

Six Creepy Sheep
ENDERLE, JUDITH ROSS

The Monster and the Tailor
GALDONE, PAUL

Tailypo: A Ghost Story
GALDONE, PAUL

Halloween
NERLOVE, MIRIAM

One Dark Night
PRESTON, EDNA MITCHELL

Thump, Thump, Thump
ROCKWELL, ANNE

The Teeny Tiny Woman
SEULING, BARBARA

Big Pumpkin
SILVERMAN, ERICA

That Terrible Hallowe'en Night
STEVENSON, JAMES

Pumpkin, Pumpkin
TETHERINGTON, JEANNE

The Little Old Lady Who Was Not Afraid of Anything
WILLIAMS, LINDA

MORE STORIES

A Woggle of Witches
ADAMS, ADRIENNE

Hester
BARTON, BYRON

Shaggy Dog's Halloween
CHARLES, DONALD

The Thirteen Days of Halloween
GREENE, CAROL

The Soup Bone
JOHNSTON, TONY

The Witch's Hat
JOHNSTON, TONY

The Gobble-uns 'll git You Ef You Don't Watch Out!
RILEY, JAMES WHITCOMB

Apples and Pumpkins
ROCKWELL, ANNE

The Witch's Hand
UTTON, PETER

NONFICTION

The Popcorn Book
DE PAOLA, TOMIE

Halloween
GIBBONS, GAIL

Things to Make and Do for Halloween
GIBBONS, GAIL

The Pumpkin Patch
KING, ELIZABETH

Happy Halloween! Things to Make and Do
SUPRANER, ROBYN

NURSERY RHYME

Peter, Peter Pumpkin Eater

Peter, Peter pumpkin eater,
Had a wife and couldn't keep her,
So he put her in a pumpkin shell,
And there he kept her very well.

To the Bat

Bat, bat, come under my hat,
And I'll give you a slice of bacon;
And when I bake, I'll give you a cake,
If I am not mistaken.

Five Little Ghostesses

Five little ghostesses,
Sitting on postesses,
Eating buttered toastesses,
Greasing their fistesses,
Up to their wristesses.
Oh what beastesses,
To make such feastesses.

FINGERPLAYS

Little Witches

One little, two little, three little witches,
Hold up fingers one by one.

Ride through the sky on a broom;
Hands clasped together in front.

One little, two little, three little witches,
Repeat action in line one.

Wink their eyes at the moon.
Wink eye while making circle overhead with arms.

A Witch

If I were a witch,
I'd ride on a broom
One fist rides on top of other, waving through air.

And scatter the ghosts
With a zoom, zoom, zoom!
Sweeping motion.

Five Little Jack-O-Lanterns

This works very well with orange pom-pom jack o'lanterns on a black glove puppet.

Five little jack-o-lanterns sitting on a gate.
Hold up five fingers.

The first one said, "My, it's getting late."
Point to thumb.

The second one said, "Sh, I hear a noise."
Pointer finger.

The third one said, "It's just a lot of boys."
Middle finger.

The fourth one said, "Come on, let's run,"
Ring finger.

The fifth one said, "It's just Halloween fun."
Little finger.

"Whooo," went the wind and out went the lights
Close fingers into fist.

And away went the jack-o-lanterns Hallowe'en night.
Open hand, run fingers behind back.

What Am I?

What am I? A face so round,
Form circle with hands.

And eyes so bright,
Touch eyes.

A nose that glows,
Touch nose.

My, what a sight!
Clasp hands.

A fiery mouth with a jolly grin,
Touch mouth and grin.

No arms, no legs, just head to chin.
Shake arms and legs, touch head and chin.

Answer: Jack-o-lantern

Five Little Goblins

Five fingers bend down one at a time.

Five little goblins on Hallowe'en night,
Made a very, very spooky sight.
The first one danced on his tippy-tip-toes;
The next one tumbled and bumped his nose;
The next one jumped high up in the air;
The next one walked like a fuzzy bear;
The next one sang a Halloween song.
Five goblins played the whole night long!

Hallowe'en

A witch once went for a ride on her broom,
Raise thumb of right hand. Zoom and dip.

Up through the frosty sky.
She zoomed and zoomed, and she dipped and zipped,
And she winked at the moon as she passed by,
Wink.

At the moon in the frosty sky.
She wore a hat that was pointed tall,
Make a pointed hat with two fingers.

And a cape that was flowing wide,
Make rippling motion with fingers.

And a fierce black cat with a stand up tail
Point forefinger up.

Rode merrily by her side,
Rode merrily by her side.
Make dipping motion with hand.

Black Cat

A big black cat with eyes so green
Point to eyes.

Went out on the night of Hallowe'en.
He saw a witch,
Bring fingertips together in a peak over head.

He saw an owl,
Form circles around eyes with fingers and thumbs.

And then he began to "Meow, meow."

What Will You Be?

I think I shall be a ghost tonight
Point to self.

Or maybe a big black bat
Arms apart for size of bat.

Would you like to be a Hallowe'en witch?
And wear a high pointed hat?
Hands together over head.

Hallowe'en Is Here

When goblins prowl
Make fingers walk.

And hoot owls howl,
Make goggles with hands around eyes.

"Whoo! whoo!"
Cup hands around mouth.

When witches fly
Flutter hands in air.

"Oooo! oooo!"
Boys and girls, don't shake with fear
It just means Hallowe'en is here!

Criss Cross Apple Sauce

Ask children to sit in a train so they can draw on one another's backs.

Criss cross
Draw an X on your partner's back.

Apple sauce,
Pat her shoulders with both hands.

Spiders crawling up your back.
Walk fingers up partner's back.

Cool breeze,
Blow on partner's neck.

Tight squeeze,
Give her a big hug from behind.

And now you've got the shivers!
Tickle your partner all over her back.

Tommy's Pumpkin

It was the biggest pumpkin
That you have ever seen.
Form large circle with arms.

It grew in Tommy's garden.
On the night of Hallowe'en
He took a knife and cut the top;
Point index finger of right hand for knife, and pretend to cut.

Then scooped it out with a spoon;
Scooping motion.

He made two round eyes,
Make circles with thumbs and index fingers.

A nose like this,
Use same fingers to form triangular nose.

And a mouth just like a moon.
Draw half moon shape.

He put a candle in it,
Hold up index finger.

And quietly as a mouse,
He crept up and placed it
In the window of his house.
Fingers creep.

And Tommy's mother cried: "Oh dear,
I fear some goblins must be hiding
Very, very near!"

Owl's Eyes

Make a mask with hands.

See my big and scary eyes,
Thumb and index fingers make owls' eyes.

Get ready for a big surprise.
Turn them upside down backwards, put them on and peer out.

BOO!

SONGS

Three Little Witches

Three fingers fly and glide.

One little, two little, three little witches,
Fly over haystacks, fly over ditches,
Slide round the moon without any hitches,
Heigh, Ho, Hallowe'en's here.

Once I Had a Pumpkin

Take a real jack o'lantern for this one. Sing to the tune of "If I Could Have a Windmill." You can listen to that song on Sharon, Lois & Bram's cassette Great Big Hits. *See music in* Sharon, Lois & Bram's Mother Goose.

Once I had a pumpkin, a pumpkin, a pumpkin,
Once I had a pumpkin with no face at all.
Show the back of the pumpkin.

With no eyes, no nose, no mouth, no teeth.
Pointing to your own eyes, nose, mouth and teeth.

Oh, once I had a pumpkin with no face at all.

Then I made a jack o'lantern, jack o'lantern,
  jack o'lantern
Then I made a jack o'lantern with a face like this.
Turn the jack o'lantern around to show its face.

It had two eyes, a nose, a mouth, and great big teeth.
Once I made a jack o'lantern with a face like this.

The Ghosts Go Gliding

Sing to the tune of "When Johnny Comes Marching Home." Sing adding ghosts to the felt board, or finger puppets to fingers. Repeat lines as in the first verse.

The ghosts go gliding one by one, Woo! Woo!
The ghosts go gliding one by one, Woo! Woo!
The ghosts go gliding one by one,
The little one tripped on a skeleton,
And they all went gliding down the street to trick
  or treat.

The ghosts go gliding two by two, Woo! Woo! . . .
The little one stopped when he heard a boo!

The ghosts go gliding three by three, Woo! Woo! . .
The little one stopped when she saw me!

The ghosts go gliding four by four, Woo! Woo! . . .
The little one stopped to knock on a door.

The ghosts go gliding five by five, Woo! Woo! . . .
The little one stopped when the owl arrived.

The ghosts go gliding six by six, Woo! Woo! . . .
The little one stopped to play some tricks.

I'm a Little Pumpkin

Sing to the tune of "I'm a Little Teapot."

I'm a little pumpkin, short and stout,
Packed full of seeds that you can scrape out.
When you're all finished, then I'll be,
The cutest jack o'lantern you ever did see.

CRAFT IDEAS

1. Make kleenex ghosts. Use two kleenexes per child. Roll one into a ball and place the other over it. Use a small elastic band or tie a string around the ball to form the ghost. Dot on eyes with a felt marker if you like.

2. Make paper bag monster masks. Use paper bags large enough to fit over the children's heads. Cut holes for eyes and mouth, then draw and colour faces and glue on various fabric scraps. Alternately, use small bags for hand puppets. Check out *Easy to Make Monster Masks and Disguises* by Frieda Gates. This is an especially appropriate activity after *Shaggy Dog's Halloween*.

3. Roast pumpkin seeds to eat or make pumpkin seed pictures after you've made your jack o'lantern.

MORE IDEAS

1. Felt stories: *The Little Old Lady Who Was Not Afraid of Anything, One Dark Night, The Big Pumpkin,* and "The Strange Visitor" from Judy Sierra's *Flannel Board Storytelling Book*.

2. "The Strange Visitor," or "Strange Company," as it is also called, makes a wonderfully spooky shadow puppet play for Halloween. Use the felt pattern for shadow puppet pieces.

3. *Humbug Witch* is fun to act out with costume and props. It also works as a felt story.

4. Use a teeny tiny witch puppet and a teeny tiny basket to tell the story of *The Teeny Tiny Woman*. She can take a teeny tiny nap in the teeny tiny folds of your teeny tiny skirt!

5. For a lovely paper cut story about a witch and a little ghost, see "The Little Orange House" in *Paper Stories* by Jean Stangl.

6. *The Bed Just So* by Jeanne Hardendorff is a little scary, easy to learn, and fun to tell at Halloween.

Houses

STORIES TO READ ALOUD

The House That Jack Built
BOLAM, EMILY

The Three Little Pigs
GALDONE, PAUL

Christina Katerina and the Box
GAUCH, PATRICIA LEE

Mr. Bear's Chair
GRAHAM, THOMAS

Lazy Lion
HADITHI, MWENYE

A House Is a House for Me
HOBERMAN, MARYANNE

The Biggest House in the World
LIONNI, LEO

The Man Who Took the Inside Out
LOBEL, ARNOLD

Is This a House for a Hermit Crab?
McDONALD, MEGAN

Too Much Noise
McGOVERN, ANN

The Mice Who Lived in a Shoe
PEPPE, RODNEY

The Big Orange Splot
PINKWATER, DANIEL

Oh! Were They Ever Happy
SPIER, PETER

The House That Jack Built
STEVENS, JANET, ILLS.

Possum Come A-Knockin'
VAN LAAN, NANCY

Where Does the Brown Bear Go?
WEISS, NICKI

The Napping House
WOOD, AUDREY

MORE STORIES

Who's in Rabbit's House?
AARDEMA, VERNA

Poinsettia and Her Family
BOND, FELICIA

The Little House
BURTON, VIRGINIA LEE

The Village of Round and Square Houses
GRIFALCONI, ANN

Alfie Gets in First
HUGHES, SHIRLEY

Rafiki
LANGNER, NOLA

London Bridge Is Falling Down
SPIER, PETER

NONFICTION

Building a House
BARTON, BYRON

How a House Is Built
GIBBONS, GAIL

Tools
ROBBINS, KEN

The Toolbox
ROCKWELL, ANNE

Moving
ROGERS, FRED

NURSERY RHYMES

This Is the House That Jack Built

This one calls for felt! Make it as short or as long as you like. Apply felt pieces as you go. Pause for children to name the additional pieces, and ask them to join in on the lines as they become familiar with the pattern.

This is the house that Jack built.

This is the malt,
That lay in the house that Jack built.

This is the rat,
That ate the malt,
That lay in the house that Jack built.

This is the cat,
That killed the rat,
That ate the malt,
That lay in the house that Jack built.

This is the dog,
That worried the cat,
That killed the rat,
That ate the malt,
That lay in the house that Jack built.

This is the cow with the crumpled horn,
That tossed the dog,
That worried the cat,
That killed the rat,
That ate the malt,
That lay in the house that Jack built.

This the maiden all forlorn,
That milked the cow with the crumpled horn, . . .

This is the man all tattered and torn,
That kissed the maiden all forlorn, . . .

This is the priest all shaven and shorn,
That married the man all tattered and torn, . . .

This is the cock that crowed in the morn,
That waked the priest all shaven and shorn, . . .

This is the farmer sowing his corn,
That kept the cock that crowed in the morn, . . .

Peter, Peter Pumpkin Eater

Peter, Peter pumpkin eater,
Had a wife and couldn't keep her,
So he put her in a pumpkin shell,
And there he kept her very well.

The Old Woman Who Lived in a Shoe

There was an old woman who lived in a shoe.
She had so many children she didn't know what to do.
She gave them some broth
And a big slice of bread
Read them all stories
And tucked them in bed.

There Was a Crooked Man

There was a crooked man
And he walked a crooked mile,
He found a crooked sixpence
Against a crooked stile.
He bought a crooked cat,
Which caught a crooked mouse,
And they all lived together
In a little crooked house.

FINGERPLAYS

A Little House

I will make a little house,
Hold hands upright with tips of fingers touching to form arch.

Where two playmates come to hide.
Slide thumbs under arch.

When I peep in at the door
Bend hands to look through arch.

They quickly run outside.
Slide thumbs out quickly.

Another Little House

I'm going to build a little house
Fingers form roof.

With windows big and bright.
Circles with index fingers and thumbs.

With chimney tall and curling smoke
Arms up in air.

Drifting out of sight.
In winter, when the snowflakes fall
Fingers flutter down.

Or when I hear a storm,
Cup hand to ear.

I'll go sit in my little house
Sit down.

Where I'll be nice and warm.
Hug chest.

A House for Me

The carpenter's hammer
Goes rap, rap, rap;
Make a fist of one hand and pound in the palm of the other.

And his saw goes see, saw, see;
Move arm in sawing motion.

He hammers and hammers,
Hammer.

And saws and saws,
Saw.

And builds a house for me.
Make house outline.

Here Is a Nest for a Robin

Here is a nest for a robin,
Cup hands.

And here is a hive for a bee.
Fists together.

Here is a hole for a bunny,
Thumb and fingers form circle.

And here is a house for me!
Fingertips together make roof overhead.

Here Is a Beehive

This is nice with finger puppets or fingers.

Here is a beehive.
Make a fist.

But where are all the bees?
Hidden away where nobody sees.
Watch them come creeping
Out of their hive.
Creep fingers.

1, 2, 3, 4, 5.
Extend fingers one at a time and count.

Bzzzzzzzzzz.
Buzz away.

Here Is the Church

Here is the church,
Interlace fingers with knuckles up.

And here is the steeple.
Point index fingers up.

Open the doors,
Turn hands over with fingers interlaced.

And here are all the people.
Wriggle fingers.

Johnny 's Hammer

Johnny pounds with one hammer, one hammer,
  one hammer,
Johnny pounds with one hammer all day long.
Pounding motion with one fist.

Johnny pounds with two hammers, two hammers,
  two hammers,
Johnny pounds with two hammers all day long.
Pounding motion with two fists.

Johnny pounds with three hammers, three hammers,
  three hammers,
Johnny pounds with three hammers all day long.
Pounding motion with two fists and one foot.

Johnny pounds with four hammers, four hammers,
  four hammers,
Johnny pounds with four hammers all day long.
Pounding motion with two fists and two feet.

Johnny pounds with five hammers, five hammers,
  five hammers,
Johnny pounds with five hammers all day long.
Pounding motion with two fists, two feet, and nod head.

Johnny now is so tired, so tired, so tired,
Johnny now is so tired all day long.
Hold hammering position.

Johnny goes to sleep now, sleep now, sleep now.
Johnny goes to sleep now all night long.
Drop head and close eyes.

Jack in the Box

Children crouch with hands over head.

Jack in the box,
Jack in the box,
Sits so still.
Will he come out?
YES HE WILL!
All jump up and shout.

Jack in the Box with the Big Red Nose

Jack in the box all shut up tight.
Children crouch down.

With the cover closed just right.
Hands on heads form lid.

Touch the spring and up she goes!
Jack in the box with the big red nose.
Jump up and point to nose.

CIRCLE GAMES

London Bridge

Listen to the tune on Bob McGrath's cassette,
Sing Along with Bob, Vol. Two. Sing it or play
it as a circle game.

London bridge is falling down,
Falling down, falling down,
London bridge is falling down,
My fair lady-o.

Additional Verses:

Build it up with iron bars, . . .
Iron bars will bend and break, . . .
Build it up with pins and needles, . . .
Pins and needles rust and bend, . . .
Build it up with sticks and stones, . . .
Sticks and stones will wash away, . . .

To play this circle game, two children form arch with
arms raised and other players march through single file.
On "My fair lady-o" the arch falls and captures a
player who is asked "gold or silver." She then starts a
row behind the appointed gold or silver representative
until all the players have been caught.

Go in and Out the Window

The tune to this song is similar to "If I Could Have
a Windmill." You can listen to that song on
Sharon, Lois & Bram's cassette Great Big Hits.
See music in Sharon, Lois & Bram's Mother
Goose.

Go in and out the window,
Go in and out the window,
Go in and out the window,
As we have done before.

Additional Verses:

Go round and round the village, . . .
Stand and face your partner, . . .
Follow me to London, . . .
Now shake his hand and leave him, . . .

For a full description of this circle game, see Singing
Bee *where the game is called "Go Round and Round*
the Village." The child who is 'It' weaves in and out of
the circle through children's raised hands. 'It' chooses a
partner to dance with, who then becomes the dancer in
the next verse. Sing and play until everyone has had a
turn.

MORE IDEAS

1. Dramatize *Who's in Rabbit's House?* with simple animal masks.

2. Have children participate in "The House That Jack Built" with a felt board version.

3. *The Three Little Pigs* can be told effectively on the felt board, or with stick or finger puppets. It's a good participation story, too, as children join in on the repetitive phrases.

4. Have a storytime on building houses with *The House That Jack Built, The Three Little Pigs, Mr. Bear's Chair,* and *A House Is a House for Me.* Promote all the wonderful new books on carpenters' tools.

5. Act out *Too Much Noise* with a blanket or a table as a prop for the house. Invite the children to come in as the various animals. If you'd like a craft to go with it, make simple headbands out of heavy paper stapled together and add cut-out animal ears. This is an effective story to tell with the felt board too.

6. *Make It with Boxes* by Joan Irvine, a nonfiction book written for older children, has lots of interesting ideas for creating play environments out of cardboard boxes: cardboard costumes, puppets, props, and stages adaptable for storytime.

Insects

STORIES TO READ ALOUD

Why Mosquitoes Buzz in People's Ears
AARDEMA, VERNA

Effie
ALLINSON, BEVERLY

Ladybird, Ladybird
BROWN, RUTH

The Big Sneeze
BROWN, RUTH

The Grouchy Ladybug
CARLE, ERIC

The Very Busy Spider
CARLE, ERIC

The Very Hungry Caterpillar
CARLE, ERIC

The Very Lonely Firefly
CARLE, ERIC

The Very Quiet Cricket
CARLE, ERIC

The Most Amazing Hide and Seek Counting Book
CROWTHER, ROBERT

Maggie and the Pirate
KEATS, EZRA JACK

Inch by Inch
LIONNI, LEO

The Giant Jam Sandwich
LORD, JOHN

The Thing that Bothered Farmer Brown
SLOAT, TERI

I Know an Old Lady Who Swallowed a Fly
WESTCOTT, NADINE

The Napping House
WOOD, AUDREY

MORE STORIES

Red Dragonfly on My Shoulder (poetry)
CASSEDEY, SYLVIA

Anansi and the Moss-Covered Rock
KIMMEL, ERIC

Anansi Goes Fishing
KIMMEL, ERIC

Anansi the Spider
McDERMOTT, GERALD

Ladybird on a Bicycle
SUEYOSHI, A.

Two Bad Ants
VAN ALLSBURG, CHRIS

NONFICTION

Spider's Web
BACK, CHRISTINE

Ant Cities
DORROS, ARTHUR

Monarch Butterfly
GIBBONS, GAIL

Spiders
GIBBONS, GAIL

The Honeybee
HOGAN, PAULA

Butterfly
TAYLOR, KIM

The Life Cycle of a Butterfly
TERRY, TREVOR

The Life Cycle of an Ant
TERRY, TREVOR

Butterfly and Caterpillar
WATTS, BARRIE

Ladybug
WATTS, BARRIE

Bees and Honey
OXFORD SCIENTIFIC FILMS

The Butterfly Cycle
OXFORD SCIENTIFIC FILMS

Dragon Flies
OXFORD SCIENTIFIC FILMS

Spider's Web
OXFORD SCIENTIFIC FILMS

NURSERY RHYMES

Ladybug, Ladybug
This is nice with a ladybug puppet.

Ladybug, ladybug,
Fly away home,
Your house is on fire
And your children all gone;
All except one
And that's little Ann
And she has crept under
The frying pan.

Little Miss Muffet
Children love to act this out.

Little Miss Muffet
Sat on a tuffet
Eating her curds and whey
Along came a spider
And sat down beside her
And frightened Miss Muffet away.

Little Miss Dimble
From Dennis Lee's Jelly Belly

Little Miss Dimble
Lived in a thimble,
Slept in a measuring spoon.
She met a mosquito
And called him "My Sweet-o,"
And married him under the moon.

FINGERPLAYS

Fuzzy Little Caterpillar

Fuzzy little caterpillar
Crawling, crawling on the ground
Fuzzy little caterpillar
Move hand forward, wiggle thumb.

Nowhere to be found,
Though we've looked and looked
And hunted everywhere around.

Roly Poly Caterpillar

Roly-poly caterpillar
Creep index finger along arm.

Into a corner crept,
Spun around himself a blanket
Spin hands around one another.

Then for a long time slept.
Rest head on hands, eyes closed.

Roly-poly caterpillar
Wakening by and by
Open eyes and stretch.

Found himself with beautiful wings
Changed to a butterfly.
Hook thumbs together and wave hands.

Arabella Miller
*Sing to the tune of "Twinkle Twinkle Little Star."
Use a caterpillar puppet for dramatic effect. The
tune is on Pat Carfra's cassette* Lullabies &
Laughter. *For music, see* Eye Winker, Tom
Tinker, Chin Chopper *by Tom Glazer.*

Little Arabella Miller
Found a wooly caterpillar.
Pretend to pick up the caterpillar.

First it crawled upon her mother,
Walk fingers of right hand up the left arm.

Then upon her baby brother;
Walk fingers of left hand up the right arm.

All said, "Arabella Miller,
Take away that caterpillar!"
Pretend to put the caterpillar down.

Here Is a Beehive

This is nice with fingers or finger puppets.

Here is a beehive
Make a fist.

But where are all the bees?
Hidden away where nobody sees.
Here they come out of their hive
Creep fingers.

1, 2, 3, 4, 5.
Extend fingers one at a a time.

Bzzzzzzzzzz.
Buzz away.

Creepy Crawly

Once there was a creepy crawly
Stand up. Creep hands up from toes.

Climbing up the castle wall-y.
Weather changed to stormy, squally
Arms up. Sway like a tree in the wind.

And the rain began to fall-y.
Flutter fingers down.

Down from the castle wall-y
Fell the little creepy crawly.
Flump!
All fall down!

Fuzzy Wuzzy Caterpillar

Play with fingers, or act it out. Children wriggle on the floor, yawn, close eyes, fall asleep, softly snore. Touch them on the head, one by one, then they wake up and fly around the room like moths.

Fuzzy wuzzy caterpillar
Creep index finger along arm.

Into a corner will creep.
He'll spin himself a blanket,
Spin hands around one another.

And then fall fast asleep.
Rest head on hands, eyes closed.

Fuzzy wuzzy caterpillar
Open eyes and stretch.

Wakes up by and by,
Stretches his lovely wings,
Hook thumbs together, wave hands.

Then away the moth will fly!

SONGS

Spider on the Floor

This one is great fun with a spider puppet. Suit actions to words. The tune is on Raffi's cassette Singable Songs for the Very Young. *Music is in* The Raffi Singable Songbook.

There's a spider on the floor, on the floor.
There's a spider on the floor, on the floor.
Who could ask for any more than a spider on the floor,
There's a spider on the floor, on the floor.

Now the spider's on my leg, on my leg.
Oh, the spider's on my leg, on my leg.
Oh, he's really big! This old spider on my leg.
There's a spider on my leg, on my leg.

Now the spider's on my stomach, on my stomach.
Oh, the spider's on my stomach, on my stomach.
Oh, he's just a dumb old lummok, this old spider on my stomach.
There's a spider on my stomach, on my stomach.

Now the spider's on my neck, on my neck,
Oh, the spider's on my neck, on my neck,
Oh, I'm gonna be a wreck, I've got a spider on my neck.
There's a spider on my neck, on my neck.

Now the spider's on my face, on my face,
Oh, the spider's on my face, on my face,
Oh, what a big disgrace, I've got a spider on my face.
There's a spider on my face, on my face.

Now the spider's on my head, on my head,
Oh, the spider's on my head, on my head,
Oh, I wish that I were dead, I've got a spider on my head.
There's s spider on my head, on my head.

Spoken: But he jumps off . . . . . .

Repeat first verse.

Eensy, Weensy Spider

Eensy weensy spider climbed up the water-spout;
Opposite thumbs and pointer fingers climb up.

Down came the rain and washed the spider out;
Flutter fingers downward. Hands sweep down.

Out came the sunshine and dried up all the rain;
Arms form circle overhead, then sweep upward.

And eensy weensy spider climbed up the spout again.
As above.

The Ants Came Marching

Sing to the tune of "When Johnny Comes Marching Home," and act it out!

The ants came marching one by one,
Hurrah! Hurrah!
The ants came marching one by one,
Hurrah! Hurrah!
The ants came marching one by one,
The little one stopped to suck his thumb,
And they all went marching down around the town.

Additional Verses:

The ants came marching two by two, . . .
The little one stopped to tie his shoe, . . .

The ants came marching three by three, . . .
The little one stopped to climb a tree, . . .

The ants came marching four by four, . . .
The little one stopped to shut the door, . . .

The ants came marching five by five, . . .
The little one stopped to take a dive, . . .

The ants came marching six by six, . . .
The little one stopped to pick up sticks, . . .

The ants came marching seven by seven, . . .
The little one stopped to go to heaven, . . .

The ants came marching eight by eight, . . .
The little one stopped to shut the gate, . . .

The ants came marching nine by nine, . . .
The little one stopped to scratch his spine, . . .

The ants came marching ten by ten, . . .
The little one stopped to say, "The end!"

Fiddle-Dee-Dee

Sing in a high little voice. The music is in
Lullabies and Night Songs by Wilder.
Fly and bee finger puppets are nice.

Refrain:
Fiddle-dee-dee, Fiddle-dee-dee,
The fly has married the bumble bee.

Says the fly, says he, "Will you marry me
And live with me, sweet bumble bee?"
    Repeat refrain.

Says the bee, says she, "I'll live under your wing,
And you'll never know that I carry a sting."
    Repeat refrain.

So when the parson had joined the pair,
They both went out to take the air.
    Repeat refrain.

And the fly did buzz and the bells did ring,
Did you ever hear so merry a thing?
    Repeat refrain.

And then to think that of all the flies,
The humble bee should carry the prize.
    Repeat refrain.

MORE IDEAS

1. Felt Stories: *The Very Hungry Caterpillar*, "I Know an Old Lady" (page 97), and "There's a Little White Duck" (page 70).

2. More felt stories: "La Hormiguita" a Mexican folktale about a little ant in Judy Sierra's *Multicultural Folktales*. "Little Cockroach Martina," a Puerto Rican tale, and "The Caterpillar," a poem by Christina Rosetti are in Judy Sierra's *Flannel Board Storytelling Book*. Highly recommended.

3. *The Very Quiet Cricket* is always a big hit. Follow-up by telling "The Cricket in the Palace" from *Listen! And Help Tell the Story* by Bernice Wells Carlson. Use a little toy cricket for the sound effects, or let the children supply the sound.

4. Tell the story of *Hubert the Caterpillar Who Thought He Was a Mustache* by Wendy Stang and Susan Richards (Harlin Quist, 1967). To make Hubert, simply attach a small piece of fuzzy fabric to your index finger with a small elastic band.

5. Craft Idea: Make egg carton caterpillars using the bumpy bottom of an egg carton cut in half lengthwise. Let children paint or decorate with felt pens and stickers. Attach pipe cleaner antennae, and draw on eyes and mouth.

7. Craft Idea: Make spiders. For small spiders, use one egg carton cup. Paint it, and attach bits of pipe cleaners for legs. For larger spiders, decorate paper plates. Fold strips of construction paper in an accordion style, and glue these to the paper plate. Attach a string to the centre of the body and hang up for a creepy jiggly-legged effect.

8. See GARDENING and SNAKES, TURTLES & LIZARDS for more ideas about creepy crawly things.

Mice

STORIES TO READ ALOUD

Who Sank the Boat
ALLEN, PAMELA

At Mary Bloom's
ALIKI

Once a Mouse
BROWN, MACIA

Elephant in a Well
ETS, MARIE HALLS

Another Mouse to Feed
KRAUS, ROBERT

Whose Mouse Are You?
KRAUS, ROBERT

The Tale of Fancy Nancy
KOENIG, MARION

Oh, A-Hunting We Will Go
LANGSTAFF, JOHN

Alexander and the Wind-Up Mouse
LIONNI, LEO

Frederick
LIONNI, LEO

The Mice Who Lived in a Shoe
PEPPE, RODNEY

But No Cheese!
PIROTTA, SAVIOUR

Mother, Mother, I Want Another
POLUSHKIN, MARIA

One Potato
PORTER, SUE

Bedtime Mouse
STODDARD, SANDOL

The Great Big Enormous Turnip
TOLSTOY

Noisy Nora (big book format)
WELLS, ROSEMARY

Seven Blind Mice
YOUNG, ED

MORE STORIES

Town Mouse, Country Mouse
BRETT, JAN

The Town Mouse and the Country Mouse
CAULEY, LORINDA BRYAN

Jessica
HENKES, KEVIN

Julius, the Baby of the World
HENKES, KEVIN

Mouse Tales (reader)
LOBEL, ARNOLD

Picnic
McCULLY, EMILY ARNOLD

The New Baby
McCULLY, EMILY ARNOLD

The Tale of Mrs. Tittlemouse
POTTER, BEATRIX

Doctor De Soto
STEIG, WILLIAM

Ernest and Celestine (many titles)
VINCENT, GABRIELLLE

NONFICTION

A Look Through a Mouse Hole
FISCHER-NAGEL, HEIDEROSE

Harvest Mouse
OXFORD SCIENTIFIC FILMS

House Mouse
OXFORD SCIENTIFIC FILMS

NURSERY RHYMES

Hickory Dickory Dock

Hickory dickory dock,
Swing arms.

The mouse ran up the clock.
Run fingers from toes up to head.

The clock struck one,
Clap.

And down he run,
Run fingers back down to your toes.

Hickory, dickory, dock.
Swing arms.

Three Blind Mice

This is fun with three little mouse finger puppets, and especially appropriate after Seven Blind Mice.

Three blind mice, three blind mice,
See how they run, see how they run.
They all ran after the farmer's wife
Who cut off their tails with the carving knife.
Did you ever see such a sight in your life
As three blind mice!

Six Little Mice

Use the fingers on one hand for mice and the other hand for the cat. Or, use a cat puppet.

Six little mice sat down to spin;
Pussy passed by and she peeped in.
What are you doing, my little men?
Weaving coats for gentlemen.
Shall I come in and cut off your threads?
No, no, Mistress Pussy, you'd bite off our heads.
Oh, no, I'll not; I'll help you to spin.
That may be so, but you can't come in!

Pussy Cat, Pussy Cat

Recite once through with a pussy cat puppet. The second time around, let children play the pussy cat and provide the responses.

Pussy cat, pussy cat, where have you been?
I've been to London to visit the Queen.
Pussy cat, pussy cat what did you there?
I frightened a little mouse under a chair.

FINGERPLAYS

Five Little Mice

Use five fingers or five mice finger puppets.

Five little mice came out to play,
Gathering crumbs up on their way;
Out came a pussy cat
Sleek and black,
Four little mice went scampering back.

Four little mice came out to play . . .

Play until all the little mice are gone.

Five Little Mice

Play this game on five fingers.

Five little mice on the pantry floor,
This little mouse peeked behind the door.
This little mouse nibbled at the cake,
This little mouse not a sound did make.
This little mouse took a bit of cheese,
This little mouse heard the kitten sneeze.
"Ah Choo," sneezed the kitten,
And, "Squeak," they all cried,
And they found a hole and ran inside.

Little Mousie

Here's a little mousie
Peeking through a hole.
Poke index finger of one hand through fist of other hand.

Peek to the left.
Wiggle finger to the left.

Peek to the right.
Wiggle finger to the right.

Pull your head back in,
Pull finger into fist.

There's a cat in sight!

MORE IDEAS

1. Felt Stories: *The Great Big Enormous Turnip, Who Sank the Boat?*, and *Elephant in a Well.*

2. Use a mouse puppet to tell *Whose Mouse Are You?*.

3. Tell "The Roly Poly Rice Ball" from *Twenty Tellable Tales* by Margaret Read MacDonald. It's a lovely participation folk tale about a magical mouse country. Musical notation for a nice little tune for the mouse music is included.

Monkeys

STORIES TO READ ALOUD

Monkey Face
ASCH, FRANK

Dear Zoo (lift the flap)
CAMPBELL, ROD

Five Little Monkeys
CHRISTELOW, EILEEN

The Cool Ride in the Sky
GALDONE, PAUL

The Monkey and the Crocodile
GALDONE, PAUL

The Turtle and the Monkey
GALDONE, PAUL

Crocodile Beat
JORGENSEN, GAIL

The Wise Monkey Tale
MAESTRO, BETSY

Mr. Monkey and the Gotcha Bird
MYERS, WALTER DEAN

Caps for Sale
SLOBODKINA, ESPHYR

MORE STORIES

Tom and Pippo (all kinds of 'em!)
OXENBURY, HELEN

Hand, Hand, Fingers, Thumb
PERKINS, AL

Curious George
REY, H. A.

NONFICTION

Monkeys
HOFFMAN, MARY

NURSERY RHYME

Pop Goes the Weasel

Round and round the cobbler's bench
The monkey chased the weasel
> *Run fingers of one hand around palm of other.*

The monkey thought 'twas all in fun
Pop! Goes the weasel!
> *Clap on "Pop."*

A penny for a spool of thread,
A penny for a needle,
That's the way the money goes,
Pop! Goes the weasel!

I've no time to sit and sigh,
No patience to wait till time goes by,
So kiss me quick, I'm off, good-bye –
Pop! Goes the weasel.

Just Like Me
> *Ask children to supply the refrain, and act it out.*

"I went up one pair of stairs."
"Just like me."
"I went up two pairs of stairs."
"Just like me."
"I went up into a room."
"Just like me."
"I looked out of a window."
"Just like me."
"And there I saw a monkey."
"Just like me."

FINGERPLAYS

Five Little Monkeys

Use with fingers, finger puppets, or act it out with as many little monkeys as you have at storytime! Carry on until the last monkey falls out, getting progressively louder as you go. End with, "Put those monkeys straight to bed!" Listen to the tune on Sharon, Lois & Bram's cassette, One Elephant.

Five little monkeys,
Five fingers up.

Jumping on the bed,
Bouncing up and down.

One fell out,
One finger down.

And hurt his head.
Hold your head.

Mother called the doctor
Pretend to use the telephone.

And the doctor said,
"No more monkeys jumping on the bed."
Shake "doctor" finger at "monkeys."

Four little monkeys . . .

And so on, until all your little monkeys are in bed.

Monkey See - Monkey Do

Use motions indicated by words.

Chorus:
Monkey see, monkey do.
Monkey does the same as you.

Oh, when you clap, clap, clap your hands,
The monkey clap, clap, claps his hands.

Repeat chorus.

Oh, when you stamp, stamp, stamp your feet,
The monkey stamp, stamp, stamps his feet.

Repeat chorus.

Oh, when you jump, jump, jump up high,
The monkey jump, jump, jumps up high.

Repeat chorus.

Oh, when you turn yourself around,
The monkey turns himself around.

Repeat chorus.

A Little Monkey Likes to Do

Perform each action as indicated. Point to children on "you and you." They then imitate your actions.

A little monkey likes to do,
Just the same as you and you;

When you sit up very tall,
Monkey sits up very tall;

When you pretend to throw a ball,
Monkey pretends to throw a ball;

When you try to touch your toes,
Monkey tries to touch his toes;

When you move your little nose,
Monkey tries to move his nose;

When you jump up in the air,
Monkey jumps up in the air;

When you sit down in a chair,
Monkey sits down in a chair.

Five Little Monkeys

Use fingers, or monkey finger puppets, and an alligator puppet.

Five little monkeys swinging from a tree,
Hold up five fingers on right hand. Swing rhythmically.

Teasing Mister Crocodile, "Can't catch me!"
Wave fingers at left hand.

Along came Mister Crocodile, slowly as could be,
Make a sneaky mouth with fingers and thumb of left hand.

SNAP!
Bite off a finger!

Four little monkeys . . .
Three little monkeys . . .
Two little monkeys . . .
One little monkey . . .

No little monkeys swinging from a tree,
I'd better watch out or he might catch me!
Point to self.

Ten Little Monkeys

One little, two little, three little monkeys,
  Holding up three fingers.
Four little, five little, six little monkeys,
  Hold up another three, and so on.
Seven little, eight little, nine little monkeys,
Ten little monkey friends.

"And do you know what they did?
They got in their boats very carefully.
Be careful you don't tip over."
  Carefully climb into imaginary boats.

They rowed, and they rowed, and they rowed to the shore.
  Rowing motion.
They rowed, and they rowed, and they rowed to the shore.
They rowed, and they rowed, and they rowed to the shore.
Ten little monkey friends.

"It was so hot, and they were tired of sitting,
So they all stood up very carefully."
  Wipe brow. Balancing motion.

They all stood up, and the boat tipped over.
  Fall to floor.
They all stood up, and the boat tipped over.
They all stood up, and the boat tipped over.
Ten little monkey friends.

"What are we going to do now?"
  Very excitedly.

They swam, and they swam, and they swam to the shore.
  Swimming motion.
They swam, and they swam, and they swam to the shore.
They swam, and they swam, and they swam to the shore.
Ten little monkey friends.

"Now, what shall we do?"

They were cold and wet, and they ran home to mother.
  Running motion.
They were cold and wet, and they ran home to mother.
They were cold and wet, and they ran home to mother.
Ten little monkey friends.

"And what do you suppose she did?"

She fed them and kissed them, and put them to bed.
  Eating motion, kissing motion and sleeping motion.
She fed them and kissed them, and put them to bed.
She fed them and kissed them, and put them to bed.
Ten little monkey friends.

Five Little Monkeys

*Use five fingers, five monkeys on the felt board
or five monkey finger puppets.*

Five little monkeys walked along the shore;
One went a-sailing,
Then there were four.
Four little monkeys climbed up a tree;
One of them tumbled down,
Then there were three.
Three little monkeys found a pot of glue;
One got stuck in it,
Then there were two.
Two little monkeys found a currant bun;
One ran away with it,
Then there was one.
One little monkey cried all afternoon,
So they put him in an aeroplane
And sent him to the moon.

Two Little Monkeys

Two little monkeys fighting in bed.
   Two index fingers fight.

One fell out and hurt his head.
   Drop one finger, hold head.

The other one called the doctor.
   Pretend to dial, hold phone to ear.

And the doctor said, "That is what
You get for fighting in bed!"
   Shake finger sternly.

MORE IDEAS

1. Felt Stories: *Caps for Sale, Monkey Face, Dear Zoo,* and "Five Little Monkeys."

2. *Caps for Sale* is a wildly popular felt story. (Six, or even three, little monkeys will do.) Children love to imitate the monkeys. Don't forget to explain what a peddler is!

3. The *Pippo* books by Helen Oxenbury and *Dear Zoo* are especially good for toddlers.

4. *Monkey Face* makes the best draw-and-tell story. It also works in felt. It's out of print, so ask your children's librarian if there is a copy hidden away somewhere.

5. This theme goes nicely with alligator and crocodile stories: Chant "Alligator Pie" after "Five little monkeys swinging from a tree." See "The Crocodile" (page 134), and alligator stories in MONSTERS, DRAGONS & WILD THINGS.

Monsters, Dragons & Wild Things

STORIES TO READ ALOUD

Go Away, Big Green Monster
EMBERLEY, ED

The Three Billy Goats Gruff
GALDONE, PAUL

The Gunniwolf
HARPER, WILHELMINA

Where's the Baby?
HUTCHINS, PAT

Crocodile Beat
JORGENSEN, GAIL

Lizzy's Lion (poetry)
LEE, DENNIS

The Wizard, the Fairy, and the Magic Chicken
LESTER, HELEN

Liza Lou and the Yeller Belly Swamp
MAYER, MERCER

There's an Alligator Under My Bed
MAYER, MERCER

There's a Nightmare in My Closet
MAYER, MERCER

The Beast
MEDDAUGH, SUSAN

Too Many Monsters
MEDDAUGH, SUSAN

The Boy in the Drawer
MUNSCH, ROBERT

The Dark
MUNSCH, ROBERT

The Paper Bag Princess
MUNSCH, ROBERT

Custard the Dragon
NASH, OGDEN

I'm Coming to Get You!
ROSS, TONY

Where the Wild Things Are
SENDAK, MAURICE

Elvira
SHANNON, MARGARET

Do Not Open
TURKLE, BRINTON

My Mama Says . . .
VIORST, JUDITH

The Judge
ZEMACH, HARVEY

MORE STORIES

Bimwili and the Zimwi
AARDEMA, VERNA

John Patrick Norman McHennessy, the Boy Who Was Always Late
BURNINGHAM, JOHN

Clyde Monster
CRAVE, ROBERT

A Promise Is a Promise
MUNSCH, ROBERT & MICHAEL KUSUGAK

The Secret in the Matchbox
WALLIS, VAL

FINGERPLAYS

See My Big and Scary Eyes
From circles around eyes with thumbs and index fingers.

See my big and scary eyes?
Get ready for a big surprise.
Boo!

Monsters

Suit actions to words. This is nice after The Boy in the Drawer.

We'll all be great big monsters,
And every one we'll scare,
With two big horns,
And bulging eyes,
And stringy, dark brown hair.
Our monster has two large scary heads
And an extra long long nose
With big enormous monster feet
And twelve big bulbous toes.
Shhh! Let's show him we're not afraid
Or he might start to grow,
We'll walk right up and kiss him SMACK!
Oh look! Where did he go?

The Monster Stomp

Look as scary as can be, gnash your terrible teeth, show your terrible claws, and suit actions to words.

If you want to be a monster, now's your chance
'Cause everybody's doing the monster dance.
You just stamp your feet,
Wave your arms around,
Stretch 'em up, stretch 'em up,
Then put them on the ground,
'Cause you're doing the monster stomp.
Ooh-Ah-Ooh-Ah-Ooh-Ah-Ooh-Ah!
Ooh-Ah-Ooh-Ah-Ooh-Ah-Ooh-Ah!

Five Little Monsters

From Blackberry Ink *by Eve Merriam. Use five monster finger puppets, or five fingers.*

Five little monsters
By the light of the moon
Stirring pudding with
A wooden pudding spoon.
The first one says,
"It mustn't be runny."
The second one says,
"That would make it taste funny."
The third one says,
"It mustn't be lumpy."
The fourth one says,
"That would make me grumpy."
The fifth one smiles,
Hums a little tune,
And licks all the drippings
From the wooden pudding spoon.

SONGS

The Crocodile

Listen to the tune on Sharon, Lois & Bram's cassette, Great Big Hits.

She sailed away on a lovely summer's day,
On the back of a crocodile.
Place right hand on back of left.

"You see," said she,
"It's as plain as plain can be,
I'll go sailing down the Nile."
Move in swaying motion.

The croc winked his eye,
Wink.

As she waved them all goodbye,
Wave.

Wearing a happy smile.
Smile.

At the end of the ride,
The lady was inside.
And the smile was on the crocodile.
Place palms together. Open and shut for crocodile's mouth.

MORE IDEAS

1. *Crocodile Beat* begs to be read aloud with an energetic rhythm. Ask children to clap in time to the music of the verse and join in on the animal sounds. Other croci-alligator stories to add for this theme are: *There's an Alligator Under My Bed, Liza Lou and the Yeller Belly Swamp,* and *Mama Don't Allow.* For action verses, see "Alligator Pie" and "Five Little Monkeys." Wind up by making alligator pie for lunch, or by making egg carton alligators (for which, see pattern in *Puppetry in Early Childhood Education* by Tamara Hunt).

2. Act out *Where the Wild Things Are.* Children pretend to be wild things by getting dressed for the story: putting on claws, gnashing their teeth, wiggling their ears, etc.

3. Tell *The Gunniwolf.*

4. Tell *The Three Billy Goats Gruff* with the felt board and have children join in on the trip traps. Use a scary voice for the troll.

5. Provide art supplies and ask children to draw pictures of monsters they've imagined.

6. Soothe any really frightened feelings by singing "If You're Happy," or "Shake My Sillies Out." See EMOTIONS.

7. If you play guitar, now would be a nice time to sing "Puff the Magic Dragon."

Mother's Day

STORIES TO READ ALOUD

The Runaway Bunny
BROWN, MARGARET WISE

Flower Garden
BUNTING, EVE

The Comic Adventures of Old Mother Hubbard and Her Dog
DE PAOLA, TOMIE

Are You My Mother?
EASTMAN, P.D.

Old Mother Hubbard
GALDONE, PAUL

Ask Mr. Bear
FLACK, MARJORIE

A Mother for Choco
KASZA, KEIKO

Little Chick's Mothers and all the Others
LUTON, MILDRED

Just for You
MAYER, MERCER

I Love You As Much
MELMED, LAURA KRAUSS

Five Minutes Peace
MURPHY, JILL

Mother, Mother, I Want Another
POLUSHKIN, MARIA

On Mother's Lap
SCOTT, ANN HERBERT

The Surprise
SHANNON, GEORGE

Owly
THALER, MIKE

My Mama Says . . .
VIORST, JUDITH

Owl Babies
WADDELL, MARTIN

Hazel's Amazing Mother
WELLS, ROSEMARY

Mr. Rabbit and the Lovely Present
ZOLOTOW, CHARLOTTE

This Quiet Lady
ZOLOTOW, CHARLOTTE

MORE STORIES

My Mom Travels a Lot
BAUER, CAROLINE FELLER

Piggybook
BROWN, ANTHONY

Mama, Do You Love Me?
JOOSSE, BARBARA M.

Blueberries for Sal
McCLOSKEY, ROBERT

Brave Irene
STEIG, WILLIAM

A Chair for My Mother
WILLIAMS, VERA

NURSERY RHYMES

Old Mother Hubbard

Old Mother Hubbard went to the cupboard
To fetch her poor doggie a bone.
But when she got there
The cupboard was bare
And so the poor doggie had none.

The Old Woman Who Lived in a Shoe

There was an old woman who lived in a shoe
She had so many children she didn't know what to do.
She gave them some broth and a big slice of bread
Kissed them all soundly and tucked them in bed.

SONGS

Over in the Meadow

*This makes a nice felt story. Raffi's version of this
traditional song is on his* Baby Beluga *cassette.
Words and music are in the* Second Raffi Songbook.

Over in the meadow in a pond in the sun,
Lived an old mother duck and her little duck one.
"Quack," said the mother, "quack," said the one,
And they quacked and were happy in the pond in the sun.

Over in the meadow in the stream so blue,
Lived an old mother fish and her little fishies two.
"Splash!" said the mother, "Splish splash," said the two,
So they splashed and were happy in the stream so blue.

Over in the meadow in a nest in a tree,
Lived an old mother bird and her little birdies three.
"Tweet! " said the mother, "tweet, tweet, " said the three,
So they sang and were happy in their nest in the tree.

Over in the meadow, on a rock by the shore,
Lived an old mother frog and her little froggies four.
"Croak!" said the mother, "croak croak," said the four,
So they croaked and were happy on a rock by the shore.

Over in the meadow in a big bee hive
Lived an old mother bee and her little bees five.
"Bzzz," said the mother, "Bzzz, Bzzz," said the five,
And they buzzed and were happy in the big bee hive.

Over in the meadow in the noon-day sun
There was a pretty mother and her little baby one.
"Listen," said the mother, "to the ducks and the bees,
To the frogs and the fish and the birds in the trees."

"Bzzz," said the five,
"Croak," said the four,
"Tweet," said the three,
"Splash," said the two,
"Quack," said the one,
And the little baby laughed just to hear such fun.

FINGERPLAYS

Five Little Pigs

Say with five fingers.

Five little pigs went out to play.
The first little pig said,
"Let's go to the woods today?"
The second little pig said,
"What will we do there?"
The third little pig said,
"We'll look for our mother."
The fourth little pig said,
"What will we do when we find her?"
"We'll hug her and kiss her and kiss her!"
Said the fifth little pig.

MORE IDEAS

1. Look for more fingerplays in FAMILIES, "Two Mother Pigs" in PIGS (page 142), "Ten Fluffy Chicks" and a Mother Hen in FARMS (page 88).

2. Change the occasion in *Mr. Rabbit and the Lovely Present* to Mother's Day instead of mother's birthday and tell it with the felt board or with puppets. Other stories on the subject of what to give Mom are: *Flower Garden*, and an adapted version of *The Birthday Thing* by Kiser.

3. Felt Stories: *The Runaway Bunny, Ask Mr. Bear, Mr. Rabbit and the Lovely Present*, and *Over in the Meadow*.

4. Other songs to sing in which mothers play a role: "Hush Little Baby" (page 19), "Five Little Ducks" (page 70), "Five Little Monkeys" (page 130), "Miss Polly Had a Dolly" (page 187), and "Three Little Kittens" (page 40).

5. Craft Idea: Make cards for moms, or presents of, say, necklaces using coloured macaroni strung with wool.

6. Plaster of paris molds of little hands make a great gift for Mother's Day, messy and fun to make. Alternately, simply make hand print pictures. Still too messy? Trace hands with crayons.

7. Draw a picture of Mom after *Monkey Face* draw-and-tell.

Music

STORIES TO READ ALOUD

Thump, Thump, Rat-a-Tat-Tat
BAER, GENE

Berlioz the Bear
BRETT, JAN

Drummer Hoff
EMBERLEY, BARBARA

Mama Don't Allow
HURD, THACHER

Ben's Trumpet
ISADORA, RACHEL

Apt. 3
KEATS, EZRA JACK

Musical Max
KRAUS, ROBERT

The Maestro Plays
MARTIN, BILL

Nicholas Cricket
MAXNER, JOYCE

Mortimer
MUNSCH, ROBERT

Max Found Two Sticks
PINKNEY, BRIAN

Charlie Parker Played Be Bop
RASCHKA, CHRIS

Dance Away
SHANNON, GEORGE

Lizard's Song
SHANNON, GEORGE

Rose and Dorothy
SCHWARTZ, ROSLYN

The Banza (folktale)
WOLKSTEIN, DIANE

MORE STORIES

Bimwili and the Zimwi (folktale)
AARDEMA, VERNA

The Bremen Town Musicians (folktale)
GRIMM BROTHERS
(MANY ILLUSTRATED VERSIONS)

Roland, the Minstrel Pig
STEIG, WILLIAM

Zeke Pippin
STEIG, WILLIAM

Orchestranimals
VAN KAMPEN, VLASTA

Ty's One-Man Band
WALTER, MILDRED PITTS

Music, Music for Everyone
WILLIAMS, VERA B.

NURSERY RHYMES

Old King Cole

*Listen to the tune on Bob McGrath's cassette,
Sing Along with Bob, Vol. Two.*

Old King Cole was a merry old soul,
And a merry old soul was he.
He called for his pipe, and he called for his bowl,
And he called for his fiddlers three.
Every fiddler he had a fine fiddle,
And a very fine fiddle had he.
Oh, there's none so rare, as can compare,
With King Cole and his fiddlers three.

Ride a Cock-horse to Banbury Cross

Ride a cock-horse to Banbury Cross
To see a fine lady upon a white horse.
With rings on her fingers and bells on her toes,
She shall have music wherever she goes.

FINGERPLAYS

The Finger Band

Start with fingers behind back. Sing to the tune of "The Mulberry Bush." This one is nice to use with Thump, Thump, Rat-a-Tat-Tat.

The Finger Band is coming to town,
Coming to town, coming to town.
The Finger Band is coming to town,
So early in the morning.
Speak softly, then louder as you bring fingers to front.

This is the way they wear their hats . . .
Hands on head to show hats.

This is the way they wave their flags . . .
Waving motion with hands.

This is the way they beat their drums . . .
Beating motion with hands.

This is the way they blow their horns . . .
Hands to mouth in blowing motion.

The Finger Band is going away,
Going away, going away.
The Finger Band is going away,
So early in the morning.
As fingers are gradually moved behind back, sound becomes softer.

Music at Our House

Imitate each instrument in turn.

Mother plays the violin,
Father plays the flute,
Little brother plays the horn,
Toot-toot-toot-toot-toot.

I Want to Lead a Band

I want to lead a band
With a baton in my hand.
Wave baton in air.

I want to make sweet music high and low.
Now first I'll beat the drum,
With a rhythmic tum-tum-tum.
Drum beating motion.

And then I'll play the bells a-ting-a-ling.
Bell ringing motion.

And next I'll blow the flute
With a cheery toot-a-toot.
Flute playing motion.

Then I'll make the violin sweetly sing.
Violin playing motion.

I Have a Red Accordion

I have a red accordion
With handles at each side.
Hold hands about ten inches apart.

And when I pull the handles out,
The bellows stretch so wide.
Pull hands further apart.

And when I push the handles in,
The bellows squeeze in tight.
Bring hands together.

And this is how I learned to make
The music come out right.
Move hands apart and together rapidly.

MORE IDEAS

1. For more fingerplays, see "Thumbelina" (page 178), "Cock-a-doodle-doo" (page 52), "Tommy Thumbs Up" (page 11).

2. Tell *Lizard's Song* with lizard and bear puppets. Ask children to join in on Lizard's refrain.

3. Take various musical instruments to show and play: a guitar, a recorder, a kazoo.

4. Make simple musical instruments children can play: paper tubes for horns, tin pie plates for cymbals, wooden spoons for rhythm sticks, yogurt containers filled with rice for shakers, and empty coffee cans for drums. Then shake and beat to the rhythm of the rhymes and songs. Make up your own marching band! For ideas, see *Musical Instruments You Can Make* by Phyllis Hayes, and *My First Music Book* by Helen Drew.

5. See "Aikendrum" (page 30), for a song to use with household instruments.

6. For wonderful ideas about using music with preschool children, listen to the way Ella Jenkins does it, particularly on her compact disc: *Play Your Instruments and Make a Pretty Sound* (Washington, DC: Smithsonian/Folkways, 1994.) She introduces children to the sounds different instruments make on this one: tuba, drums, piano, trumpet, trombone, clarinet, harmonica, the whole band! And all the different kinds of music the instruments can play.

7. Read stories in which music saves the day with: *The Gunniwolf, Dance Away, The Banza,* and *Bimwili and the Zimwi*.

8. Introduce children to illustrated song books. See the list in RECOMMENDED RESOURCES at the back of this book for suggestions.

Pets

STORIES TO READ ALOUD

At Mary Bloom's
ALIKI

Dear Zoo
CAMPBELL, ROD

May I Bring a Friend?
DE REGNIERS, BEATRICE

Play with Me
ETS, MARIE HALLS

A Bag Full of Pups
GACKENBACH, DICK

I Love You Mouse
GRAHAM, JOHN

Pet Show
KEATS, EZRA JACK

The Mysterious Tadpole
KELLOG, STEVEN

Lizzy's Lion
LEE, DENNIS

What Do You Do with a Kangaroo?
MAYER, MERCER

The Box with Red Wheels
PETERSHAM, MAUD

Crictor
UNGERER, TOMI

MORE STORIES

The Dead Bird
BROWN, MARGARET WISE

The Accident
CARRICK, CAROL

Carl Goes to Day Care
DAY, ALEXANDRA

I Want a Dog
KHALSA, DAYAL KAUR

The Big Pets
SMITH, LANE

NONFICTION

Kitten
BURTON, JANE

Puppy
BURTON, JANE

Pets
(EYE OPENERS SERIES)

Spiders
(and other titles in the *Keeping Minibeasts* series)
HENWOOD, CHRIS

Taking My Cat to the Vet
KUKLIN, SUSAN

Rabbits
(and other titles in the *First Pets* series)
PETTY, KATE

When a Pet Dies
ROGERS, FRED

Hamster
WATTS, BARRIE

NURSERY RHYMES

Two Little Dogs

Two little dogs sat by the fire
Over a fender of coal-dust;
Said one little dog
To the other little dog,
If you don't talk,
Why, I must.

FINGERPLAYS

My Pets

Hold up five fingers. Starting with the little finger, point to each as the verse progresses.

I have five pets
That I'd like you to meet.
They all live on Mulberry Street.
This is my chicken,
The smallest of all.
He comes running whenever I call.
This is my duckling.
He says: "Quack, quack, quack"
As he shakes the water from his back.
Here is my rabbit, he runs from his pen.
Then I must put him back again.
This is my kitten.
Her coat is black and white.
She loves to sleep on my pillow at night.
Here is my puppy who has lots of fun.
He chases the others and makes them run.
Move thumb slowly and fingers rapidly.

I Had a Little Turtle

I had a little turtle,
Make a fist with thumb sticking out.

He lived in a box.
Cup hands together for box.

He swam in a puddle
Wiggle hand for swimming.

He climbed on the rocks.
Fingers climb up other fist.

He snapped at a mosquito,
Snap fingers.

He snapped at a flea,
Snap.

He snapped at a minnow
Snap.

And he snapped at me!
Snap.

He caught the mosquito,
Clap, gulp.

He caught the flea,
Clap, gulp.

He caught the minnow,
Clap, gulp.

But he didn't catch me!
Wag pointer finger back and forth.

SONGS

Ha Ha This A-Way

Listen to Raffi's version on his Everything Grows *cassette. Words and music in* The Raffi Everything Grows Songbook. *Add other animals; a lion, a snake; ask children for suggestions.*

Chorus:
Ha Ha this a-way
Hands on waist, bend to right.

Ha Ha that a-way,
Hands on waist, bend to left.

Ha Ha this a-way,
Hands on waist, bend to right again.

Then oh then . . .
Clap hands and stamp feet three times, once on each word.

Verses:
Once I had a pussy cat, pussy cat, pussy cat,
Once I had a pussy cat, then oh then . . .
Clap and stamp feet as in chorus,

She said meow, meow, meow.
Imitate a cat.

Repeat chorus.

Once I had a puppy dog, puppy dog, puppy dog,
Once I had a puppy dog, then oh then . . .
Clap and stamp feet as in chorus,

He said woof, woof, woof.
Imitate a dog.

Repeat chorus.

Mary Had a Little Lamb
See page 168.

MORE IDEAS

1. See CATS, DOGS, RABBITS, DUCKS, and FARMS for lots of nursery rhymes, fingerplays and songs.

2. Felt Storie: *I Love You Mouse* is a lovely story about caring for pets.

3. Make paper bag pet puppets. Use small paper bags to fit over children's hands. Draw faces on and add pre-cut ears, tongues, etc.

4. Show children nonfiction books on pets and pet care.

5. Have a weird pets program and read stories about snakes and spiders, introducing the *Keeping Minibeasts* series.

Pigs

STORIES TO READ ALOUD

Harvey, the Foolish Pig
GACKENBACK, DICK

The Old Woman and Her Pig
GALDONE, PAUL

The Three Little Pigs
GALDONE, PAUL

The Three Little Pigs
GAY, MARIE-LOUISE

The Pig's Wedding
HEINE, HELME

This Little Pig (pop-up)
HELLARD SUSAN

The Pigs' Picnic
KASZA, KEIKO

Geraldine's Blanket
KELLER, HOLLY

Book of Pigericks (poetry)
LOBEL, ARNOLD

A Treeful of Pigs
LOBEL, ARNOLD

Yummers (and *Yummers Too*)
MARSHALL, JAMES

Pigs Aplenty, Pigs Galore!
McPHAIL, DAVID

Pigs
MUNSCH, ROBERT

Hamilton
PECK, ROBERT

Piggy in the Puddle
POMERANTZ, CHARLOTTE

Mrs. Pig's Bulk Buy
RAYNER, MARY

Pig in the Pond
WADDELL, MARTIN

Wiggles, the Little Wishing Pig
WATSON, PAULINE

Piggies
WOOD, AUDREY

MORE STORIES

Poinsettia and Her Family
BOND, FELICIA

Piggybook
BROWNE, ANTHONY

Pig William (and other titles)
DUBANEVICH, ARLENE

The Amazing Pig
GALDONE, PAUL

The Wonderful Pigs of Jillian Jiggs
GILMAN, PHOEBE

The Tale of Little Pig Robinson
POTTER, BEATRIX

The Tale of Pigling Bland
POTTER, BEATRIX

The True Story of the Three Little Pigs
SCIESZKA, JON

The Amazing Bone
STEIG, WILLIAM

The Three Little Wolves and the Big Bad Pig
TRIVIZAS, EUGENE

Tales of Amanda Pig (reader series)
VAN LEEUWEN, JEAN

NONFICTION

Pig
LING, BILL

NURSERY RHYMES

To Market, to Market

To market, to market, to buy a fat pig.
Home again, home again, jiggity jig.
To market, to market, to buy a fat hog.
Home again, home again, jiggity jog.
To market, to market, to buy a plum bun,
Home again, home again, market is done.

Dickery Dickery Dare

Dickery, dickery, dare,
The pig flew up in the air;
The man in brown
Soon brought him down,
Dickery, dickery, dare.

Elsie Marley

Elsie Marley is grown so fine,
She won't get up to feed the swine,
But lies in bed till eight or nine.
Lazy Elsie Marley.

Lazy Lousy Liza Briggs

From Jelly Belly *by Dennis Lee.*

Lazy lousy Liza Briggs
Wouldn't get up to feed the pigs
The pigs pulled off the comforter
And jumped right into bed with her.

FINGERPLAYS

Five Little Pigs

Play this game on five fingers.

Five little pigs went out to play.
The first little pig said,
"Let's go to the woods today."
The second little pig said,
"What will we do there?"
The third little pig said,
"We'll look for our mother."
The fourth little pig said,
"What will we do when we find her?"
"We'll hug her and kiss her and kiss her!"
Said the fifth little pig.

Five Little Piggies

Five little piggies had my dad,
Good one, bad one, gay one, sad one,
And this little piggy who was mad, mad, mad!
Five little piggies had my dad.

Two Mother Pigs

Two mother pigs lived in a pen,
Two thumbs up.
Each had four babies and that made ten.
Wiggle four fingers on each hand.
These four babies were black and white.
Wiggle four fingers of one hand.
These four babies were black as night.
Wiggle four fingers of other hand.
All eight babies loved to play.
Wiggle eight fingers.
And they rolled and they rolled in the mud all day.
Roll hands.
At night, with their mother,
They curled up in a heap,
Make fists, palms up.
And squealed and squealed
'Til they went to sleep.
Tuck thumbs under fingers.

This Little Pig

This little pig had a scrub-a-dub,
This little pig had a rub-a-dub,
This little pig-a-wig ran upstairs,
This little pig-a-wig called out "Bears!"
Down came the jar with a loud slam, bam,
And this little pig had all the jam.

This Little Piggie

*Play this familiar rhyme for toes on five
fingers instead.*

This little piggie went to market,
This little piggie stayed home,
This little piggie had roast beef,
This little piggie had none,
This little piggie went wee, wee, wee, wee,
All the way home.

MORE IDEAS

1. Felt stories: *The Old Woman and Her Pig, The Pig's Picnic,* and *The Three Little Pigs.*

2. Puppets: *The Three Little Pigs.*

3. Five pig finger puppets for "Five Little Pigs," or two pig finger puppets for "Piggy Wig and Piggy Wee," which is in FARMS (page 87).

4. Sing: "Old MacDonald" (page 89).

5. Craft: Make paper plate pig masks and act out the story of *The Three Little Pigs.*

Rabbits

STORIES TO READ ALOUD

Goodnight Moon
BROWN, MARGARET WISE

Home for a Bunny
BROWN, MARGARET WISE

The Runaway Bunny
BROWN, MARGARET WISE

Henry and the Red Stripes
CHRISTELOW, EILEEN

In the Rabbit Garden
LIONNI, LEO

Let's Make Rabbits
LIONNI, LEO

Foolish Rabbit's Big Mistake
MARTIN, RAFE

Guess How Much I Love You
McBRATNEY, SAM

In a Cabin in a Wood
McNALLY, DARCIE

Dance Away
SHANNON, GEORGE

The Tortoise and the Hare
STEVENS, JANET

Mr. Rabbit and the Lovely Present
ZOLOTOW, CHARLOTTE

MORE STORIES

Who's in Rabbit's House?
AARDEMA, VERNA

The Tale of Peter Rabbit
BEATRIX POTTER

Doctor Rabbit's Foundling
WAHL, JAN

NONFICTION

The Wild Rabbit
OXFORD SCIENTIFIC FILMS

Rabbits
PETTY, KATE

Rabbit
WATTS, BARRIE

The Life Cycle of a Rabbit
WILLIAMS, JOHN

FINGERPLAYS

Ears So Funny

Here is a bunny with ears so funny,
Hold up two fingers, bent over.
And here is his home in the ground.
*Make a circle with thumb and index finger
of other hand.*
When a noise he hears, he pricks up his ears,
Straighten fingers.
And he jumps to his home in the ground.
Two fingers dive into circle of other hand.

Robbie the Rabbit

Robbie the Rabbit is fat, fat, fat.
Pat stomach.
His soft little paws go pat, pat, pat.
Pat hands.
His soft little ears go flop, flop, flop.
Flop hands on head.
And when Robbie runs, he goes hop, hop, hop.
Hop forward three times.

Little Rabbit

I saw a little rabbit go hop, hop, hop.
Hold up two fingers and go hop, hop, hop.

I saw his long ears go flop, flop, flop.
Place hands above head and flop at wrists.

I saw his little eyes go wink, wink, wink.
Wink.

I saw his little nose go twink, twink, twink.
Wiggle nose.

I said, "Little Rabbit, won't you stay?"
Make beckoning motion.

He looked at me and hopped away.
Make two finger hop away.

Tired Bunnies

"Come my bunnies, it's time for bed."
Beckoning motion with hand.

That's what mother bunny said,
"But first I'll count you just to see
Finger on chin contemplating.

If you have all come back to me.
Bunny one, bunny two, bunny three, oh dear,
Hold up each finger as bunnies are counted.

Bunny four, bunny five, yes you're all here.
You're the sweetest things alive.
My bunnies one, two, three, four, five."
Hug bunnies to chest.

Not Say a Single Word

A good hand rhyme or action rhyme.

I can hop, hop, hop like a bunny,
Hopping motion.

And run, run, run like a dog;
Running motion.

I can walk, walk, walk like an elephant,
Walking motion.

And jump, jump, jump like a frog.
Jumping motions.

I can swim, swim, swim like a fish,
Swimming motion.

And fly, fly, fly like a bird;
Flying motion.

I can sit right down and fold my hands,
Fold hands in lap.

And not say a single word!

Little Bunny

This is just like "There Was a Little Turtle."

There was a little bunny who lived in the wood.
Hold up two fingers.

He wiggled his ears as a good bunny should.
Place forefingers on either side of head and wiggle.

He hopped by a squirrel.
Two fingers hop down arm.

He hopped by a tree.
Repeat.

He hopped by a duck.
Repeat.

And he hopped by me.
Hop over opposite fist.

He stared at the squirrel
Stare.

He stared at the tree.
Stare.

He stared at the duck.
Stare.

But he made faces at me!
Wiggle nose rabbit fashion.

Five Little Rabbits

Use five fingers or five bunny finger puppets.

Five little rabbits under a log;
Hold up fingers of one hand.

This one said, "Shh! I hear a dog!"
Point to first finger.

This one said, "I see a man!"
Point to second finger.

This one said, "Run while you can!"
Point to third finger.

This one said, "I'm not afraid!"
Point to fourth finger.

This one said, "Let's hide in the shade!"
Point to thumb.

A man and his dog went hurrying by,
Thumb and fingers of other hand hurry by.

And you should have seen those rabbits fly!
Move fingers quickly away.

Little Rabbit Foo Foo

Celebrate this naughty rabbit with gusto. Sing to the tune of "Alouette." Listen to the tune on Sharon, Lois & Bram's cassette Great Big Hits.

Sing:
Little Rabbit Foo Foo hopping through the forest,
Hold up two fingers and hop along.

Scooping up the field mice, smack 'em on the head.
Scoop with cupped hands, smack motion.

Speak:
Down came the good fairy, and she said,
Float good fairy down from the sky and wag finger.

"Little Rabbit Foo Foo, I don't like your attitude
Scooping up the field mice, smack 'em on the head,
I'll give you three chances,
Hold up three fingers.

And if you don't stop that,
I'll turn you into a goon, Phoof!"
Make a funny face on "goon," throw arms out on "poof."

Next morning, Little Rabbit Foo Foo wakes up and says,
"Oh, what a beautiful morning, I think I'll take a walk.
I really shouldn't, I really, really shouldn't, but I will."

Little Rabbit Foo Foo hopping through the forest,
Scooping up the field mice, smack 'em on the head.

Down came the good fairy, she said
"Little Rabbit Foo Foo, I don't like your attitude
Scooping up the field mice, smack 'em on the head,
I'll give you two more chances,
And if you don't stop that,
I'll turn you into a goon, Phoof!"

Next morning, Little Rabbit Foo Foo wakes up and says,
"Oh, what a beautiful morning, I think I'll take a walk.
I really shouldn't, I really, really shouldn't, but I will."

Little Rabbit Foo Foo hopping through the forest,
Scooping up the field mice, smack 'em on the head.

Down came the good fairy, she said
"Little Rabbit Foo Foo, I don't like your attitude
Scooping up the field mice, smack 'em on the head,
I'll give you one more chance,
And if you don't stop that,
I'll turn you into a goon, Phoof!"

Next morning, Little Rabbit Foo Foo wakes up and says,
"Oh, what a beautiful morning, I think I'll take a walk.
I really shouldn't, I really, really shouldn't, but I will."

Little Rabbit Foo Foo hopping through the forest,
Scooping up the field mice, smack 'em on the head.

Down came the good fairy, she said
"Little Rabbit Foo Foo, I gave you three chances,
And you didn't stop, now you are a goon! Phoof!"
Make a goon face.

And the moral of the story is hare today,
  goon tomorrow.

In a Cottage in a Wood

In a cottage in a wood,
Make roof of a cottage with hands.

A little man at the window stood,
Make glasses with fingers.

Saw a rabbit hopping by,
Hopping motion with fingers.

Knocking at his door.
Knocking.

Help me! Help me! Help me! he said,
Raise hands from shoulders.

Or the hunter will shoot me dead,
Make gun with right hand.

Come little rabbit, come with me,
Beckon with finger.

Happy we will be.
Pat left hand with right.

A Poem in Praise of Rabbits

From Marshmallow *by Clare Newberry.*
Tell with a bunny puppet.

A bunny is a quiet pet,
A bunny is the best thing yet,
A bunny never makes a sound,
A bunny's nice to have around.

Puppies whimper, bark, and growl;
Kittens mew, and tom cats yowl;
Birdies twitter, chirp, and tweet;
Moo-cows moo, and lambkins bleat;

Some creatures bellow, others bray;
Some hoot, or honk, or yap, or neigh;
Most creatures make annoying noises,
Even little girls and boyses.

A bunny, though, is never heard,
He simply never says a word.
A bunny's a delightful habit,
No home's complete without a rabbit.

John the Rabbit

You say the lines; the children echo "Yes ma'am."
You can listen to this on the cassettes Songs &
Games for Toddlers by Bob McGrath and
Katharine Smithrim, or on Lullabies & Laughter
by Pat Carfra.

Mr. John the Rabbit,
Yes Ma'am.
You've got a mighty bad habit.
Yes Ma'am.
Of comin' into my garden,
Yes Ma'am.
And eating up all my cabbage,
Yes Ma'am.
My sweet potatoes,
Yes Ma'am.
My red tomatoes.
Yes Ma'am.
And if I live to see next fall,
I ain't gonna have no vegetables at all.
Yes Ma'am!

Little Peter Rabbit

Sing to the tune of "John Brown's Body."
Listen to the tune on Bob McGrath's cassette,
Sing Along with Bob, Vol. Two.

Little Peter Rabbit had a flea upon his ear.
Little Peter Rabbit had a flea upon his ear.
Little Peter Rabbit had a flea upon his ear.
And he flicked it till it flew away.

> *For Peter Rabbit, hold up two fingers.*
> *For the flea, wiggle thumb and baby finger on one*
>   *hand.*
> *For ear, pull your ear.*
> *For flick, flick ear.*
> *Fly away with both arms flapping.*

This is an elimination song. Sing the verse through
once with actions. Then each time you sing the verse
eliminate one more part, Peter Rabbit, flea, ear, and
replace with actions only. Speed it up as you go.

MORE IDEAS

1. Felt stories: *The Runaway Bunny.*

2. Dramatize *Who's in Rabbit's House?* with simple animal masks.

3. Bunnies are not always soft and cuddly sweet blah things, they can have a lot of spunk. The rabbit in *The Tortoise and the Hare* is rather naughty for teasing turtle. Follow up with "Little Rabbit Foo Foo," and "Mr. John the Rabbit."

4. Display various illustrated versions of Aesop's classic tale of *The Hare and the Tortoise.*

5. Bring a real bunny for show and tell.

6. Here is an opportunity to introduce the trickster, Brer Rabbit, from the southern tradition, with tales eloquently told by Jackie Torrence, available on cassette.

7. Promote the video recording *Rabbit Tales* (Montreal: National Filmboard of Canada, 1992). It's a wonderful show in which puppeteer Noreen Crone-Findlay tells stories to her rabbit friend, Lagomorphis. The stories included are: Miss Lucy's Medicine Show, Auntie's Knitting a Baby, Elsie and the Dragonstone, The Little Red Hen, and The Emperor's New Clothes.

Royalty

STORIES TO READ ALOUD

A Lion in the Night
ALLEN, PAMELA

The Princess and the Pea
ANDERSEN, H.C.

May I Bring a Friend?
DE REGNIERS, BEATRICE

The Amazing Pig
GALDONE, PAUL

The Most Wonderful Egg in the World
HEINE, HELME

The Missing Tarts
HENNESSY, B.G.

Prince Bertram the Bad
LOBEL, ARNOLD

The Paper Bag Princess
MUNSCH, ROBERT

The King's Tea
NOBLE, TRINKA HAKES

Sing a Song of Sixpence
PEARSON, TRACEY

One Monday Morning
SHULEVITZ, URI

King Bidgood's in the Bathtub
WOOD, AUDREY

MORE STORIES

Medieval Feast
ALIKI

The Emperor's New Clothes
ANDERSON, H.C.

Prince Cinders
COLE, BABETTE

Princess Smartypants
COLE, BABETTE

King at the Door
COLE, BROCK

The Balloon Tree
GILMAN, PHOEBE

The Queen Who Couldn't Bake Gingerbread
VAN WOERKOM, DOROTHY

NURSERY RHYMES

Humpty Dumpty

Humpty Dumpty sat on a wall.
Humpty Dumpty had a great fall;
All the King's horses, and all the King's men,
Couldn't put Humpty together again.

The Queen of Hearts

The Queen of Hearts made some tarts
All on a summer's day.
The Knave of Hearts stole those tarts
And took them far away.
The King of Hearts called for the tarts
And beat the Knave full sore.
The Knave of Hearts returned the tarts
And vowed he'd steal no more.

Pussy Cat, Pussy Cat

Pussy cat, pussy cat, where have you been?
I've been to London to visit the Queen.
Pussy cat, pussy cat what did you there?
I frightened a little mouse under a chair.

The Lord Mayor

A face rhyme!

Here sits the Lord Mayor
Here sit his two men,
Here sits the cock
Here sits the hen.
Here sit the little chickens
Here they run in.
Chin-chopper, chin-chopper, chin-chopper, chin!

Old King Cole

*Listen to the tune on Bob McGrath's cassette
Sing Along With Bob, Vol. Two.*

Old King Cole was a merry old soul,
And a merry old soul was he.
He called for his pipe, and he called for his bowl,
And he called for his fiddlers three.
Every fiddler he had a fine fiddle,
And a very fine fiddle had he.
Oh, there's none so rare, as can compare,
With King Cole and his fiddlers three.

Lavender's Blue

*Listen to the tune on Sharon, Lois & Bram's
cassette, Mainly Mother Goose. See more verses
on page 196.*

Lavender's blue, dilly dilly, lavender's green,
When I am King, dilly dilly, you shall be Queen.
Who told you so, dilly dilly, who told you so?
'Twas my own heart, dilly dilly, that told me so.

SONGS

Sing a Song of Sixpence

Sing a song of sixpence,
A pocketful of rye;
Four-and-twenty blackbirds,
Baked in a pie!

When the pie was opened,
The birds began to sing;
Wasn't that a dainty dish,
To set before the King?

The King was in his counting-house,
Counting out his money;
The queen was in the parlor,
Eating bread and honey.

The maid was in the garden,
Hanging out the clothes;
When down came a blackbird,
And snapped off her nose!

The Grand Old Duke of York

A marching song.

The grand old Duke of York,
He had ten thousand men.
He marched them up to the top of the hill
March on tiptoes.
And he marched them down again.
March in a crouching position.
And when they were up they were up.
March on tiptoes again.
And when they were down they were down.
March down in the crouching position.
But when they were only half way up,
They were neither up nor down.
March in a stooped position.

MORE IDEAS

1. Felt Stories: *May I Bring a Friend?* and *The Princess and the Pea*. Invite children to pile the mattresses (felt pieces) on the board for *The Princess and the Pea*.

2. *The Princess and the Pea* is also nice with prince and princess puppets. Put on a crown and you can be the prince's mother. Use felt pieces for the mattresses and let the children participate by piling them on your knee.

3. Tell *The Paper Bag Princess*. It's fun on its own, or with hand or finger puppets.

4. Tell "The Drake's Tail," from Judy Sierra's *Multicultural Folktales*. It's about a duck who becomes king.

5. See BIRDS for ideas about the presentation of "Sing a Song of Six Pence." Act it out with crowns for the king and queen.

6. Sing or play "London Bridge Is Falling Down" (page 122).

7. Craft Idea: Have a special royalty day. Make crowns out of heavy paper with notches cut on top. Staple ends together. Have children decorate them using felt markers, sticky paper shapes, tin foil, or sparkle dust. Provide colourful scarves and make pointed princess hats. You could then invite Humpty Dumpty and serve egg salad sandwiches for lunch!

8. Game: The Grand Old Duke of York. Make a circle, hands dropped. March around in a circle on the first two lines. March toward the centre on the third line and back to original places on the fourth line.

Safety

STORIES TO READ ALOUD

Mr. Gumpy's Outing
BURNINGHAM, JOHN

The Gunniwolf
HARPER, WILHELMINA

Pig Pig Rides
MCPHAIL, DAVID

Wings: A Tale of Two Chickens
MARSHALL, JAMES

Tikki Tikki Tembo
MOSEL, ARLENE

MORE STORIES

Little Red Riding Hood
HYMAN, TRINA SCHART
(AND OTHER ILLUSTRATORS)

Blue Bug's Safety Book
POULET, VIRGINIA

Curious George Rides a Bike
REY, H. A.

NONFICTION

Dinosaurs Alive and Well
BROWN, LAURENE KRASNY

Dinosaurs, Beware!
BROWN, MARC

Playing on the Playground
CHLAD, DOROTHY

When I Cross the Street
CHLAD, DOROTHY

Fire! Fire!
GIBBONS, GAIL

I Read Signs
HOBAN, TANA

I Read Symbols
HOBAN, TANA

Fire Engines
ROCKWELL, ANNE

NURSERY RHYMES

Ladybird

Ladybird, ladybird, fly away home!
Your house is on fire, your children all gone,
All but one, and her name is Ann
And she crept under the pudding pan.

Ding, Dong, Bell

Ding, dong, bell,
Pussy's in the well!
Who put her in?
Little Johnny Green.
Who pulled her out?
Little Tommy Stout.
What a naughty boy was that
To try to drown poor pussycat,
Who never did him any harm,
And killed the mice in his father's barn.

FINGERPLAYS

Stop Says the Red Light
*Singing tune is an upbeat first two lines of
"Twinkle Twinkle Little Star."*

Stop says the red light
Go says the green.
Slow says the yellow light in between.
Stop says the red light,
Go says the green,
We must obey them, even the queen!

Safety

Red says STOP.
Hold right hand in "stop" gesture.

And green says GO.
Extend right arm with index finger pointed.

Yellow says WAIT:
You'd better go slow!
With index finger draw a line across your chest from right to left.

When I reach a crossing place,
Cross arms at wrists.

To left and right I turn my face.
Turn head left, then right.

I walk, not run, across the street,
Demonstrate walking.

And use my head to guide my feet.
Point to head, then feet.

Look Both Ways

Step on the corner
Watch for the light.
Look to the left,
Look to the right.
If nothing is coming
Then start and don't talk.
Go straight across
Be careful and walk.

Traffic Lights

Do you know what traffic lights say to you?
Do you know what traffic lights say to do?
Yellow says, "Be careful,"
Hold arm straight out.

Green says, "You may go,"
Lower arm.

But red is most important,
Raise arm up.

It says, "Stop!" you know.

Helping Daddy Drive
Suit actions to words.

Open the car door. Climb inside.
I get to help my daddy drive.
Fasten the seat belt. Shut the door.
Start the motor. Hear it roar.
Brr! Brr! Brr! Turn the corner, step on the gas.
If the road is clear we may pass.

The Corner

Little Jack Horner stood on the corner
Stand with feet together.

Watching the traffic go by
Look to left and right.

And when it passed, he crossed at last
Take two steps forward.

And said, "What a safe boy am I."
Thumbs under arms.

Stood Up Dangerously

Silly little Teddy Bear
Stood up in a rocking chair.
Make rocking movement

Now he has to stay in bed
Lay head on hands

With a bandage 'round his head.
Circular movement of hand about head.

MORE IDEAS

1. See "Five Little Monkeys" jumping on the bed, and "Ten Little Monkey" rowing to the shore in MONKEYS.

2. Tell "The Rainhat" from *Just Enough to Make a Story* by Nancy Schimmel. In it, a resourceful little girl makes a rainhat, a fire fighter's helmet, a pirate hat, a boat and, finally, a life jacket to wear when her boat sinks — all out of one piece of paper!

3. Focus on traffic safety, water safety, fire safety, and safety with strangers. Use easy-to-make props: traffic lights with big red, yellow and green circles, and walk-don't walk signs for traffic safety.

4. Help children memorize their own names and telephone numbers. Play telephone to learn how to dial the local emergency number.

5. Unfortunately there are not so many good books yet available on this extremely important theme. You want to teach children how to look after themselves in an emergency and how to avoid trouble, without instilling fear. Talk about safety. Improvise and adapt where you can.

St. Patrick's Day

STORIES TO READ ALOUD

The Terrible Finn MacCoul
HARPUR, TOM

Those Green Things
STINSON, KATHY

MORE STORIES

Field of Buttercups: An Irish Story
BODEN, ALICE

St. Patrick's Day in the Morning
BUNTING, EVE

The Hungry Leprechaun
CALHOUN, MARY

Fin M'Coul: The Giant of Knockmany Hill
DE PAOLA, TOMIE

NONFICTION

St. Patrick's Day
GIBBONS, GAIL

FINGERPLAYS

Happy St. Patrick's Day
Hold up one finger at a time, or put five little leprechauns on the felt board.

Five little leprechauns dressed in green
They're the happiest I've ever seen.
This leprechaun has a big gold ring.
This leprechaun has a song to sing.
This leprechaun wears a funny wig.
This leprechaun likes to dance the jig.
This leprechaun nods his head to say,
"We wish you a happy St. Patrick's Day!"

Five Little Leprechauns
Use five fingers or five leprechauns on the felt board.

Five little leprechauns knocked at my door,
One chased a rainbow, then there were four.
Four little leprechauns oh so wee,
One picked a shamrock, then there were three.
Three little leprechauns hiding in my shoe,
One found a toadstool, then there were two.
Two little leprechauns dancing in the sun,
One went in search of gold, then there was one.
One little leprechaun on the run,
He shined his shoe buckles, then there was none.

Elfman

I met a little elf-man
Down where the lilies blow,
Use thumb and pointer finger to indicate size.

I asked him why he was so small
And why he didn't grow.
Shrug shoulders, hands out at sides, palms up.

He slightly frowned and with his eyes
He looked me through and through.
Tilt head to side and look serious.

"I'm just as big for me," said he,
"As you are big for you."
Place hands on hips.

Suppose

Do you suppose a giant
Who is tall, tall, tall,
Reach toward ceiling and stand on tiptoe.

Could ever be a brownie
Who is small, small, small?
Crouch down on floor.

But the brownie who is tiny
Will try, try, try
To reach up to the giant
Who is high, high, high.
Reach toward ceiling.

The Owl and the Brownies

An owl sat alone on the branch of a tree,
Fold hands.

And he was as quiet as quiet could be.
Whisper.

It was night and his eyes were round like this.
Make circles around eyes with fingers.

He looked all around: not a thing did he miss.
Turn head from side to side.

Some brownies crept up on the branch of the tree,
Make fingers creep up opposite arm.

And they were as quiet as quiet could be.
Whisper.

Said the wise old owl, "To-whooo, to-whooo."
Up jumped the brownies and away they flew.
Hands move behind back.

An owl sat alone on the branch of a tree,
And he was as quiet as quiet could be.
Fold hands and whisper.

The Fairies' Wash Day

This is the fairies' wash day,
With acorn cups for tubs,
Cup hands.

And tiny leaves for wash boards,
Show palms.

Each fairy rubs and rubs.
Scrubbing motion.

The fairy sheets so white and fine
Upon the grass are lying.
Spreading motion.

The spider spins a line for them,
Twirl finger.

And now the clothes are drying.

An Irish Benediction

May the road rise up to meet you;
Rising motion with hands.

May the wind be always at your back;
Hands over shoulders.

May the sun shine warm upon your face;
Hands on face.

May the rain fall soft upon your fields;
Flutter fingers down.

And until we meet again,
Point to audience, then to self.

May your God hold you
Hand extended palm up.

In the palm of his hand.
Close fingers of other hand in palm.

SONGS
Cockles and Mussels
Sing an Irish song!

Chorus:
Alive, alive oh! Alive, alive oh!
Crying, "Cockles and Mussels, alive, alive oh!"

In Dublin's fair city, where girls are so pretty,
I first set my eyes on sweet Molly Malone;
She drove her wheelbarrow through streets old
    and narrow,
Crying, "Cockles and Mussels, alive, alive oh!"

She was a fishmonger, but sure 'twas no wonder,
For so were her father and mother before;
And they each wheel'd their barrow through
    streets old and narrow,
Crying, "Cockles and Mussels, alive, alive oh!"

She died of a fever, and no one could save her,
And that was the end of Sweet Molly Malone;
Her ghost wheels her barrow through streets old
    and narrow,
Crying, "Cockles and Mussels, alive, alive oh!"

MORE IDEAS

1. Songs to sing: "If You're Wearing Green Today" instead of "If You're Wearing Red Today" (see page 59). When all the children are standing, clap and sing "Rig-a-Jig-Jig" (page 106). You can also adapt "Mary Wore Her Red Dress" (page 59).

2. Hide shamrocks around the room before storytime. Ask children to find just one, then sit down. Sing "If you've found a shamrock, please stand up." Alternately, give out little green shamrocks at the end of the program for children to take home.

3. There are not many stories about Saint Patrick's Day that are just right for storytime, but you can rely on giants and green things.

4. Craft: Make shamrock potato prints and use green paint to make St. Patrick's Day pictures.

5. Craft: Have precut green shamrocks ready and let children decorate shamrock men by gluing on black hats, eyes, shoes and buckles. Draw on facial features.

6. Frogs, of course, are green. You could also give them frogs. A *Frog and Toad* puppet show maybe.

School

STORIES TO READ ALOUD

The Most Amazing Hide and Seek Alphabet Book
CROWTHER, ROBERT

The Most Amazing Hide and Seek Counting Book
CROWTHER, ROBERT

John Patrick Norman McHennesy
BURNINGHAM, JOHN

Bill and Pete
DE PAOLA, TOMIE

Mary Had a Little Lamb
HALE, SARAH

Spot Goes to School
HILL, ERIC

Crictor
UNGERER, TOMI

The Secret in the Matchbox
WALLIS, VAL

MORE STORIES

Starting School
AHLBERG, JANET

Franklin Goes to School
BOURGEOIS, PAULETTE

Will I Have a Friend?
COHEN, MIRIAM

School Bus
CREWS, DONALD

Chrysanthemum
HENKES, KEVIN

Lucy & Tom Go to School
HUGHES, SHIRLEY

School (wordless)
McCULLY, EMILY ARNOLD

Annabelle Swift, Kindergartner
SCHWARTZ, AMY

Timothy Goes to School
WELLS, ROSEMARY

Morris Goes to School
WISEMAN, BERNARD

NONFICTION

Going to Nursery School
ANHOLT, LAURENCE

Going to My Nursery School
KUKLIN, SUSAN

My Nursery School
ROCKWELL, HARLOW

Going to Daycare
ROGERS, FRED

NURSERY RHYMES

Mary Had a Little Lamb
See page 168.

FINGERPLAYS

Ready for School

Two little houses closed up tight,
Fists closed up tight, thumbs in.

Let's open up the windows and let in some light.
Make finger circles.

Ten little finger people tall and straight,
Hold fingers erect.

Ready for the bus at half-past eight.
Fingers run to catch bus.

The Night Before School

Repeat for the little boy who is going to bed.

This little girl is going to bed,
  Lay pointer in palm.

Down on the pillow she lays her head.
  Thumb acts as pillow.

She covers herself with the blankets so tight,
  Wrap fingers around girl finger.

And this is the way she sleeps all night.
  Close eyes.

Morning comes, and she opens her eyes,
  Open eyes.

Throws back the covers, and up she flies.
  Open fingers.

Soon she is up and dressed and away,
  Pointer stands straight.

Ready for school and ready for play.

MORE IDEAS

1. This is a good theme to use in September when children are entering preschool and older siblings are going back to school. This usually entails a shopping trip for supplies and new clothes. Talk about all the interesting activities the children will experience when they get to school: reading and writing and singing and drawing and painting and recess and new friends. See ALPHABET BOOKS, COUNTING, COLOUR & ART, and FRIENDS for more ideas.

2. Sing the Alphabet song.

3. Have *Crictor*, a stuffed snake who goes to school, act out the letters of the alphabet. *The Most Amazing Hide and Seek Alphabet Book* is a wonderful enticement to learning the alphabet.

4. Tell and draw *Monkey Face* by Frank Asch. Monkey draws a picture of his mother at school.

5. *Timothy Goes to School* makes a tale for two tellers using giant (adult sized) clothes cut-outs as props. Great for a back-to-school performance!

Sea & Seashore

STORIES TO READ ALOUD

Who Sank the Boat?
ALLEN, PAMELA

The Lighthouse Keeper's Lunch
ARMITAGE, RONDA

Just Like Daddy
ASCH, FRANK

Sand Cake
ASCH, FRANK

Mr. Gumpy's Outing
BURNINGHAM, JOHN

One-Eyed Jake
HUTCHINS, PAT

The Owl and the Pussy Cat
LEAR, EDWARD

Fish Is Fish
LIONNI, LEO

Swimmy
LIONNI, LEO

My Camera at the Aquarium
MARSHALL, JANET PERRY

Is This a House for a Hermit Crab?
McDONALD, MEGAN

Row, Row, Row Your Boat
MULLER, ROBIN

Baby Beluga
RAFFI

At the Beach
ROCKWELL, ANNE

Do Not Open
TURKLE, BRINTON

Harry by the Sea
ZION, GENE

MORE STORIES

Bimwili and the Zimwi (folktale)
AARDEMA, VERNA

By the Sea: An Alphabet Book
BLADES, ANN

A Salmon for Simon
BLADES, ANN

Why the Tides Ebb and Flow (folktale)
BOWDEN, J.C.

Grandma and the Pirates
GILMAN, PHOEBE

By the Sea
HOFFSTRAND, MARY

Lucy & Tom at the Seaside
HUGHES, SHIRLEY

Kate's Castle
LAWSON, JULIE

A Morning to Polish and Keep
LAWSON, JULIE

Our Home Is the Sea
LEVINSON, SONIA

The Great White Man-Eating Shark
MAHY, MARGARET

Picnic
McCULLY, EMILY ARNOLD

Jessie's Island
McFARLANE, SHERYL

Waiting for the Whales
McFARLANE, SHERYL

The Whale's Song
SHELDON, DYAN

Amos and Boris
STEIG, WILLIAM

NONFICTION

Fish Eyes: A Book You Can Count On
EHLERT, LOIS

Surrounded by the Sea: Life on a New England Fishing Island
GIBBONS, GAIL

An Octopus Is Amazing
LAUBER, PATRICIA

Big City Port
MAESTRO, BETSY

Ocean Parade: A Counting Book
MacCARTHY, PATRICIA

Between the Tides
MORRIS, MARY

Jellyfish and Other Sea Creatures
OXFORD SCIENTIFIC FILMS

The Ocean Alphabet Book
PALLOTTA, JERRY

Shells
ROYSTON, ANGELA

Fish Faces
WU, NORBERT

NURSERY RHYMES

Rub a Dub Dub

Rub-a-dub-dub, three men in a tub,
And who do you think they be?
The butcher, the baker, the candlestick maker
And all of them gone to sea.

If All the Seas Were One Sea

If all the seas were one sea,
What a great sea that would be!
And if all the trees were one tree,
What a great tree that would be!
And if all the axes were one axe.
What a great axe that would be!
And if all the men were one man,
What a great man he would be!
And if the great man took the great axe
And cut down the great tree,
And let it fall into the great sea,
What a splish splash that would be!

Catch Me and Kiss Me

From Catch Me and Kiss Me and Say It Again.

Catch me and kiss me and say it again
Set sail in a cockle shell boat.
If no one fell out, then who stayed in?
Catch me and kiss me and say it again.

FINGERPLAYS

Ocean Shell

I found a great big shell one day,
Cup hands as if holding large shell.

Upon the ocean floor.
Pick it up from the floor.

I held it close up to my ear,
Hold cupped hands to ear.

I heard the ocean roar!
I found a tiny little shell one day.
Pretend to roll shell between fingers.

Upon the ocean sand.
The waves had worn it nice and smooth.
It felt nice in my hand.
Place little shell in palm of other hand.

Here Is the Sea

Teach children how to make the wavy sea motion, and how to make the boat before your start.

Here is the sea, the wavy sea,
Indicate small waves with hands.

Here is the boat and here is me.
Cup one hand for the boat, and stick a finger from other hand up from below.

All the little fishes down below
Put hands down low, and point to the floor.

Wriggle their tails, and away they all go!
Wriggle fingers behind your back, then push hands up and away behind you.

Two Little Fishes

Two little fishes side by side
Hold up two index fingers, side by side.

Swim through the water,
Swim through the tide.
Swimming motion.

They don't need a motor
And they don't need a sail.
Shake head, and shake head.

They just wiggle their fins
Wiggle hands at sides.

And wiggle their tails.
Wiggle hands behind your back.

Little Fish

Little fish goes out to play
> *Put one hand on top of other, both palms down,
> with thumbs outstretched.*

He wiggles his fins,
> *Wiggle thumbs.*

Then swims away.
> *Move fingers up and down in unison.*

He swims and swims in the water bright.
He opens his mouth and takes a bite.
> *Move fingers of lower hand.*

Mmmmmmmm! Tastes good!
> *Rub your tummy.*

Once I Caught a Fish Alive

One, two, three, four, five,
> *Count on fingers.*

Once I caught a fish alive.
> *Wriggle hand like a fish.*

Six, seven, eight, nine, ten,
> *Count fingers.*

Then I let him go again.
> *Pretend to throw fish back.*

Why did you let him go?
Because he bit my finger so.
> *Shake hand.*

Which one did he bite?
This little finger on the right.
> *Hold up little finger on right hand.*

Five Little Fishes
> *Use fingers or finger puppets.*

Five little fishes were swimming near the shore.
One took a dive and then there were four.
Four little fishes were swimming out to sea.
One went for food and then there were three.
Three little fishes said, "Now what shall we do?"
One swam away and then there were two.
Two little fishes were having great fun,
But one took a plunge and then there was one.
One little fish said, "I like the warm sun."
Away he went and then there was none.

Fred and His Fishes

Fred had a fish bowl.
> *Form shape of bowl with hands.*

In it was a fish.
> *Hold up one finger.*

Swimming around
> *Make swimming motions.*

With a swish, swish, swish!
Fred said, "I know what I will do.
I'll buy another and that will make ___."
> *Children supply number and hold up two fingers.*

Fred said, "I'm sure it would be
Very, very nice if I just had ___. "
> *Children supply number and hold up three fingers.*

Fred said, "If I just had one more
That would make one, two, three ___. "
> *Children supply number and hold up four fingers.*

Fred said, "What fun to see them dive.
One, two, three, four, ___."
> *Children supply number and hold up five fingers.*

How many fishes do you see?
How many fishes? Count them with me!
> *Children count to five.*

SONGS

My Big Blue Boat
> *On first and third verses, pretend to row sitting on
> the floor. Two children can sit facing one another
> holding hands, pulling back and forth. Parents can
> hold children on laps facing you. On second verse,
> raise arms above head and wave them gently like
> sails.*

I love to row in my big blue boat,
My big blue boat, my big blue boat;
I love to row in my big blue boat,
Out on the deep blue sea.

My big blue boat has two red sails,
Two red sails, two red sails;
My big blue boat has two red sails,
Two red sails.

So come for a ride in my big blue boat,
My big blue boat, my big blue boat;
So come for a ride in my big blue boat,
Out on the deep blue sea.

There's a Hole in the Bottom of the Sea

Make a felt story out of this one or follow the actions. See music in Tom Glazer's Eye Winker, Tom Tinker, Chin Chopper.

Refrain:
There's a hole, there's a hole,
There's a hole in the bottom of the sea.
Describe circle with forefinger pointing downward. Repeat this at the end of each verse.

There's a log in the hole in the bottom of the sea . . .
Hold up forearm. Repeat twice, then repeat the refrain.

There's a bump on the log, in the hole, in the bottom of the sea . . .
Slam fist down on the word "bump". Repeat as above.

There's a frog on the bump, on the log, in the hole, in the bottom of the sea . . .
Hold fist up then slam down on word "bump"

There's a wart on the frog, on the bump, on the log, in the hole, in the bottom of the sea . . .
Make small circle in front of you with thumb and finger.

There's a hair on the wart, on the frog, on the bump, on the log, in the hole, in the bottom of the sea . . .
Point to hair.

There's a flea on the hair, on the wart, on the frog, on the bump, on the log, in the hole, in the bottom of the sea . . .
Hold pinky up.

There's a germ on the flea, on the hair, on the wart, on the frog, on the bump, on the log, in the hole, in the bottom of the sea . . .
Hold forefinger just over thumb without touching.

There's a "pst" on the germ, on the flea, on the hair, on the wart, on the frog, on the bump, on the log, in the hole, in the bottom of the sea . . .
Whisper.

Seashell, Seashell

This is a lovely tune to sing before "Here Is the Sea." Listen to the tune on the cassette Songs and Games for Toddlers, *by Bob McGrath and Katherine Smithrim.*

Seashell, seashell,
Sing a song for me.
Tell me about the ocean,
Tell me about the sea.

Row, Row, Row Your Boat

Row, row, row your boat
Gently down the stream.
Merrily, merrily, merrily, merrily,
Life is but a dream.

MORE IDEAS

1. Felt stories: *Mr. Gumpy's Outing, The Owl and the Pussy Cat,* and *There's a Hole in the Bottom of the Sea.*

2. Tell the story of "Charlotte," a rare little story about a crab, from *Cut & Tell Scissor Stories for Spring* by Jean Warren.

3. Sing "Baby Beluga" from Raffi's *Baby Beluga* cassette. Words and music are in *The Second Raffi Songbook.*

4. Sing "Octopus's Garden" on Raffi's *One Light, One Sun* cassette. Words and music are in *The Second Raffi Songbook* ("I'd like to be . . . . under the sea . . . ").

5. Practice fishy kisses! Open and shut lips silently like goldfish.

6. Take a conch shell for the children to listen to after *Bimwili and the Zimwi* and use it to introduce children to various kinds of shells. Take a collection for them to touch.

7. Focus on a day at the beach and all the things that can be seen there. If you're planning a trip to the beach, collect objects to make a beach collage when you get home. Make a Japanese sand garden for children to draw pictures in while at the beach, as in *Sand Cake.* Collect some sand and make beach paintings applying sand for texture.

8. Introduce children to fresh and salt water fish and different types of sea creatures that like different environments. Salmon like the Pacific, lobsters like the Atlantic, and bass and trout like freshwater lakes and streams. Collect magazine photographs of different kinds of fish and make a collage. End up with a fishy snack: tuna or smoked salmon.

9. Art: Make an undersea collage using strips of coloured cellophane, or use a blue watercolour wash over crayon drawings. Have children add their own little Swimmys.

10. Art: Make fish prints!

11. For more ideas see DUCKS & GEESE, FROGS, and SNAKES, TURTLES & LIZARDS.

Spring

STORIES TO READ ALOUD

Annie and the Wild Animals
BRETT, JAN

The Short Tree and the Bird That Could Not Sing
FOON, DENNIS

Hamilton Duck's Springtime Story
GETZ, ARTHUR

Spring Is Here
GOMI, TARO

Jenny's Hat
KEATS, EZRA JACK

The Quangle Wangle's Hat
LEAR, EDWARD

Who Took the Farmer's Hat?
NODSET, JOAN

My Spring Robin
ROCKWELL, ANNE

MORE STORIES

It's Spring
MINARIK, ELSE

First Comes Spring
ROCKWELL, ANNE

This Year's Garden
RYLANT, CYNTHIA

Chicken Soup with Rice
SENDAK, MAURICE

Simon Welcomes Spring
TIBO, GILES

NONFICTION

Spring
HIRSCHI, RON

In a Spring Garden (haiku poetry)
LEWIS, RICHARD, ED.

NURSERY RHYMES

Hickety, Pickety, My Black Hen

> *See* Pocketful of Puppets: Mother Goose *by Tamara Hunt and Nancy Renfro for a great puppetry idea to go with this rhyme.*

Hickety, Pickety, my black hen,
She lays eggs for gentlemen.
Gentlemen come every day
To see what my black hen doth lay.
Sometimes nine and sometimes ten,
Hickety, Pickety, my black hen.

Little Robin Redbreast

Little Robin Redbreast
> *Hold up thumb and little finger for head and tail.*

Sat upon a rail;
Niddle noodle went his head,
> *Wiggle thumb.*

Wiggle waggle went his tail.
> *Wiggle little finger.*

FINGERPLAYS

Pussy Willow

Children crouch on the floor in cat positions. Rise slowly through the verse, then down again on the meows. Jump up on SCAT.

I know a little pussy,
Her coat is silver grey;
She lives down in the meadow,
Not very far away.
Although she is a pussy,
She'll never be a cat,
For she's a pussy willow.
Now what do you think of that?
Meow, meow, meow, meow,
Meow, meow, SCAT!

The Rain

Pitter-patter, raindrops,
Falling from the sky;
Flutter fingers down from the sky.

Here is my umbrella,
Cup one hand over erect pointer finger of other hand.

To keep me safe and dry.
Hold overhead.

When the rain is over,
And the sun begins to glow,
Make a big circle with your arms.

Little flowers start to bud,
Cup two hands together.

And grow and grow and grow!
Spread hands apart slowly.

Pretty Nest

For a pretty tune, see This Little Puffin, *1969 edition.*

I have made a pretty nest,
Look inside, look inside.
Interlock fingers, palms upwards.

Hungry birdies with their beaks
Open wide, open wide.
Place index fingers and thumbs of each hand together, and open and close them.

See my little birdies grow
Day by day, day by day,
Gradually spread hands apart.

Till they spread their little wings,
And then they fly away.
Cross arms at wrist and flap hands.

The Flower

Here's a green leaf,
Show hand.

And here's a green leaf;
Show other hand.

That, you see, makes two.
Hold up two fingers.

Here is a bud
Cup hands together.

That makes a flower;
Watch it bloom for you!
Open cupped hands gradually.

MORE IDEAS

1. Sing "Everything Grows" from Raffi's album of the same name. Words and music are in *The Raffi Everything Grows Songbook*. Sing "Over in the Meadow" (page 136).

2. See GARDENING, EASTER, BIRDS, and WEATHER – RAINY DAY for more ideas.

3. *Jenny's Hat* by Ezra Jack Keats makes a lovely story to tell with props. Develop a spring hat theme around this story. See CLOTHING for more titles. For a follow up craft, have lots of colourful ribbons, feathers and paper flowers available and make spring hats by gluing these on to paper plates. Punch holes in the sides to tie them on to little heads.

4. Tell "Grandfather Bear Is Hungry" in *Look Back and See* by Margaret Read MacDonald. This is a wonderful tellable tale about a bear who is hungry when he wakes up in spring.

5. Have an Egg storytime with *The Most Wonderful Egg in the World*, *The Egg Book*, and *Who Took the Farmer's Hat*.

6. Make pussy willow pictures. Start with plain dark construction paper with twigs drawn on. Have children dip their fingers in white paint and print pussy willows along the stems. Plan the program using stories about other things that are soft and furry from CATS & KITTENS.

6. Make a spring blossom picture after reading *Hamilton Duck's Springtime Story*. Try blown ink branches. Place a dab of ink on a piece of paper and blow through a straw to move it around. Dip and glue small pieces of scrunched-up tissue paper onto the branches for blossoms.

Summer

STORIES TO READ ALOUD

Maisy Goes Swimming (pop-up)
COUSINS, LUCY

Jamberry
DEGEN, BRUCE

Take Me Out to the Ballgame
KOVALSKI, MARYANN

Froggy Learns to Swim
LONDON, JONATHAN

Pig Pig Goes to Camp
McPHAIL, DAVID

Farmer Joe's Hot Day
RICHARDS, NANCY WILCOX

The Relatives Came
RYLANT, CYNTHIA

Pig in the Pond
WADDELL, MARTIN

The Little Mouse, the Red Ripe Strawberry and the Big Hungry Bear
WOOD, AUDREY

Peanut Butter and Jelly: A Play Rhyme
WESTCOTT, NADINE

MORE STORIES

The Grey Lady and the Strawberry Snatcher
BANG, MOLLY

The Picnic
DENTON, KADY MacDONALD

Bailey Goes Camping
HENKES, KEVIN

Amy Loves the Sun
HOBAN, JULIA

Blueberries for Sal
McCLOSKEY, ROBERT

Picnic (wordless)
McCULLY, EMILY ARNOLD

The Car Trip
OXENBURY, HELEN

Simon in Summer
TIBO, GILES

My Family Vacation
KHALSA, DAYAL KAUR

NONFICTION

Dinosaurs Travel
BROWN, LAURENE KRASNEY

NURSERY RHYMES

Billy Boy

See complete version on page 197.

Can she bake a cherry pie?
Billy Boy, Billy Boy,
Can she bake a cherry pie,
Charming Billy,
She can bake a cherry pie
Fast as a cat can wink his eye,
She's a young thing and cannot leave her mother.

Simple Simon

Simple Simon met a pieman
Going to the fair.
Said Simple Simon to the pieman,
"Let me taste your ware."
Said the man to Simple Simon,
"Show me first your penny."
Said Simple Simon to the pieman,
"Indeed, I have not any."

Peanut Butter

Rehearse the chorus of this popular chant first, then repeat after each verse. Check out the slightly different verse and slap-clap pattern in Peanut Butter and Jelly, *available in big book format.*

Chorus:

Peanut butter, peanut butter,
Both hands are thrust up and to the right, twice,

Jelly, jelly.
Hands are thrust down to your left, dramatically,

Verses:

First you take the peanuts and you dig 'em, you
dig 'em.
You dig 'em, dig 'em, dig 'em.
Dig with an invisible shovel.

Then you crush 'em, you crush 'em,
You crush 'em, crush 'em, crush 'em.
Squash 'em in the palms of your hands.

And you spread 'em, you spread 'em,
You spread 'em, spread 'em, spread 'em.
Use finger as knife. Spread on palm of other hand.

Repeat chorus

Then you take the berries and you pick 'em,
you pick 'em.
You pick 'em, pick 'em, pick 'em.
Pick your berries out of the air.

And you crush 'em, you crush 'em,
You crush 'em, crush 'em, crush 'em.
Squash these in the palms of your hands too.

Then you spread 'em, you spread 'em,
You spread 'em, spread 'em, spread 'em.
Use finger as knife. Spread on palm of hand again.

Repeat chorus

Then you take the sandwich and you bite it,
you bite it,
You bite it, bite it, bite it.
Take an exaggerated bite of your sandwich.

And you munch it, you munch it,
You munch it, munch it, munch it.
Chew with your worst manners.

And you swallow, you swallow,
You swallow, swallow, swallow.
Gulp 'er down!

Repeat chorus.

SONGS

She'll Be Comin' 'Round the Mountain

So . . . the relatives are coming for a visit! Run through all the sounds backwards after each verse when children are familiar with this song. Listen to the tune on Sharon, Lois & Bram's Great Big Hits.

She'll be comin' 'round the mountain when she
comes. Toot, Toot.
She'll be comin' 'round the mountain when she
comes. Toot, Toot.
She'll be comin' 'round the mountain,
She'll be comin' 'round the mountain,
She'll be comin' 'round the mountain when she
comes. Toot, Toot!

She'll be driving six white horses when she comes.
Whoa Back . . .

We'll all go out to meet her when she comes.
Hi babe . . .

We'll all have chicken and dumplings when she
comes. Yum, yum . . .

She'll be wearin' red pajamas when she comes.
Scratch, scratch . . .

She'll have to sleep with Grandma when she comes.
Move over . . .

We'll have a great big party when she comes.
Ya-hoo . . .

Mr. Sun

See WEATHER – RAINY DAY, page 202.

MORE IDEAS

1. Develop themes on vacations, picnics, camping out, ball games, swimming, gardening, or hot days.

2. Going Fishing? Going to the beach? See SEA & SEASHORE. Make collage pictures with sand and beach objects.

3. Have a berry celebration. Display different kinds of berries, read *Blueberries for Sal, The Little Mouse, the Red Ripe Strawberry and the Big Hungry Bear, Jamberry, Peanut Butter and Jelly,* and *The Giant Jam Sandwich.* Then have a berry feast! Use fingerplays from FOOD. Visit a berry patch if you can.

4. Hot day stories: *Maisy Goes Swimming, Pig in the Pond, Farmer Joe's Hot Day,* and *Froggy Learns to Swim.*

Fall

STORIES TO READ ALOUD

Red Leaf, Yellow Leaf
EHLERT, LOIS

Ska-tat!
KNUTSON, KIMBERLY

Rain Makes Apple Sauce
SHEER, JULIAN

The Bears' Autumn
TEJIMA, KEIZABURO

Pumpkin, Pumpkin
TETHERINGTON, JEANNE

The Great Big Enormous Turnip
TOLSTOY

Apple Pie
WELLINGTON, ANNE

The Little Red Hen
ZEMACH, MARGOT

MORE STORIES

Every Autumn Comes the Bear
ARNOSKY, JIM

Raccoons and Ripe Corn
ARNOSKY, JIM

The Cinnamon Hen's Autumn Day
DUTTON, SANDRA

The Seasons of Arnold's Apple Tree
GIBBONS, GAIL

The Year at Maple Hill Farm
PROVENSEN, ALICE

The Life Cycle of the Oak Tree
HOGAN, PAULA

November Boots
HUNDAL, NANCY

Apple Pigs
ORBACH, RUTH

Apples and Pumpkins
ROCKWELL, ANNE

Autumn Harvest
TRESSELT, ALVIN

Johnny Maple-Leaf
TRESSELT, ALVIN

NONFICTION

The Pumpkin Patch
KING, ELIZABETH

Apple Tree
PARNALL, PETER

NURSERY RHYMES

Little Boy Blue

Little Boy Blue, come Blow your horn!
The sheep's in the meadow,
The cow's in the corn.
Where is the boy
Who looks after the sheep?
He's under a haystack, fast asleep.
Will you wake him? No, not I,
For if I do, he's sure to cry.

FINGERPLAYS

October Gave a Party

October gave a party,
The leaves by hundreds came.
The ashes, oaks, and maples
And leaves of every name.
The sunshine spread a carpet
And everything was grand.
Miss Weather led the dancing,
Professor Wind the band.

Way Up High in the Apple Tree

Way up high in the apple tree,
Hold arms up high.

Two red apples looked down at me.
Make fists for apples.

I shook that tree as hard as I could,
Shake the tree.

And down fell the apples
Hands fall to the ground.

Mmmm were they good!
Take a bite, and rub your tummy.

The Apple Tree

Sing to the tune of "Rock-a-bye Baby."

Here is a tree with leaves so green.
Forearms together, elbows to wrists, hands spread.

Here are the apples that hang between.
Clench fists for apples.

When the wind blows the apples will fall.
Wave arms in the wind and let apples fall suddenly.

Here is a basket to gather them all.
Make a basket with both hands, fingers interlocked.

SONGS

Autumn Leaves Are Falling Down

Sing to the tune of "London Bridge" and act it out. End by sitting down for a cup of hot chocolate after the work is done.

Autumn leaves are falling down,
Falling down, falling down,
Autumn leaves are falling down,
All over town.

The cold wind blows them all around,
All around, all around,
The cold wind blows them all around,
All over town.

They're drifting gently to the ground,
To the ground, to the ground,
They're drifting gently to the ground,
All over town.

Take a rake and rake them up,
Rake them up, rake them up,
Take a rake and rake them up,
All over town.

I Wish I Were a Leaf

*Children raise arms and sing together, then float, twirl, and fall down like leaves in the wind.
Sing to the tune of "If I Had a Windmill." Listen to that song on Sharon, Lois & Bram's cassette* Great Big Hits. *See music in* Sharon, Lois & Bram's Mother Goose.

I wish I were a leaf
A leaf, a leaf.
If I were a leaf,
I'd float in the wind like this.

I wish I were a leaf
A leaf, a leaf.
If I were a leaf,
I'd twirl in the wind like this.

I wish I were a leaf
A leaf, a leaf.
If I were a leaf,
I'd fall down to the ground like this.

Five Red Apples

See GARDENING, page 110.

MORE IDEAS

1. Felt Stories: *The Great Big Enormous Turnip, The Little Red Hen,* and *Apple Pie.*

2. Cut and tell "The Little Brown Cradle" (a cocoon) from *Paper Stories* by Jean Stangl.

3. If autumn leaves are the focus of your program, take a small collection of leaves to storytime. Throw a few into the air and watch them float to the floor. Make leaf rubbings using different colours of crayons and paper; or make pictures for the window by pressing leaves between pieces of clear mactac. Identify the varieties of trees the leaves have come from. Go for a walk, collect leaves, and see what kinds of trees live in your neighbourhood.

4. Follow up apple stories with an apple snack, and apple identification. See what different kinds of apples the children like best. Have apple sauce after *Rain Makes Apple Sauce.*

5. Say goodbye to the DUCKS & GEESE flying south for the winter.

6. Other themes for other directions: harvest moon stories in BEDTIME & MOON STORIES, owl stories in BIRDS, and others in WEATHER – WINDY DAY, THANKSGIVING, and HALLOWEEN.

Winter

STORIES TO READ ALOUD

The Mitten
BRETT, JAN

Sleepy Bear
DABCOVICH, LYDIA

Charlie Needs a Cloak
DE PAOLA, TOMIE

The Short Tree and the Bird That Could Not Sing
FOON, DENNIS

Hamilton Duck
GETZ, ARTHUR

I Love to Play Hockey
KLASSEN, DALE

What's That Noise?
LEMIEUX, MICHELLE

Frederick
LIONNI, LEO

Amos's Sweater
LUNN, JANET

Froggy Gets Dressed
LONDON, JONATHAN

Mrs. McDockerty's Knitting
MARTINEZ, RUTH

Thomas's Snowsuit
MUNSCH, ROBERT

50 Below Zero
MUNSCH, ROBERT

White Bear, Ice Bear
RYDER, JOANNE

Fox's Dream
TEJIMA

Little Mo
WADDELL, MARTIN

The Winter Picnic
WELBER, ROBERT

MORE STORIES

The Very Last First Time
ANDREWS, JAN

Mary of Mile 18
BLADES, ANNE

A Winter Day
FLORIAN, DOUGLAS

Winter Magic
HASLER, EVELINE

Norman's Snowball
HUTCHINS, HAZEL

Baseball Bats for Christmas
KUSUGAK, MICHAEL

A Promise Is a Promise
MUNSCH, ROBERT & MICHAEL KUSUGAK

Something Is Going to Happen
ZOLOTOW, CHARLOTTE

NURSERY RHYMES

The Cold Wind Doth Blow

The cold wind doth blow
And we shall have snow
And what will the robin do then?
Poor thing.
He'll sit in a barn,
And keep himself warm,
And hide his head under his wing,
Poor thing.

FINGERPLAYS

My Snowsuit

This one is perfect after Thomas's Snowsuit.

My zipper suit is bunny brown.
Point to chest.

The top zips up,
Draw fingers up from tummy to chin.

The legs zip down.
Draw fingers down leg to ankle.

I wear it every day.
My daddy brought it out from town.
Zip it up and zip it down,
*Draw fingers up from tummy to chin,
then down leg to ankle.*

And hurry out to play!

Things I Can Do

Suit actions to words.

Hat on head, chin strap here,
Snap just so, you see;
I can put my cap on
All by myself, just me!

One arm in, two arms in,
Buttons one, two, three;
I can put my coat on
All by myself, just me!

Toes in first, heels push down,
Pull, pull, pull and "whee!"
I can put my boots on
All by myself, just me!

Fingers here, thumbs right here,
Hands are warm as can be;
I can put my mittens on
All by myself, just me.

The Mitten Song

"Thumb in the thumb place
Hold up one hand, fingers together, thumb apart.

Fingers all together!"
This is the song we sing in mitten weather.
When it's cold,
Rub hands together.

It doesn't matter whether,
Mittens are wool,
Or made of finest leather.
Hold up two hands, fingers together, thumb apart.

This is the song we sing in mitten weather,
"Thumb in thumb place
Repeat action.

Fingers all together!"

Come Sing a Song of Winter

Sing to the tune of "The More We Get Together."

Come sing a song of winter,
Of winter, of winter,
Come sing a song of winter,
The cold days are here.
Clap out this verse in double time.

With snowing and blowing
Flutter fingers down, wave arms about.

And rosy cheeks glowing,
Point to cheeks.

Come sing a song of winter,
The cold days are here.
Return to clapping double time.

Three Little Kittens

See CATS & KITTENS, page 40.

MORE IDEAS

1. Read stories about winter hibernation with: *Sleepy Bear, What's That Noise?*, and *Froggie Gets Dressed.*

2. Bird migration is another good topic: See *The Short Tree and the Bird That Could Not Sing* and other stories in BIRDS. Follow up by making bird feeders to hang for the birds who've stayed behind.

3. See WEATHER – SNOWY DAY for a snowy winter theme, and WEATHER – RAINY DAY for a rainy winter theme.

4. Dress up for the cold weather with these stories: *Froggy Gets Dressed, Amos's Sweater, Mrs. McDockerty's Knitting,* and *The Mitten.* Sheep rhymes are appropriate here.

5. Dress up for rainy weather with these stories: *Big Sarah's Little Boots, The Mud Puddle,* and "The Rainhat."

Sheep

STORIES TO READ ALOUD

Borreguita and the Coyote (folktale)
AARDEMA, VERNA

Sheep, Sheep, Sheep, Help Me Fall Asleep
ALDA, ARLENE

Charlie Needs a Cloak
DE PAOLA, TOMIE

Little Bo-Peep
GALDONE, PAUL

Six Sleepy Sheep
GORDON, JEFFIE ROSS

Mary Had a Little Lamb
HALE, SARAH (ills. by De Paola)

Mary Had a Little Lamb
HALE, SARAH (photos by Bruce McMillan)

Amos's Sweater
LUNN, JANET

Mrs. McDockerty's Knitting
MARTINEZ, RUTH

Three Bags Full
SCAMELL, RAGNHILD

Sheep in a Jeep (and other sheep titles)
SHAW, NANCY

The Lamb and the Butterfly
SUNDGAARD, ARNOLD

MORE STORIES

In the Moonlight, Waiting
CARRICK, CAROL

Ten Sleepy Sheep
KELLER, HOLLY

Emma's Lamb
LEWIS, KIM

NONFICTION

Lamb
ROYSTON, ANGELA

The Sheep
ROYSTON, ANGELA

NURSERY RHYMES

Little Boy Blue

*This is a nice one for the felt board. All you'll
need is a haystack and a boy dressed in blue.*

Little Boy Blue,
Come Blow your horn!
The sheep's in the meadow,
The cow's in the corn.
Where is the boy
Who looks after the sheep?
He's under a haystack, fast asleep.
Will you wake him?
No, not I,
For if I do,
He's sure to cry.

Baa Baa Black Sheep

*Repeat for the little girl who lives down the lane.
Sing to the tune of "Twinkle Twinkle Little Star."*

Baa, Baa, Black Sheep,
Have you any wool?
Yes, sir, yes, sir,
Three bags full.
One for my master,
One for my dame,
And one for the little boy
Who lives down the lane.
Baa, Baa, Black Sheep,
Have you any wool?
Yes, sir, yes, sir,
Three bags full.

Mary Had a Little Lamb

Mary had a little lamb
Little lamb, little lamb,
Mary had a little lamb,
Whose fleece was white as snow.

And everywhere that Mary went,
Mary went, Mary went,
Everywhere that Mary went,
The lamb was sure to go.

It followed her to school one day,
School one day, school one day,
It followed her to school one day,
Which was against the rule.

It made the children laugh and play,
Laugh and play, laugh and play,
It made the children laugh and play,
To see a lamb at school.

"Why does the lamb love Mary so?
Mary so? Mary so?
Why does the lamb love Mary so?"
The eager children cry.

"Why, Mary loves the lamb, you know!
Lamb, you know! Lamb, you know!
Why, Mary loves the lamb, you know!"
The teacher did reply.

Little Bo-Peep

Little Bo-peep has lost her sheep,
And doesn't know where to find them.
Leave them alone, and they'll come home,
Bringing their tails behind them.

Little Bo-peep fell fast asleep,
And dreamed she heard them bleating,
But when she awoke, she found it a joke,
For they were still a-fleeting.

Then up she took her little crook,
Determined for to find them;
She found them indeed, but it made her heart bleed,
For they'd left their tails behind them.

It happened one day, as Bo-peep did stray
Into a meadow hard by;
There she espied their tails side by side,
All hung on a tree to dry.

She heaved a sigh and wiped her eye,
And over the hillocks went rambling;
And tried what she could, as a shepherdess should,
To tack again each to its lambkin.

MORE IDEAS

1. Other stories to use in which sheep make an appearance: *Mr. Gumpy's Outing,* and *Old MacDonald Had a Farm.*

2. *Amos's Sweater* is a classic to use here. Tell the story with a sheep puppet and an old sweater that almost fits.

3. Add woolly mittens with *Three Little Kittens,* and *The Mitten.*

4. All of the nursery rhymes here are fun to sing as you add pieces to the felt board.

5. Use finger puppets as you sing "Baa Baa Black Sheep." All you need is a man, a woman, a boy, a girl, and a little black sheep.

6. Bring in a sack of raw wool for children to feel. Make little sheep pictures by gluing clumps onto construction paper. Draw on little faces and feet.

Shopping

STORIES TO READ ALOUD

The Shopping Basket
BURNINGHAM, JOHN

Baby-O
CARLSTROM, NANCY WHITE

The Comic Adventures of Old Mother Hubbard and Her Dog
DE PAOLA, TOMIE

Corduroy
FREEMAN, DON

Don't Forget the Bacon
HUTCHINS, PAT

Mrs. Pig's Bulk Buy
RAYNER, MARY

Max's Dragon Shirt
WELLS, ROSEMARY

MORE STORIES

Not So Fast Songololo
DALY, NIKI

The Shopping Trip
OXENBURY, HELEN

A Chair for My Mother
WILLIAMS, VERA

NONFICTION

Department Store
GIBBONS, GAIL

NURSERY RHYMES

To Market to Market
Clap it out!

To market, to market, to buy a fat pig,
Home again, home again, jiggety jig,
To market, to market, to buy a fat hog,
Home again, home again, jiggety jog.
To market, to market, to buy a plum bun,
Home again, home again, shopping is done.

Simple Simon

Simple Simon met a pieman
Going to the fair.
Said Simple Simon to the pieman,
"Let me taste your ware."
Said the man to Simple Simon,
"Show me first your penny."
Said Simple Simon to the pieman,
"Indeed, I have not any."

The Muffin Man
Listen to the tune on Bob McGrath's cassette, Sing Along with Bob, Vol. One. *Words and music are in Sharon, Lois & Bram's* Elephant Jam.

Oh, do you know the muffin man,
The muffin man, the muffin man,
Oh, do you know the muffin man,
Who lives on Drury Lane?

Oh, yes, I know the muffin man,
The muffin man the muffin man,
Oh, yes, I know the muffin man,
Who lives on Drury Lane?

Now we all know the muffin man,
The muffin man, the muffin man,
Now we all know the muffin man,
Who lives on Drury Lane.

FINGERPLAYS

The Shopping Trip

Older children will get a kick out of this.

We're going on a shopping trip
In a big department store.
Name a local store.

We're going to buy a pair of scissors first.
Cutting motion with forefinger and middle finger of right hand.

We need a new set of steps for the back porch.
Walking motion with feet.

There was a sale of rocking chairs,
Rocking motion back and forth while walking and cutting.

So we bought one.
We got thirsty walking around,
So we bought some bubble gum.
Make lump in cheek with tongue and begin chewing.

At this moment our heads began to itch.
Scratch heads while continuing previous motions.

The salesman came up to us and asked
If we wanted to buy anything else.
Shake head from side to side continuing all motions.

Going Shopping

Come to the store with me,
Beckon.

Just down the street.
Point.

We don't need a car.
Pretend to steer a car.

We can go on our feet.
Tap feet in place.

Daddy wants cherries
Make small circles with fingers.

And apples and steak.
Big circle for steak.

Mother wants bread
Make long shapes for bread.

And strawberry cake.
Rub tummy, smack lips.

The Corner Grocery Store

Listen to the tune on The Corner Grocery Store *cassette. Words and music are in* The Raffi Singable Songbook.

There was cheese, cheese, walkin' on its knees,
In the store, in the store.
There was cheese, cheese, walkin' on its knees,
In the corner grocery store.

Chorus:
My eyes are dim, I cannot see,
I have not brought my specs with me,
I have not brought my specs with me.

Additional Verses:
There were plums, plums, twiddling their
thumbs . . .
There was corn, corn, blowin' on a horn . . .
There were beans, beans, tryin' on some jeans . . .
There was more, more, just inside the door . . .

Hot Cross Buns

See music in Singing Bee.

Hot cross buns! Hot cross buns!
One a penny, two a penny,
Hot cross buns!
If you have no daughters,
Give them to your sons.
One a penny, two a penny,
Hot cross buns!
But if you have none of these little elves,
Then you just eat them all yourselves.

MORE IDEAS

1. If you want to go shopping for clothes, see CLOTHING for some ideas. *Caps for Sale* fits nicely here.

2. Perhaps you want to go shopping for a pet. See DOGS for "How Much Is That Doggie in the Window."

3. Talk about money. See Tana Hoban's *26 Letters and 99 Cents.* Follow up with a coin rubbing activity.

4. If you're going shopping for food, sing "The Corner Grocery Store," and see more ideas in FOOD.

Sickness & Health

STORIES TO READ ALOUD

Chicken Pox
ANFOUSSE, GINETTE

I Wish I Was Sick Too
BRANDENBERG, FRANZ

Mother, Mother, I Feel Sick
CHARLIP, REMY

Who's Sick Today?
CHERRY, LYNNE

Hunky Dory Ate It
EVANS, KATIE

Teddy Bears Cure a Cold
GRETZ, SUSANNA

Rachel Fister's Blister
MacDONALD, AMY

Bear's Toothache
McPHAIL, DAVID

Gregory, the Terrible Eater
SHARMAT, MITCHELL

*Alexander and the Terrible, Horrible,
No Good Very Bad Day*
VIORST, JUDITH

The Lady with the Alligator Purse
WESTCOTT, NADINE

Mr. Nick's Knitting
WILD, MARGARET

Carousel
WILDSMITH, BRIAN

MORE STORIES

Madeline
BEMELMANS, LUDWIG

Miss Tizzy
GRAY, LIBBA MOORE

Curious George Goes to the Hospital
REY, H.A.

Doctor De Soto (dentist)
STEIG, WILLIAM

Doctor De Soto Goes to Africa
STEIG, WILLIAM

Feel Better, Ernest!
VINCENT, GABRIELLE

Just Awful (cut finger)
WHITNEY, ALMA

Albert's Toothache
WILLIAMS, BARBARA

Betsy and the Chicken Pox
WOLDE, GUNILLA

NONFICTION

Germs Make Me Sick
BERGER, MELVIN

Dinosaurs Alive and Well
BROWN, LAURENE KRASNY

When I See My Dentist
KUKLIN, SUSAN

When I See My Doctor
KUKLIN, SUSAN

My Dentist
ROCKWELL, HARLOW

My Doctor
ROCKWELL, HARLOW

Going to the Doctor
ROGERS, FRED

Going to the Dentist
ROGERS, FRED

Going to the Hospital
ROGERS, FRED

NURSERY RHYMES

Jack and Jill

Jack and Jill went up the hill
To fetch a pail of water.
Jack fell down and broke his crown,
And Jill came tumbling after.

Up Jack got and home did trot,
As fast as he could caper;
He jumped into bed and wrapped his head
In vinegar and brown paper.

Humpty Dumpty

Humpty Dumpty sat on a wall,
Humpty Dumpty had a great fall;
All the King's horses and all the King's men
Couldn't put Humpty together again.

Doctor Foster

Doctor Foster went to Gloucester
In a shower of rain.
He stepped in a puddle right up to his middle
And never went there again.

FINGERPLAYS

Little Froggie

Play on five fingers, or five toes.

This little froggie broke his toe.
This little froggie said, "Oh, oh, oh,"
This little froggie laughed and was glad,
This little froggie cried and was sad,
But this little froggie, so thoughtful and good
Ran for the doctor as fast as he could.

Five Little Monkeys

See MONKEYS, page 130.

SONGS

Miss Polly Had a Dolly

Miss Polly had a dolly who was sick, sick, sick,
  Rock arms.
So she called for the doctor to come quick, quick, quick.
  Dial and listen.
The doctor came with his bag and his hat.
  Hold bag and touch hat.
And he knocked on the door with a rat-a-tat-a-tat.
  Knock on door.
He looked at the dolly and he shook his head.
  Shake head.
He said, "Miss Polly, put her straight to bed."
  Shake finger sternly.
He wrote on a paper for a pill, pill, pill.
  Write on paper.
Said, "I'll be back in the morning with my bill, bill, bill."

John Brown's Baby

Sing to the tune of "John Brown's Body." Repeat several times, each time leaving out one more word which you mime instead.

John Brown's baby had a cold upon its chest,
John Brown's baby had a cold upon its chest,
John Brown's baby had a cold upon its chest,
And they rubbed it with camphorated oil.

Replace "baby" with rocking motion.
Replace "cold" with a sneeze.
Replace "chest" with a fist on your chest.
Replace "rubbed" it with circular motion on chest.
Replace "camphorated" with nose-holding.

MORE IDEAS

1. Use this theme in winter when several children come down with colds. If one of the children is sick, make get well cards or pictures as the children do in *Carousel*.

2. Use *Gregory, the Terrible Eater* to chat about healthy foods to eat. Sing *I Know an Old Lady Who Swallowed a Fly* (page 97).

3. It's always fun to play doctor and patient with pretend stethoscopes, popsicle sticks, medicine, bandages and band-aids. Talk about what doctors, dentists and other health professionals do. Let girls know that they can be doctors and boys that they can be nurses.

4. *The Lady with the Alligator Purse* is fun to tell with finger puppets.

Snakes, Turtles & Lizards

STORIES TO READ ALOUD

The Hare and the Tortoise
AESOP

Turtle Tale
ASCH, FRANK

The Greedy Python
BUCKLEY, RICHARD

The Mixed-Up Chameleon
CARLE, ERIC

Tomorrow, Up and Away!
COLLINS, PAT LOWERY

The Turtle and the Monkey
GALDONE, PAUL

Jump, Frog, Jump
KALAN, ROBERT

The Snake that Sneezed
LEYDENFROST, ROBERT

Fish Is Fish
LIONNI, LEO

The Name of the Tree
LOTTERIDGE, CELIA

I Wish I Could Fly
MARIS, RON

Lizard in the Sun
RYDER, JOANNE

Lizard's Song
SHANNON, GEORGE

Crictor
UNGERER, TOMI

MORE STORIES

The Animal
BALIAN, LORNA

A Snake Is Totally Tail
BARRETT, JUDI

Franklin Fibs (and other *Franklin* titles)
BOURGEOIS, PAULETTE

The Day Jimmy's Boa Ate the Wash
NOBLE, TRINKA HAKES

Yertle the Turtle and Other Stories
SEUSS, DR.

Snake
WABER, BERNARD

Albert's Toothache
WILLIAMS, BARBARA

FINGERPLAYS

A Slippery, Slithery Snake

I saw a slippery, slithery snake,
> *Hold up index finger of one hand.*

Slide through the grasses, making them shake.
> *Weave index finger through fingers of other hand.*

He looked at me with his beady eye.
> *Fingers and thumbs make goggle eyes.*

"Go away from my pretty green garden," said I.
> *Make shooing movements with hand.*

"Sssssss," said the slippery, slithery snake,
As he slid through the grasses, making them shake.
> *Repeat first movement. Wiggle fingers.*

A Snake!

Here's a box
   Make a fist as if holding a bunch of flowers.

And here's the lid.
   Cover with palm of other hand.

I wonder whatever inside is hid?
   Pause and peek.

Why, it's a SNAKE!
   Quickly throw up hands.

A Snake

Use one arm resting on a table to represent the snake. Make his head by touching thumb to fingertips.

Down in the grass, curled up in a heap,
Lies a big snake, fast asleep.
When he hears the grasses blow,
He moves his body to and fro.
Up and down and in and out,
See him slowly move about.
Now his jaws are open, so . . .
Snap! He's caught my finger! Oh!
   Pretend to catch finger of other hand.

There Was a Little Turtle

There was a little turtle,
   Make a fist with thumb sticking out.

He lived in a box.
   Cup hands together for box.

He swam in a puddle,
   Wiggle hand for swimming.

He climbed on the rocks.
   Fingers climb up other fist.

He snapped at a mosquito,
   Snap fingers.

He snapped at a flea,
   Snap.

He snapped at a minnow,
   Snap.

And he snapped at me!
   Snap.

He caught the mosquito,
   Clap, gulp.

He caught the flea,
   Clap, gulp.

He caught the minnow,
   Clap, gulp.

But he didn't catch me!
   Move pointer finger back and forth.

My Turtle

This is my turtle,
   Make fist, extend thumb.

He lives in a shell.
   Hide thumb in fist.

He likes his home very well.
He pokes his head out when he wants to eat.
   Extend thumb.

And pulls it back in when he wants to sleep.
   Hide thumb in fist.

MORE IDEAS

1. Felt Stories: *The Snake That Sneezed* and "The Little White Duck" (page 70). Hiss like a snake in rehearsal for "The Little White Duck."

2. Tell the story of *The Snake That Sneezed* adding a child for each animal in a line behind the snake's head, the storyteller. Weave the line in and out as the story is told. At the "sneeze" everyone falls down.

3. Make a stuffed snake and have *Crictor* act out the letters and numbers as the story is told. Ask children to name the shapes. Other props you will need are: a baby bottle, a scarf, and a medal. A hat box for Crictor's arrival is nice. I use a bamboo steamer with a bow on top.

4. Tell the poem "Boa Constrictor" by Shel Silverstein, in *Where the Sidewalk Ends.*

5. Tell "Turtle of Koka," an easy-to-learn participation story for preschoolers. This is in *The Storyteller's Start-Up Book* by Margaret Read MacDonald.

6. Tell "The Tortoise and the Hare" with lap puppets. For a storytelling idea see *Storytelling Made Easy with Puppets* by Jan VanSchuyver.

7. *Lizard's Song* is a wonderful participation story to tell with lap puppets.

8. Have a lizard storytime with: *Lizard's Song, The Mixed-Up Chameleon,* and "Gecko," a participation story about perseverance, also in *The Storyteller's Start-Up Book* by Margaret Read MacDonald.

Space

STORIES TO READ ALOUD

Mooncake
ASCH, FRANK

I Want to Be an Astronaut
BARTON, BYRON

Moon Rope
EHLERT, LOIS

Regards to the Man in the Moon
KEATS, EZRA JACK

First Flight
McPHAIL, DAVID

Penguin Moon
MITRA, ANNIE

Louis and the Night Sky
MORGAN, NICOLA

Angela's Airplane
MUNSCH, ROBERT

What Faust Saw
OTTLEY, MATT

Squawk to the Moon, Little Goose
PRESTON, EDNA MITCHELL

The Architect of the Moon
WYNNE-JONES, TIM

The Last Piece of Sky
WYNNE-JONES, TIM

NONFICTION

Airport
BARTON, BYRON

Flying
CREWS, DONALD

Flying
GIBBONS, GAIL

Planes
ROCKWELL, ANNE

Going on an Airplane
ROGERS, FRED

NURSERY RHYMES

Flying-Man, Flying-Man

Flying-man, Flying-man,
Up in the sky,
Where are you going to,
Flying so high?

Over the mountains
And over the sea,
Flying-man, Flying-man,
Can't you take me?

There Was an Old Woman

For felt pieces you will need: an old woman with a broom, a basket, and stringy stars for the sky.

There was an old woman tossed up in a basket,
Seventeen times as high as the moon.
Where she was going I couldn't but ask it,
For in her hand she carried a broom.
Old woman, old woman, old woman, quoth I,
Where are you going to up so high?
To brush the cobwebs off the sky!
May I go with you? Aye, by and by.

The Man in the Moon

The man in the moon
Looked out of the moon,
Looked out of the moon and said,
It's time, I think, for all good children
To think about going to bed.

Aikendrum

Sing to the tune of "Here We Go Round the Mulberry Bush." Listen to the tune on Raffi's Singable Songs for the Very Young *cassette. Music is in* The Raffi Singable Songbook.

There was a man lived in the moon
In the moon, in the moon
There was a man lived in the moon
And his name was Aikendrum.

And he played upon a ladle
A ladle, a ladle
He played upon a ladle
And his name was Aikendrum.

And his hat was made of cream cheese . . .
And his coat was made of roast beef . . .
And his pants were made of haggis . . .
There was a man lived in the moon . . .

Twinkle, Twinkle, Little Star

Twinkle, twinkle, little star,
How I wonder what you are.
Up above the world so high,
Like a diamond in the sky.
Twinkle, twinkle, little star,
How I wonder what you are.

Star Light, Star Bright

Star light, star bright,
First star I see tonight,
I wish I may,
I wish I might,
Have this wish,
I wish tonight.

FINGERPLAYS

Moon Ride

Do you want to go up with me to the moon?
Point to friend, self, then to sky.
Let's get in our rocket ship and blast off soon!
Pretend to climb in ship.
Faster and faster we reach to the sky.
Swish hands quickly. Jump and reach.
Isn't it fun to be able to fly?
We're on the moon, now all take a look,
Look down.
And gently sit down and I'll show you a book.
Sit down gently.

Bend and Stretch

Bend and stretch, reach for the stars.
There goes Jupiter, here comes Mars.
Bend and stretch, reach for the sky
Stand on tip-e-toe, oh! so high!

Zoom, Zoom, Zoom

Zoom, zoom, zoom,
Hand in prayer position. Brush up three times.
We're going to the moon.
Point up into the sky.
If you want to take a trip,
Climb aboard my rocket ship.
Climbing motion.
Zoom, zoom, zoom,
We're going to the moon.
Repeat first actions with hands.
10, 9, 8, 7, 6, 5, 4, 3, 2, 1,
With hands together as before, bend down into a crouching position.
Blast off!
Jump up and shoot arms up into the air!
Zoom, zoom, zoom,
We're going to the moon.

Ring Around the Rocket Ship

Sing to the tune of "Ring Around the Rosie."

Ring around the rocket ship,
All join hands in a circle and walk to the right.
Reach for a star,
Drop hands and reach up.
Stardust, stardust,
Fall where you are.
Fall to the floor.

MORE IDEAS

1. Felt Stories: *Squawk to the Moon, Little Goose,* "Aikendrum," "Flying Man," and "The Old Lady Tossed Up in a Basket."

2. Develop a flying theme with *Angela's Airplane* and *First Flight.* Sing Raffi's lovely song, "Riding in My Airplane" on his *One Light, One Sun* cassette. Music is in *The Second Raffi Songbook.*

3. Construct a space ship with the children out of a large cardboard box, as the little bear does in *Mooncake.* The spaceship can then be used for a prop as you act out *Mooncake* or *The Architect of the Moon.*

4. For more moon stories, see BEDTIME & MOON STORIES.

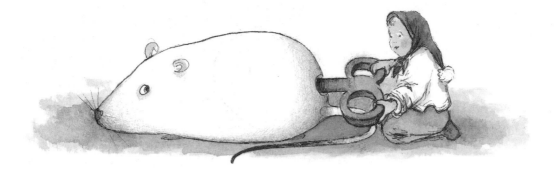

Teeny Tiny Things

STORIES TO READ ALOUD

Effie
ALLINSON, BEVERLY

Turtle Tale
ASCH, FRANK

The Very Hungry Caterpillar
CARLE, ERIC

A Bed Just So
HARDENDORF, JEANNE

Titch
HUTCHINS, PAT

You'll Soon Grow into Them, Titch
HUTCHINS, PAT

Fat Cat
KENT, JACK

The Carrot Seed (big book format)
KRAUSS, RUTH

The Biggest House in the World
LIONNI, LEO

Inch by Inch
LIONNI, LEO

Swimmy
LIONNI, LEO

Big or Little
STINSON, KATHY

The Teeny Tiny Woman
SEULING, BARBARA

The Napping House
WOOD, AUDREY

NONFICTION

Big Ones, Little Ones
HOBAN, TANA

NURSERY RHYMES

There Was a Maid on Scrabble Hill

A felt idea: make a tall felt maid, a crescent moon, and some clothes to hang on it.

There was a maid on Scrabble Hill,
And if not dead, she lives there still.
She grew so tall, she reached the sky,
And on the moon hung clothes to dry.

The Old Woman Who Lived in a Shoe

There was an old woman
Who lived in a shoe.
She had so many children,
She didn't know what to do.
So she gave them some broth,
And a big piece of bread,
Kissed them all soundly
And tucked them in bed.

Ladybird

Ladybird, ladybird, fly away home,
Your house is on fire, your children all gone;
All but one, and her name is Ann,
And she crept under the pudding pan.

Little Miss Dimble

From Jelly Belly *by Dennis Lee.*

Little Miss Dimble
Lived in a thimble,
Slept in a measuring spoon.
She met a mosquito
And called him "My sweet-o,"
And married him under the moon.

Thumbelina

From Jelly Belly by Dennis Lee.

Thumbelina came to town.
Pigtails up and petticoats down,
All the children crowding round -
Tiny Thumbelina!

Thumbelina, dance on my thumb,
Tap your toes with a rum-tum-tum!
Boy on piano, girls on drum
Play for Thumbelina!

Jerry Hall

Make a little felt person with a tall felt hat.

Jerry Hall
He is so small,
A rat could eat him,
Hat and all!

FINGERPLAYS

Sometimes I'm Tall

Sometimes I'm tall.
Stand a full height.

Sometimes I'm small.
Bend down close to floor.

Sometimes I'm very, very, tall.
Stretch on tiptoes.

Sometimes I'm very, very, small.
Bend close to the floor.

Sometime tall, sometimes small,
Stretch high, bend low.

See how I am now.
Stand normally.

Tall As a Tree

Act it out.

Tall as a tree.
Wide as a house.
Thin as a pin.
Small as a mouse.

Thumbkin

Sing to the tune of "Frère Jacques." Everybody hides hands behind backs to start.

Where is thumbkin?
Where is thumbkin?
Here I am!
Bring out one hand, thumb up.

Here I am!
Bring out the other hand, thumb up.

How are you today, sir?
Nod one thumb.

Very well, I thank you.
Nod the other thumb.

Run away, run away,
Hide hands behind back again.

Run away and hide.
One at a time.

Repeat using "Pointer," "Tall Man," "Ring Man," and "the Baby" in place of Thumbkin.

Tommy Thumbs

Tommy Thumbs up and
Thumbs up, both hands.

Tommy Thumbs down,
Thumbs down.

Tommy thumbs dancing
Thumbs up and bounce to the right.

All around the town.
Bounce to the left.

Dance 'em on your shoulders,
Bounce them on your shoulders.

Dance 'em on your head,
Bounce them on your head.

Dance 'em on your knees and
Bounce them on your knees.

Tuck them into bed.
Fold arms hiding hands.

Peter Pointer up . . .
Repeat using index finger.

Toby Tall up . . .
Repeat using tall finger, and so on.

Ring Man up . . .
Baby Finger up . . .
Finger Family up . . .

Mr. Tall and Mr. Small

From Listen: And Help Tell the Story *by*
Bernice Wells Carlson.

Once there was a man
Who was tall, tall, tall.
Stand on tiptoes, reach up as far as possible.

And he had a friend
Who was small, small, small.
Kneel and bend 'way down.

The man who was small
Would try to call
To the man who was tall,
Cup hands near mouth, look up.

"Hello, up there!"
In high voice.

The man who was tall
Stand on tiptoes.

At once would call
To the man who was small,
Bend from waist.

"Hello, down there."
Use deep voice.

Stand straight.

Then each tipped his hat
Tip an imaginary hat.

And made this reply,
"Good-bye, my friend."
Look up, speak in high voice.

"Good-bye, good-bye."
Bow, and speak in deep voice.

Eensy, Weensy Spider

Eensy weensy spider
Climbed up the water-spout;
Thumbs and pointer fingers climb up each other.

Down came the rain
Raise hands and lower wriggling fingers.

And washed the spider out;
Sweep arms out to the side.

Out came the sunshine
Raise hands above head and form circle.

And dried up all the rain;
And eensy weensy spider
Climbed up the spout again.
Repeat climbing motion.

There was a Little Turtle

There was a little turtle,
Make a fist with thumb sticking out.

He lived in a box.
Cup hands together for box.

He swam in a puddle
Wiggle hand for swimming.

He climbed on the rocks.
Fingers climb up other fist.

He snapped at a mosquito,
Snap fingers.

He snapped at a flea,
Snap.

He snapped at a minnow,
Snap.

And he snapped at me!
Snap.

He caught the mosquito,
Clap, gulp.

He caught the flea,
Clap, gulp.

He caught the minnow,
Clap, gulp.

But he didn't catch me!
Point to self.

Elfman

I met a little elf-man
Down where the lilies blow,
Use thumb and pointer finger to indicate size.

I asked him why he was so small
And why he didn't grow.
Shrug shoulders, hands out at sides, palms up.

He slightly frowned and with his eyes
He looked me through and through.
Tilt head to side and look serious.

"I'm just as big for me," said he,
"As you are big for you."
Place hands on hips.

Tom Thumb

Now I'll tell you a story, and this story is new,
So you listen carefully, and do as I do.
This is Tom Thumb, and this is his house;

> *Hold up thumb, then make a roof shape with two
> forefingers.*

These are his windows, and this is Squeaky, his
mouse.

> *Make 'spectacles,' then hold up one finger for the
> mouse.*

One morning very early the sun began to shine;

> *Indicate sunshine with arms held high,
> gradually lower.*

Squeaky mouse sat up in bed and counted up to
nine.

> *Wriggle the 'mouse' finger and point to nine
> fingers in turn.*

Then Squeaky made a jump, right on to Tom
Thumb's bed;

> *Jump 'mouse' finger onto other hand.*

She quickly ran right up his arm and sat upon
his head.

> *Run finger right up arm and on to head.*

Squeaky pulled his hair, and Squeaky pulled his
nose,

> *Pretend to pull hair and nose.*

Until Tom Thumb jumped out of bed
And put on all his clothes.

> *Run thumb and forefinger down 'Tom Thumb' to
> indicate dressing.*

Then they sat down to breakfast,
And ate some crusty bread,

> *Mime the actions.*

And when that was all quite finished,
Little Tom Thumb said,
Now I'll tell you a story, and this story is new . . .

MORE IDEAS

1. Felt Stories: *The Very Hungry Caterpillar* and *Fat Cat.*

2. *The Bed Just So* is a wonderful story, easy to learn and fun to tell. The hudgin character is so small, he is only a tiny voice! Hold out a walnut shell at the end for a bed and a fine finishing touch.

3. Tell "The Knee-High Man," a story about a little man who wants to be big. The story and pattern for the felt board are in *Multicultural Folktales* by Judy Sierra.

4. Tell "Gecko," from *The Storyteller's Start-Up Book* by Margaret Read MacDonald.

5. Make this an "I'm Growing" theme with: *The Very Hungry Caterpillar, Titch,* and *Big or Little.*

6. Make this a "Power of the Small" theme with: *The Very Hungry Caterpillar, Titch, Elephant in a Well, Effie, Swimmy,* and *The Great Big Enormous Turnip.*

7. Tell "One Inch Tall" from *Where the Sidewalk Ends* by Shel Silverstein.

8. See GIANTS for more ideas of contrast.

9. Sing "The Ants Came Marching" (page 126). See this and more ideas in INSECTS.

Thanksgiving

STORIES TO READ ALOUD

Over the River and Through the Wood
CHILD, LYDIA MARIA

Nuts to You!
EHLERT, LOIS

The Great Big Enormous Turnip
TOLSTOY

The Giant Vegetable Garden
WESTCOTT, NADINE

MORE STORIES

Sometimes It's Turkey, Sometimes It's Feathers
BALIAN, LORNA

Thanksgiving Treat
STOCK, CATHERINE

Autumn Harvest
TRESSELT, ALVIN

Thanksgiving at Our House
WATSON, WENDY

Chester Chipmunk's Thanksgiving
WILLIAMS, BARBARA

NONFICTION

Turkeys, Pilgrims, and Indian Corn: The Story of the Thanksgiving Symbols (adult)
BARTH, EDNA

Things to Make and Do for Thanksgiving
CAULEY, LORINDA BRYAN

The Dragon Thanksgiving Feast: Things to Make and Do
LEEDY, LOREEN

It's Thanksgiving (poetry)
PRELUTSKY, JACK

FINGERPLAYS

A Turkey

A turkey I saw on Thanksgiving,
His tail was spread so wide,
Hands together, fingers spread, thumbs touching.
And he said, "Sh . . . don't tell that you've seen me,
Finger to lips.
For I'm running away to hide."
Use two fingers to run away.

Mr. Turkey

Mr. Turkey's tail is big and wide.
Spread fingers.
He swings it when he walks.
Swing hands.
His neck is long.
Stretch neck.
His chin is red,
Stroke chin.
And he gobbles when he talks.
Open and close hands, and gobble.

Little Leaves

Little leaves fall gently down,
Red and yellow, orange and brown.
Raise hands and flutter fingers down like falling leaves.
Whirling, whirling round and round,
Quietly without a sound.
Whirl around quietly.
Falling softly to the ground,
Down - and - down - and - down - and - down!
Lower bodies gradually to floor.

When Thanksgiving Comes

Every day when we eat our dinner,
Our table is just this small.
> *Interlace fingers, palms down. Thumbs point down for legs.*

Just room for mother, father, sister,
Brother and me, that's all.
> *Point to each finger of left hand.*

But when it's Thanksgiving and company comes,
You'd hardly believe your eyes,
That very self-same table
Stretches out until it's this size!
> *Expand hands as far as possible while keeping fingertips touching.*

The Farm Yard

In the farm yard at the end of the day,
All the animals politely say,
"Thank you for my food today."
The cow says, "Moo."
> *Point to thumb.*

The pigeon, "Coo."
> *Point to index finger.*

The sheep says, "Baa."
> *Point to middle finger.*

The lamb says, "Maaa."
> *Point to fourth finger.*

The hen, "Cluck, cluck, cluck."
> *Point to little finger.*

> *Point to fingers of the opposite hand for remaining animals:*

"Quack," says the duck.
The dog, "Bow wow."
The cat, "Meow."
The horse, "Neigh."
The pig grunts, "Oink."
Then the barn is locked up tight,
And the farmer says, "Goodnight."
> *Hands together against cheek.*

Thanksgiving Day

Five little children on Thanksgiving day
The first one said, "I'll have cake if I may."
The second one said, "I'll have turkey roasted."
The third one said, "I'll have chestnuts toasted."
The fourth one said, "I'll have a pumpkin pie."
The fifth one said, "Cranberries I spy."
But before they ate any turkey or dressing
They all sat down and said a blessing.

Gray Squirrel

See page 16.

SONGS

Thanks a Lot

> *Listen to the tune on Raffi's* Baby Beluga *cassette. Words and music are in* The Second Raffi Songbook. *Children sing the echo, "thanks a lot," each time you sing it.*

Thanks a lot,
Thanks for the sun in the sky.
Thanks a lot,
Thanks for the clouds so high.

Thanks a lot,
Thanks for the whispering wind.
Thanks a lot,
Thanks for the birds in the spring.

Thanks a lot,
Thanks for the moonlit night.
Thanks a lot,
Thanks for the stars so bright.

Thanks a lot,
Thanks for the wonder in me.
Thanks a lot,
Thanks for the way I feel.

Thanks for the animals, thanks for the land,
Thanks for the people everywhere.
Thanks a lot,
Thanks for all I've got,
Thanks for all I've got.

MORE IDEAS

1. Felt Stories: *The Great Big Enormous Turnip, The Great Big Enormous Pumpkin* (a simple adaptation of The GBE Turnip), and "Old MacDonald Had a Farm" (page 89).

2. Craft: Have children make hand prints on a sheet of paper with thumbs and fingers spread wide. Or simply draw around hand to make a turkey shape. Then add an eye and a beard on the thumb, and add some feet. They look remarkably like little turkeys!

3. Craft: Provide the materials and show the children how to make crayon rubbings over the texture of gathered leaves.

4. Celebrate the harvest! For more ideas, see FARMS; to celebrate the season, see SEASONS – FALL. For pumpkin ideas, see HALLOWEEN.

Time

STORIES TO READ ALOUD

The Grouchy Ladybug
CARLE, ERIC

The Sun's Day
GERSTEIN, MORDICAI

Just a Minute
HARPER, ANITA

Clocks and More Clocks
HUTCHINS, PAT

Around the Clock with Harriet
MAESTRO, BETSY

NONFICTION

Clocks and How They Go
GIBBONS, GAIL

Big Time Bears
KRENSKY, STEPHEN

Time To . . .
McMILLAN, BRUCE

My First Look at Time
RANDOM HOUSE

Time
THOMPSON, CAROL

NURSERY RHYMES

The Man in the Moon

The man in the moon
Looked out of the moon,
Looked out of the moon and said,
    Raise arms up in a circle over your head.
It's time, I think, for all good children
To think about going to bed.
    Cup hands to mouth.

Wee Willie Winkie

Wee Willie Winkie runs through the town,
Upstairs and downstairs, in his nightgown,
Rapping at the window,
Crying through the lock,
"Are the children in their beds?
For now it's eight o'clock."

Hickory Dickory Dock

Hickory dickory dock,
    Swing arms like a pendulum.
The mouse ran up the clock.
    Run two fingers up your arm.
The clock struck one,
    Hold up one finger.
And down he run,
    Run two fingers back down your arm.
Hickory, dickory, dock.
    Swing arm like a pendulum again.

Hickory Dickory Dock

    Repeat this game playing faster and faster, then in slow motion.

Hickory dickory dock,
    Swing arms back and forth.
Tick tock!
    Clap, clap.
The mouse ran up the clock.
    Run hands from your toes to the top of your head.
Tick tock!
    Clap, clap.
The clock struck one,
    Hold up one finger.
And down he run,
    Run hands back down to toes.
Hickory, dickory, dock.
    Swing arms.
Tick tock!
    Stamp feet.

Bell Horses

Strike a little bell or shake a jingle bell in time to the rhythm of the verse. Listen to the tune on Bob McGrath's cassette, Songs and Games for Toddlers.

Bell horses, bell horses,
What's the time of day?
One o'clock, two o'clock,
Time to go away.
Hide bell behind back.

Little bell, little bell,
Where are you?
Whisper.

Here I am, here I am,
How do you do.
Bring bell back and shake loudly.

FINGERPLAYS

The Big Old Clock

The big old clock goes tick tock, tick tock.
Loud voice, slowly sway from side to side.

That is the noise of the big old clock.
Dong, dong, dong.
Move backwards and forwards slowly.

The middle-sized clock goes tick tock, tick tock, tick tock.
Normal voice, sway from side to side a little faster.

That is the noise of the middle sized clock.
Ding dong, ding dong, ding dong.
Move backwards and forwards quickly.

The little cuckoo clock goes tick tock, tick tock, tick tock.
Soft voice, sway quickly.

That is the noise of the little cuckoo clock.
Cuckoo, cuckoo, cuckoo.
Make quick little moves back and forth.

Hear the Steeple Clock

Hear the steeple clock go tick-tock, tick-tock,
Slowly, loudly.

Hear the little mantle clock go tick-tock, tick tock.
Bit faster, bit softer.

Now hear the little wrist watch go tick-tick-tick-tick-tick-tick-tick-tick.
Furiously fast, softly.
Stop!

SONG

Brush Your Teeth

Load up your toothbrushes! Children will join in on the sound effects. The tune is on Raffi's Singable Songs for the Very Young *cassette. Words and music in* The Raffi Singable Songbook.

When you wake up in the morning and it's quarter to one,
And you want to have a little fun,
You brush your teeth, ch ch ch ch, ch ch ch ch ch,
You brush your teeth.

When you wake up in the morning and it's quarter to two,
And you want to find something to do,
You brush your teeth, ch ch ch ch, ch ch ch ch ch,
You brush your teeth.

When you wake up in the morning and it's quarter to three,
And your mind starts humming twiddle de dee,
You brush your teeth, ch ch ch ch, ch ch ch ch ch,
You brush your teeth.

When you wake up in the morning and it's quarter to four,
And you think you hear a knock on your door,
You brush your teeth, ch ch ch ch, ch ch ch ch ch,
You brush your teeth.

When you wake up in the morning and it's quarter to five,
And you just can't wait to come alive,
You brush your teeth, ch ch ch ch, ch ch ch ch ch,
You brush your teeth.

MORE IDEAS

1. This theme connects nicely to BEDTIME, perhaps the first and best known time to children.

2. Use chopsticks or wooden spoons to beat time to the rhymes here. Strike a little bell for "Bell Horses."

Toys

STORIES TO READ ALOUD

Beady Bear
FREEMAN, DON

Corduroy
FREEMAN, DON

A Pocket for Corduroy
FREEMAN, DON

Christina Katerina and the Box
GAUCH, PATRICIA LEE

Teddy Bears 1 to 10
GRETZ, SUSANNA

This Is the Bear and the Scary Night
HAYES, SARAH

Tidy Titch
HUTCHINS, PAT

Peter's Chair
KEATS, EZRA JACK

Alexander and the Wind-Up Mouse
LIONNI, LEO

Mine!
ORAM, HIAWYN

The Wedding Procession of the Rag Doll . . .
SANDBURG, CARL

The Piney Woods Peddler
SHANNON, GEORGE

Ira Sleeps Over
WABER, BERNARD

Hazel's Amazing Mother
WELLS, ROSEMARY

The Architect of the Moon
WYNNE-JONES, TIM

Hush Little Baby
ZEMACH, MARGOT

Only the Best
ZOLA, MEGUIDO

MORE STORIES

Good As New
DOUGLASS, BARBARA

Laura Charlotte
GALBRAITH, KATHRYN O.

Fix-It
McPHAIL, DAVID

Curious George Flies a Kite
REY, H. A.

William's Doll
ZOLOTOW, CHARLOTTE

NURSERY RHYMES

Tweedledum and Tweedledee

Tweedledum and Tweedledee
Agreed to have a battle,
For Tweedledum said Tweedledee
Had spoiled his nice new rattle.
Just then flew by a monstrous crow
As black as a tar-barrel,
Which frightened both the heroes so,
They quite forgot their quarrel.

FINGERPLAYS

My Red Balloon

I had a little red balloon
Make a ball with two hands.

And I blew and blew and blew
Blow into it three times.

Until it grew and grew and grew.
Stretch hands apart.

I tossed it in the air
Tossing motion.

And never let it drop.
Shake head.

I bounced it on the ground
Bounce with one hand.

Until it suddenly went, "POP!"
Clap hands for a pop.

Jack in the Box

Jack in the box
Jack in the box
Sits so still.
*Children crouch with hands over heads
as if in a box.*

Will he come out?
YES HE WILL!
All jump up and shout.

Jack in the Box

This is Jack
Clench left fist with thumb extended.

In a box.
*Put thumb in fist and cover with palm of right
hand.*

Open the lid,
Lift right hand.

And out Jack pops!
Pull thumb out of fist with a jerk.

Rag Doll

Flop your arms, flop your feet,
Let your hands go free,
Be the raggiest rag doll,
Your ever did see.

Flopsy Flora

I'm just like Flopsy Flora,
A doll that's made of rags.
My arms go flop, my feet go plop,
My head just wigs and wags.

I'm just like Wooden William,
Who stands up straight and tall,
My arms and legs are wooden,
They just don't move at all.

I'm a Little Puppet Clown

I'm a funny little puppet clown
Bend at knees.

When my strings move up and down.
Bounce up and down.

First, I'll stand up
Stand up straight.

Then I'll fall down.
Fall to floor.

I'm a funny little puppet clown.

I'm a funny little puppet gay.
Repeat first action.

Move my strings and watch me play.
Now I'm stiff,
Stand tall, arms at sides.

Now I'm tall
Stretch on tip-toes.

Let my strings go,
And I will fall.
Fall to floor.

I Am a Top

I am a top all wound up tight;
Clasp hands tightly together.

I whirl and whirl with all my might;
Make hands spin around each other quickly.

And now the whirls are out of me
Stop whirling.

So I will rest as still as can be.
Fold hands.

I Have a Dear Little Dolly

I have a dear little dolly,
Who has eyes of bright blue.
Point to eyes.

She can open and shut them,
Open and shut eyes.

And she smiles at me too.
Smile.

In the morning I dress her,
And she goes out to play.
Index and middle fingers of one hand walk on open palm.

But I like best to rock her
At the end of the day.
Pretend to rock doll in arms.

SONGS

The Chinese Fan

Sit on floor with legs out straight.

My ship sailed from China with a cargo of tea,
All laden with presents for you and for me.
They brought me a fan.
Just imagine my bliss,
When I fan myself daily, like this, like this,
Like this, like this.

Repeat song five times. Each time "like this" is sung, fan yourself as follows:

First verse: With your right hand in rhythm.

Second verse: With both hands.

Third verse: With both hands as you sweep your right foot up and over your left foot in rhythm.

Fourth verse: With both hands as you sweep your right foot across the left, then the left across the right in rhythm.

Fifth verse: With both hands, both feet, as you nod your head forward and backward.

Miss Polly Had a Dolly

Miss Polly had a dolly who was sick, sick, sick,
Rock arms.

So she called for the doctor to come quick, quick, quick.
Dial and listen.

The doctor came with his bag and his hat,
Hold bag and touch hat.

And he knocked on the door with a rat-a-tat-a-tat.
Knock on door.

He looked at the dolly and he shook his head.
Shake head.

He said, "Miss Polly, put her straight to bed."
Shake finger sternly.

He wrote on a paper for a pill, pill, pill.
Write on paper.

Said, "I'll be back in the morning with my bill, bill, bill."

Hambone

This is a wonderful rhythmic chant. Ask children simply to clap with you as you repeat the call and the response.

Hambone, Hambone where you been?
'Round the world and back again!

Hambone, Hambone where's your wife?
In the kitchen cooking rice.

Hambone, Hambone have you heard?
Papa's gonna buy me a mockingbird.

If that mockingbird don't sing,
Papa's gonna buy me a diamond ring.

If that diamond ring don't shine,
Papa's gonna buy me a fishing line.

Hambone, Hambone where you been?
'Round the world and I'm goin' again!

Hush Little Baby
See BABIES, page 20.

MORE IDEAS

1. Hambone is a call and response song from the African-American tradition. Make up your own clapping pattern, or, for an original pattern, see *Shake It to the One That You Love the Best* by Cheryl Warren-Mattox. This book comes with a cassette. Talk about how children have made toys out of ordinary household objects, even hambones. Think of other toys and rhythm instruments to make. See MUSIC for ideas.

2. Take a favourite or unusual toy to show the children. A hambone, a wish bone, an antique, or a homemade toy. Ask children to bring a favourite toy for show and tell, or ask them to describe their favourite toys.

3. Talk about all the special times we give one another toys as presents: birthdays, Christmas, special days.

4. Make toys out of ordinary things: puppets out of wooden spoons or paper bags, masks representing story characters out of paper plates.

5. See BEARS & TEDDY BEARS for more ideas.

6. Sing "Puff the Magic Dragon."

7. Make simple paper finger puppets, toys children can take home.

Transportation

STORIES TO READ ALOUD

Mr. Gumpy's Motor Car
BURNINGHAM, JOHN

Mr. Gumpy's Outing
BURNINGHAM, JOHN

The Bus Stop
HELLEN, NANCY

Regards to the Man in the Moon
KEATS, EZRA JACK

The Wheels on the Bus
KOVALSKI, MARYANN

The Train
McPHAIL, DAVID

Angela's Airplane
MUNSCH, ROBERT

Jonathan Cleaned Up
MUNSCH, ROBERT

Tooth-Gnasher, Superflasher
PINKWATER, DANIEL

The Little Engine That Could
PIPER, WATTY

The Wheels on the Bus
ZELINSKY, PAUL

MORE STORIES

Mike Mulligan and His Steam Shovel
BURTON, VIRGINIA LEE

My Family Vacation
KHALSA, DAYAL KHUR

Ferryboat
MAESTRO, BETSY

Train Song
SIEBERT, DIANE

NONFICTION

Airport
BARTON, BYRON

Dinosaurs Travel: A Guide for Families
BROWN, LAURENE KRASNY

Flying
CREWS, DONALD

Carousel
CREWS, DONALD

Freight Train
CREWS, DONALD

Harbor
CREWS, DONALD

Truck
CREWS, DONALD

Cars and How They Go
COLE, JOANNA

Trucks
(EYE OPENERS SERIES)

Flying
GIBBONS, GAIL

New Road!
GIBBONS, GAIL

Fill It Up!
GIBBONS, GAIL

Trucks
(see also *Trains* and *Boat Book*)
GIBBONS, GAIL

Boats
ROBBINS, KEN

Boats
ROCKWELL, ANNE

Planes
ROCKWELL, ANNE

NURSERY RHYMES

Flying-Man, Flying-Man

Flying-man, Flying-man,
Up in the sky,
Where are you going to,
Flying so high?
Over the mountains
And over the sea,
Flying-man, Flying-man,
Can't you take me?

Ride a Cock-Horse

Ride a cock-horse to Banbury Cross,
To see a fine lady upon a white horse;
With rings on her fingers and bells on her toes,
She shall have music wherever she goes.

To Market, to Market

Hold reigns and pretend to ride on a pig!

To market, to market to buy a fat pig.
Home again, home again jiggity jig.
To market, to market to buy a fat hog.
Home again, home again, jiggity jog.
To market, to market to buy a plum bun.
Home again, home again, shopping is done.

FINGERPLAYS

Helping Mommy Drive

Suit actions to words.

Open the car door. Climb inside.
I get to help my mommy drive.
Fasten the seat belt. Shut the door.
Start the motor. Hear it roar.
Brr! Brr! Brr! Turn the corner, step on the gas.
If the road is clear we may pass.

Safety

Red says STOP.
  Hold right hand in "stop" gesture.

And green says GO.
  Extend right arm with index finger pointed.

Yellow says WAIT:
You'd better go slow!
  With index finger draw a line across your chest
  from right to left.

When I reach a crossing place,
  Cross arms at wrists.

To left and right I turn my face.
  Turn head left, then right.

I walk, not run, across the street,
  Demonstrate walking.

And use my head to guide my feet.
  Point to head, then feet.

The Airplane

The airplane has great big wings
  Arms outstretched.

Its propeller spins around and sings,
  Make one arm go around.

"Vvvvvvvv!"
The airplane goes up;
  Lift arms.

The airplane goes down;
  Lower arms.

The airplane files high
All over our town!
  Arms outstretched, turn body around.

Choo-Choo Train

This is a choo-choo train,
  Bend arms at elbows.

Puffing down the track.
  Rotate forearms in rhythm.

Now it's going forward,
  Push arms forward; continue rotating motion.

Now it's going back.
  Pull arms back; continue rotating motion.

Now the bell is ringing,
  Pull bell cord with closed fist.

Now the whistle blows.
  Hold fist near mouth and blow.

What a lot of noise it makes,
  Cover ears with hand.

Everywhere it goes.
  Stretch out arms.

Engine, Engine, Number 9

Chug shoulders and arms in rhythm. Repeat singing faster, then repeat singing slower. After the last verse, hold thumb up and toot your whistle three times. Listen to the tune on the cassette Songs and Games for Toddlers, *by Bob McGrath and Katharine Smithrim.*

Engine, engine, number 9,
Coming down the Vancouver line.
If the train goes off the track,
Do you want your money back.
Yes, no, maybe so.
Clap five times.

My Bicycle

One wheel, two wheels on the ground;
Revolve hand in forward circle to form each wheel.

My feet make the pedals go round and round.
Move feet in pedaling motion.

Handle bars help me steer so straight,
Pretend to steer bicycle.

Down the sidewalk, through the gate.

Riding

Suit actions to words.

Riding in a train I go,
Rocking, rocking, to and fro,
Side to side and to and fro,
Riding in a train I go.

In an aeroplane I fly,
Up, up, up, into the sky,
Up, up, up, so very high,
In an aeroplane I fly.

Riding on my bike today,
Pedal, pedal, all the way,
Pedal fast and pedal slow,
Riding on my bike I go.

SONGS

Row Row Row Your Boat

Row, row, row your boat,
Gently down the stream.
Merrily, merrily, merrily, merrily,
Life is but a dream.

Down by the Station

Stand up and march to the beat. Listen to the tune on Sharon, Lois & Bram's cassette Great Big Hits. *Music is in* Elephant Jam.

Down by the station, early in the morning.
See the little puffer-bellies
All in a row.
Point to imaginary engines standing in a row.

Hear the station master
Shouting, "All aboard now!"
Cup hands to mouth.

Chug! Chug! Toot! Toot!
Bend elbows and chug. Pull the whistle.

Off we go.

The Wheels on the Bus

Act it out! Or sing it using one of the picture books. Listen to the tune on Raffi's Rise and Shine *cassette. Music is in* The Second Raffi Songbook.

The wheels on the bus go round and round,
Round and round, round and round.
The wheels on the bus go round and round
All around the town.

The people on the bus go up and down . . .
The wipers on the bus go swish, swish, swish . . .
The horn on the bus goes beep, beep, beep . . . .
The money on the bus goes plink, plink, plink . . .
The lights on the bus go on, off, on . . .
The babies on the bus go, "Waa, waa, waa," . . .
The mothers on the bus go, "Shh, shh, shh," . . .
The driver on the bus says, "Move on back," . . .
The driver on the bus says, "Move up front," . . .
The doors on the bus go open and shut . . .
The wheels on the bus . . .

My Big Blue Boat

On the first and third verses, pretend to row. On the second verse, raise arms above head and wave gently like sails. Two children can sit facing each other holding hands and pulling back and forth.

I love to ride in my big blue boat,
My big blue boat, my big blue boat;
I love to ride in my big blue boat,
Out on the deep blue sea.

My big blue boat has two red sails,
Two red sails, two red sails;
My big blue boat has two red sails,
Two red sails.

So come for a ride in my big blue boat,
My big blue boat, my big blue boat;
So come for a ride in my big blue boat,
Out on the deep blue sea.

My Little Red Wagon

All sit in a circle, legs stretched in toward centre. Bounce up and down on bottoms. Listen to the tune on Raffi's Singable Songs for the Very Young *cassette. Music is in* The Raffi Singable Songbook.

Bumping up and down in my little red wagon.
Bumping up and down in my little red wagon.
Bumping up and down in my little red wagon.
Won't you be my darlin!

One wheel's off and the axle's broken. . .
Freddie's gonna fix it with his hammer . . .
Laura's gonna fix it with her pliers . . .
Bumping up and down in my little red wagon . . .

I've Been Workin on the Railroad

Listen to the music on Raffi's More Singable Songs *cassette. Words and music are in* The Raffi Singable Songbook.

I've been working on the railroad,
All the live-long day.
I've been working on the railroad,
Just to pass the time away.
Can't you hear the whistle blowing,
Rise up so early in the morn,
Can't you hear the captain shouting,
"Dinah, blow your horn."

Dinah, won't you blow,
Dinah, won't you blow,
Dinah, won't you blow your horn?
Dinah, won't you blow,
Dinah, won't you blow,
Dinah, won't you blow you horn.

Someone's in the kitchen with Dinah,
Someone's in the kitchen, I know,
Someone's in the kitchen with Dinah,
Strummin' on the old banjo.

Singing
Fee-fi-fiddle-ee-i-o,
Fee-fi-fiddle-ee-i-o-o-o-o,
Fee-fi-fiddle-ee-i-o,
Strummin' on the old banjo.

Michael Rowed the Boat Ashore

Listen to the tune on Raffi's Bananaphone *cassette.*

Chorus: Repeat between verses:
Michael row the boat ashore, hallelujah,
Michael row the boat ashore, hallelujah.

Sister help to trim the sail, hallelujah,
Sister help to trim the sail, hallelujah.

The River Jordan is chilly and cold, hallelujah,
Chills the body but not the soul, hallelujah.

Jordan's river is deep and wide, hallelujah,
Milk and honey on the other side, hallelujah.

GAME

Ring Around the Rocket Ship

Play this version of "Ring Around the Rosie." All join hands in a circle and slide to the right. Reach up high for a star, and fall to the floor. Repeat verse sliding to the left.

Ring around the rocket ship,
Reach for a star,
Stardust, stardust,
Fall where you are.

MORE IDEAS

1. Felt Stories: "My Little Red Wagon," *Mr. Gumpy's Outing* and *Mr. Gumpy's Motor Car.* Use the same animals for the Mr. Gumpys, if you like. All you need then is an extra long boat and an extra big car and you have two felt stories.

2. Going places? Sing "She Sailed Away" (page 134). Go for a ride on a giant cat with *The Big Pets* by Lane Smith. Tell *The Gingerbread Man* and go for a ride on a fox's back. Tell "The Rainhat" (see reference in WEATHER – RAINY DAY) and go for a ride in a boat you can make yourself.

3. Sing "This Train." This African-American spiritual is a classic and unforgettable tune, and it's easy to bring to life on the felt board. All you need is a train, a bike, a car, a plane and a boat. Alternately, props can be children's toys. See adapted words and music in Tom Glazer's *Eye Winker, Tom Tinker, Chin Chopper.*

4. Sing "She'll Be Comin' Round the Mountain," one of the first American railway songs (page 162).

Valentine's Day

STORIES TO READ ALOUD

Traveling to Tondo
AARDEMA, VERNA

The Princess and the Pea
ANDERSON, H. C. (ILLS. BY GALDONE)

Valentine Bears
BUNTING, EVE

Anancy and Mr. Dry-Bone
FRENCH, FIONA

I Love You Mouse
GRAHAM, JOHN

The Pig's Wedding
HEINE, HELME

Jake Baked the Cake
HENNESSY, B.G.

Little Mouse's Big Valentine
HURD, THACHER

The Tale of Fancy Nancy
KOENIG, MARION

Brenda and Edward
KOVALSKI, MARYANN

Frog Went A-Courtin'
LANGSTAFF, JOHN

The Owl and the Pussycat
LEAR, EDWARD

Just for You
MAYER, MERCER

The Paper Bag Princess
MUNSCH, ROBERT

The Wedding Procession of the Rag Doll and the Broom Handle and Who Was in it
SANDBURG, CARL

Red Is Best
STINSON, KATHY

Do You Know What I'll Do?
ZOLOTOW, CHARLOTTE

MORE STORIES

Arthur's Valentine
BROWN, MARC

"Bee My Valentine!"
COHEN, MIRIAM

Cranberry Valentine
DEVLIN, WENDE

A Kiss for Little Bear
MINARIK, ELSE

Little Mouse's Valentine
ROSS, DAVE

The Best Valentine in the World Holiday
SHARMAT, MARJORIE

Happy Valentine's Day, Emma!
STEVENSON, JAMES

Caleb and Kate
STEIG, WILLIAM

Tiffky Doofky
STEIG, WILLIAM

Hug Me
STREN, PATTI

NONFICTION

Things to Make and Do for Valentine's Day
DE PAOLA, TOMIE

Valentine's Day
GIBBONS, GAIL

Valentine's Day: Things to Make and Do
SUPRANER, ROBYN

NURSERY RHYMES

The Queen of Hearts

The Queen of Hearts made some tarts,
All on a summer's day;
The Knave of Hearts stole those tarts
And took them far away.
The King of Hearts called for the tarts,
And beat the Knave full sore;
The Knave of Hearts returned the tarts,
And vowed he'd steal no more.

Hey Diddle, Diddle

Hey, diddle, diddle,
The cat and the fiddle,
The cow jumped over the moon.
The little dog laughed to see such sport,
And the dish ran away with the spoon.

Georgie Porgie

Georgie Porgie, pudding and pie,
Kissed the girls and made them cry;
When the boys came out to play,
Georgie Porgie ran away.

Bobby Shafto

Bobby Shafto's gone to sea,
Silver buckles on his knee.
He'll come back and marry me,
Bonny Bobby Shafto.

Bobby Shafto's bright and fair,
Combing down his yellow hair.
He's my love for evermore,
Bonny Bobby Shafto.

Bobby Shafto's gone to sea,
Silver buckles on his knee.
He'll come back and marry me,
Bonny Bobby Shafto.

Little Miss Dimble

From Dennis Lee's Jelly Belly.

Little Miss Dimble
Lived in a thimble
Slept in a measuring spoon.
She met a mosquito
And called him, "My Sweet-o,"
And married him under the moon.

FINGERPLAYS

Five Little Valentines

This one is nice with valentines on a glove puppet or on the felt board.

Five little valentines were having a race.
The first little valentine was frilly with lace.
The second little valentine had a funny face.
The third little valentine said, "I love you."
The fourth little valentine said, "I do, too."
The fifth little valentine was sly as a fox.
She ran the fastest to your valentine box.

How Many Valentines?

Valentines, valentines;
How many do you see?
Valentines, valentines;
Can you count them with me?
One for father,
Hold up thumb.
One for mother,
Pointer finger.
One for grandma, too
Hold up middle finger.
One for sister,
Ring finger.
One for brother,
Little finger.
And here is one for you!
Make heart shape with thumbs and pointer fingers.

Five Gay Valentines

Use a glove puppet with five coloured valentines, or hold up five fingers and bend down one by one as the verse progresses.

Five gay valentines from the ten-cent store.
I sent one to mother, now there are four.
Four gay valentines, pretty ones to see.
I gave one to brother, now there are three.
Three gay valentines, yellow, red and blue.
I gave one to sister, now there are two.
Two gay valentines, my we have fun.
I gave one to daddy, now there is one.
One gay valentine, the story is almost done.
I gave it to baby, now there are none.

What Color Are You Wearing?

Suit actions to words. Repeat until most of the common colours are used.

Leader says:
Red, red, red, red,
Who is wearing red today?
Red, red, red, red,
Who is wearing red?

All children with red showing say:
I am wearing red today.
Look at me and you will say
Red, red, red, red,
I am wearing red.

POEMS

Roses Are Red

Roses are red
Violets are blue
Honey is sweet
And so are you.

Good Morrow 'tis St. Valentine's Day

Shakespeare

Good morrow 'tis St. Valentine's Day
All in the morning time
And I a maid at your window
To be your valentine.

SONGS

If You're Wearing Red Today

Sing to the tune of "Mary Had a Little Lamb." Add more colours. When all are standing up, form a circle and play a circle game.

If you're wearing red today,
Red today, red today,
If you're wearing red today,
Please stand up.

Mary Wore Her Red Dress

This is very nice after Red Is Best. *Listen to the tune of this lovely simple song on Raffi's* Everything Grows *cassette. Words and music are in* The Raffi Everything Grows Songbook.

Mary wore her red dress, red dress, red dress,
Mary wore her red dress all day long.

Mary wore her red hat . . . all day long.
Mary wore her red shoes . . . all day long.
Mary wore her red gloves . . . all day long.
Mary was a red bird . . . all day long.
Mary wore her red dress . . . all day long.

Whistle or hum a verse.

Skinnamarink

Listen to the tune of this wildly popular song on Sharon, Lois & Bram's Great Big Hits *cassette. Music is in* Elephant Jam.

Skinnamarinky dinky dink,
Place right elbow in left hand and wave fingers of right hand.
Skinnamarinky doo,
Switch to left elbow in right hand.
I
Point to eye.
love
Place both hands on heart and flutter.
you!
Point to the audience.
Skinnamarinky dinky dink,
Repeat actions.
Skinnamarinky doo,
I . . . love . . . you.
I love you in the morning,
Clasp hands at knee level for the sun in the morning, and sway in rhythm.
And in the afternoon,
Raise clasped hands to waist level.
I love you in the evening
Raise clasped hands high overhead.
Underneath the moon.
Swing arms open for the moon.
Skinnamarinky dinky dink,
Repeat actions of first verse.
Skinnamarinky doo,
I . . . love . . . you.

Fiddle-Dee-Dee

Ask children to join in on the refrain of this delightful song after each verse. Fly and bee finger puppets are nice. For music, see Lullabies and Night Songs *by Wilder.*

Chorus:
Fiddle-dee-dee, Fiddle-dee-dee,
The fly has married the bumble bee.

Says the fly, says he, "Will you marry me
And live with me, sweet bumble bee?"
    Chorus.

Says the bee, says she, "I'll live under your wing,
And you'll never know that I carry a sting."
    Chorus.

So when the parson had joined the pair,
They both went out to take the air.
    Chorus.

And the fly did buzz and the bells did ring,
Did you ever hear so merry a thing?
    Chorus.

And then to think that of all the flies,
The humble bee should carry the prize.

Mail Myself to You

Listen to Fred Penner's adaptation of this Woody Guthrie song on Penner's cassette Special Delivery. *Words and music are in* Fred Penner's Sing Along Play Along Song and Activity Book.

I'm gonna wrap myself in paper;
I'm gonna dab myself with glue.
Stick some stamps on top of my head;
I'm gonna mail myself to you.

I'm gonna tie me up in a red string;
I'm gonna tie blue ribbons, too.
I'm gonna climb up in my mail box;
I'm gonna mail myself to you.

When you see me in your mail box,
Cut the string and let me out.
Wash the glue off my fingers;
Stick some bubble-gum in my mouth.

Take me out of my wrapping paper;
Wash the stamps off my head.
Pour me full of ice cream sodies,
Put me in my nice warm bed.

Lavender's Blue

Listen to the tune on Sharon, Lois & Bram's Mainly Mother Goose *cassette.*

Lavender's blue, dilly, dilly,
Lavender's green;
When I am king, dilly, dilly,
You shall be queen.

Call up your men, dilly, dilly,
Set them to work,
Some to the plough, dilly, dilly,
Some to the cart.

Some to make hay, dilly, dilly,
Some to thresh corn,
Whilst you and I, dilly, dilly,
Keep ourselves warm.

Lavender's green, dilly, dilly,
Lavender's blue;
If you love me, dilly, dilly,
I will love you.

Call up your maids, dilly, dilly,
Set them to work,
Some to the wheel, dilly, dilly,
Some to the rock.

Let the birds sing, dilly, dilly,
Let the lambs play;
Whilst you and I, dilly, dilly,
Stay out of harm's way.

Rig-A-Jig-Jig

Listen to this tune on Bob McGrath's Sing Along with Bob, Vol. Two. *For music, see* Singing Bee. *Stand in a circle to sing the middle verse. Skip in a circle with partners to rig-a-jig-jig.*

Rig-a-jig-jig and away we go,

'Way we go, 'way we go;
Rig-a-jig-jig and away we go,
Heigh-ho, heigh-ho, heigh-ho!

As I was walking down the street,
Down the street, down the street,
A pretty girl (boy) I chanced to meet,
Heigh-ho, heigh-ho, heigh-ho!

Rig-a-jig-jig and away we go,
'Way we go, 'way we go;
Rig-a-jig-jig and away we go,
Heigh-ho, heigh-ho, heigh-ho!

Billy Boy

See music in Singing Bee.

Oh where have you been, Billy Boy, Billy Boy?
Oh where have you been, charming Billy?
I have been to seek a wife, she's the joy of my life,
She's a young thing and cannot leave her mother.

Did she ask you to come in, Billy Boy, Billy Boy?
Did she ask you to come in, charming Billy?
Yes, she asked me to come in,
There's a dimple in her chin,
She's a young thing and cannot leave her mother.

Can she make a cherry pie, Billy Boy, Billy Boy?
Can she make a cherry pie, charming Billy?
She can make a cherry pie,
Quick as a cat can wink its eye,
She's a young thing and cannot leave her mother.

How old is she, Billy Boy, Billy Boy?
How old is she, charming Billy?
Three times six and three times seven
Twenty-eight and eleven,
She's a young thing and cannot leave her mother.

Frog Went A-Courtin'

Frog went a courtin', he did ride, ah-hum, ah-hum.
Frog went a courtin', he did ride.
With a sword and pistol by his side, ah-hum,
  ah-hum, ah-hum.

He rode up to Miss Mousie's den, ah-hum, ah-hum.
He rode up to Miss Mousie's den
Said, "Please, Miss Mousie, are you within,"
  ah-hum, ah-hum, ah-hum.

"Yes, Sir Frog, I sit and spin," ah-hum, ah-hum.
"Yes, Sir Frog, I sit and spin.
Please, Mister Froggie, won't you come on in?"
  ah-hum, ah-hum, ah-hum.

The Froggie said, "I've come to see," ah-hum,
  ah-hum.
The Froggie said, "I've come to see,
If you Miss Mousie will marry me," ah-hum,
  ah-hum, ah-hum.

"Oh yes, Sir Frog, I'll Marry you," ah-hum,
  ah-hum.
"Oh yes, Sir Frog, I'll Marry you,
And we'll have children two by two," ah-hum,
  ah-hum, ah-hum.

The frog and the mouse they went to France,
  ah-hum, ah-hum.
The frog and the mouse they went to France,
And that's the end of my romance, ah-hum,
  ah-hum, ah-hum.

You Are My Sunshine

Listen to the tune of this old favourite on Bob
McGrath's cassette Sing Along with Bob, Vol.
Two.

You are my sunshine,
My only sunshine,
You make me happy when skies are grey.
You'll never know, dear,
How much I love you.
Please don't take my sunshine away.

The other night, dear,
As I lay sleeping,
I dreamed I held you in my arms.
But when I woke, dear,
I was mistaken,
And I hung my head and I cried.

Repeat first verse.

CIRCLE GAMES

Little Sally Waters

For music see Singing Bee. *Listen to Sharon, Lois*
& Bram's version on their Smorgasbord *cassette.*
See music in Elephant Jam. *Or, listen to the tune*
on the cassette that goes with Shake It to the One
That You Love the Best *by Cheryl Warren-*
Mattox.

Little Sally Waters, sitting in the sun,
Crying and weeping, lonesome little one.
Rise, Sally, rise; wipe off your eyes;
Fly to the East, Sally
Fly to the West, Sally,
Fly to the one you love the very best.

One child sits in the middle of the ring pretending to
weep while others circle around and sing. She rises, flies
to the east and then to the west, and then to her very
best friend. Repeat until everyone has had a turn as
Sally Waters.

Skip to My Lou

A circle game to play or sing and clap to. Listen to the tune on Sharon, Lois & Bram's cassette, Mainly Mother Goose.

Chorus: Repeat between verses:
Skip, skip, skip to my Lou,
Skip, skip, skip to my Lou,
Skip, skip, skip to my Lou,
Skip, skip, skip to my Lou, my Darling!

Verses:
Lost my partner, what'll I do?
Lost my partner, what'll I do?
Lost my partner, what'll I do?
Skip, skip, skip to my Lou, my Darling!

I'll find another one, prettier, too,
I'll find another one, prettier, too,
I'll find another one, prettier, too,
Skip, skip, skip to my Lou, my Darling!

Can't get a red bird, blue bird'll do,
Can't get a red bird, blue bird'll do,
Can't get a red bird, blue bird'll do,
Skip, skip, skip to my Lou, my Darling!

Flies in the buttermilk, shoo, fly, shoo,
Flies in the buttermilk, shoo, fly, shoo,
Flies in the buttermilk, shoo, fly, shoo,
Skip, skip, skip to my Lou, my Darling!

Children stand with partners in a circle, one child in the centre. All sing and clap. On "Lost my partner," the child in the centre chooses a partner from the circle and the two skip around outside the circle together. Others clap in time. All skip around to the left on the chorus. The child who lost his partner stands in the centre of the ring, chooses another one on "I'll get another one," and takes his turn skipping around the outside of the circle. Continue until all the children have had a turn in the centre of the ring.

A Tisket, a Tasket

For this circle game that extends the Valentine letter idea, see DOGS, page 68.

MORE IDEAS

1. Felt Stories: *I Love You Mouse, The Owl and the Pussycat, Hug Me,* and *A Kiss for Little Bear.*

2. Tell "The Elegant Rooster," from Judy Sierra's *Multicultural Folktales.* A rooster gets his beak dirty on his way to a friend's wedding and has a terrible time getting it clean again. Felt patterns are in the book.

3. Cut and tell "A Valentine for Kitten" or "Six Little Girls and One Valentine" from *Paper Stories* by Jean Stangl.

4. Tell and draw "Claudette's Valentines" from Richard Thompson's *Frog's Riddle and Other Draw-and-Tell Stories.*

5. Puppetry: *Hug Me* makes a nice short puppet show. Use fuzzy fabric for porcupine puppets. Other stories that adapt well to the stage on Valentine's Day are: "The Kiss" from *George and Martha* by James Marshall (two hippos); "The Letter" and "Cookies" from *Frog and Toad* by Arnold Lobel; *A Kiss for Little Bear* by Else Minarik; and *Happy Valentine's Day, Emma* by James Stevenson.

6. Teach children to say "I love you" in sign, and substitute these actions when you sing "Skinnamarink." A wonderful little poem to go along with this that is especially appropriate for older children is "Deaf Donald" by Shel Silverstein in *Where the Sidewalk Ends.*

7. If you play the recorder, now would be a good time to take it to storytime. Set the mood with the Friendly Giant's theme song, "Early One Morning," or with "Greensleeves."

8. Sing "A You're Adorable," Sharon, Lois & Bram's lovable alphabet song. Listen to the tune on their *Great Big Hits* cassette.

9. Give children little valentine treats: dime store cards, little red hearts, or valentine-shaped balloons.

10. Make valentine cookies to take to storytime for this special occasion.

Rainy Day

STORIES TO READ ALOUD

Bringing the Rain to Kapiti Plain
AARDEMA, VERNA

Big Sarah's Little Boots
BOURGEOIS, PAULETTE

Mr. Gumpy's Motor Car
BURNINGHAM, JOHN

Rainy Day Magic
GAY, MARIE-LOUISE

Mushroom in the Rain
GINSBURG, MIRRA

Rain Puddle
HOLL, ADELAIDE

Muddigush
KNUTSON, KIMBERLY

It's Going to Rain
LITCHFIELD, ADA

The Mud Puddle
MUNSCH, ROBERT

Piggy in the Puddle
POMERANTZ, CHARLOTTE

Rain Makes Applesauce
SCHEER, JULIAN

April Showers
SHANNON, GEORGE

It Looked Like Spilt Milk
SHAW, CHARLES

Wet World
SIMON, NORMA

The Lady Who Saw the Good Side of Everything
TAPIO, PAT DECKER

MORE STORIES

November Boots
HUNDAL, NANCY

Listen to the Rain
MARTIN, BILL

A Walk in the Rain
SCHEFFTER, UNSEL

Rain Rain Rivers
SHULEVITZ, URI

Peter Spier's Rain
SPIER, PETER

Rain Drop Splash
TRESSELT, ALVIN

Umbrella
YASHIMA, TARO

The Storm Book
ZOLOTOW, CHARLOTTE

NURSERY RHYMES

Doctor Foster

Doctor Foster went to Gloucester
In a shower of rain,
He stepped in a puddle
Right up to his middle
And never went there again.

It's Raining, It's Pouring

It's raining, it's pouring,
The old man is snoring.
He fell out of bed and bumped his head
And couldn't get up in the morning!

One Misty, Moisty Morning

Use two thumbs for this conversation.

One misty, moisty morning,
When cloudy was the weather,
I chanced to meet an old man
Clothed all in leather.
He began to compliment,
And I began to grin,
How do you do, and how do you do,
And how do you do again?

FINGERPLAYS

Falling Raindrops

Raindrops, raindrops,
Falling all around.
> *Flutter fingers down to imitate falling rain.*

Pitter-patter on the rooftops,
> *Flutter up high.*

Pitter-patter on the ground.
> *Flutter down to the floor.*

Here is my umbrella.
> *Cup hand over index finger.*

It will keep me dry.
When I go walking in the rain,
> *Hold it over head.*

I hold it up so high.
> *Hold it high in air.*

Rain

The storm came up so very quick,
It couldn't have been quicker.
I should have brought my hat along,
> *Place flat palm on top of head.*

I should have brought my slicker.
> *Indicate slicker.*

My hair is wet, my feet are wet,
> *Point to head and feet.*

I couldn't be much wetter.
I fell into a river once,
But this is even wetter.

I Hear Thunder

Sing to the tune of "Frère Jacques."

I hear thunder,
I hear thunder,
> *Drum with hands or feet.*

Hark, don't you?
Hark, don't you?
> *Hand behind ear to listen.*

Pitter, patter raindrops,
Pitter, patter raindrops,
> *Flutter hands down.*

I'm wet through.
I'm wet through.
> *Shake hands.*

I see blue skies,
I see blue skies,
> *Look up to the sky.*

Way up high.
Way up high.
> *Reach way up high.*

Hurry up the sunshine,
Hurry up the sunshine,
> *Roll hands in front of chest.*

I'll soon dry.
I'll soon dry.
> *Sweep hands back and forth to dry.*

Clouds

What's fluffy-white
> *Look toward sky and point finger.*

And floats up high
Like piles of ice cream
In the sky?
And when the wind
Blows hard and strong,
> *Sway arms back and forth.*

What very gently floats along?
What brings the rain?
> *Raise arms high, flutter fingers to the ground.*

What brings the snow,
That showers down on us below?
What seems to have just lots of fun
Peek-a-booing with the sun?
> *Place hand over eyes with fingers spread and peek through.*

When you look in the high, blue sky,
What are those things you see floating by?

April Trickery

The big round sun
In an April sky,
Form a circle with fingers of both hand.

Winked at a cloud
That was passing by.
Raise arms to form large circle over head.

The gray cloud laughed
As it scattered rain.
Pretend to scatter rain with fingers.

Then out came the big
Round sun again.
Form circle with fingers of both hands.

Rainy Day Fun

Suit actions to words.

Slip on your raincoat,
Pull on galoshes;
Wading in puddles
Make splishes and sploshes!

Rain

Rain on the green grass,
Flutter fingers up and down.

And rain on the tree,
Raise both hands to form tree.

Rain on the roof top,
Touch fingertips above head to form roof.

But not on me.
Point to self and shake head.

Storm

Black clouds are giants hurrying
Across the field of the sky.
Make circle with arms and move quickly across the room.

And they slip out bolts of lightning
As they go racing by.
Flash arms up and out.

When they meet each other
They shake hands and thunder
Pretend to shake hands.

How do you do! How do you do!
HOW DO YOU DO!
In a thunderous voice.

Eensy, Weensy Spider

Eensy weensy spider
Climbed up the water-spout;
Thumbs and pointer fingers climb up each other.

Down came the rain
Raise hands and lower wriggling fingers.

And washed the spider out;
Sweep arms out to the side.

Out came the sunshine
Raise hands above head and form circle.

And dried up all the rain;
And eensy weensy spider
Climbed up the spout again.
Repeat climbing motion.

SONGS

Rain Rain Go Away

Substitute children's names for 'Johnny,' or just say 'I want to go out and play.'

Rain rain go away
Come again another day.
Rain rain go away
Little Johnny wants to play.

Rain Is Falling Down

Rain is falling down,
Raise hands up high and flutter fingers down.

Splash!
Slap the floor with gusto.

Rain is falling down,
Hands up high and flutter fingers down again.

Splash!
Slap the floor.

Pitter patter, pitter patter,
Quietly. Flutter fingers delicately.

Rain is falling down,
Flutter fingers down.

Splash!
Slap the floor with gusto.

Mr. Sun

Listen to the tune on Raffi's Singable Songs for the Very Young cassette. Words and music are in The Raffi Singable Songbook.

Oh Mister Sun, Sun, Mister Golden Sun,
Please shine down on me.
Oh Mr. Sun, Sun, Mister Golden Sun,
Hiding behind a tree.
These little children are asking you
To please come out so we can play with you.
Oh Mister Sun, Sun, Mister Golden Sun,
Please shine down on me.

Whistle for the second verse.
Sing a verse for Mr. Moon.
Repeat Mister Sun for the last verse.

Row, Row, Row Your Boat

Get into boats, very carefully, and row together.

Row, row, row your boat,
Gently down the stream.
Merrily, merrily, merrily, merrily,
Life is but a dream.

MORE IDEAS

1. Felt Stories: *Mr. Gumpy's Motor Car, Mushroom in the Rain*, and the classic, *It Looked Like Spilt Milk*.

2. Tell "The Rainhat" from *Just Enough to Make a Story* by Nancy Schimmel. After this story, hand out newsprint and teach the children how to make rainhats of their own.

3. *The Mud Puddle* by Robert Munsch is easy to learn, fun to tell with sound effects, and the children love to join in on the repetition with Jule Ann. You can hear the story the way Munsch tells it on his cassette *Munsch Favourite Stories* (Toronto, ON: Kids' Records, 1983. Distributed by A&M Records of Canada.)

4. Act out *Mushroom in the Rain* with a big umbrella. The storyteller holds the mushroom umbrella while the kids come under as various animals. Simple animal masks can make the play even more elaborate. Use paper headbands with animal ears glued on, or use animal snouts.

5. For another rainy day song with a lovely tune, sing "Listen to the Water" on Charlotte Diamond's cassette *My Bear Gruff* (Vancouver, BC: Hug Bug Records, 1992). Cup hand to ear as you listen to the water, and roll hands on "rollin' down the river."

6. See related songs and rhymes in SEA & SEASHORE.

Snowy Day

STORIES TO READ ALOUD

Annie and the Wild Animals
BRETT, JAN

The Mitten
BRETT, JAN

Take Time to Relax!
CARLSON, NANCY

Stopping by Woods on a Snowy Evening
(poetry)
FROST, ROBERT

Snowfeather
GAGNON, CECILE

The Runaway Giant
HOLL, ADELAIDE

The Snowy Day
KEATS, EZRA JACK

Geraldine's Big Snow
KELLER, HOLLY

Round Robin
KENT, JACK

Froggy Gets Dressed
LONDON, JONATHAN

Sadie and the Snowman
MORGAN, ALLEN

Thomas's Snowsuit
MUNSCH, ROBERT

50 Below Zero
MUNSCH, ROBERT

White Bear, Ice Bear
RYDER, JOANNE

The Mitten
TRESSELT, ALVIN

Has Winter Come?
WATSON, WENDY

MORE STORIES

Katy and the Big Snow
BURTON, VIRGINIA LEE

Snowman
BRIGGS, RAYMOND

The Snow Lady
HUGHES, SHIRLEY

Geraldine's Big Snow
KELLER, HOLLY

The Snow Cat
KHALSA, DAYAL KAUR

First Snow
McCULLY, EMILY ARNOLD

*"What Will Little Bear Wear?" in *Little Bear*
MINARIK, ELSE

The First Snowfall
ROCKWELL, ANNE

Brave Irene
STEIG, WILLIAM

Sledding
WINTHROP, ELIZABETH

Something Is Going to Happen
ZOLOTOW, CHARLOTTE

NURSERY RHYMES

The Cold Wind Doth Blow

The cold wind doth blow
And we shall have snow
And what will the robin do then?
Poor thing.
He'll sit in a barn,
And keep himself warm,
And hide his head under his wing,
Poor thing.

Three Little Kittens

Make two-sided finger puppets, one side without mittens, one side with, and turn the kittens around for the second verse. See complete version in CATS & KITTENS, page 40.

Three little kittens lost their mittens
And they began to cry.
Oh Mother, dear, see here, see here,
Our mittens we have lost.
What! Lost your mittens you naughty kittens
Now you shall have no pie.

Three little kittens found their mittens
And they began to sigh.
Oh Mother, dear, see here, see here,
Our mittens we have found.
What! Found your mittens you darling kittens.
Now you shall have some pie.
Meow, meow, meow, meow,
Now you shall have some pie.

FINGERPLAYS

Dressing for Winter Weather

Let's put on our mittens
Put on mittens.

And button up our coat.
Button coat.

Wrap a scarf snugly
Throw scarf around neck.

Around our throat.
Tug one end of the scarf down.

Pull on our boots,
Pull on boots with both hands.

Fasten the straps,
Fasten straps with fingers.

And tie on tightly
Our warm winter caps.
Pull on cap with both hands and tie.

Then open the door
*Turn imaginary doorknob, and pull open the door.
Step through.*

And out we go
Into the soft and feathery snow.
Hold out hands to catch snow and look up.

The Snow Fell Softly

This one sets a nice mood for Stopping by Woods on a Snowy Evening.

The snow fell softly all the night,
Flutter fingers in a downward motion.

It made a blanket soft and white.
Spread out the blanket.

It covered houses, flowers and ground,
Make a house with a pointed roof, ten fingers up for flowers, and lay hands flat for the ground.

But never made a single sound.
Whisper.

The Mitten Song

"Thumb in the thumb place
Hold up one hand, fingers together, thumb apart,

Fingers all together!"
This is the song we sing in mitten weather.
When it's cold
Rub hands together.

It doesn't matter whether
Mittens are wool
Or made of finest leather.
Hold up two hands, fingers together, thumb apart.

This is the song we sing in mitten weather,
"Thumb in thumb place
Repeat action.

Fingers all together!"

Let's Go Walking in the Snow

Let's go walking in the snow
Walk.

Walking, walking on tiptoe.
Walk on tiptoe.

Lift your one foot way up high
Hop on one foot.

Then the other to keep it dry.
Change feet.

All around the yard we skip
Skip in circle.

Watch your step or you might slip.
All fall down.

Lying on Things

From Dennis Lee's Alligator Pie.

After it snows
I go and lie on things.
I lie on my back
And make snow-angel wings.
I lie on my front
And powderpuff my nose.
I always lie on things
Right after it snows.

Let's Make a Snowman

Start with a very tiny snowball,
Form a fist.

And roll it through the snow.
Roll hands.

Over and over and over again,
Each turn makes it grow.
*Pretend you're pushing a big ball through the
snow.*

Now the ball is big and round,
Make ball with arms.

Make it broad and tall.
Make it bigger and taller.

Add a head and then some arms,
Set on the head and pack on the arms.

Firm so they won't fall.
Now we'll be the snowmen!
Here are buttons for his coat,
Place buttons on.

A broom for him to hold.
Pretend to hold a broom.

Let's put a hat upon his head,
Pretend to put a hat on your head.

So he won't get cold.
Pose as a cold stiff snowman.

I Am a Snowman

Now I am a snowman
Stand with arms out.

Standing on the lawn.
I melt and melt and melt
And pretty soon I'm gone.
Body slumps and voice fades.

Five Little Snowmen

*Hold up five fingers. Bend down one at a time. Use
fingers or snowmen finger puppets. Children can
stand up and melt to the floor with each snowman.*

Five little snowmen all made of snow,
Five little snowmen standing in a row.
Out came the sun and stayed all day,
And one little snowman melted away.

Four little snowmen . . .
Three little snowmen . . .
Two little snowmen . . .

One little snowman made of snow
One little snowman left in the row
Out came the sun and stayed all day
And the last little snowman melted away.

Five Little Snowmen

Use fingers or snowmen finger puppets.

Five little snowmen happy and gay,
The first one said, "What a lovely day."
The second one said, "We'll never have tears."
The third one said, "We'll stay for years."
The fourth one said, "But what happens in May?"
The fifth one said, "Look! We're melting away."

Chubby Little Snowman

A chubby little snowman
*Make a fist with left hand and draw circles around it
with right index finger.*

Had a carrot nose.
Make thumb stick out through fingers.

Along came a bunny
Make a bunny with two fingers of right hand.

And what do you suppose?
That hungry little bunny
Looking for his lunch,
Bunny hops along.

Ate that little snowman's nose
Make thumb disappear.

Nibble, nibble, crunch.
Bunny crunches.

Snowflakes

Flutter fingers high in the air, slowly falling to the ground. Sing to the tune of "Merrily We Roll Along," or "Mary Had a Little Lamb."

Snowflakes whirling all around,
All around, all around,
Snowflakes whirling all around,
Until they cover all the ground.

Snow Men

Five little snow men
Hold up five fingers.

Standing in a row,
Each with a hat
Join thumbs and index fingers and place on top of head.

And a big red bow.
Join thumbs and index fingers together to make bow under chin.

Five little snowmen
Hold up five fingers.

Dressed for a show,
Now they are ready,
Where will they go?
Wait till the sun shines;
Make circle with arms above head.

Soon they will go
Down through the fields
Bring arms down to lap.

With the melting snow.

SONG

Frosty the Snowman

Listen to the tune on Raffi's Christmas Album.

Frosty the Snowman, was a jolly happy soul,
With a corncob pipe and a button nose,
And two eyes made out of coal.
Frosty the Snowman, was a fairy tale they say,
He was made of snow but the children know,
How he came to life one day.
There must have been some magic in,
That old silk hat they found.
For when they placed it on his head he began to
    dance around.

Frosty the Snowman, was alive as he could be,
And the children say he could laugh and play,
Just the same as you and me.
He led them down the streets of town,
Right to the traffic cop,
And he only paused a moment when he heard
    him holler STOP!

For Frosty the Snowman, had to hurry on his way,
But he waved goodbye saying don't you cry,
I'll be back again some day.
Thumpety thump bump,
Thumpety thump bump,
Look at Frosty go.
Thumpety thump bump,
Thumpety thump bump.
Over the hills of snow.

MORE IDEAS

1. Felt Stories: *It Looked Like Spilt Milk, The Mitten,* and the entire version of *The Three Little Kittens* —wash tub, clothesline, and all!

CRAFT IDEAS

1. Make snow pictures. Using dark coloured construction paper for the background, have children draw snow scenes using chalk. Glue on cotton balls.

2. Make *Snowfeather* with chalk on blue construction paper. Glue on pieces of red wool for his mouth.

3. Make all kinds of snowmen. Prepare variously-sized circles of heavy white construction paper, and lots of decorating supplies: black felt hats, coloured feathers, orange carrot shapes for noses, black bits for eyes and buttons. Decorate with glue. Each snowman will be unique.

4. Make popcorn snowmen. Use heavy construction paper to cut out snowmen shapes. Apply glue to the whole surface and sprinkle on the popcorn. Use raisins and bits of candied fruit for eyes, nose, mouth and buttons. Snack as you create!

5. Make snowy day pictures à la Ezra Jack Keats with potato prints: blue paint on white paper, or white paint on blue paper.

Windy Day

STORIES TO READ ALOUD

My Red Umbrella
BRIGHT, ROBERT

Gilberto and the Wind
ETS, MARIE HALLS

Mrs. Mopple's Washing Line
HEWETT, ANITA

The Wind Blew
HUTCHINS, PAT

Too Much Noise
McGOVERN, ANN

Millicent and the Wind
MUNSCH, ROBERT

Who Took the Farmer's Hat?
NODSET, JOAN

MORE STORIES

Follow That Hat
PRATT, PIERRE

Brave Irene
STEIG, WILLIAM

Simon and the Wind
TIBO, GILES

NURSERY RHYMES

The Cold Wind

The cold wind doth blow,
And we shall have snow,
And what will the robin do then?
Poor thing.
He'll sit in the barn
And keep himself warm,
And hide his head under his wing.
Poor thing!

FINGERPLAYS

When Cold Winds Blow

When cold winds blow,
 Blow.
And bring us snow,
 Flutter fingers.
At night what I like most,
 Point to self.
Is to climb in bed,
 Pretend to climb in bed.
And hide my head,
 Hands over eyes.
And sleep as warm as toast.
 Place head on hands.
"Shhhhhh - good night!"

Winds

 Hold up five fingers, and, starting with thumb,
 bend down one at a time as verse progresses.

This little wind blows silver rain,
This little wind drifts snow,
This little wind sings a whistled tune,
This little wind croons low,
And this little wind rocks baby birds
Tenderly to and fro.
 Rock hands.

Wind Tricks

The wind is full of tricks today,
  Make sweeping motion with one hand for wind.

He blew my daddy's hat away.
  Pretend to sweep hat off head.

He chased our paper down the street.
  Roll hands.

He almost blew us off our feet.
  Almost fall.

He makes the trees and bushes dance.
  With raised arms, make dancing motions.

Just listen to him howl and prance.
  Cup hand to ear.

The Wind

The wind came out to play one day.
He swept the clouds out of his way;
  Make sweeping motion with arms.

He blew the leaves and away they flew.
  Make fluttering motions with fingers.

The trees bent low, and their branches did too.
  Lift arms and lower them.

The wind blew the great big ships at sea;
  Repeat sweeping motions.

The wind blew my kite away from me.
  Let imaginary string go up and away, raise hand to brow and look up.

I Wish I Were a Leaf

  *Sing to the tune of "If I Had a Windmill."
  Children raise arms and sing together, then float,
  twirl, and fall down like leaves in the wind.*

I wish I were a leaf
A leaf, a leaf.
If I were a leaf,
I'd float in the wind like this.

I wish I were a leaf
A leaf, a leaf.
If I were a leaf,
I'd twirl in the wind like this.

I wish I were a leaf
A leaf, a leaf.
If I were a leaf,
I'd fall down to the ground like this.

Autumn Leaves

Leaves are floating softly down.
  Flutter fingers in downward motion.

They make a carpet on the ground.
  Spread hands over ground.

Then, swish, the wind comes whistling by
  Arms move side to side.

And sends them dancing to the sky.
  Hands flutter into air.

SONGS

If I Could Have a Windmill
  See DUCKS & GEESE, page 71.

POEM

Who Has Seen the Wind
  *By Christina Rosetti. As you recite the poem, make
  your fingers tremble on the first verse and your
  head bow down on the second.*

Who has seen the wind?
Neither I nor you:
But when the leaves hang trembling
The wind is passing through.

Who has seen the wind?
Neither you nor I:
But when the trees bow down their heads
The wind is passing by.

MORE IDEAS

1. Felt Stories: *My Red Umbrella, Mrs. Mopple's Washing Line, The Wind Blew, Too Much Noise,* and *Who Took the Farmer's Hat?*.

2. Take a wind chime for show and tell.

3. Craft: Decorate simple paper kites, tie bows of colourful ribbon onto tails, and hang from the ceiling.

4. Craft: Make simple pinwheels with the children, like Titch's pinwheel in Pat Hutchins' story, *Titch*. The children decorate both sides of a paper square. There is a simple pattern for this in *I Can Make a Rainbow* by Marjorie Frank, pages 208-209.

Zoos

STORIES TO READ ALOUD

Dear Zoo (lift the flap)
CAMPBELL, ROD

The Happy Lion
FATIO, LOUISE

Be Nice to Spiders
GRAHAM, MARGARET BLOY

Greedy Zebra
HADITHI, MWENYE

A Children's Zoo
HOBAN, TANA

My Camera at the Zoo
MARSHALL, JANET PERRY

Bruno Munari's Zoo
MUNARI, BRUNO

Sam Who Never Forgets
RICE, EVE

MORE STORIES

Gorilla
BROWNE, ANTHONY

If I Ran the Zoo
SEUSS, DR.

NONFICTION

1, 2, 3 to the Zoo: A Counting Book
CARLE, ERIC

Zoo Animals
(EYE OPENERS SERIES)

Zoo
GIBBONS, GAIL

What Do You Do at a Petting Zoo?
MACHOTKA, HANA

When We Went to the Zoo
ORMEROD, JAN

A Visit to the Zoo
TESTER, SYLVIA ROOT

NURSERY RHYMES

Little Miss Muffet

Act it out!

Little Miss Muffet
Sat on a tuffet,
Eating her curds and whey;
Along came a spider
And sat down beside her
And frightened Miss Muffet away.

FINGERPLAYS

The Yellow Giraffe

The yellow giraffe is tall as can be,
Reach up high.
His lunch is a bunch of leaves off a tree.
Pretend hand is nibbling leaves.
He has a very long neck and his legs are long too.
Stretch neck and legs.
And he can run faster than his friends in the zoo.
Run on the spot.

The Brown Kangaroo

The brown kangaroo is very funny
She leaps and runs and hops like a bunny.
Two fingers up. Hop like a bunny.
And on her stomach is a pocket so wide,
Place other hand on stomach.
Her baby can jump in and go for a ride.
First hand jumps into "pocket."

An Elephant

An elephant goes like this and that.
> *Pat knees.*

He's terrible big,
> *Hands up high.*

And he's terrible fat.
> *Hand out wide.*

He has no fingers
> *Wriggle fingers.*

And he has no toes,
> *Touch toes.*

But goodness gracious, what a nose!
> *Make curling movement away from nose.*

Elephant

Right foot, left foot; see me go.
> *Put weight on first one foot, then other, swaying from side to side.*

I am gray and big and very slow.
When I come walking down the street
I bring my trunk and four big feet.
> *Extend arms together in front and swing like a trunk.*

Eensy, Weensy Spider

> *See INSECTS, page 125.*

Five Little Monkeys

> *See MONKEYS, page 130.*

SONGS

Spider on the Floor

> *This one is great fun with a spider puppet.*
> *See INSECTS, page 125.*

One Elephant

> *See ELEPHANTS, page 78.*

MORE IDEAS

1. Keeping animals in captivity is a controversial issue these days. Nevertheless, many zoos still exist, and lots of children are still taken to the zoo to see animals, like elephants and giraffes, that they would not otherwise see. Older children may enjoy Anthony Browne's indictment of zoos in his book *Zoo*.

2. Felt Stories: *Greedy Zebra* and *Dear Zoo*.

3. Sing Tom Paxton's song "Going to the Zoo." The tune is on Raffi's *Singable Songs for the Very Young* cassette. Words and music are in *The Raffi Singable Songbook*.

4. There are lots of books in the library on individual animals that are just right for preschool children. Include the giraffe, the zebra, the elephant, the crocodile, the ostrich and other exotic animals. Look in the J599 section.

5 See: ANIMALS OF THE WILD, BEARS, BIRDS, ELEPHANTS, MONKEYS, and RABBITS for more ideas.

Recommended Resources

This section contains bibliographies of resource materials that are valuable for further research. The topics included are: Arts, Crafts & Activities, Folk & Fairy Tales, Fingerplays & Action Rhymes, Nursery Rhymes (Single Editions and Collections), Song Books (Single Editions and Collections), Songs on Sound Recordings, Storytelling, and Professional Books. The books are arranged in alphabetical order by author, followed by publication information, in each category.

ARTS, CRAFTS & ACTIVITIES

Borycki, Barb and Jo-Anne Sotski-Engele. *The Best in Kids: Creative Activities for Preschool Children.* Saskatoon, SK: The Best in Kids, 1988. (A valuable little book full of fingerplays, crafts and recipes, arranged by theme.)

Bowden, Marcia. *Nature for the Very Young: A Handbook of Indoor & Outdoor Activities.* New York: Wiley, 1989.

Brown, Sam. *Bubbles, Rainbows & Worms: Science Experiments for Pre-school Children.* Mt. Rainier, MD: Gryphon House, 1981.

Cech, Maureen. *Globalchild: Multicultural Resources for Young Children.* Ottawa, ON: Health and Welfare Canada, 1990. (A treasure trove of simple multicultural stories and activities that celebrate cultural diversity around the year.)

Cole, Ann. *A Pumpkin in a Pear Tree: Creative Ideas for Twelve Months of Holiday Fun.* Boston: Little, Brown, 1976. (Crafts)

Cole, Ann. *I Saw a Purple Cow and 100 Other Recipes for Learning.* Boston: Little, Brown, 1972. (Crafts)

Connolly, Ann Marie and Helen Gibson. *Rainy Day Activities for Preschoolers.* Mercer Island Preschool Assoc., Box 464, Mercer Island, WA 98040, 1988. (Recipes and crafts.)

Coombs, Ernie. *Mr. Dressup's 50 More Things to Make and Do: Year-Round Activities from Mr. Dressup.* Toronto: Stoddart, 1991.

Coombs, Ernie. *Mr. Dressup's Things to Make and Do.* Don Mills, ON: Stoddart, 1991.

Frank, Marjorie. *I Can Make a Rainbow: Things to Create and Do for Children.* Nashville: Incentive Publications, 1976. (Art experiences for older children, many adaptable for preschoolers. Full of recipes.)

Irving, Jan. *Full Speed Ahead! Stories and Activities for Children on Transportation.* Littleton, CO: Libraries Unlimited, 1988.

Irving, Jan. *Glad Rags: Stories and Activities Featuring Clothes for Children.* Littleton, CO: Libraries Unlimited, 1987.

Irving, Jan. *Mudluscious: Stories and Activities Featuring Food for Preschool Children.* Littleton, CO: Libraries Unlimited, 1986.

Jenkins, Peggy Davidson. *Art for the Fun of It: A Guide for Teaching Young Children.* Englewood Cliffs, NJ: Prentice Hall, 1980. (Philosophy & method.)

Kohl, Mary Ann F. *Scribble Cookies and Other Independent Creative Art Experiences for Children.* Bellingham, WA: Bright Ring Publishing, 1985. (Distributed by Gryphon House.)

Mackenzie, Jennie. *Creative Fun Crafts for Kids.* Menlo Park, CA: Sunset Publishing, 1993.

Mackenzie, Jennie. *Kids Craft and Play Ideas.* Pymble, NSW, Australia: Bay Books, 1993. (Easy and colourful craft ideas for kindergarten and preschool with rhymes to accompany each activity.)

Martin, Elaine. *Kids' Games: Creative Games and Activities: A Parents' Guide to Playing with Your Three to Six Year Old.* Mississauga, ON: Random House of Canada, 1989. (A great cache of games and activities.)

Moxley, Juliet. *150 Things to Make and Do with Your Children.* London: Vermillion, 1993.

Rockwell, Robert E. *Hug a Tree and Other Things to Do Outdoors with Young Children.* Mt. Rainier, MD: Gryphon House, 1983.

Tanaka, Shelley. *Mr. Dressup's Birthday Party Book: Painless Parties for Young Children and Their Parents.* Vancouver, BC: Douglas & McIntyre, 1988.

Williams, Robert A. *Mudpies to Magnets: A Preschool Science Curriculum.* Mt. Rainier, MD: Gryphon House, 1987.

FOLK & FAIRY TALES

Aardema, Verna. *Who's in Rabbit's House?* Ills. by Leo & Diane Dillon. New York: Dial Press, 1977.

Aardema, Verna. *Why Mosquitoes Buzz in People's Ears.* New York: Dial Press, 1975.

Aardema, Verna. *Bringing the Rain to Kapiti Plain: A Nandi Tale.* Ills. by Beatriz Vidal. New York: Dial Press, 1981.

Aardema, Verna. *Bimwili and the Zimwi.* Ills. by Susan Meddaugh. New York: Dial Press, 1985.

Aardema, Verna. *Borreguita and the Coyote.* Ills. by Petra Mathers. New York: Knopf, 1991.

Barton, Byron. *The Three Bears.* New York: HarperCollins, 1991.

Bennet, Jill. *Teeny Tiny.* Ills. by Tomie DePaola. New York: G.P. Putnam's Sons, 1985.

Brett, Jan. *Goldilocks and the Three Bears.* New York: G.P. Putnam's, 1987.

Brown, Marcia. *Stone Soup.* New York: C. Scribner's Sons, 1975.

Cleaver, Elizabeth. *The Enchanted Caribou.* Toronto: Oxford University Press, 1985.

De la Mare, Walter. *Molly Whuppie.* Ills. by Errol Le Cain. New York: Farrar, Straus, Giroux, 1983.

Galdone, Paul. *The Hare and the Tortoise.* New York: McGraw-Hill, 1962.

Galdone, Paul. *Henny Penny.* New York: Clarion Books, 1968.

Galdone, Paul. *The Three Billy Goats Gruff.* Boston: Houghton Mifflin, 1987.

Galdone, Paul. *The Three Little Pigs.* New York: Seabury Press, 1970.

Jacobs, Joseph. *Jack and the Beanstalk.* Ills. by Lorinda Bryan Cauley. New York: G.P. Putnam, 1983.

Kimmel, Eric. *The Gingerbread Man.* Ills. by Megan Lloyd. New York: Holiday House, 1993.

Louie, Ai-Ling. *Yeh Shen: A Cinderella Story from China.* Ills. by Young, Ed. New York: Philomel, 1982.

Marshall, James. *Little Red Riding Hood.* New York: Dial Books for Young Readers, 1987.

McDermott, Gerald. *Raven : A Trickster Tale from the Pacific Northwest.* San Diego: Harcourt Brace Jovanovich, 1993.

Seuling, Barbara. *The Teeny Tiny Woman: An Old English Ghost Tale.* New York: Viking, 1976.

Toye, William. *The Loon's Necklace.* Ills. by Elizabeth Cleaver. Toronto: Oxford University Press, 1977.

Wolkstein, Diane. *The Banza: A Haitian Story.* Ills. by Marc Brown. New York: Dial Press, 1981.

Young, Ed. *Lon Po Po: Red Riding Hood Story from China.* New York: Philomel Books, 1989.

Zemach, Margot. *The Little Red Hen.* New York: Farrar, Straus, & Giroux, 1983.

FINGERPLAYS & ACTION RHYMES - COLLECTIONS

Brown, Marc. *Finger Rhymes.* New York: E. P. Dutton, 1980.

Brown, Marc. *Hand Rhymes.* New York: E. P. Dutton, 1985.

Brown, Marc. *Party Rhymes.* New York: E.P. Dutton, 1988.

Carlson, Bernice Wells. *Listen! And Help Tell the Story.* New York: Abingdon Press, 1965.

Defty, Jeff. *Creative Fingerplays & Action Rhymes: An Index and Guide to their Use.* Phoenix: Oryx Press, 1992. (A complete index with an intelligent commentary on the multiple uses of fingerplays and the importance of selecting only the best.)

Glazer, Tom. *Do Your Ears Hang Low?: Fifty More Musical Fingerplays.* Garden City, NY: Doubleday, 1980.

Glazer, Tom. *Eye Winker Tom Tinker Chin Chopper: Fifty Musical Fingerplays.* Garden City, NY: Doubleday, 1973.

Grayson, Marion. *Let's Do Fingerplays.* Ills. by Nancy Weyl. Washington: Robert B. Luce, 1962.

Hammond, Linda. *One Blue Boat: Finger Fun and Action Rhymes for Every Day of the Year.* Ills. by Julie Park. Markham, ON: Penguin, 1991.

Hayes, Sarah. *Clap Your Hands: Finger Rhymes.* Ills. by Toni Goffe. New York: Lothrop, Lee & Shepard, 1988.

Hayes, Sarah. *Stamp Your Feet: Action Rhymes.* Ills. by Toni Goffe. New York: Lothrop, Lee & Shepard, 1988.

King, Karen. *Oranges and Lemons.* Ills. by Ian Beck. Oxford; Toronto: Oxford University Press, 1985.

Matterson, Elizabeth. *This Little Puffin . . . Nursery Songs and Rhymes.* London, England; Toronto: Penguin Books Canada, 1969. Revised edition 1991. (A classic collection.)

Ring a Ring O' Roses: Stories, Games and Finger Plays for Pre-school Children. Flint, Michigan: Flint Public Library, 1981. (A classic collection.)

Williams, Sarah. *Ride a Cock-Horse: Knee-Jogging Rhymes, Patting Songs & Lullabies.* Ills. by Ian Beck. Oxford University Press, 1986.

Williams, Sarah. *Round and Round the Garden: Play Rhymes for Young Children.* Ills. by Ian Beck. Oxford; New York: Oxford University Press, 1983.

NURSERY RHYMES - SINGLE EDITIONS

Aliki. *Hush Little Baby*. Englewood Cliffs, NJ: Prentice Hall, 1968.

Bolam, Emily. *The House That Jack Built*. London: Pan MacMillan Children's Books, 1992.

Cauley, Lorinda Bryan. *The Three Little Kittens*. New York: Clarion Books, 1986.

Galdone, Paul. *Little Bo-Peep*. New York: Clarion Books, 1986.

Galdone, Paul. *Three Little Kittens*. New York: Clarion Books, 1986.

Martin, Sarah Catherine. *The Comic Adventures of Old Mother Hubbard and Her Dog*. Ills. by Tomie De Paola. New York: Harcourt Brace Jovanovich, 1981.

Hayes, Sarah. *Mary Had a Little Lamb*. Ills. by Tomie De Paola. New York : Holiday House, 1984.

Ivimey, John W. *The Complete Story of the Three Blind Mice*. New York: Clarion, 1987.

Provensen, Alice and Martin. *Old Mother Hubbard*. New York: Random House, 1977.

Spier, Peter. *London Bridge Is Falling Down!* Garden City, NY: Doubleday, 1967.

Stevens, Janet. *The House That Jack Built*. New York: Holiday, 1985.

Stobbs, William. *Pat-A-Cake*. London: Bodley Head, 1985.

NURSERY RHYMES & POETRY - COLLECTIONS

Briggs, Raymond. *The Mother Goose Treasury*. London: Hamish Hamilton, 1966.

De Angeli, Marguerite. *Book of Nursery and Mother Goose Rhymes*. Garden City, NY: Doubleday, 1954.

DePaola, Tomie. *Tomie De Paola's Mother Goose*, New York: G. P. Putnam, 1985.

Foreman, Michael. *Michael Foreman's Mother Goose*. San Diego: Harcourt Brace Jovanovich, 1991.

Lee, Dennis. *Alligator Pie*. Ills. by Frank Newfeld. Toronto: Macmillan of Canada, 1974.

Lee, Dennis. *Garbage Delight*. Ills. by Frank Newfeld. Toronto: Macmillan of Canada, 1977.

Lee, Dennis. *Jelly Belly*. Ills. by Juan Wijngaard. Toronto: Macmillan of Canada, 1983.

Lobel, Arnold. *The Random House Book of Mother Goose*. New York: Random House, 1986.

The Nursery Treasury: A Collection of Baby Games, Rhymes and Lullabies. Selected by Sally Emerson. Ills. by Moira and Colin Maclean. New York: Doubleday, 1988.

Opie, I. *Oxford Dictionary of Nursery Rhymes*. London: Oxford University Press, 1975. (Adult reference. Histories and full text for traditional nursery rhymes.)

Sutherland, Zena. *The Orchard Book of Nursery Rhymes*. Ills. by Faith Jaques. New York: Orchard Books, 1990. (Beautiful suggestive illustrations for felts.)

Prelutsky, Jack. *Read-Aloud Rhymes for the Very Young*. Ills. by Marc Brown. New York: Knopf, 1986. (Required reading! Poems for every occassion.)

Reid, Barbara. *Sing a Song of Mother Goose*. Richmond Hill, ON: North Winds, 1987.

Watson, Clyde. *Catch Me and Kiss Me and Say It Again*. Ills. by Wendy Watson. New York: Collins,World: 1978.

Watson, Clyde. *Father Fox's Feast of Songs*. Ills. by Wendy Watson. New York: Philomel Books, 1983. (Lovely original rhymes with familiar rhythms to say or sing.)

Wildsmith, Brian. *Brian Wildsmith's Mother Goose: A Collection of Nursery Rhymes*. New York: Franklin Watts, 1965.

SONG BOOKS - SINGLE EDITIONS

Aliki. *Hush Little Baby*. Englewood Cliffs, NJ: Prentice-Hall, 1968.

Conover, Chris. *Six Little Ducks*. New York: Crowell, 1976.

Spier, Peter. *The Fox Went Out on a Chilly Night*. Garden City, NY: Doubleday, 1961.

Spier, Peter. *London Bridge Is Falling Down*. Garden City, NY: Doubleday, 1967.

Galdone, Paul. *Cat Goes Fiddle-i-Fee*. New York: Clarion Books, 1985.

Galdone, Paul. *Over in the Meadow: An Old Nursery Counting Rhyme*. Englewood Cliffs, NJ: Prentice-Hall, 1986.

Hale, Sarah. *Mary Had a Little Lamb*. Ills. by Tomie De Paola. New York: Holiday House, 1984.

Harrison, Ted. *O Canada*. Toronto: Kids Can Press, 1992.

Kennedy, Jimmy. *Michael Hague's Illustrated the Teddy Bear's Picnic*. New York: H. Holt, 1992.

King, Bob. *Sitting on the Farm*. Ills. by Bill Slavin. Toronto: Kids Can Press, 1991.

Kovalski, Maryann. *Jingle Bells*. Toronto: Kids Can Press, 1988.

Kovalski, Maryann. *Take Me Out to the Ball Game*. Richmond Hill, ON: North Winds Press, 1992.

Kovalski, Maryann. *The Wheels on the Bus*. Toronto: Kids Can Press, 1987.

Langstaff, John. *Oh, A-Hunting We Will Go.* Ills. by Nancy Winslow Parker. New York: Atheneum, 1974.

Langstaff, John. *Over in the Meadow.* Ills. by Feodor Rojankovsky. New York: Harcourt, Brace & World, 1957.

McNally, Darcie. *In a Cabin in a Wood.* Ills. by Robin Michal Koontz. New York: Cobblehill/Dutton, 1991.

Nichol, B.P. *Once, a Lullaby.* Ills. by Anita Lobel. New York: Greenwillow Books, 1983.

Old MacDonald Had a Farm. Ills. by Lorinda Bryan Cauley. New York: Putnam, 1989.

Pearson, Tracey Campbell. *Sing a Song of Sixpence.* New York: Dial Books for Young Readers, 1985.

Peek, Merle. *Mary Wore Her Red Dress and Henry Wore His Green Sneakers.* New York: Clarion Books, 1985.

Rae, Mary Maki. *The Farmer in the Dell: A Singing Game.* New York: Viking Kestrel, 1988.

Raffi. *Five Little Ducks.* Ills. by Jose Aruego & Ariane Dewey. New York: Crown, 1989.

Rees, Mary. *Ten in a Bed.* Boston: Joy Street Books, 1988.

Reid, Barbara. *Two by Two.* Richmond Hill, ON: North Winds Press, 1992.

Slavin, Bill. *The Cat Came Back: A Traditional Story.* Toronto: Kids Can Press, 1992.

Sowden, Harry. *The Grand Old Duke of York.* London: V. Gollancz, 1988.

Staines, Bill. *All God's Critters Got a Place in the Choir.* Ills. by Margot Zemach. New York: E.P. Dutton, 1989.

Sweet, Melissa. *Fiddle-i-Fee: A Farmyard Song for the Very Young.* Boston: Little, Brown, 1992.

This Old Man. Ills. by Carol Jones. Boston: Houghton Mifflin, 1990.

Watson, Wendy. *Wendy Watson's Frog Went A-Courting.* New York: Lothrop, Lee & Shepard Books, 1990.

Westcott, Nadine. *I Know an Old Lady Who Swallowed a Fly.* Boston: Little, Brown, 1980.

Westcott, Nadine. *The Lady with the Alligator Purse.* Boston: Joy Street Books, 1988.

Westcott, Nadine. *Skip to My Lou.* Boston: Joy Street Books, 1989.

Westcott, Nadine. *There's a Hole in My Bucket.* New York: Harper & Row, 1990.

Zelinsky, Paul O. *Wheels on the Bus.* New York: E.P. Dutton, 1990. (movable parts)

SONG BOOKS - COLLECTIONS

De Paola, Tomie. *Tomie De Paola's Book of Christmas Carols.* New York: G.P. Putnam's Sons, 1987.

Glazier, Tom. *Do Your Ears Hang Low? 50 More Musical Fingerplays.* New York: Doubleday, 1980.

Glazier, Tom. *Eye Winker, Tom Tinker, Chin Chopper: Fifty Musical Fingerplays.* New York: Doubleday, 1973.

Glazier, Tom. *The Mother Goose Songbook.* Ills. by David McPhail. New York: Doubleday, 1990.

Go In and Out the Window: An Illustrated Songbook for Young People. New York: Metropolitan Museum of Art: Henry Holt, 1987. (Sixty-one traditional songs illustrated with art works from the Metropolitan Museum of Art.)

Hart, Jane. *Singing Bee!* Ills. by Anita Lobel. New York: Lothrop, Lee & Shepard Books, 1982.

Larrick, Nancy. *Songs from Mother Goose: With the Traditional Melody for Each.* Ills. by Robin Spowart. New York: Harper & Row, 1989.

Mahoney, Judy. *Teach Me French.* Minneapolis: Teach Me Tapes, Inc., 1993. (Books and cassettes for children learning other languages, include popular preschool songs. Also available in Spanish, German, Hebrew, Italian, Japanese and Russian.)

Penner, Fred. *Fred Penner's Sing Along Play Along Song & Activity Book.* Scarborough, ON: McGraw-Hill Ryerson,1990.

Raffi. *The Raffi Everything Grows Songbook: A Collection of Songs from Raffi's Album Everything Grows.* New York: Crown, 1989.

Raffi. *The Raffi Christmas Treasury: Fourteen Illustrated Songs and Musical Arrangements.* New York: Crown Publishers, 1988.

Raffi. *The Raffi Singable Songbook: A Collection of 51 Songs from Raffi's First Three Records for Young Children.* Toronto: Chappell, 1980.

Raffi. *The Second Raffi Songbook.* Willowdale, ON: Homeland Publishing, 1986.

Sharon, Lois & Bram. *Elephant Jam: Songs to Play and Games to Sing.* 2nd Edition. Toronto: McGraw-Hill Ryerson, 1989.

Sharon, Lois & Bram. *Sharon, Lois & Bram's Mother Goose.* Vancouver, BC: Douglas and McIntyre, 1985.

Warren, Jean. *Piggyback Songs: New Songs Sung to the Tune of Childhood Favorites.* Everett, WA: Warren Pub. House; Mt. Rainier, MD, distributed by Gryphon House, 1983.

Warren-Mattox, Cheryl. *Shake It to the One That You Love the Best: Play Songs and Lullabies from Black Musical Traditions*. Warren-Mattox Productions, 1989. (A great little collection of clapping rhymes, circle games and call and response rhymes. Comes with a cassette. Warren-Mattox Productions, 3817 San Pablo Dam Road #336, El Sobrante, CA 94803.)

SONGS ON SOUND RECORDINGS

All recordings are on cassette tape, unless otherwise noted.

Carfra, Pat. *Babes, Beasts and Birds*. Scarborough, ON: A&M Records, 1978. ("Skip to My Lou," "Over in the Meadow.")

Carfra, Pat. *Lullabies and Laughter*. Scarborough, ON: A&M Records, 1982. ("Hush Pretty Baby," "Morningtown Ride," "Cobbler's Bench," "One Elephant," "Eensy Weensy Spider," "Down by the Station," "John, the Rabbit.")

Jenkins, Ella. *Ella Jenkins Live! at the Smithsonian* [videorecording] Cambridge, MA: Rounder Records, 1991.

Jenkins, Ella. *You'll Sing a Song and I'll Sing a Song*. [compact disc] Washington, DC: Smithsonian /Folkways, 1989. ("This Train," "Did You Feed My Cow?" "Miss Mary Mack.")

McGrath, Bob. *If You're Happy and You Know It, Sing Along with Bob. Vol. One*. Toronto, ON: Kids Records, 1985. ("If You're Happy and You Know It," "The Wheels on the Bus," "Six Little Ducks," "Five Little Monkeys," "Head and Shoulders," "Skip to My Lou," "Aikendrum," "Mr. Sun," "Where is Thumbkin?" "My Dog Rags," "She'll Be Comin' Round the Mountain.")

McGrath, Bob. *Sing Along with Bob. Vol. Two*. Toronto, ON: Kids Records, 1985. ("You'll Sing a Song and I'll Sing a Song," "Little Peter Rabbit," "Rig a Jig-Jig," "Do You Know the Muffin Man," "Bingo," "Do Your Ears Hang Low," "Put Your Finger in the Air," "London Bridge," "Three Blind Mice," "Old King Cole," "Your Are My Sunshine," "Little Tommy Tinker," "I've Been Workin on the Railroad," "Hush Little Baby.")

McGrath, Bob, and Kathrine Smithrim. *Songs and Games for Toddlers*. Toronto, ON: Kids Records, 1985. ("Rig a Jig Jig," "Engine, Engine," "Tommy Thumbs Up," "Zoom, Zoom, Zoom," "Bumpin' Up and Down," "John the Rabbit," "Jelly in the Bowl," "Five Little Ducks," "This Old Man," "Bell Horses," "Frère Jacques," "Seashell.")

Raffi. *Baby Beluga*. Willowdale, ON: Troubadour Records, 1980. ("Oats and Beans and Barley," "Over in the Meadow," "Morningtown Ride.")

Raffi. *Bananaphone*. Willowdale, ON: Troubadour Records, 1994. ("Michael Row the Boat Ashore," "Down by the Riverside.")

Raffi. *Corner Grocery Store*. Willowdale, ON: Troubadour Records, 1979. ("You'll Sing a Song, and I'll Sing a Song," "Pick a Bale O' Cotton," "Frère Jacques," "Goodnight Irene.")

Raffi. *Everything Grows*. Willowdale, ON: Shoreline/A&M Records, 1987. ("Brown Girl in the Ring," "Mary Wore Her Red Dress." "Ha Ha Thisaway," "Little White Duck.")

Raffi. *More Singable Songs*. Willowdale, ON: Troubadour Records, 1977. ("Six Little Ducks," "Shake My Sillies Out," "I've Been Workin' on the Railroad.")

Raffi. *One Light, One Sun*. Willowdale, ON: Troubadour Records, 1985. ("Apples and Bananas," "Down on Grandpa's Farm.")

Raffi with Ken Whiteley. *Raffi's Christmas Album*. Willowdale, ON: Troubadour Records, 1983. ("Must Be Santa," "Rudolph the Red-Nosed Reindeer," "Away in a Manger.")

Raffi. *Rise and Shine*. Willowdale, ON: Troubadour Records, 1982. ("Wheels on the Bus," "Tête Epaules," "I'm in the Mood.")

Raffi. *Singable Songs for the Very Young*. Willowdale, ON: Troubadour Records, 1976. ("The More We Get Together," "Bumping Up and Down," "Spider on the Floor," "Willoughby Wallaby Woo," "Mr. Sun.")

Sharon, Lois & Bram. *Great Big Hits*. Toronto: Elephant Records, 1984. (CD 1992) ("One Elephant," "She'll Be Comin' Round the Mountain," "Jenny Jenkins," "If I Could Have a Windmill," "Pop Goes the Weasel," "Little Rabbit Foo Foo," "How Much Is that Doggie in the Window," "Rags," "The Smile Was on the Crocodile," "Pufferbellies," "Skinnamarink.")

Sharon, Lois & Bram. *Mainly Mother Goose*. Toronto: Elephant Records, 1984. (CD 1991) ("Eensy Weensy Spider," "Old King Cole," "Bluebird," "Three Little Kittens," "Three Blind Mice," "Pop Goes the Weasel," "Little Rabbit Foo Foo," "Tom Tom the Piper's Son," "Jack and Jill," "Skip to My Lou," "Little Arabella Miller," "Lavender's Blue.")

Smithrim, Katharine. *Songs and Games for Toddlers*. [videorecording] Racine, WI: Golden Book Video, 1986. (Learn all kinds of songs here and enjoy seeing the way someone else does it.)

STORYTELLING

Anderson, Dr. Paul S. *Storytelling with the Flannel Board*. Minneapolis: Denison, 1970. (Dated, but if you need patterns to trace for felts, this is one book for it.)

Baltuck, Naomi. *Crazy Gibberish and other Story Hour Stretches from a Storyteller's Bag of Tricks*. Ills. by Doug Cushman. Hamden, CT: Linnet Books, 1993. (A great little cache of "one minute miracles." Cassette available too.)

Bauer, Caroline Feller. *Handbook for Storytellers*. Chicago: American Library Association, 1977. (A classic. New edition 1993.)

Carlson, Bernice Wells. *Listen! And Help Tell the Story*. New York: Abingdon Press, 1965.

Cech, Maureen. *Globalchild: Multicultural Resources for Young Children*. Ottawa, ON: Health and Welfare Canada, 1990. (A treasure trove of simple multicultural stories and activities. A unique offering!)

Hunt, Tamara and Nancy Renfro. *Pocketful of Puppets: Mother Goose*. Austin, TX: Nancy Renfro Studios, 1982. (Simple puppetry and dramatization ideas for storytellers.)

Hunt, Tamara and Nancy Renfro. *Puppetry in Early Childhood Education*. Austin, TX: Nancy Renfro Studios, 1982.

MacDonald, Margaret Read. *Twenty Tellable Tales: Audience Participation Folktales for the Beginning Storyteller*. Bronx, NY: H. W. Wilson, 1986. (For more collections see MacDonald's *Look Back and See, The Storyteller's Start-Up Book,* and *When the Lights Go Out: Twenty Scary Stories to Tell*.)

Peterson, Carolyn Sue. *Story Programs: A Source Book of Materials*. Metuchen, NJ: Scarecrow, 1980.

Schimmel, Nancy. *Just Enough to Make a Story*. Berkeley: Sisters' Choice Press, 1978. ("The Rainhat" and "The Frog Trap" are favourites.)

Sierra, Judy. *Flannel Board Storytelling Book*. Bronx, NY: H.W. Wilson Co., 1987. (A treasure trove of stories and patterns for the felt board.)

Sierra, Judy. *Multicultural Folktales: Stories to Tell Young Children*. Phoenix: Oryx Press, 1991. (An excellent collection.)

Stangl, Jean. *Paper Stories*. Belmont, CA: David S. Lake Publishers, 1984. (31 original cut and tell stories.)

Thompson, Richard. *Draw-and-Tell*. Willowdale, ON: Annick Press, 1988. (See also *Frog's Riddle and Other Draw-and-Tell Stories*.)

VanSchuyver, Jan. *Storytelling Made Easy with Puppets*. Phoenix: Oryx Press, 1993. (Very useful, straight to the point, easy to use.)

Warren, Jean. *"Cut & Tell" Scissor Stories For . . . Spring, Fall, Winter*. Mt. Rainier, MD: Gryphon House, 1984. (Three books. Short original stories, paper plate cut-outs with patterns.)

Wright, Lyndie. *Masks*. New York: Franklin Watts, 1990. (Mask-making ideas for storytelling props.)

PROFESSIONAL BOOKS

This is a small selection of books useful for storytime planning. All have something valuable to offer.

Lerach, Helen. *Creative Storytimes: A Resource Book For Child Care Workers*. Regina, SK: Regina Public Library. 1993.

Lerach, Helen. *Storytime Handbook For Daycare Workers*. Regina, SK: Regina Public Library, 1990. (These two are good for follow-up crafts, films and music. They include Canadian titles.)

Lima, Carolyn W. *A to Zoo: Subject Access to Children's Picture Books*. 4th edition. New York: Bowker, 1993. (An invaluable tool, the only published index so far that offers subject access to picture books. However, it only includes books published or co-published in the United States. It excludes, therefore, many wonderful Canadian titles.)

MacDonald, Margaret Read. *Booksharing: 101 Programs To Use With Preschoolers*. Hamden, CT: Library Professional Publication, 1988. (Unique themes for planning, packed with ideas, although no Canadian books.)

Mahoney, Ellen. *Ready, Set, Read: Best Books To Prepare Preschoolers*. Metuchen, NJ: Scarecrow, 1985. (Commentary with annotated booklists good for each year of development.)

Marino, Jane. *Sing Us a Story: Using Music in Preschool and Family Storytimes*. Bronx, NY: H.W. Wilson, 1994.

Nichols, Judy. *Storytime For Two-Year-Olds*. Chicago: American Library Assn, 1987. (This is the only book available so far on storytime ideas for toddlers.)

Oppenheim, Joanne, et al. *Choosing Books For Kids: How To Choose The Right Book For The Right Child At The Right Time*. New York: Random House, 1986.

Sitarz, Paula Gaj. *Picture Book Story Hours*. Englewood, CO: Libraries Unlimited, 1987.

Sitarz, Paula Gaj. *More Picture Book Story Hours*. Englewood, CO: Libraries Unlimited, 1990. (These two by Sitarz are good for publicity ideas and introductory comments for themes and books. Also includes the concept of booktalking books not used at storytime. No Canadian books.)

Bibliography

This bibliography is arranged in three sections: STORIES TO READ ALOUD, MORE STORIES, and NONFICTION, just as the books are arranged within each theme. Within each section, the books are arranged alphabetically by the authors' last names. Illustrators, when they are not also the authors of the books, are mentioned after the titles. The relevant themes for each book appear in parentheses after the publication information.

STORIES TO READ ALOUD

Aardema, Verna. *Borreguita and the Coyote*. Ills. by Petra Mathers. New York: Knopf, 1991. (Foxes & Wolves, Sheep)

Aardema, Verna. *Bringing the Rain to Kapiti Plain*. Ills. by Beatriz Vidal. New York: Dial Press, 1981. (Weather – Rainy Day)

Aardema, Verna. *Traveling to Tondo*. Ills. by Will Hillenbrand. New York: Knopf, 1991. (Valentine's Day)

Aardema, Verna. *Why Mosquitoes Buzz in People's Ears*. Ills. by Leo and Diane Dillon. New York: Dial Press, 1975. (Animals of the Wild, Cats, Insects)

Aesop. *The Hare and the Tortoise*. Ills. by Paul Galdone. New York: McGraw-Hill, 1962. (Snakes, Turtles & Lizards)

Ahlberg, Janet. *Each Peach Pear Plum*. Middlesex, England: Viking Kestrel, 1979. (Food)

Alda, Arlene. *Sheep, Sheep, Sheep, Help Me Fall Asleep*. New York: Doubleday, 1992. (Sheep)

Aliki. *At Mary Bloom's*. New York: Greenwillow Books, 1976. (Mice, Pets)

Aliki. *Go Tell Aunt Rhody*. New York: Macmillan, 1974. (Ducks & Geese)

Aliki. *Hush Little Baby*. Englewood Cliffs, NJ: Prentice Hall, 1968. (Babies, Bedtime, Toys)

Allen, Pamela. *A Lion in the Night*. New York: Putnam, 1985. (Royalty)

Allen, Pamela. *Mr. Archimedes' Bath*. New York: Lothrop, Lee & Shepard Books, 1980. (Bathtime)

Allen, Pamela. *Who Sank the Boat?* New York: Coward - McCann, Inc., 1982. (Mice, Sea & Seashore)

Allinson, Beverly. *Effie*. Ills. by Barbara Reid. Toronto: Summerhill Press, 1990. (Elephants, Friends, Giants, Insects, Teeny Tiny Things)

Andersen, H. C. *The Princess and the Pea*. Ills. by Paul Galdone. New York: Seabury Press, 1978. (Bedtime, Royalty, Valentine's Day)

Armitage, Ronda. *The Lighthouse Keeper's Lunch*. London: Deutsch, 1977. (Birds, Food, Sea & Seashore)

Asbjornsen, P.C. *The Runaway Pancake*. Ills. by Svend Otto. New York: Larousse, 1980. (Food)

Asch, Frank. *Happy Birthday, Moon*. Englewood Cliffs, NJ: Prentice-Hall, 1982. (Bedtime, Birthdays)

Asch, Frank. *Just Like Daddy*. Englewood Cliffs, NJ: Prentice-Hall, 1981. (Families, Father's Day, Sea & Seashore)

Asch, Frank. *Monkey Face*. New York: Parents' Magazine Press, 1977. (Colour & Art, Monkeys)

Asch, Frank. *Moonbear*. New York: Simon & Schuster, 1993. (Bears, Bedtime)

Asch, Frank. *Mooncake*. Englewood Cliffs, NJ: Prentice-Hall, 1983. (Space)

Asch, Frank. *Popcorn*. New York: Parent's Magazine Press, 1979. (Halloween)

Asch, Frank. *Sand Cake*. New York: Parents' Magazine Press, 1978. (Food, Sea & Seashore)

Asch, Frank. *Turtle Tale*. New York: Dial Press, 1978. (Snakes, Turtles & Lizards, Teeny Tiny Things)

Baer, Gene. *Thump, Thump, Rat-a-Tat-Tat*. Ills. by Lois Ehlert. New York: HarperCollins, 1991. (Music)

Baker, Keith. *Big Fat Hen*. San Diego: Harcourt, Brace, 1994. (Easter, Farms)

Balian, Lorna. *Humbug Witch*. Nashville: Abingdon Press, 1965. (Halloween)

Bang, Molly. *Ten, Nine, Eight*. New York: Greenwillow Books, 1983. (Bedtime, Counting)

Barrett, Judith. *Animals Should Definitely Not Wear Clothing*. New York: Aladdin Books, 1989, c1970. (Clothing)

Barton, Byron. *I Want to Be an Astronaut*. New York: Crowell, 1988. (Space)

Biro, Val. *Jack and the Beanstalk*. Oxford: Oxford University Press, 1989. (Giants)

Blake, Quentin. *Mister Magnolia*. London: J. Cape, 1980. (Clothing)

Blos, Joah W. *Lottie's Circus*. illustrated by Irene Trivas. New York: Morrow, 1989. (Circus)

Bolam, Emily. *The House That Jack Built*. London: Pan MacMillan Children's Books, 1992. (Houses)

Bornstein, Ruth. *Little Gorilla*. New York: Seabury Press, 1976. (Birthdays)

Bourgeois, Paulette. *Big Sarah's Little Boots*. Ills. by Brenda Clark. Toronto: Kids Can Press, 1987. (Clothing, Colour & Art, Weather – Rainy Day)

Brandenberg, Franz. *Aunt Nina and Her Nephews and Nieces*. Ills. by Aliki. New York: Greenwillow Books, 1983. (Birthdays, Families)

Brandenberg, Franz. *I Wish I Was Sick Too*. Ills. by Aliki. New York: Greenwillow Books, 1976. (Sickness & Health)

Brett, Jan. *Annie and the Wild Animals*. Boston: Houghton Mifflin, 1985. (Animals of the Wild, Cats, Seasons – Spring, Weather – Snowy Day)

Brett, Jan. *Berlioz the Bear*. New York: Putnam, 1991. (Music)

Brett, Jan. *The Mitten*. New York: Putnam, 1989. (Clothing, Seasons – Winter, Weather – Snowy Day)

Bright, Robert. *My Red Umbrella*. New York:Wm. Morrow, 1959. (Weather – Windy Day)

Brown, Craig. *Tractor*. New York: Greenwillow, 1995. (Farms)

Brown, Marcia. *Once a Mouse*. New York: Scribner, 1961. (Mice)

Brown, Marcia *Stone Soup*. New York: Scribner's, 1975. (Food)

Brown, Margaret Wise. *The Golden Egg Book*. Ills. by Leonard Weisgard. New York: Simon, 1947. (Easter)

Brown, Margaret Wise. *Goodnight Moon Room: A Pop-up Book*. Ills. by Clement Hurd. New York: Harper & Row, 1984. (Easter)

Brown, Margaret Wise. *Goodnight Moon*. Ills. by Clement Hurd. New York: Harper, 1947. (Bedtime, Rabbits)

Brown, Margaret Wise. *Home for a Bunny*. Ills. by Garth Williams. Racine, WI: Golden Press, 1956. (Easter, Rabbits)

Brown, Margaret Wise. *The Runaway Bunny*. Ills. by Clement Hurd. New York: Harper & Row, 1972. (Easter, Families, Mothers, Rabbits)

Brown, Ruth. *The Big Sneeze*. Toronto: Stoddart, 1985. (Insects)

Brown, Ruth. *A Dark, Dark Tale*. New York: Dial Books, 1981. (Halloween, Cats)

Brown, Ruth. *Ladybird, Ladybird*. Toronto: Stoddart, 1988. (Insects)

Brown, Ruth. *Our Cat Flossie*. Toronto: Stoddart, 1986. (Cats)

Brown, Ruth. *Our Puppy's Holiday*. Toronto: Stoddart, 1987. (Dogs)

Buckley, Richard. *The Greedy Python*. Ills. by Eric Carle. Picture Book Studio USA, 1985. (Snakes, Turtles & Lizards)

Bunting, Eve. *Flower Garden*. Ills. by Kathryn Hewitt. San Diego: Harcourt Brace & Co., 1994. (Gardening, Mother's Day)

Bunting, Eve. *In the Haunted House*. Ills. by Susan Meddaugh. New York: Clarion Books, 1990. (Halloween)

Bunting, Eve. *Scary, Scary Halloween*. Ills. by Jan Brett. New York: Clarion Books, 1986. (Halloween)

Bunting, Eve. *Valentine Bears*. Ills. by Jan Brett. New York: Clarion Books, 1983. (Valentine's Day)

Burningham, John. *Avocado Baby*. London: J. Cape, 1982. (Babies, Families, Food)

Burningham, John. *Harvey Slumfenburger's Christmas Present*. Cambridge, MA: Candlewick, 1993. (Christmas)

Burningham, John. *John Patrick Norman McHennesy*. New York: Crown, 1987. (School)

Burningham, John. *Mr. Gumpy's Motor Car*. New York: Crowell, 1976, c1973. (Transportation, Weather – Rainy Day)

Burningham, John. *Mr. Gumpy's Outing*. London: J. Cape, 1970. (Friends, Safety, Sea & Seashore, Transportation,)

Burningham, John. *The Shopping Basket*. New York: Crowell, 1980. (Food, Shopping)

Butterworth, Nick & Mick Inkpen. *Jasper's Beanstalk*. London: Hodder & Stoughton, 1992. (Gardening)

Campbell, Rod. *Dear Zoo*. New York: Macmillan, 1986. (Pets, Zoos)

Carle, Eric. *The Grouchy Ladybug*. New York: T.Y. Crowell, 1977. (Friends, Insects, Time)

Carle, Eric. *The Mixed-Up Chameleon*. New York: Thomas Y. Crowell, 1975, 1984. (Snakes, Turtles & Lizards)

Carle, Eric. *Pancakes, Pancakes!*. New York: Scholastic Inc., 1990. (Food)

Carle, Eric. *The Rooster Who Set Out to See the World*. New York: Franklin Watts, 1972. (Counting)

Carle, Eric. *The Secret Birthday Message*. New York: T.Y. Crowell, 1972. (Birthdays)

Carle, Eric. *Today Is Monday*. New York: Philomel Books, 1993. (Food)

Carle, Eric. *The Very Busy Spider*. New York: Philomel Books, 1984. (Insects)

Carle, Eric. *The Very Hungry Caterpillar*. New York: Philomel Books, 1985. (Counting, Food, Insects, Teeny Tiny Things)

Carle, Eric. *The Very Lonely Firefly*. New York: Philomel Books, 1995. (Insects)

Carle, Eric. *The Very Quiet Cricket*. New York: Philomel Books, 1990. (Insects)

Carlstrom, Nancy White. *Baby-O*. Ills. by Sucie Stevenson. Boston: Little, Brown, 1992. (Families, Shopping)

Carlstrom, Nancy White. *Jesse Bear, What Will You Wear?* New York: Macmillan, 1986. (Bears, Clothing)

Carlson, Nancy White. *Take Time to Relax!* New York: Viking, 1991. (Weather – Snowy Day)

Carrick, Carol. *Paul's Christmas Birthday*. New York: Greenwillow Books, 1978. (Birthdays)

Carter, David. *Jingle Bugs*. New York: Simon & Shuster, 1992. (Christmas)

Carroll, Kathleen. *One Red Rooster*. Ills. by Suzette Barbier. Boston: Houghton Mifflin, 1992. (Counting)

Cauley, Lorinda. *Goldilocks and the Three Bears*. New York: Putnam, 1981. (Bears)

Cauley, Lorinda. *Jack and the Beanstalk*. New York: G.P. Putnam, 1983. (Giants)

Cauley, Lorinda. *Old MacDonald Had a Farm*. New York: G.P. Putnam's Sons, 1989. (Farms)

Charlip, Remy. *Fortunately*. New York: Parents' Magazine Press, 1964. (Birthdays)

Charlip, Remy. *Mother, Mother, I Feel Sick*. New York: Four Winds Press, 1966. (Food, Sickness & Health)

Chase, Edith Newlin. *The New Baby Calf*. Ills. by Barbara Reid. Toronto: Scholastic, 1984. (Farms)

Chelsea, Jane. *Salt Hands*. Ills. by Ted Rand. New York: Dutton, 1989. (Animals of the Wild)

Cherry, Lynne. *Who's Sick Today?* New York: Dutton, 1988. (Sickness & Health)

Child, Lydia Maria. *Over the River and Through the Wood: A Song for Thanksgiving*. Ills. by Nadine Bernard Westcott. New York: HarperCollins, 1993. (Thanksgiving)

Christelow, Eileen. *Five Little Monkeys Jumping on the Bed*. New York: Clarion Books, 1989. (Monkeys)

Christelow, Eileen. *Henry and the Red Stripes*. New York: Clarion Books, 1982. (Rabbits)

Cole, Brock. *No More Baths*. New York: Farrar, Straus & Giroux, 1989. (Bathtime)

Collins, Pat Lowery. *Tomorrow, Up and Away!* Ills. by Lynn Munsinger. Boston: Houghton Mifflin, 1990. (Snakes, Turtles & Lizards)

Cousins, Lucy. *Maisy goes Swimming*. Boston: Little, Brown, 1990. (Bathtime, Clothing, Seasons – Summer)

Cowcher, Helen. *Tigress*. New York: Farrar, Straus, & Giroux, 1991. (Animals of the Wild)

Crowther, Robert. *The Most Amazing Hide and Seek Alphabet Book*. New York: Viking Press, 1977. (Alphabet Books, School)

Crowther, Robert. *The Most Amazing Hide and Seek Counting Book*. New York: Viking Kestrel, 1981. (Counting, Insects, School)

Dabcovich, Lydia. *Sleepy Bear*. New York: Dutton, 1982. (Seasons – Winter)

Davis, Virginia. *Simply Ridiculous*. Ills. by Russ Williams. Toronto: Kids Can Press, 1995. (Babies)

De Paola, Tomie. *Bill and Pete*. New York: Putnam, 1978. (Alphabet Books, Friends, School)

De Paola, Tomie. *Charlie Needs a Cloak*. Englewood Cliffs, NJ: Prentice-Hall, 1973. (Clothing, Seasons – Winter, Sheep)

De Paola, Tomie. *The Comic Adventures of Old Mother Hubbard and Her Dog*. New York: Harcourt Brace Jovanovich, 1981. (*Dogs,* Food, Mother's Day, Shopping)

De Regniers, Beatrice. *It Does Not Say Meow*. Ills. by Paul Galdone. Boston: Houghton Mifflin, 1979. (Cats)

De Regniers, Beatrice. *May I Bring a Friend?* Ills. by Beni Montresor. New York: Atheneum, 1964. (Animals of the Wild, Friends, Pets, Royalty)

Degen, Bruce. *Jamberry*. New York: Harper & Row, 1983. (Seasons – Summer)

Denton, Kady MacDonald. *The Christmas Boot*. Boston: Little, Brown & Co., 1990. (Christmas)

Denton, Kady MacDonald. *Dorothy's Dream*. New York: M.K. McElderry Books, 1989. (Bedtime)

Denton, Kady MacDonald. *Granny Is a Darling*. Toronto: Kids Can Press, 1988. (Bedtime, Families)

Dunbar, Joyce. *A Cake for Barney*. Ills. by Emilie Boon. New York: Orchard Books, 1987. (Food)

Dunbar, Joyce. *Four Fierce Kittens*. Ills. by Jakki Wood. New York: Scholastic, 1991. (Cats)

Eastman, P.D. *Are You My Mother?* New York: Beginner Books, 1960. (Mother's Day)

Ehlert, Lois. *Circus*. New York: HarperCollins, 1992. (Circus)

Ehlert, Lois. *Feathers for Lunch*. San Diego: Harcourt Brace Jovanovich, 1990. (Birds, Cats)

Ehlert, Lois. *Growing Vegetable Soup*. San Diego: Harcourt Brace Jovanovich, 1987. (Gardening)

Ehlert, Lois. *Mole's Hill*. San Diego: Harcourt Brace Jovanovich, 1994. (Gardening)

Ehlert, Lois. *Moon Rope*. San Diego: Harcourt Brace Jovanovich, 1992. (Space)

Ehlert, Lois. *Nuts to You!* San Diego: Harcourt Brace Jovanovich, 1993. (Animals of the Wild, Thanksgiving)

Ehlert, Lois. *Planting a Rainbow*. San Diego: Harcourt Brace Jovanovich, 1988. (Colour & Art, Gardening)

Ehlert, Lois. *Red Leaf, Yellow Leaf*. San Diego: Harcourt Brace Jovanovich, 1991. (Seasons – Fall)

Emberley, Barbara. *Drummer Hoff*. Ills. by Ed Emberley. New York: Simon & Shuster, 1985. (Music)

Emberley, Ed. *Go Away, Big Green Monster*. Boston: Little Brown & Co., 1992. (Monsters)

Enderle, Judith Ross. *Six Creepy Sheep*. Ills. by John O'Brien. Honesdale, PA: Caroline House, 1992. (Halloween)

Ets, Marie Hall. *Elephant in a Well.* New York: Viking Press, 1972. (Elephants, Mice)

Ets, Marie Hall. *Gilberto and the Wind.* New York: Viking Press, 1963. (Weather – Windy Day)

Ets, Marie Hall. *Play with Me.* New York: Viking Press, 1955. (Friends, Pets)

Evans, Katie. *Hunky Dory Ate It.* Ills. by Janet Morgan Stoeke. New York: Dutton Children's Books, 1992. (Dogs, Sickness & Health)

Fatio, Louise. *The Happy Lion.* Ills. by Roger Duvoisin. New York: McGraw-Hill, 1954. (Zoos)

Flack, Marjorie. *Angus and the Cat.* Garden City, NY: Doubleday, 1931. (Cats, Dogs)

Flack, Marjorie. *Angus and the Ducks.* Garden City, NY: Doubleday, 1930. (Dogs, Ducks & Geese)

Flack, Marjorie. *Angus Lost.* Garden City, NY: Doubleday, 1932. (Dogs)

Flack, Marjorie. *Ask Mr. Bear.* New York: Macmillan, 1958, c1932. (Bears, Birthdays, Mother's Day)

Flack, Marjorie. *The Story About Ping.* New York: Viking Press, 1933. (Ducks & Geese)

Foon, Dennis. *The Short Tree and the Bird That Could Not Sing.* Ills. by John Bianchi. Vancouver, BC: Douglas & McIntyre, 1986. (Birds, Seasons – Spring, Seasons – Winter)

Fox, Mem. *Hattie and the Fox.* Ills. by Patricia Mullins. New York: Bradbury Press, 1986. (Foxes & Wolves)

Fox, Mem. *Night Noises.* Ills. by Terry Denton. San Diego: Harcourt Brace Jovanovich, 1989. (Birthdays)

Fox, Mem. *Shoes from Grandpa.* Ills. by Patricia Mullins. New York: Orchard Books, 1990. (Clothing)

Fox, Mem. *Time for Bed.* Ills. by Jane Dyer. San Diego: Harcourt, Brace, 1993. (Bedtime)

Fox, Mem. *Wilfrid Gordon MacDonald Partridge.* Ills. by Julie Vivas. Brooklyn, NY: Kane/Miller Book Publishers, 1985. (Friends)

Freeman, Don. *Beady Bear.* New York: Viking Press, 1954. (Bears, Toys)

Freeman, Don. *Bearymore.* New York: Viking Press, 1976. (Circus)

Freeman, Don. *Corduroy.* New York: Viking Press, 1968. (Bears, Friends, Shopping, Toys)

Freeman, Don. *Dandelion.* New York: Viking Press, 1964. (Cats)

Freeman, Don. *A Pocket for Corduroy.* New York: Viking Press, 1978. (Toys)

Freeman, Don. *Rainbow of My Own.* New York: Viking Press, 1966. (Colour & Art)

French, Fiona. *Anancy and Mr. Dry-Bone.* Boston: Little, Brown, 1991. (Valentine's Day)

French, Vivian. *Red Hen and Sly Fox.* Ills. by Sally Hobson. New York: Simon & Shuster, 1994. (Foxes & Wolves)

Frost, Robert. *Stopping by Woods on a Snowy Evening.* Ills. by Susan Jeffers. New York: Dutton, 1978. (Weather – Snowy Day)

Gackenbach, Dick. *A Bag Full of Pups.* New York: Clarion Books, 1981. (Dogs)

Gackenback, Dick. *Claude the Dog: A Christmas Story.* New York: Seabury Press, 1974. (Christmas)

Gackenback, Dick. *Harvey, the Foolish Pig.* New York: Clarion Books, 1988. (Pigs)

Gag, Wanda. *Millions of Cats.* New York: Coward-McCann, 1928. (Cats)

Gage, Wilson. *Cully Cully and the Bear.* New York: Greenwillow Books, 1983. (Bears)

Gagnon, Cecile. *Snowfeather.* Toronto: James Lorimer, 1981. (Weather – Snowy Day)

Galdone, Paul. *The Amazing Pig.* New York: Houghton Mifflin/Clarion Books, 1981. (Royalty)

Galdone, Paul. *Cat Goes Fiddle-i-fee.* New York: Clarion Books, 1985. (Farms)

Galdone, Paul. *Gertrude the Goose Who Forgot.* New York: Franklin Watts, 1975. (Ducks & Geese)

Galdone, Paul. *The Gingerbread Boy.* New York: Seabury Press, 1975. (Food)

Galdone, Paul. *Henny Penny.* New York, Seabury Press, 1968. (Birds, Ducks & Geese, Farms, Foxes & Wolves, Space)

Galdone, Paul. *The History of Mother Twaddle and Her Son Jack.* New York: Seabury Press, 1974. (Giants)

Galdone, Paul. *Little Bo-Peep.* New York: Clarion Books, 1986. (Sheep)

Galdone, Paul. *Little Red Hen.* New York: Clarion Books, 1973. (Birds, Farms)

Galdone, Paul. *The Magic Porridge Pot.* New York: Seabury Press, 1976. (Food)

Galdone, Paul. *The Monkey and the Crocodile.* New York: Seabury Press, 1969. (Animals of the Wild, Monkeys)

Galdone, Paul. *The Monster and the Tailor: A Ghost Story.* New York: Clarion Books, 1982. (Halloween)

Galdone, Paul. *The Old Woman and Her Pig.* New York: McGraw-Hill, 1960. (Farms, Pigs)

Galdone, Paul. *Over in the Meadow.* Englewood Cliffs, NJ: Prentice-Hall, 1986. (Counting)

Galdone, Paul. *Tailypo: A Ghost Story.* New York: Seabury Press, Clarion Books, 1977. (Halloween)

Galdone, Paul. *The Three Billy Goats Gruff.* New York: Houghton Mifflin/Clarion Books, 1973. (Farms, Monsters)

Galdone, Paul. *Three Little Kittens.* New York: Clarion Books, 1986. (Cats, Clothing)

Galdone, Paul. *The Three Little Pigs.* New York: Seabury Press, Clarion Books, 1970. (Foxes & Wolves, Houses, Pigs)

Galdone, Paul. *The Turtle and the Monkey.* New York: Clarion Books, 1983. (Monkeys; Snakes, Turtles & Lizards)

Galdone, Paul. *What's in Fox's Sack.* New York: Clarion Books, 1982. (Foxes & Wolves)

Gantos, Jack. *Greedy Greeny.* Garden City, NY: Doubleday, 1979. (Food)

Gauch, Patricia Lee. *Christina Katerina and the Box.* Ills. by Doris Burn. New York: Coward, McCann & Geoghen, 1971. (Houses, Toys)

Gay, Marie-Louise. *Fat Charlie's Circus.* Don Mills, ON: Stoddart, 1989. (Circus)

Gay, Marie-Louise. *Moonbeam on a Cat's Ear.* Toronto: Stoddart, 1986 . (Bedtime)

Gay, Marie-Louise. *Rainy Day Magic.* Toronto: Stoddart, 1987. (Weather – Rainy Day)

Gay, Marie-Louise. *The Three Little Pigs.* Toronto: Groundwood, 1994. (Pigs)

Gerstein, Mordicai. *The Sun's Day.* New York: Harper & Row, 1989. (Time)

Getz, Arthur. *Hamilton Duck.* New York: Golden Press, 1972. (Seasons – Winter)

Getz, Arthur. *Hamilton Duck's Springtime Story.* New York: Golden Press, 1974. (Seasons – Spring)

Gibson, Betty. *The Story of Little Quack.* Ills. by Kady MacDonald Denton. Toronto: Kids Can Press, 1990. (Ducks & Geese, Farms)

Gilman, Phoebe. *Something from Nothing.* Richmond Hill, ON: North Winds Press, 1992. (Clothing)

Ginsburg, Mirra. *The Chick and the Duckling.* Ills. by Jose Aruego & Ariane Dewey. New York: Macmillan, 1972. (Birds, Ducks & Geese)

Ginsburg, Mirra. *Four Brave Sailors.* Ills. by Nancy Tafuri. New York: Greenwillow Books, 1987. (Bedtime)

Ginsburg, Mirra. *Good Morning, Chick.* Ills. by Byron Barton. New York: Greenwillow Books, 1980. (Farms)

Ginsburg, Mirra. *Mushroom in the Rain.* Ills. by Jose Aruego & Ariane Dewey. New York: Macmillan Pub. Co., 1974. (Foxes & Wolves, Gardening, Weather – Rainy Day)

Ginsburg, Mirra. *Two Greedy Bears.* Ills. by Jose Aruego & Ariane Dewey. New York: Macmillan, 1976. (Bears, Emotions, Food)

Ginsburg, Mirra. *Where Does the Sun Go at Night?* Ills. by Jose Aruego & Ariane Dewey. New York: Wm. Morrow, 1981. (Bedtime)

Goffin, Josse. *Yes.* New York: Lothrop, Lee & Shepard, 1994. (Easter, Farms)

Gomi, Taro. *Spring Is Here.* San Francisco: Chronicle Books, 1989. (Seasons – Spring)

Gordon, Jeffie Ross. *Six Sleepy Sheep.* Ills. by John O'Brien. Honesdale, PA: Caroline House, 1991. (Sheep)

Graham, John. *I Love You Mouse.* Ills. by Tomie De Paola. New York: Harcourt Brace Jovanovich, 1976. (Pets, Valentine's Day)

Graham, Margaret Bloy. *Be Nice to Spiders.* New York: Harper & Row, 1967. (Zoos)

Graham, Thomas. *Mr. Bear's Chair.* New York: Dutton, 1987. (Bears, Houses)

Gretz, Susanna. *Teddy Bears 1 to 10.* New York: Four Winds Press, 1986. (Toys)

Gretz, Susanna. *Teddy Bears Cure a Cold.* New York: Four Winds Press, 1984. (Sickness & Health)

Hadithi, Mwenye. *Crafty Chameleon.* Ills. by Adrienne Kennaway. Boston: Little, Brown, 1987. (Animals of the Wild)

Hadithi, Mwenye. *Greedy Zebra.* Ills. by Adrienne Kennaway. Boston: Little, Brown, 1984. (Animals of the Wild, Zoos)

Hadithi, Mwenye. *Lazy Lion.* Ills. by Adrienne Kennaway. Boston: Little, Brown, 1990. (Animals of the Wild, Cats, Houses)

Hague, Kathleen. *The Man Who Kept House.* New York: Harcourt Brace Jovanovich, 1981. (Farms, Father's Day)

Hale, Sarah. *Mary Had a Little Lamb.* Photos by Bruce McMillan. New York: Scholastic, 1990. (Sheep)

Hale, Sarah. *Mary Had a Little Lamb.* Ills. by Tomie De Paola. New York: Holiday House, 1984. (School, Sheep)

Hardendorf, Jeanne. *The Bed Just So.* New York: Four Winds, 1975. (Halloween, Teeny Tiny Things)

Harper, Anita. *Just a Minute.* Ills. by Susan Hellard. New York: Putnam, 1987. (Time)

Harper, Wilhelmena. *The Gunniwolf.* Ills. by William Wiesner. New York: Dutton, 1967, c1918. (Emotions, Foxes & Wolves, Monsters, Music, Safety)

Harpur, Tom. *The Terrible Finn MacCoul.* Ills. by Linda Hendry. Toronto: Oxford University Press, 1990. (St. Patrick's Day)

Hayes, Sarah. *This Is the Bear and the Scary Night.* Ills. by Helen Craig. Boston: Little, Brown, 1992. (Bears, Toys)

Heine, Helme. *The Most Wonderful Egg in the World.* New York: Atheneum, 1983. (Easter, Royalty)

Heine, Helme. *The Pig's Wedding.* New York: Margaret K. McElderry Books, 1978. (Pigs, Valentine's Day)

Hellard Susan. *This Little Piggy.* New York: Putnam, 1989. (Pigs)

Hennessy, B.G. *Jake Baked the Cake*. Ills. by Mary Morgan. New York: Viking Kestrel, 1990. (Valentine's Day)

Hennessy, B.G. *The Missing Tarts*. New York: Viking Kestrel, 1989. (Royalty)

Hewett, Anita. *Mrs. Mopple's Washing Line*. Ills. by Robert Broomfield. New York: McGraw-Hill, 1966. (Clothing, Farms, Weather – Windy Day)

Hill, Eric. *Spot Goes to School*. New York: Putnam, 1984. (School)

Hill, Eric. *Spot's Birthday Party*. New York: Putnam, 1982. (Birthdays)

Hill, Eric. *Spot's First Christmas*. New York: Putnam, 1983. (Christmas)

Hill, Eric. *Where's Spot?* New York: Putnam, 1980. (Dogs)

Hoban, Tana. *A Children's Zoo*. New York: Greenwillow Books, 1985. (Zoos)

Hoban, Tana. *Where Is It?* New York: Macmillan, 1974. (Rabbits)

Hoberman, Maryanne. *A House Is a House for Me*. Ills. by Betty Fraser. New York: Viking Press, 1978. (Houses)

Hogrogian, Nonny. *One Fine Day*. New York: Macmillan, 1971. (Foxes & Wolves)

Hoguet, Susan Ramsay. *I Unpacked My Grandmother's Trunk*. New York: E.P. Dutton. (Alphabet Books)

Holl, Adelaide. *Rain Puddle*. Ills. by Roger Duvoisin. New York: Lothrop, Lee & Shepard, 1965. (Weather – Rainy Day)

Holl, Adelaide. *The Runaway Giant*. Ills. by Mamoru Funai. New York: Lothrop, Lee & Shepard, 1967. (Weather – Snowy Day)

Hong, Lily Toy. *Two of Everything*. Morton Grove, IL: A. Whitman, 1993. (Gardening)

Howe, John. *Jack and the Beanstalk*. Boston: Little, Brown, 1989. (Giants)

Hurd, Thacher. *Little Mouse's Big Valentine*. New York: Harper & Row, 1990. (Valentine's Day)

Hurd, Thacher. *Mama Don't Allow*. New York: Harper & Row, 1984. (Music)

Hutchins, Pat. *1 Hunter*. New York: Greenwillow Books, 1982. (Counting)

Hutchins, Pat. *Clocks and More Clocks*. Toronto: Maxwell Macmillan Publishing, 1994, c1970. (Time)

Hutchins, Pat. *Don't Forget the Bacon*. New York: Greenwillow Books, 1976. (Shopping)

Hutchins, Pat. *The Doorbell Rang*. New York: Greenwillow Books, 1986. (Food, Counting)

Hutchins, Pat. *Goodnight, Owl*. New York: Macmillan, 1972. (Bedtime, Birds)

Hutchins, Pat. *Happy Birthday, Sam*. New York: Greenwillow Books, 1978. (Birthdays)

Hutchins, Pat. *My Best Friend*. New York: Greenwillow Books, 1993. (Friends)

Hutchins, Pat. *One-Eyed Jake*. New York: Greenwillow Books, 1979. (Sea & Seashore)

Hutchins, Pat. *Rosie's Walk*. New York: Macmillan, 1968. (Birds)

Hutchins, Pat. *The Surprise Party*. New York: Macmillan, 1969. (Birthdays)

Hutchins, Pat. *Tidy Titch*. New York: Greenwillow Books, 1991. (Families, Toys)

Hutchins, Pat. *Titch*. New York: Macmillan, 1971. (Families, Gardening, Teeny Tiny Things)

Hutchins, Pat. *Where's the Baby?* New York: Greenwillow Books, 1988. (Babies, Monsters)

Hutchins, Pat. *The Wind Blew*. New York: Macmillan, 1974. (Weather – Windy Day)

Hutchins, Pat. *You'll Soon Grow into Them, Titch*. New York: Greenwillow Books, 1983. (Clothing, Teeny Tiny Things)

Isadora, Rachel. *Ben's Trumpet*. New York: Greenwillow, 1979. (Music)

Jennings, Sharon. *Jeremiah and Mrs. Ming*. Willowdale, ON: Annick Press, 1990. (Bedtime)

Jorgensen, Gail. *Crocodile Beat*. Ills. by Patricia Mullins. Adelaide: Omnibus Books, 1988. (Cats; Monsters, Dragons & Wild Things)

Kalan, Robert. *Jump, Frog, Jump*. Ills. by Byron Barton. New York: Greenwillow Books, 1981. (Frogs; Snakes, Turtles & Lizards)

Kasza, Keiko. *A Mother for Choco*. New York: Putnam, 1992. (Mother's Day)

Kasza, Keiko. *The Pigs' Picnic*. New York: Putnam, 1988. (Food, Pigs)

Kasza, Keiko. *The Wolf's Chicken Stew*. New York: Putnam, 1987. (Foxes & Wolves)

Keats, Ezra Jack. *Apt. 3*. New York: Macmillan, 1971. (Music)

Keats, Ezra Jack. *Dreams*. New York: Macmillan, 1974. (Bedtime)

Keats, Ezra Jack. *Hi, Cat!* New York: Macmillan, 1970. (Cats)

Keats, Ezra Jack. *Jennie's Hat*. New York: Harper & Row, 1966. (Birds, Clothing, Easter, Seasons – Spring)

Keats, Ezra Jack. *Letter to Amy*. New York: Harper & Row, 1968. (Birthdays)

Keats, Ezra Jack. *Maggie and the Pirate*. New York: Four Winds Press, 1979. (Insects)

Keats, Ezra Jack. *Pet Show!* New York: Macmillan, 1972. (Cats, Pets)

Keats, Ezra Jack. *Peter's Chair*. New York: Harper & Row, 1967. (Babies, Emotions, Families, Toys)

Keats, Ezra Jack. *Regards to the Man in the Moon*. New York : Aladdin Books, 1987, c1981. (Space, Transportation)

Keats, Ezra Jack. *The Snowy Day.* New York: Viking Press, 1962. (Weather – Snowy Day)

Keats, Ezra Jack. *Whistle for Willie.* New York: Viking Press, 1964. (Dogs)

Keller, Holly. *Geraldine's Big Snow.* New York: Greenwillow Books, 1988. (Weather – Snowy Day)

Keller, Holly. *Geraldine's Blanket.* New York: Greenwillow Books, 1984. (Pigs)

Keller, Holly. *Horace.* New York: Greenwillow Books, 1991. (Pigs)

Kellog, Steven. *The Mysterious Tadpole.* New York: Dial Press, 1977. (Birthdays, Frogs, Pets)

Kennedy, Jimmy. *Teddy Bears' Picnic.* New York: H. Holt, 1992. (Bears)

Kent, Jack. *The Caterpillar and the Polliwog.* Englewood Cliffs, NJ: Prentice-Hall, 1982. (Frogs)

Kent, Jack. *Fat Cat.* New York: Parent's Magazine Press, 1971. (Cats, Food, Teeny Tiny Things)

Kent, Jack. *Round Robin.* Englewood Cliffs, NJ: Prentice-Hall, 1982. (Birds, Weather – Snowy Day)

Kent, Jack. *Silly Goose.* Englewood Cliffs, NJ: Prentice-Hall, 1983. (Ducks & Geese)

Kent, Jack. *Socks for Supper.* New York: Parents' Magazine Press, 1978. (Clothing, Food)

Kiser, Suann & Kevin. *The Birthday Thing.* New York: Greenwillow Books, 1989. (Birthdays)

Klassen, Dale. *I Love to Play Hockey.* Ills. by Rhian Brynjolson. Winnipeg: Pemmican, 1994. (Seasons – Winter)

Knutson, Kimberly. *Muddigush.* New York: Maxwell Macmillan, 1992. (Weather – Rainy Day)

Knutson, Kimberly. *Ska-tat!* New York: Maxwell Macmillan, 1993. (Weather – Rainy Day)

Koenig, Marion. *The Tale of Fancy Nancy.* London: Chatto, 1977. (Mice, Valentine's Day)

Koscielniak, Bruce. *Bear and Bunny Grow Tomatoes.* New York: Alfred A. Knopf, 1993. (Gardening)

Kovalski, Maryann. *Brenda and Edward.* Toronto: Kids Can Press, 1984. (Dogs, Valentine's Day)

Kovalski, Maryann. *Jingle Bells.* Toronto: Kids Can Press, 1988. (Christmas)

Kovalski, Maryann. *Take Me Out to the Ballgame.* Richmond Hill, ON: North Winds Press, 1992. (Seasons – Summer)

Kovalski, Maryann. *The Wheels on the Bus.* Toronto: Kids Can Press, 1987. (Transportation)

Kraus, Robert. *Another Mouse to Feed.* Ills. by Jose Aruego & Ariane Dewey. New York: Simon & Schuster, 1980. (Babies, Mice)

Kraus, Robert. *Leo the Late Bloomer.* Ills. by Jose Aruego. New York: Windmill Books, 1971. (Cats, Families)

Kraus, Robert. *Milton the Early Riser.* Ills. by Jose & Ariane Aruego. New York: Windmill Books, 1972. (Bears)

Kraus, Robert. *Musical Max.* Ills. by Jose Aruego & Ariane Dewey. New York: Simon & Schuster, 1990. (Music)

Kraus, Robert. *Owliver.* Ills. by Jose Aruego & Ariane Dewey. New York: Simon & Schuster, 1974. (Birds)

Kraus, Robert. *Whose Mouse Are You?* Ills. by Jose Aruego. New York: Macmillan, 1970. (Babies, Families, Mice)

Lane, Megan Halsey. *Something to Crow About.* New York: Dial, 1990. (Farms, Friends)

Langstaff, John. *Frog Went A-Courtin'.* Ills. by Feodor Rojankovsky. San Diego, CA: Harcourt Brace Jovanovich, 1983. (Frogs, Valentine's Day)

Langstaff, John. *Oh A-Hunting We Will Go.* Ills. by Nancy Winslow Parker. New York: Atheneum, 1974. (Bears, Mice)

Langstaff, John. *Over in the Meadow.* Ills. by Feodor Rojankovsky. New York: Harcourt, Brace & World, 1957. (Counting, Frogs)

Lear, Edward. *The Owl and the Pussy Cat.* Ills. by Ron Berg. Richmond Hill, ON: North Winds Press, 1984. (Birds, Cats, Sea & Seashore, Valentine's Day)

Lear, Edward. *The Quangle Wangle's Hat.* Ills. by Helen Oxenbury. New York: Watts, 1970. (Clothing)

Lee, Dennis. *Alligator Pie.* Ills. by Frank Newfeld. Toronto: Macmillan of Canada, 1974. (Food)

Lee, Dennis. *Jelly Belly.* Ills. by Juan Wijngaard. Toronto: Macmillan of Canada, 1983. (Giants)

Lee, Dennis. *Lizzy's Lion.* Ills. by Marie-Louise Gay. Toronto: Stoddart, 1984. (Cats, Monsters, Pets)

Lemieux, Michelle. *What's That Noise?* London: Methuen Children's Books, 1984. (Bears, Seasons – Winter)

Lester, Helen. *It Wasn't My Fault.* Ills. by Lynn Munsinger. Boston: Houghton Mifflin, 1985. (Emotions)

Lester, Helen. *A Porcupine Named Fluffy.* Ills. by Lynn Munsinger. Boston: Houghton Mifflin, 1986. (Friends)

Lester, Helen. *Tacky the Penguin.* Ills. by Lynn Munsinger. Boston: Houghton Mifflin, 1988. (Birds)

Lester, Helen. *The Wizard, the Fairy, and the Magic Chicken.* Ills. by Lynn Munsinger. Boston: Houghton Mifflin, 1983. (Friends, Monsters)

Lewison, Wendy Cheyette. *Going to Sleep on the Farm.* Ills. by Juan Wijngaard. New York: Dial Books for Young Readers, 1992. (Farms)

Leydenfrost, Robert. *The Snake That Sneezed.* New York: Putnam, 1970. (Animals of the Wild; Snakes, Turtles & Lizards)

Lindbergh, Reeve. *Midnight Farm.* Ills. by Susan Jeffers. New York: Dial Books for Young Readers, 1987. (Bedtime)

Lindbergh, Reeve. *The Day the Goose Got Loose.* Ills. by Steven Kellogg. New York: Dial Books for Young Readers, 1990. (Ducks & Geese)

Lindgren, Astrid. *The Tomten and the Fox.* New York: Coward, McCann & Geoghen, 1966. (Foxes & Wolves)

Lindgren, Barbro. *The Wild Baby.* Ills. by Eva Eriksson. New York: Greenwillow Books, 1981. (Babies)

Lionni, Leo. *Alexander and the Wind-Up Mouse.* New York: Pantheon, 1969. (Mice, Toys)

Lionni, Leo. *The Biggest House in the World.* New York: Pantheon, 1968. (Houses, Teeny Tiny Things)

Lionni, Leo. *A Colour of His Own.* New York: Pantheon, 1975. (Colour & Art)

Lionni, Leo. *Fish Is Fish.* New York: Pantheon Books, 1970. (Sea & Seashore; Snakes, Turtles & Lizards)

Lionni, Leo. *Frederick.* New York: Pantheon, 1967. (Colour & Art, Mice, Seasons – Winter)

Lionni, Leo. *In the Rabbit Garden.* New York: Pantheon, 1975. (Rabbits)

Lionni, Leo. *Inch by Inch.* New York: Obolensky, 1960. (Gardening, Insects, Teeny Tiny Things)

Lionni, Leo. *Let's Make Rabbits.* New York: Pantheon, 1982. (Colour & Art, Rabbits)

Lionni, Leo. *Little Blue and Little Yellow.* New York: Mc Dowell, Obolensky, 1959. (Colour & Art)

Lionni, Leo. *Swimmy.* New York: Pantheon, 1963. (Sea & Seashore, Teeny Tiny Things)

Litchfield, Ada Bassett. *It's Going to Rain.* Ills. by Ruth M. Hartshorn. New York: Atheneum, 1980. (Weather – Rainy Day)

Lobel, Arnold. *Book of Pigericks.* New York: Harper & Row, 1983. (Pigs)

Lobel, Arnold. "The Garden" in *Frog and Toad Together.* New York: Harper & Row, 1972. (Gardening)

Lobel, Arnold. *Giant John.* New York: Harper & Row, 1964. (Giants)

Lobel, Arnold. *The Great Blueness and Other Predicaments.* New York: Harper & Row, 1968. (Colour & Art)

Lobel, Arnold. *The Man Who Took the Inside Out.* New York: Harper & Row, 1974. (Father's Day, Houses)

Lobel, Arnold. *Prince Bertram the Bad.* New York: Harper & Row, 1963. (Emotions, Royalty)

Lobel, Arnold. *The Rose in My Garden.* Ills. by Anita Lobel. New York: Greenwillow Books, 1984. (Gardening)

Lobel, Arnold. *A Treeful of Pigs.* New York: Greenwillow Books, 1979. (Farms, Pigs)

London, Jonathan. *Froggy Gets Dressed.* Ills. by Frank Remkiewicz. New York: Viking, 1992. (Clothing, Frogs, Weather – Snowy Day)

London, Jonathan. *Froggy Learns to Swim.* Ills. by Frank Remkiewicz. New York: Viking, 1995. (Frogs, Seasons – Summer)

Lord, John. *The Giant Jam Sandwich.* London: J. Cape, 1972. (Food, Giants, Insects, Seasons – Summer)

Lotteridge, Celia. *The Name of the Tree.* Ills. by Ian Wallace. Toronto: Groundwood Books, 1989. (Animals of the Wild; Cats; Elephants; Snakes, Turtles & Lizards)

Lotteridge, Celia. *One Watermelon Seed.* Ills. by Karen Patkau. Toronto: Oxford University Press, 1986. (Gardening)

Lunn, Janet. *Amos's Sweater.* Ills. by Kim LaFave. Toronto: Groundwood Books, 1988. (Clothing, Sheep, Weather – Winter)

Lunn, Janet. *Duck Cakes for Sale.* Ills. by Kim LaFave. Toronto: Groundwood Books, 1989. (Ducks & Geese)

Luton, Mildred. *Little Chick's Mothers and all the Others.* Ills. by Mary Maki Rae. New York: Viking Press, 1983. (Mother's Day)

MacDonald, Amy. *Rachel Fister's Blister.* Ills. by Marjorie Priceman. Boston: Houghton Mifflin, 1990. (Sickness & Health)

Mack, Stan. *Ten Bears in My Bed.* New York: Pantheon Books, 1974. (Bears)

Maestro, Betsy. *The Wise Monkey Tale.* New York: Crown, 1975. (Monkeys)

Maestro, Betsy. *Around the Clock with Harriet.* New York: Crown Publishers, 1984. (Time)

Maestro, Betsy. *Harriet Goes to the Circus.* New York: Crown Publishers, 1977. (Circus)

Maris, Ron. *I Wish I Could Fly.* New York: Greenwillow Books, 1986. (Birds; Snakes, Turtles & Lizards)

Marshall, James. *Wings: A Tale of Two Chickens.* New York: Viking Kestrel, 1986. (Birds, Foxes & Wolves, Safety)

Marshall, James. *Yummers!* Boston: Houghton Mifflin, 1972. (Food, Pigs)

Marshall, Janet Perry. *My Camera at the Aquarium.* Boston: Little, Brown & Co., 1989. (Sea & Seashore)

Marshall, Janet Perry. *My Camera at the Zoo.* Boston: Little, Brown & Co., 1989. (Zoos)

Martin, Bill. *Brown Bear, Brown Bear.* Ills. by Eric Carle. New York: Henry Holt and Co., 1992. (Bears, Colour & Art)

Martin, Bill. *Chicka, Chicka Boom Boom.* Ills. by Lois Ehlert. New York: Simon & Schuster Books for Young Readers, 1989. (Alphabet Books)

Martin, Bill. *The Maestro Plays*. Ills. by Vladimir Radunsky. New York: H. Holt, 1994. (Music)

Martin, Bill. *Polar Bear, Polar Bear, What Do You Hear?* Ills. by Eric Carle. New York: H. Holt, 1991. (Animals of the Wild)

Martin, Rafe. *Foolish Rabbit's Big Mistake*. Ills. by Ed Young. New York: Putnam, 1985. (Cats, Rabbits)

Martinez, Ruth. *Mrs. McDockerty's Knitting*. Ills. by Catherine O'Neill. Toronto: Douglas & McIntyre, 1990. (Clothing, Farms, Seasons – Winter, Sheep)

Marzollo, Jean. *Close Your Eyes*. Ills. by Susan Jeffers. New York: Dial Press, 1978. (Bedtime, Father's Day)

Maxner, Joyce. *Nicholas Cricket*. Ills. by William Joyce. New York: Harper & Row, 1989. (Music)

Mayer, Mercer. *Just for You*. New York: Golden, 1975. (Families, Mother's Day, Valentine's Day)

Mayer, Mercer. *Just Me and My Dad*. New York: Golden, 1977. (Father's Day)

Mayer, Mercer. *Liza Lou and the Yeller Belly Swamp*. New York: Four Winds Press, 1980. (Monsters)

Mayer, Mercer. *Me Too!* New York: Golden, 1985. (Families)

Mayer, Mercer. *There's a Nightmare in My Closet*. New York: Dial Press, 1968. (Bedtime, Emotions, Monsters)

Mayer, Mercer. *There's an Alligator Under My Bed*. New York: Dial Books for Young Readers, 1987. (Bedtime, Monsters)

Mayer, Mercer. *What Do You Do with a Kangaroo?* New York: Scholastic, 1973. (Bedtime, Pets)

McBratney, Sam. *Guess How Much I Love You*. Ills. by Anita Jeram. Cambridge, MA: Candlewick, 1994. (Father's Day, Rabbits)

McDonald, Megan. *Is This a House for a Hermit Crab?* New York: Orchard Books, 1990. (Houses, Sea & Seashore)

McGovern, Ann. *Too Much Noise*. Ills. by Simms Taback. Boston: Houghton Mifflin, 1967. (Farms, Houses, Weather – Windy Day)

McNally, Darcie. *In a Cabin in a Wood*. Ills. by Robin Michal Koontz. New York: Cobblehill/Dutton, 1991. (Rabbits)

McPhail, David. *Andrew's Bath*. Boston: Little, Brown, 1984. (Bathtime)

McPhail, David. *Bear's Toothache*. Boston: Little, Brown, 1972. (Bears, Sickness & Health)

McPhail, David. *Emma's Pet*. New York: Dutton, 1985. (Bears)

McPhail, David. *First Flight*. Boston: Little, Brown, 1987. (Bears, Space)

McPhail, David. *Pig Pig Goes to Camp*. New York: Dutton, 1983. (Seasons – Summer)

McPhail, David. *Pigs Aplenty, Pigs Galore!*. New York: Dutton, 1993. (Pigs)

McPhail, David. *Pig Pig Rides*. New York: Dutton, 1982. (Safety)

McPhail, David. *The Train*. Boston: Little, Brown, 1977. (Transportation)

McPhail, David. *Where Can an Elephant Hide*. Garden City, NY: Doubleday, 1979. (Elephants)

Meddaugh, Susan. *The Beast*. Boston: Houghton Mifflin, 1981. (Monsters)

Meddaugh, Susan. *Too Many Monsters*. Boston: Houghton, Mifflin, 1982. (Monsters)

Melmed, Laura Krauss. *I Love You As Much*. Ills. by Henri Sorensen. New York: Lothrop, 1993. (Mother's Day)

Mitra, Annie. *Penguin Moon*. New York: Holiday House, 1989. (Bedtime, Birds, Space)

Modell, Frank. *Ice Cream Soup*. New York: Greenwillow Books, 1988. (Birthdays)

Modell, Frank. *Seen Any Cats?* New York: Greenwillow, 1979. (Cats)

Mohr, Joseph. *Silent Night*. Ills. by Susan Jeffers. New York: Dutton, 1984. (Christmas)

Moore, Clement. *The Night Before Christmas*. Ills. by Tomie De Paola. New York: Holiday House, 1980. (Christmas)

Morgan, Allen. *Sadie and the Snowman*. Ills. by Brenda Clark. Toronto: Kids Can Press, 1985. (Weather – Snowy Day)

Morgan, Nicola. *Louis and the Night Sky*. Toronto: Oxford University Press, 1990. (Bedtime, Space)

Mosel, Arlene. *Tikki Tikki Tembo*. Ills. by Blair Lent. New York: Holt, Rinehart and Winston, 1968. (Safety)

Muller, Robin. *Row, Row, Row Your Boat*. Richmond Hill, ON: Scholastic, 1993. (Sea & Seashore)

Munari, Bruno. *Bruno Munari's Zoo*. New York: World Publishing, 1963. (Zoos)

Munari, Bruno. The *Elephant's Wish*. New York: William Collins, 1980. (Birthdays, Elephants)

Munsch, Robert. *50 Below Zero*. Ills. by Michael Martchenko. Toronto: Annick Press, 1986. (Seasons – Winter, Weather – Snowy Day)

Munsch, Robert. *Angela's Airplane*. Ills. by Michael Martchenko. Toronto: Annick Press, 1988. (Space, Transportation)

Munsch, Robert. *The Boy in the Drawer*. Michael Martchenko. Toronto: Annick Press, 1986. (Emotions, Monsters)

Munsch, Robert. *The Dark*. Ills. by Sami Suomalainen. Toronto: Annick Press, 1984. (Bedtime, Monsters)

Munsch, Robert. *David's Father*. Ills. by Michael Martchenko. Toronto: Annick Press, 1983. (Emotions, Families, Father's Day, Friends, Giants)

Munsch, Robert. *Jonathan Cleaned Up.* Ills. by Michael Martchenko. Toronto: Annick Press, 1981. (Transportation)

Munsch, Robert. *Millicent and the Wind.* Ills. by Suzanne Duranceau. Toronto: Annick Press, 1984. (Friends, Weather – Windy Day)

Munsch, Robert. *Moira's Birthday.* Ills. by Michael Martchenko. Toronto: Annick Press, 1987. (Birthdays)

Munsch, Robert. *Mortimer.* Ills. by Michael Martchenko. Toronto: Annick Press, 1985. (Bedtime, Music)

Munsch, Robert. *The Mud Puddle.* Ills. by Sami Suomalainen. Toronto: Annick Press, 1979. (Bathtime, Weather – Rainy Day)

Munsch, Robert. *Murmel, Murmel, Murmel.* Ills. by Michael Martchenko. Toronto: Annick Press, 1982. (Babies, Families, Father's Day)

Munsch, Robert. *The Paper Bag Princess.* Ills. by Michael Martchenko. Toronto: Annick Press, 1980. (Clothing, Monsters, Royalty, Valentine's Day)

Munsch, Robert. *Pigs.* Ills. by Michael Martchenko. Toronto: Annick Press, 1989. (Pigs)

Munsch, Robert. *Thomas's Snowsuit.* Ills. by Michael Martchenko. Toronto: Annick Press, 1985. (Clothing, Seasons – Winter, Weather – Snowy Day)

Murphy, Jill. *Five Minutes Peace.* London: Walker, 1986. (Bathtime, Families, Mother's Day)

Murphy, Jill. *Peace at Last.* New York: Dial Press, 1980. (Bears, Bedtime, Father's Day)

Myers, Walter Dean. *Mr. Monkey & the Gotcha Bird.* Ills. by Leslie Morrill. New York: Delacorte Press, 1984. (Birds, Monkeys)

Nash, Ogden. *Custard the Dragon.* Boston: Little, Brown, 1959. (Monsters)

Nerlove, Miriam. *Halloween.* Niles, Ill: A. Whitman, 1989. (Halloween)

Noble, Trinka Hakes. *The King's Tea.* New York: Dial Press, 1979. (Royalty)

Nodset, Joan. *Who Took the Farmer's Hat?* Ills. by Fritz Siebel. New York: Harper & Row, 1963. (Birds, Clothing, Farms, Seasons – Spring, Weather – Windy Day)

Oppenheim, Joanne. *Have You Seen Birds?* Ills. by Barbara Reid. Richmond Hill, ON: North Winds Press, 1986. (Birds)

Oram, Hiawyn. *Mine!* Ills. by Mary Rees. Hauppauge, NY: Barron's, 1992. (Toys)

Ottley, Matt. *What Faust Saw.* Rydalmere, NSW, Australia: Hodder Children's Books, 1995. (Dogs, Space)

Parker, Nancy Winslow. *Love from Uncle Clyde.* New York: Dodd, Mead, 1977. (Birthdays)

Patz, Nancy. *Nobody Knows I Have Delicate Toes.* New York: Franklin Watts, 1980. (Bathtime, Elephants)

Pearson, Tracey. *Sing a Song of Sixpence.* New York: Dial Books for Young Readers, 1985. (Birds, Royalty)

Peck, Robert. *Hamilton.* Ills. by Laura Lydecker. Boston: Little, Brown, 1976. (Pigs)

Peek, Merle. *Mary Wore Her Red Dress and Henry Wore His Green Sneakers.* New York: Clarion Books, 1985. (Birthdays, Clothing, Colour & Art)

Peek, Merle. *The Balancing Act: A Counting Song.* New York: Clarion Books, 1987. (Counting)

Peek, Merle. *Roll Over: A Counting Song.* New York: Houghton Mifflin / Clarion Books, 1981. (Counting)

Peppe, Rodney. *The Mice Who Lived in a Shoe.* Harmondsworth, England: Kestrel Books, 1981. (Families, Houses, Mice)

Petersham, Maud. *The Box with Red Wheels.* New York: Macmillan, 1949. (Farms, Pets)

Petersham, Maud. *Circus Baby.* New York: Macmillan, 1950. (Circus, Elephants)

Pinkney, Brian. *Max Found Two Sticks.* New York: Simon & Shuster, 1994. (Music)

Pinkwater, Daniel. *Bear's Picture.* New York: Dutton, 1984, c1972. (Bears, Colour & Art))

Pinkwater, Daniel. *The Big Orange Splot.* New York: Hastings House, 1977. (Colour & Art, Houses)

Pinkwater, Daniel. *Tooth-Gnasher, Superflasher.* New York: Four Winds Press, 1981. (Transportation)

Piper, Watty. *The Little Engine That Could.* New York: Platt & Munk, 1954. (Transportation)

Pirotta, Saviour & Kate Simpson. *But No Cheese!* London: Hodder & Stoughton, 1992. (Food, Mice)

Polushkin, Maria. *Mother, Mother I Want Another.* Ills. by Diane Dawson. New York: Crown Publishers, 1978. (Bedtime, Families, Mice, Mother's Day)

Pomerantz, Charlotte. *Here Comes Henny.* Ills. by Nancy Winslow Parker. New York: Greenwillow, 1994. (Food)

Pomerantz, Charlotte. *Piggy in the Puddle.* Ills. by James Marshall. New York: Macmillan, 1974. (Bathtime, Farms, Pigs, Weather – Rainy Day)

Porter, Sue. *Little Wolf and the Giant.* New York: Simon & Schuster, 1990. (Foxes & Wolves, Giants)

Porter, Sue. *One Potato.* Toronto: Doubleday, 1989. (Food, Mice)

Preston, Edna Mitchell. *One Dark Night.* Ills. by Kurt Werth. New York: Viking Press, 1969. (Halloween)

Preston, Edna Mitchell. *Squawk to the Moon, Little Goose*. Ills. by Barbara Cooney. New York: Viking Press, 1974. (Bedtime, Birds, Ducks & Geese, Space)

Rae, Mary Maki. *The Farmer in the Dell*. New York: Viking Kestrel, 1988. (Farms)

Raffi. *Baby Beluga*. Ills. by Ashley Wolff. New York: Crown, 1990. (Sea & Seashore)

Raschka, Chris. *Charlie Parker Played Be Bop*. New York: Orchard Books, 1992. (Music)

Raschka, Chris. *Yo! Yes?* New York: Orchard, 1993. (Friends)

Rayner, Mary. *Mrs. Pigs Bulk Buy*. London : Macmillan Children's Books, 1981. (Families, Food, Pigs, Shopping)

Rice, Eva. *Benny Bakes a Cake*. New York: Greenwillow Books, 1981. (Birthdays, Food)

Rice, Eve. *Sam Who Never Forgets*. New York: Greenwillow Books, 1977. (Zoos)

Richards, Nancy Wilcox. *Farmer Joe's Hot Day*. Ills. by Werner Zimmermann. Richmond Hill, ON: North Winds Press; Scholastic, 1987. (Seasons – Summer)

Rockwell, Anne. *At the Beach*. New York: Macmillan, 1987. (Sea & Seashore)

Rockwell, Anne. *My Spring Robin*. New York: Macmillan, 1989. (Seasons – Spring)

Rockwell, Anne. *Poor Goose*. New York: Crowell, 1976. (Ducks & Geese)

Rockwell, Anne. *Thump, Thump, Thump*. New York: Dutton, 1981. (Halloween)

Roddie, Shen. *Hatch, Egg, Hatch: A Touch-and-Feel Action Flap Book*. Ills. by Frances Cony. Boston: Joy Street Books, 1991. (Easter)

Rosen, Michael. *We're Going on a Bear Hunt*. Ills. by Helen Oxenbury. New York: Macmillan, 1989. (Bears)

Ross, Tony. *I'm Coming to Get You!* London: Andersen, 1984. (Monsters)

Roy, Ron. *Three Ducks Went Wandering*. Ills. by Paul Galdone. New York: Houghton Mifflin, 1979. (Ducks & Geese)

Ruck-Pauquet, Gina. *Mumble Bear*. Ills. by Erika Dietzsch-Capelle. New York: G. P. Putnam's Sons, 1983. (Bears)

Ryder, Joanne. *Lizard in the Sun*. Ills. by Michael Rothman. New York: Morrow, 1990. (Snakes, Turtles & Lizards)

Ryder, Joanne. *The Snail's Spell*. Ills. by Lynne Cherry. New York: F. Warne, 1982. (Gardening)

Ryder, Joanne. *White Bear, Ice Bear*. Ills. by Michael Rothman. New York: Morrow Junior Books, 1989. (Animals of the Wild, Bears, Seasons – Winter, Weather – Snowy Day)

Rylant, Cynthia. *Night in the Country*. Ills. by Mary Szilagyi. New York: Bradbury Press, 1986. (Bedtime)

Rylant, Cynthia. *The Relatives Came*. Ills. by Stephen Gammell. New York: Bradbury Press, 1985. (Families, Seasons – Summer)

Sandburg, Carl. *The Wedding Procession of the Rag Doll and the Broom Handle and Who Was in It*. New York: Harcourt, Brace & World, 1967. (Toys, Valentine's Day)

Saunders, Davie and Julie. *Dibble and Dabble*. New York: Bradbury Press, 1990. (Ducks & Geese)

Scamell, Ragnhild. *Buster's Echo*. Ills. by Genvieve Webster. New York: HarperCollins, 1993. (Dogs)

Scamell, Ragnhild. *Three Bags Full*. Ills. by Sally Hobson. New York: Orchard Books, 1993. (Sheep)

Scharer, Niko. *Emily's House*. Ills. by Joanne Fitzgerald. Toronto: Groundwood Books, 1990. (Farms)

Scheer, Julian. *Rain Makes Applesauce*. New York: Holiday House, 1964. (Fall, Weather – Rainy Day)

Schneider, Rex. *The Wide-Mouthed Frog*. Owings Mills, MD: Stemmer House, 1980. (Animals of the Wild, Frogs)

Schwartz, Roslyn. *Rose and Dorothy*. Toronto: Kids Can Press, 1990. (Elephants, Friends, Music)

Scott, Ann Herbert. *On Mother's Lap*. Ills. by Glo Coalson. New York: Clarion Books, 1992. (Babies, Mother's Day)

Seeger, Pete. *Abiyoyo*. Ills. by Michael Hays. New York : Macmillan: Collier Macmillan, 1986. (Giants)

Seeger, Pete. *Foolish Frog*. Ills. by Miloslav Jagr. New York: MacMillan, 1973. (Frogs)

Sendak, Maurice. *In the Night Kitchen*. New York: Harper & Row, 1970. (Bedtime, Food)

Sendak, Maurice. *Where the Wild Things Are*. New York: Harper & Row, 1963. (Emotions, Monsters)

Serfozo, Mary. *Who Said Red?* Ills. by Keiko Narahashi. New York: M.K. McElderry Books, 1988. (Colour & Art)

Seuling, Barbara. *The Teeny Tiny Woman*. New York: Viking Press, 1976. (Halloween, Teeny Tiny Things)

Shannon, George. *April Showers*. Ills. by Jose Aruego and Ariane Dewey. New York: Greenwillow Books, 1995. (Frogs, Weather – Rainy Day)

Shannon, George. *Dance Away*. Ills. by Jose Aruego and Ariane Dewey. New York: Greenwillow Books, 1982. (Foxes & Wolves, Music, Rabbits)

Shannon, George. *Lizard 's Song*. Ills. by Jose Aruego and Ariane Dewey. New York: Greenwillow Books, 1981. (Bears; Music; Snakes, Turtles & Lizards)

Shannon, George. *The Piney Woods Peddler.* Ills. by Nancy Tafuri. New York: Greenwillow Books, 1981. (Father's Day, Toys)

Shannon, George. *The Surprise.* Ills. by Jose Aruego and Ariane Dewey. New York: Greenwillow Books, 1983. (Birthdays, Mother's Day)

Shannon, Margaret. *Elvira.* New York: Ticknor & Fields, 1993. (Monsters, Dragons & Wild Things)

Sharmat, Marjorie W. *Big Fat Enormous Lie.* Ills. by David McPhail. New York: Dutton, 1978. (Emotions)

Sharmat, Mitchell. *Gregory, the Terrible Eater.* Ills. by Jose Aruego and Ariane Dewey. New York: Four Winds Press, 1980. (Food, Sickness & Health)

Shaw, Charles. *It Looked Like Spilt Milk.* New York: Harper, 1947. (Weather – Rainy Day)

Shaw, Nancy. *Sheep in a Jeep.* Ills. by Margot Apple. Boston: Houghton Mifflin, 1986. (Sheep)

Shulevitz, Uri. *One Monday Morning.* New York: Scribner, 1967. (Royalty)

Simon, Norma. *Wet World.* Ills. by Alexi Natcher. Cambridge, MA: Candlewick, 1995. (Weather – Rainy Day)

Silverman, Erica. *Big Pumpkin.* Ills. by S.D. Schindler. New York : Macmillan, 1992. (Halloween)

Slavin, Bill. *The Cat Came Back.* Toronto, ON: Kids Can Press, 1992. (Cats)

Slobodkina, Esphyr. *Caps for Sale.* New York: Harper Collins, 1984, c1968. (Clothing, Monkeys)

Slote, Teri. *The Thing that Bothered Farmer Brown.* Ills. by Nadine Bernard Westcott. New York: Orchard Books, 1995. (Bedtime, Farms, Insects)

Spier, Peter. *Oh! Were They Ever Happy.* Garden City, NY: Doubleday, 1978. (Colour & Art, Families, Houses)

Stevens, Janet, ills. *The House That Jack Built.* New York: Holiday House, 1985. (Houses)

Stevens, Janet, ills. *The Tortoise and the Hare.* New York: Holiday House, 1984. (Rabbits)

Stevenson, James. *That Terrible Hallowe'en Night.* New York: Greenwillow Books, 1980. (Halloween)

Stevenson, James. *The Great Big Especially Beautiful Easter Egg.* New York: Greenwillow Books, 1983. (Easter)

Stevenson, James. *We Can't Sleep.* New York: Greenwillow Books, 1982. (Bedtime)

Stinson, Kathy. *Big or Little.* Ills. by Robin Baird Lewis. Toronto: Annick Press, 1983. (Teeny Tiny Things)

Stinson, Kathy. *Red Is Best.* Ills. by Robin Baird Lewis. Toronto: Annick Press, 1982. (Clothing, Colour & Art, Valentine's Day)

Stinson, Kathy. *Those Green Things.* Ills. by Mary McLoughlin. Toronto: Annick Press, 1985. (St. Patrick's Day)

Stoddard, Sandol. *Bedtime Mouse.* Ills. by Lynn Munsinger. Boston: Houghton Mifflin, 1981. (Bedtime, Mice)

Sundgaard, Arnold. *The Lamb and the Butterfly.* Ills. by Eric Carle. New York: Orchard Books, 1988. (Friends, Sheep)

Tapio, Pat Decker *The Lady Who Saw the Good Side of Everything.* Ills. by Paul Galdone. New York: Seabury Press, 1975. (Weather – Rainy Day)

Tejima. *Bear's Autumn.* New York: Philomel Books, 1993. (Seasons – Fall)

Tejima. *Fox's Dream.* New York: Philomel Books, 1987. (Foxes & Wolves, Seasons – Winter)

Tejima. *Owl Lake.* New York: Philomel Books, 1987. (Birds)

Tetherington, Jeanne. *Pumpkin, Pumpkin.* New York: Greenwillow Books, 1986. (Halloween, Seasons – Fall)

Thaler, Mike. *Owly.* Ills. by David Wiesner. New York: Harper & Row, 1982. (Birds, Mother's Day)

Tolstoy. *The Great Big Enormous Turnip.* Ills. by Helen Oxenbury. London: Heinemann, 1989, c1985. (Gardening, Mice, Seasons – Fall, Thanksgiving)

Tresselt, Alvin. *The Mitten.* Ills. by Yaroslava. New York: Lothrop, Lee & Shepard, 1964. (Cats, Clothing, Weather – Snowy Day)

Turkle, Brinton. *Do Not Open.* New York: Dutton, 1981. (Cats, Monsters, Sea & Seashore)

Ungerer, Tomi. *Crictor.* New York: Harper & Row, 1958. (Alphabet Books; Counting; Pets; School; Snakes, Turtles & Lizards)

Van Laan, Nancy. *The Big Fat Worm.* Ills. by Marisabina Russo. New York: Knopf, 1987. (Birds, Gardening)

Van Laan, Nancy. *Possum Come a-Knockin'.* Ills. by George Booth. New York: Knopf, 1990. (Houses)

Viorst, Judith. *Alexander and the Terrible, Horrible, No Good, Very Bad Day.* Ills. by by Ray Cruz. New York: Atheneum, 1972. (Emotions, Sickness & Health)

Viorst, Judith. *My Mama Says There Aren't any Zombies, Ghosts, Vampires, Creatures, Demons, Monsters, Fiends, Goblins or Things . . .* Ills. by Kay Chorao. New York: Atheneum, 1973. (Emotions, Monsters, Mother's Day)

Vipont, Elfrida. *The Elephant and the Bad Baby.* Ills. by Raymond Briggs. London: Hamilton, 1969. (Babies, Elephants)

Waber, Bernard. *Ira Sleeps Over.* Boston: Houghton Mifflin, 1972. (Bears, Bedtime, Emotions, Friends, Toys)

Waddell, Martin. *Farmer Duck*. Ills. by Helen Oxenbury. Cambridge, MA: Candlewick Press, 1991. (Ducks & Geese, Farms*)*

Waddell, Martin. *Little Mo*. Ills. by Jill Barton. Cambridge, MA: Candlewick Press, 1993. (Seasons – Winter)

Waddell, Martin. *Owl Babies*. Ills. by Patrick Benson. Cambridge, MA: Candlewick Press, 1992. (Babies, Mothers)

Waddell, Martin. *Pig in the Pond*. Ills. by Jill Barton. Cambridge, MA: Candlewick Press, 1992. (Farms, Pigs, Seasons – Summer)

Waddell, Martin. *Sam Vole and His Brothers*. Cambridge, MA: Candlewick Press, 1992. (Families)

Wagner, Jenny. *The Bunyip of Berkely Creek*. Ills. by Ron Brooks. Harmondsworth, England: Kestrel Books, 1973. (Friends)

Wagner, Jenny. *John Brown, Rose, and the Midnight Cat*. Ills. by Ron Brooks. Scarsdale, NY: Bradbury Press, 1978. (Cats, Dogs)

Wallis, Val. *The Secret in the Matchbox*. Ills. by John Shelley. New York: Farrar, Straus & Giroux, 1988. (School)

Watanabe, Shigeo. *How Do I Put It On?* Ills. by Yasuo Ohtomo. New York: Philomel Books, 1980. (Bears, Clothing)

Watson, Clyde. *Midnight Moon*. New York: St. Martin's Press, 1985. (Bedtime)

Watson, Pauline. *Wiggles, the Little Wishing Pig*. Ills. by Paul Galdone. New York: Seabury Press, 1978. (Pigs)

Watson, Wendy. *Has Winter Come?* New York: Collins & World, 1978. (Weather – Snowy Day)

Weiss, Nicki. *Where Does the Brown Bear Go?* New York : Greenwillow Books, 1989. (Houses)

Welber, Robert. *The Winter Picnic*. Ills. by Deborah Ray. New York: Random House, 1970. (Seasons – Winter)

Willington, Anne. *Apple Pie*. Ills. by Nina Sowter. Englewood Cliffs, NJ:Prentice-Hall, 1978. (Seasons – Fall)

Wells, Rosemary. *Hazel's Amazing Mother*. New York: Dial Books for Young Readers, 1985. (Families, Mother's Day, Toys)

Wells, Rosemary. *A Lion for Lewis*. New York: Dial Press, 1982. (Cats)

Wells, Rosemary. *Max's Chocolate Chicken*. New York: Dial Books for Young Readers, 1989. (Easter)

Wells, Rosemary. *Max's Christmas*. New York: Dial Books for Young Readers, 1986. (Christmas)

Wells, Rosemary. *Max's Dragon Shirt*. New York: Dial Books for Young Readers, 1991. (Clothing, Shopping)

Wells, Rosemary. *Morris's Disappearing Bag*. New York: Dial Press, 1975. (Christmas)

Wells, Rosemary. *Noisy Nora*. New York: Dial Press, 1973. (Babies, Emotions, Families, Mice)

Westcott, Nadine. *The Giant Vegetable Garden*. Boston: Little, Brown, 1981. (Gardening, Giants, Thanksgiving)

Westcott, Nadine. *I Know an Old Lady Who Swallowed a Fly*. Boston: Little, Brown, 1980. (Farms, Food, Insects)

Westcott, Nadine. *The Lady with the Alligator Purse*. Boston: Joy Street Books, 1988. (Sickness & Health)

Westcott, Nadine. *Peanut Butter and Jelly: A Play Rhyme*. New York: E.P. Dutton, 1987. (Food, Seasons – Summer)

Westwood, Jennifer. *Going to Squintum's: A Foxy Folktale*. Ills. by Fiona French. New York: Dial Books for Young Readers, 1985. (Foxes & Wolves)

Wild, Margaret. *Mr. Nick's Knitting*. Ills. by Dee Huxley. San Diego: Harcourt Brace Jovanovich, 1989. (Friends, Sickness & Health)

Wild, Margaret. *Our Granny*. Ills. by Julie Vivas. New York: Ticknor & Fields, 1994. (Families)

Wildsmith, Brian. *Carousel*. New York: Knopf, 1988. (Sickness & Health)

Wildsmith, Brian. *What the Moon Saw*. New York: Oxford University Press, 1978. (Bedtime)

Williams, Garth. *The Chicken Book*. New York: Delacorte Press, 1970. (Birds, Farms)

Williams, Linda. *The Little Old Lady Who Was Not Afraid of Anything*. Ills. by Megan Lloyd. New York: Crowell, 1986. (Halloween)

Williams, Sue. *I Went Walking*. Ills. by Julie Vivas. San Diego: Harcourt Brace Jovanovich, 1990. (Colour & Art)

Wishinsky, Frieda. *Oonga Boonga*. Ills. by Sucie Stevenson. Boston: Little, Brown, 1990. (Babies)

Wolkstein, Diane. *The Banza*. Ills. by Marc Brown. New York: Dial Press, 1981. (Music)

Wood, Audrey. *King Bidgood's in the Bathtub*. Ills. by Don Wood. San Diego: Harcourt Brace Jovanovich, 1985. (Bathtime, Royalty)

Wood, Audrey. *The Little Mouse, the Red Ripe Strawberry and the Big Hungry Bear*. Ills. by Don Wood. New York: Child's Play, 1990. (Seasons – Summer)

Wood, Audrey. *The Napping House*. Ills. by Don Wood. San Diego: Harcourt Brace Jovanovich, 1984. (Bedtime, Houses, Insects, Teeny Tiny Things)

Wood, Audrey. *Piggies*. Ills. by Don Wood. San Diego: Harcourt Brace Jovanovich, 1991. (Pigs)

Wood, Audrey. *Rude Giants*. San Diego: Harcourt Brace Jovanovich, 1993. (Giants)

Wynne-Jones, Tim. *Architect of the Moon*. Ills. by Ian Wallace. Vancouver, BC: Douglas and McIntyre, 1988. (Space, Toys)

Wynne-Jones, Tim. *The Hour of the Frog*. Ills. by Catherine O'Neill. Vancouver, BC: Douglas and McIntyre, 1989. (Frogs)

Wynne-Jones, Tim. *The Last Piece of Sky*. Ills. by Marie-Louise Gay. Toronto: Groundwood Books, 1993. (Space)

Xiong, Blia. *Nine-In-One, Grr! Grr!* Ills. by Nancy Hom. San Francisco: Children's Book Press. 1989. (Cats)

Yolen, Jane. *Mouse's Birthday*. Ills. by Bruce Degen. New York: Putnam's, 1993. (Birthdays)

Young, Ed. *Seven Blind Mice*. New York: Philomel Books, 1991. (Elephants, Mice)

Zelinsky, Paul O. *Wheels on the Bus*. New York: E.P. Dutton, 1990. (Transportation)

Zemach, Harvey. *The Judge*. Ills. by Margot Zemach. New York: Farrar, Straus & Giroux, 1969. (Monsters)

Zemach, Margot. *The Little Red Hen*. New York: Farrar, Straus & Giroux, 1983.. (Fall, Farms, Food, Gardening)

Zemach, Margot. *The Three Wishes: An Old Story*. New York: Farrar, Straus, & Giroux, 1986. (Birthdays, Food)

Zion, Gene. *Harry by the Sea*. Ills. by Margaret Bloy Graham. New York: Harper & Row, 1965. (Sea & Seashore)

Zion, Gene. *Harry, the Dirty Dog*. Ills. by Margaret Bloy Graham. New York: Harper & Row, 1956. (Bathtime, Dogs)

Zion, Gene. *No Roses for Harry*. Ills. by Margaret Bloy Graham. New York: Harper & Row, 1958. (Birthdays)

Zola, Meguido. *Only the Best*. Ills. by Valerie Littlewood. New York: Julia MacRae Books, 1981. (Father's Day, Toys)

Zolotow, Charlotte. *Do You Know What I'll Do?* Ills. by Garth Williams. New York: Harper & Row, 1958. (Babies, Families, Valentine's Day)

Zolotow, Charlotte. *Mr. Rabbit and the Lovely Present*. Ills. by Maurice Sendak. New York: Harper & Row, 1962. (Birthdays, Colour & Art, Easter, Mother's Day, Rabbits)

Zolotow, Charlotte. *This Quiet Lady*. Ills. by Anita Lobel. New York: Greenwillow Books, 1992. (Mother's Day)

MORE STORIES

Aardema, Verna. *Bimwili and the Zimwi*. Ills. by Susan Meddaugh. New York: Dial Books for Young Readers, 1985. (Monsters, Music, Sea & Seashore)

Aardema, Verna. *Who's in Rabbit's House?* Ills. by Leo and Diane Dillon. New York: Dial Press, 1977. (Animals of the Wild, Houses, Rabbits)

Adams, Adrienne. *The Easter Egg Artists*. New York: Scribner, 1976. (Easter)

Adams, Adrienne. *A Woggle of Witches*. New York: Scribner, 1971. (Halloween)

Ahlberg, Janet. *Starting School*. London: Viking Kestrel, 1988. (School)

Alexander, Martha. *Nobody Asked Me If I Wanted a Baby Sister*. New York: Dial Press, 1971. (Babies)

Aliki. *Medieval Feast*. New York: Crowell, 1983. (Food, Royalty)

Aliki. *We Are Best Friends*. New York: Greenwillow Books, 1982. (Friends)

Andersen, H. C. *The Emperor's New Clothes*. Ills. by Nadine Westcott. Boston: Little, Brown, 1984. (Clothing, Royalty)

Andrews, Jan. *The Auction*. Ills. by Karen Reczuch. Toronto: Groundwood Books, 1990. (Farms)

Andrews, Jan. *The Very Last First Time*. Ills. by Ian Wallace. Vancouver, BC: Douglas & McIntyre, 1985. (Seasons – Winter)

Anfousse, Ginette. *Chicken Pox*. Toronto: NC Press, 1981. (Sickness & Health)

Anholt, Catherine & Laurence. *Here Come the Babies*. Cambridge, MA: Candlewick Press, 1993. (Babies)

Arnosky, Jim. *Deer at the Brook*. New York: Lothrop, Lee & Shepard Books, 1986. (Animals of the Wild)

Arnosky, Jim. *Every Autumn Comes the Bear*. New York: G.P. Putnam, 1993. (Seasons – Fall)

Arnosky, Jim. *Otters Under Water*. New York: Putnam, 1992. (Animals of the Wild)

Arnosky, Jim. *Raccoons and Ripe Corn*. New York: Lothrop, Lee & Shepard Books, 1987. (Animals of the Wild, Fall)

Arnosky, Jim. *Watching Foxes*. New York: Lothrop, Lee & Shepard Books, 1985. (Animals of the Wild)

Auch, Mary Jane. *Peeping Beauty*. New York: Holiday House, 1993. (Ducks & Geese)

Balian, Lorna. *The Animal*. Nashville: Abingdon Press, 1972. (Snakes, Turtles & Lizards)

Balian, Lorna. *Humbug Rabbit*. Nashville: Abingdon, 1974. (Easter)

Balian, Lorna. *Sometimes It's Turkey, Sometimes It's Feathers.* New York: Abingdon, 1987. (Thanksgiving)

Bang, Molly. *Dawn.* New York: W. Morrow, 1983. (Ducks & Geese)

Bang, Molly. *The Grey Lady and the Strawberry Snatcher.* New York: Four Winds Press, 1980. (Seasons – Summer)

Bannatyne-Cugnet, Jo. *A Prairie Alphabet.* Ills. by Yvette Moore. Montreal: Tundra Books, 1992. (Alphabet Books, Farms)

Barrett, Judi. *A Snake Is Totally Tail.* Ills. by L.S. Johnson. New York: Atheneum, 1983. (Snakes, Turtles & Lizards)

Barton, Byron. *Hester.* New York: Greenwillow, 1975. (Halloween)

Bauer, Caroline Feller. *My Mom Travels A Lot.* Ills. by Nancy Winslow Parker. New York: F. Warne, 1981. (Mother's Day)

Bemelmans, Ludwig. *Madeline.* New York: Viking Press, 1939. (Sickness & Health)

Beskow, Elsa. *Pelle's New Suit.* New York: Harcourt, Brace Jovanovich, 1929. (Clothing)

Blades, Ann. *A Salmon for Simon.* Vancouver, BC: Douglas & McIntyre, 1978. (Sea & Seashore)

Blades, Ann. *By the Sea: An Alphabet Book.* Toronto: Kids Can Press, 1985. (Alphabet Books, Sea & Seashore)

Blades, Anne. *Mary of Mile 18.* Montreal: Tundra Books, 1971. (Seasons – Winter)

Boden, Alice. *Field of Buttercups: An Irish Story.* London: Hamish Hamilton, 1974. (St. Patrick's Day)

Bogart, Jo Ellen. *10 for Dinner.* Ills. by Carlos Freire. Richmond Hill, ON: North Winds Press, 1989. (Birthdays)

Bogart, Jo Ellen. *Daniel's Dog.* Ills. by Janet Wilson. Richmond Hill, ON: North Winds Press, 1990. (Babies)

Bogart, Jo Ellen. *Malcolm's Runaway Soap.* Ills. by Linda Hendry. Richmond Hill, ON: North Winds Press, 1988. (Bathtime)

Bond, Felicia. *Poinsettia and Her Family.* New York: Crowell, 1981. (Pigs, Houses)

Bouchard, Dave. *If You're Not From the Prairies.* Ills. by Henry Ripplinger. Vancouver, BC: Raincoast & Summerwild Productions, 1993. (Farms)

Bourgeois, Paulette. *Franklin Fibs.* Ills. by Brenda Clark. Toronto: Kids Can Press, 1991. (Snakes,Turtles & Lizards)

Bourgeois, Paulette. *Franklin Goes to School.* Ills. by Brenda Clark. Toronto: Kids Can Press, 1995. (School)

Bourgeois, Paulette. *Franklin in the Dark.* Ills. by Brenda Clark. Toronto: Kids Can Press, 1986. (Emotions)

Bowden, J.C. *Why the Tides Ebb and Flow.* Ills. by Marc Brown. Boston: Houghton Mifflin, 1979. (Sea & Seashore)

Brett, Jan. *Town Mouse, Country Mouse.* New York: Putnam's, 1994. (Mice)

Briggs, Raymond. *Jim and the Beanstalk.* London: Hamilton, 1970. (Gardening, Giants)

Briggs, Raymond. *Snowman.* London: Hamish Hamilton, 1988, c1978. (Weather – Snowy Day)

Brown, Marc. *Arthur's Valentine.* Boston: Little, Brown, 1980. (Valentine's Day)

Brown, Margaret Wise. *Christmas in the Barn.* Ills. by Barbara Cooney. New York: Crowell, 1952. (Christmas)

Brown, Margaret Wise. *On Christmas Eve.* Ills. by Beni Montresor. New York: Young Scott Books, 1938. (Christmas)

Brown, Margaret Wise. *The Dead Bird.* Ills. by Remy Charlip. New York: W. R. Scott, 1958. (Pets)

Browne, Anthony. *Gorilla.* New York: Knopf, 1983. (Zoos)

Browne, Anthony. *The Piggybook.* New York: Knopf, 1986. (Families, Mother's Day, Pigs)

Browne, Antony. *Willy the Wimp.* New York : Knopf, 1984. (Emotions)

Bruna, Dick. *My Shirt Is White.* London: Methuen, 1972. (Clothing)

Bruneel, Etienne. *A Whale of a Bath.* Ills. by Tess Holloway. Edmonton: Tree Frog Press, 1990. (Bathtime)

Bunting, Eve. *St. Patrick's Day in the Morning.* Ills. by Jan Brett. New York: Clarion Books, 1980. (St. Patrick's Day)

Burningham, John. *Cannonball Simp.* London: Cape, 1966. (Circus)

Burningham, John. *John Patrick Norman McHennessy, The Boy Who Was Always Late.* New York: Crown, 1987. (Monsters)

Burningham, John. *Time to Get Out of the Bath, Shirley.* New York: Crowell, 1978. (Bathtime)

Burton, Virginia Lee. *Katy and the Big Snow.* Boston: Houghton Mifflin company, 1943. (Weather – Snowy Day)

Burton, Virginia Lee. *Mike Mulligan and His Steam Shovel.* Boston: Houghton Mifflin, 1939. (Transportation)

Burton, Virginia Lee. *The Little House.* Boston: Houghton Mifflin, 1969, c1942. (Houses)

Calhoun, Mary. *The Hungry Leprechaun.* Ills. by Roger Duvoisin. New York: Wm. Morrow & Co., 1962. (St. Patrick's Day)

Carle, Eric. *The Tiny Seed*. Natick, MA : Picture Book Studio, 1987. (Gardening)

Carrick, Carol. *The Accident*. Ills. by Donald Carrick. New York: Seabury Press, 1976. (Pets)

Carrick, Carol. *In the Moonlight, Waiting*. Ills. by Donald Carrick. New York: Clarion, 1990. (Sheep)

Carrick, Carol. *Paul's Christmas Birthday*. Ills. by Donald Carrick. New York: Greenwillow Books, 1978. (Christmas)

Carrick, Carol. *A Rabbit for Easter*. Ills. by Donald Carrick. New York: Greenwillow Books, 1979. (Easter)

Carrick, Donald. *Morgan and the Artist*. New York: Clarion Books, 1985. (Colour & Art)

Cassedey, Sylvia. *Red Dragonfly on My Shoulder*. Ills. by Molly Bang. New York: Harper Collins, 1992. (Insects)

Cauley, Lorinda Bryan. *The Town Mouse and the Country Mouse*. New York: G.P. Putnam, 1984. (Mice)

Charles, Donald. *Shaggy Dog's Halloween*. Chicago: Childrens Press, 1984. (Halloween)

Cleaver, Elizabeth. *ABC*. Toronto: Oxford University Press, 1984. (Alphabet Books)

Cohen, Miriam. *"Bee My Valentine!"* Ills. by Lillian Hoban. New York: Greenwillow Books, 1978. (Valentine's Day)

Cohen, Miriam. *Best Friends*. Ills. by Lillian Hoban. New York: Macmillan, 1971. (Friends)

Cohen, Miriam. *No Good in Art*. Ills. by Lillian Hoban. New York: Greenwillow Books, 1980. (Colour & Art)

Cohen, Miriam. *Will I Have a Friend?* Ills. by Lillian Hoban. New York: Macmillan, 1967. (School)

Cole, Babette. *Prince Cinders*. London: Hamilton, 1987. (Royalty)

Cole, Babette. *Princess Smartypants*. London: Hamilton, 1986. (Royalty)

Cole, Brock. *The Giant's Toe*. New York: Farrar, Straus & Giroux, 1986. (Giants)

Cole, Brock. *The King at the Door*. Garden City, NY: Doubleday, 1979. (Royalty)

Cooney, Barbara. *Miss Rumphius*. New York: Viking Press, 1982. (Families, Gardening)

Crave, Robert L. *Clyde Monster*. Ills. by Kay Chorao. New York: Dutton, 1976. (Monsters)

Crews, Donald. *Carousel*. New York: Greenwillow Books, 1982. (Circus, Colour & Art)

Crews, Donald. *Freight Train*. New York: Greenwillow Books, 1978. (Colour & Art, Transportation)

Crews, Donald. *Parade*. New York: Greenwillow, 1983. (Circus)

Crews, Donald. *School Bus*. New York: Greenwillow, 1984. (School)

Cutler, Jane. *Darcy and Gran Don't Like Babies*. New York: Scholastic, 1993. (Babies)

Daly, Niki. *Not So Fast Songololo*. New York : Atheneum, 1986. (Clothing, Shopping)

Day, Alexandra. *Carl Goes to Day Care*. New York: Farrar, Straus & Giroux, 1993. (Pets)

Day, Alexandra. *Carl's Masquerade*. New York: Farrar, Straus & Giroux, 1992. (Dogs)

De Brunhoff, Jean. *Babar and Father Christmas*. New York: Random House, 1940. (Christmas)

De Brunhoff, Jean. *The Story of Babar*. New York: Random House, 1961, c1933. (Elephants)

De Brunhoff, Laurent. *Babar's ABC*. New York: Random House, 1983. (Alphabet Books)

De Brunhoff, Laurent. *Babar's Birthday Surprise*. New York: Random House, 1970. (Birthdays)

De La Mare, Walter. *Molly Whuppie*. Ills. by Errol Le Cain. New York: Farrar, Straus & Giroux, 1983. (Giants)

De Paola, Tomie. *The Art Lesson*. New York: Putnam, 1989. (Colour & Art)

De Paola, Tomie. *Fin M'Coul: The Giant of Knockmany Hill*. New York: Holiday House, 1981. (Giants, St. Patrick's Day)

De Paola, Tomie. *The Friendly Beasts: An Old English Christmas Carol*. New York: Putnam, 1981. (Christmas)

De Paola, Tomie. *Legend of the Indian Paintbrush*. New York: Putnam, 1988. (Colour & Art)

De Paola, Tomie. *Strega Nona*. Englewood Cliffs, NJ: Prentice-Hall, 1975. (Food)

Demi. *Liang and the Magic Paintbrush*. Toronto: Doubleday Canada, 1989. (Colour & Art)

Denton, Kady Macdonald. *The Picnic*. London: Methuen Children's Books, 1988. (Seasons – Summer)

Devlin, Wende. *Cranberry Valentine*. New York: Four Winds, 1986. (Valentine's Day)

Douglass, Barbara. *Good As New*. Ills. by Patience Brewster. New York: Lothrop, Lee & Shepard, 1982. (Toys)

Dubanevich, Arlene. *Pig William*. New York: Bradbury Press, 1985. (Pigs)

Dutton, Sandra . *The Cinnamon Hen's Autumn Day*. New York: Atheneum, 1988. (Seasons – Fall)

Duvoisin, Roger. *Crocus*. New York: Knopf, 1977. (Farms)

Duvoisin, Roger. *Petunia*. New York: Knopf, 1950. (Ducks & Geese, Farms)

Duvoisin, Roger. *Petunia's Christmas*. New York: Knopf, 1952. (Christmas)

Ehlert, Lois. *Eating the Alphabet: Fruits and Vegetable from A to Z.* San Diego: Harcourt Brace Jovanovich, 1989. (Alphabet Books)

Ehlert, Lois. *Planting a Rainbow.* San Diego: Harcourt Brace Jovanovich, 1988. (Gardening)

Emberly, Ed. *The Wing on a Flea: A Book About Shapes.* Boston: Little, Brown & Co., 1961. (Colour & Art)

Eyvindson, Peter. *Kyle's Bath.* Ills. by Wendy Wolsak. Winnipeg, MB: Pemmican Publications, 1988, c1984. (Bathtime)

Eyvindson, Peter. *Old Enough.* Ills. by Wendy Wolsak. Winnipeg, MB: Pemmican, 1986. (Father's Day)

Farmer, Patti. *I Can't Sleep.* Ills. by Ron Lightburn. Victoria, BC: Orca, 1992. (Bedtime)

Feldman, Judy. *The Alphabet in Nature.* Chicago: Childrens Press, 1991. (Alphabet Books)

Florian, Douglas. *A Winter Day.* New York: Greenwillow Books, 1987. (Seasons – Winter)

Fowler, Susi Gregg. *I'll See You When the Moon Is Full.* New York: Greenwillow, 1994. (Father's Day)

Friedrich, Priscilla. *The Easter Bunny That Overslept.* Ills. by Adrienne Adams. New York: Lothrop, Lee & Shepard, 1983, c1957. (Easter)

Galbraith, Kathryn O. *Laura Charlotte.* Ills. by Floyd Cooper. New York: Philomel, 1990. (Toys)

Galdone, Paul. *The Amazing Pig.* New York: Houghton Mifflin/Clarion Books, 1981. (Pigs)

Galdone, Paul. *Puss in Boots.* New York: Seabury Press, 1976. (Cats)

Gay, Marie Louise. *Angel and the Polar Bear.* Don Mills, ON: Stoddart, 1988. (Bears)

George, William T. *Beaver at Long Pond.* New York: Greenwillow, 1988. (Animals of the Wild)

Gibbons, Gail. *The Seasons of Arnold's Apple Tree.* San Diego: Harcourt Brace Jovanovich, 1984. (Seasons – Fall)

Gilman, Phoebe. *The Balloon Tree.* Richmond Hill, ON: North Winds Press, 1984. (Royalty)

Gilman, Phoebe. *Grandma and the Pirates.* Richmond Hill, ON: Northwinds Press, 1990. (Sea & Seashore)

Gilman, Phoebe. *The Wonderful Pigs of Jillian Jiggs.* Richmond Hill, ON: North Winds Press, 1988. (Pigs)

Ginsburg, Mirra. *The Sun's Asleep Behind the Hill.* Ills. by Paul O. Zelinsky. New York: Greenwillow, 1982. (Bedtime)

Gray, Libba Moore. *Miss Tizzy.* Ills. by Jada Rowland. New York: Simon & Schuster, 1993. (Friends, Sickness & Health)

Greeley, Valerie. *White Is the Moon.* New York: Macmillan, 1991. (Colour & Art)

Greene, Carol. *The Thirteen Days of Halloween.* Chicago: Childrens Press, 1983. (Halloween)

Grifalconi, Ann. *The Village of Round and Square Houses.* Boston: Little, Brown, 1986. (Houses)

Grimm Brothers. *The Bremen Town Musicians.* Ills. by Hans Wilhelm. New York: Scholastic, 1992. (Music)

Grindley, Sally. *Shhh! Lift the Flaps But Don't Wake Up the Giant!* Ills. by Peter Utton. Boston: Joy Street Books, 1992. (Giants)

Hale, Trina. *Brown Bear in a Brown Chair.* New York: Atheneum, 1983. (Bears, Clothing)

Harpur, Tom. *The Terrible Fin MacCoul.* Ills. by Linda Hendry. Toronto: Oxford University Press, 1990. (Giants)

Harrison, Ted. *A Northern Alphabet.* Montreal: Tundra Books, 1982. (Alphabet Books)

Hasler, Eveline. *Winter Magic.* Ills. by Michele Lemieux. New York: Wm. Morrow, 1984. (Seasons – Winter)

Heine, Helme. *Friends.* New York: Atheneum, 1983. (Friends)

Hellen, Nancy. *The Bus Stop.* New York: Orchard, 1988. (Transportation)

Henkes, Kevin. *Bailey Goes Camping.* New York: Greenwillow Books, 1985. (Seasons – Summer)

Henkes, Kevin. *Chester's Way.* New York: Greenwillow Books, 1988. (Friends)

Henkes, Kevin. *Chrysanthemum.* New York: Greenwillow Books, 1991. (School)

Henkes, Kevin. *Jessica.* New York: Greenwillow Books, 1989. (Friends, Mice)

Henkes, Kevin. *Julius, the Baby of the World.* New York: Greenwillow Books, 1990. (Babies, Mice)

Henkes, Kevin. *Sheila Rae, the Brave.* New York: Greenwillow Books, 1987. (Families)

Hoban, Julia. *Amy Loves the Sun.* Ills. by Lillian Hoban. New York: Harper & Row, 1988. (Seasons – Summer)

Hoban, Lillian. *Bread and Jam for Frances.* Ills. by Lillian Hoban. New York: Harper & Row, 1964. (Food)

Hoban, Russell. *A Baby Sister for Frances.* Ills. by Lillian Hoban. New York: Harper Collins, 1992. (Families)

Hoban, Russell. *A Birthday for Frances.* Ills. by Lillian Hoban. New York: Harper & Row, 1968. (Birthdays)

Hoban, Russell. *Bedtime for Frances.* Ills. by Garth Williams. New York: Harper, 1960. (Bedtime)

Hoban, Russell. *Best Friends for Frances.* Ills. by Lillian Hoban. New York: Harper & Row, 1969. (Friends)

Hoffstrand, Mary. *By the Sea.* New York: Atheneum, 1989. (Sea & Seashore)

Hogan, Paula. *The Life Cycle of the Oak Tree*. Milwaukee: Raintree Childrens Books, 1979. (Seasons – Fall)

Hughes, Shirley. *Alfie Gets in First*. New York: Lothrop, Lee & Shepard, 1981. (Houses)

Hughes, Shirley. *Alfie Gives a Hand*. New York: Lothrop, Lee & Shepard, 1983. (Birthdays)

Hughes, Shirley. *Alfie's Feet*. New York: Lothrop, Lee & Shepard, 1982. (Clothing)

Hughes, Shirley. *Colours*. Vancouver, BC: Douglas & McIntyre, 1986. (Colour & Art)

Hughes, Shirley. *David and Dog*. New York: Lothrop, Lee & Shepard, 1988. (Dogs, Friends, Pets)

Hughes, Shirley. *Lucy & Tom's 1 2 3*. Vancouver, BC: Douglas & McIntyre, 1987. (Counting)

Hughes, Shirley. *Lucy & Tom's ABC*. New York: Viking Kestrel, 1986, c1984. (Alphabet Books)

Hughes, Shirley. *Lucy & Tom at the Seaside*. London: Gollancz, 1982, c1976. (Sea & Seashore)

Hughes, Shirley. *Lucy & Tom Go to School*. London: Gollancz, 1991. (School)

Hughes, Shirley. *Lucy & Tom's Christmas*. London: Gollancz, 1981. (Christmas)

Hughes, Shirley. *The Snow Lady*. Vancoucer, BC: Douglas & McIntyre, 1990. (Weather – Snowy Day)

Hundal, Nancy. *November Boots*. Ills. by Marilyn Mets. Toronto: Harper Collins, 1993. (Clothing, Seasons – Fall, Weather – Rainy Day)

Hutchins, Hazel. *Norman's Snowball*. Ills. by Ruth Ohi. Willowdale, ON: Annick Press, 1989. (Seasons – Winter)

Hutchins, Pat. *Rosie's Walk*. New York: Macmillan, 1968. (Farms, Foxes & Wolves)

Hutchins, Pat. *The Silver Christmas Tree*. New York: Macmillan, 1974. (Christmas)

Hyman, Trina Schart. *Little Red Riding Hood*. New York: Holiday House, 1983. (Foxes & Wolves, Safety)

Isadora, Rachel. *At the Crossroads*. New York: Greenwillow, 1991. (Father's Day)

Jackson, Ellen B. *The Bear in the Bathtub*. Ills. by Margot Apple. Reading, MA: Addison-Wesley, 1981. (Bathtime)

Johnston, Tony. *The Soup Bone*. Ills. by Margot Tomes. San Diego: Harcourt Brace Jovanovich, 1990. (Halloween)

Johnston, Tony. *The Witch's Hat*. Ills. by Margot Tomes. New York: Putnam, 1984. (Halloween)

Joosse, Barbara M. *Mama, Do You Love Me?* Ills. by Barbara Lavallee. San Francisco, CA: Chronicle Books, 1991. (Mother's Day)

Keats, Ezra Jack. *The Little Drummer Boy*. New York: Collier-Macmillan, 1968. (Christmas)

Keller, Holly. *Ten Sleepy Sheep*. New York: Greenwillow, 1983. (Sheep)

Kesselman, Wendy. *Emma*. Ills. by Barbara Cooney. New York: Dell, 1993, c1980. (Colour & Art)

Khalsa, Dayal Kaur. *Cowboy Dreams*. Montreal: Tundra Books, 1990. (Farms)

Khalsa, Dayal Kaur. *How Pizza Came to Our Town*. Montreal: Tundra Books, 1989. (Food)

Khalsa, Dayal Kaur. *I Want a Dog*. Montreal: Tundra Books, 1987. (Dogs, Pets)

Khalsa, Dayal Kaur. *Julian*. Montreal: Tundra Books, 1989. (Dogs)

Khalsa, Dayal Kaur. *My Family Vacation*. Montreal: Tundra Books, 1988. (Families, Seasons – Summer, Transportation)

Khalsa, Dayal Kaur. *Sleepers*. Montreal: Tundra Books, 1988. (Bedtime)

Khalsa, Dayal Kaur. *Tales of a Gambling Grandma*. Montreal: Tundra Books, 1986. (Families)

Khalsa, Dayal Kaur. *The Snow Cat*. Montreal: Tundra Books, 1992. (Weather – Snowy Day)

Kimmel, Eric. *Anansi and the Moss-Covered Rock*. Ills. by Janet Stevens. New York: Holiday House, 1988. (Insects)

Kimmel, Eric. *Anansi Goes Fishing*. Ills. by Janet Stevens. New York: Holiday House, 1991. (Insects)

Kipling, Rudyard. *The Elephant's Child*. Ills. by Arlette Lavie. Swindon, England: Child's Play, 1986. (Elephants)

Konigsburg, E.L. *Samuel Todd's Book of Great Colours*. New York: Atheneum, 1990. (Colour & Art)

Krauss, Ruth. *The Carrot Seed*. Ills. by Crockett Johnson. New York: Harper & Row, 1945. (Gardening, Teeny Tiny Things)

Kusugak, Michael. *Baseball Bats for Christmas*. Ills. by Vladyana Krykorka. Toronto, ON: Annick Press, 1990. (Seasons – Winter)

Langner, Nola. *Rafiki*. New York: Viking, 1977. (Houses)

Lavut, Karen. *Jacques' Jungle Ballet*. Ills. by Nicola Rigg. New York: H. Holt, 1989. (Elephants)

Lawson, Julie. *A Morning to Polish and Keep*. Ills. by Sheena Lott. Red Deer, AB: Red Deer College Press, 1992. (Sea & Seashore)

Lawson, Julie. *Kate's Castle*. Ills. by Frances Tyrrell. Toronto: Oxford University Press, 1992. (Sea & Seashore)

Lewis, Kim. *Emma's Lamb*. London: Walker Books, 1991. (Sheep)

Lindenbaum, Pija. *Else-Marie and her Seven Little Daddies*. Vancouver, Toronto: Douglas & McIntyre, 1991. (Father's Day)

Lobel, Arnold. *Frog and Toad All Year*. New York: Harper & Row, 1976. (Frogs)

Lobel, Arnold. *Frog and Toad Are Friends.* New York: Harper Collins, 1970. (Friends)

Lobel, Arnold. *Mouse Tales.* New York: Harper & Row, 1972. (Mice)

Lobel, Arnold. *On Market Street.* Ills. by Anita Lobel. New York: Greenwillow Books, 1981. (Alphabet Books)

Lobel, Arnold. *Uncle Elephant.* New York: Harper & Row, 1981. (Elephants)

Loewen, Iris. *My Kokum Called Today.* Ills. by Gloria Miller. Winnipeg, MB: Pemmican, 1993. (Families)

Lord, John. *Mr. Mead and His Garden.* London: J. Cape, 1974. (Gardening)

Maestro, Betsy. *Ferryboat.* New York: Crowell, 1986. (Transportation)

Mahy, Margaret. *17 Kings and 42 Elephants.* Ills. by Patricia MacCarthy. New York: Dial Books for Young Readers, 1987. (Elephants)

Mahy, Margaret. *The Great White Man-Eating Shark.* Ills. by Jonathan Allen. New York: Dial Books for Young Readers, 1990. (Sea & Seashore)

Marshall, James. *George and Martha.* Boston: Houghton Mifflin, 1972. (Friends)

Martin, Bill. *Listen to the Rain.* Ills. by James Endicott. New York: H. Holt, 1988. (Weather – Rainy Day)

McCloskey, Robert. *Blueberries for Sal.* New York: Viking Press, 1948. (Bears, Mother's Day, Seasons – Summer)

McCloskey, Robert. *Make Way for Ducklings.* New York: The Viking press, 1941. (Ducks & Geese)

McCully, Emily Arnold. *The Christmas Gift.* New York: Harper & Row, 1988. (Christmas)

McCully, Emily Arnold. *First Snow.* New York: Harper & Row, 1985. (Weather – Snowy Day)

McCully, Emily Arnold. *Mirette on the High Wire.* New York: G.P. Putnam's Sons, 1992. (Circus)

McCully, Emily Arnold. *The New Baby.* New York: Harper & Row, 1988. (Babies, Families, Mice)

McCully, Emily Arnold. *Picnic.* New York: Harper & Row, 1984. (Families, Food, Mice, Sea & Seashore, Seasons – Summer)

McCully, Emily Arnold. *School.* New York: Harper Row, 1987. (School)

McCully, Emily Arnold. *Speak Up, Blanche!* New York: HarperCollins, 1991. (Colour & Art)

McDermott, Gerald. *Anansi the Spider.* New York: Holt, Rinehart and Winston 1972. (Insects)

McFarlane, Sheryl. *Jessie's Island.* Ills. by Sheena Lott. Victoria, BC: Orca Book Publishers, 1992. (Sea & Seashore)

McFarlane, Sheryl. *Waiting for the Whales.* Ills. by Ron Lightburn. Victoria, BC: Orca Book Publishers, 1991. (Sea & Seashore)

McKissack, Patricia. *Flossie and the Fox.* Ills. by Rachel Isadora. New York: Dial, 1986. (Foxes & Wolves)

McPhail, David. *Farm Morning.* San Diego: Harcourt Brace Jovanovich, 1985. (Father's Day)

McPhail, David. *Fix-it.* New York: E.P. Dutton, 1984. (Toys)

Melmed, Laura Krauss. *I Love You As Much.* Ills. by Henri Sorensen. New York: Lothrop, 1993. (Mother's Day)

Minarik, Else. *It's Spring.* Ills. by Margaret Bloy Graham. New York: Greenwillow Books, 1989. (Seasons – Spring)

Minarik, Else. *A Kiss for Little Bear.* Ills. by Maurice Sendak. New York: Harper & Row, 1968. (Valentine's Day)

Minarik, Else. "Birthday Soup" in *Little Bear.* Ills. by Maurice Sendak. New York: Harper, 1957. (Birthdays)

Minarik, Else . "What Will Little Bear Wear?" in *Little Bear.* Ills. by Maurice Sendak. New York: Harper & Row, 1957. (Weather – Snowy Day)

Morgan, Allen. *Nicole's Boat.* Ills. by Jirina Marton. Toronto: Annick Press, 1986. (Bedtime)

Munsch, Robert & Michael Kusugak. *A Promise Is a Promise.* Ills. by Vladyana Krykorka. Toronto: Annick Press, 1988. (Monsters, Seasons – Winter)

Murdoch, Patricia. *Deep Thinker and the Stars.* Ills. by Kellie Jobson. Toronto: Three Trees Press, 1987. (Babies)

Noble, Trinka Hakes. *The Day Jimmy's Boa Ate the Wash.* Ills. by Steven Kellogg. New York: Dial, 1980. (Snakes, Turtles & Lizards)

Oppenheim, Joanne. *The Story Book Prince.* Ills. by Rosanne Litzinger. San Diego: Harcourt Brace Jovanovich, 1987. (Bedtime)

Orbach, Ruth. *Apple Pigs.* New York: Philomel, 1976. (Seasons – Fall)

Ormerod, Jan. *101 Things to Do with a Baby.* New York: Lothrop, Lee & Shepard, 1984. (Babies)

Ormerod, Jan. *Moonlight.* New York: Lothrop, Lee & Shepard Books, 1982. (Bathtime, Bedtime, Father's Day)

Ormerod, Jan. *Sunshine.* New York: Lothrop, Lee & Shepard, 1982. (Families)

Oxenbury, Helen. *The Car Trip.* New York: Dial Books for Young Readers, 1983. (Seasons – Summer)

Oxenbury, Helen. *The Shopping Trip.* New York: Dial Books for Young Readers, 1982. (Shopping)

Oxenbury, Helen. *Tom and Pippo Go for a Walk* (and other Pippo titles). New York: Aladdin Books, 1988. (Monkeys)

Pearson, Tracey Campbell. *Old MacDonald Had a Farm*. New York: Dial Books for Young Readers, 1984. (Farms)

Peet, Bill. *Randy's Dandy Lions*. Boston: Houghton Mifflin, 1964. (Circus)

Peppe, Rodney. *Circus Numbers*. New York: Delacorte Press, 1986. (Circus)

Perkins, Al. *Hand, Hand, Fingers, Thumb*. Ills. by Eric Gurney. New York: Random House, 1969. (Monkeys)

Potter, Beatrix. *The Tale of Little Pig Robinson*. London: F. Warne, 1987. (Pigs)

Potter, Beatrix. *The Tale of Mrs. Tittlemouse*. London: F. Warne, 19—. (Mice)

Potter, Beatrix. *The Tale of Peter Rabbit*. London: F. Warne, 1987. (Rabbits)

Potter, Beatrix. *The Tale of Pigling Bland*. London: F. Warne, 19—. (Pigs)

Potter, Beatrix. *The Tale of Tom Kitten*. New York : F. Warne, 19—. (Cats)

Potter, Beatrix. *The Tale of Two Bad Mice*. London: F. Warne, 1987, c1904. (Mice)

Poulet, Virginia. *Blue Bug's Safety Book*. Chicago: Chicago Press, 1973. (Safety)

Poulin, Stephan. *Can You Catch Josephine?* Montreal: Tundra Books, 1987. (Cats)

Pratt, Pierre. *Follow That Hat*. Willowdale, ON: Annick Press, 1992. (Weather – Windy Day)

Price, Matthew. *The Christmas Stockings*. Ills. by Errol Le Cain. New York: Barron's, 1987. (Christmas)

Priceman, Marjorie. *Friend or Frog*. Boston: Houghton Mifflin, 1989. (Frogs)

Provensen, Alice. *Our Animal Friends on Maple Hill Farm*. New York: Random House, 1974. (Farms)

Provensen, Alice. *The Year at Maple Hill Farm*. New York: Random House, 1978. (Farms, Seasons – Fall)

Quinlan, Patricia. *My Dad Takes Care of Me*. Ills. by Vlasta van Kampen. Toronto: Annick Press, 1987. (Father's Day)

Rey, H. A. *Curious George*. Boston: Houghton Mifflin, 1941. (Monkeys)

Rey, H. A. *Curious George Goes to the Hospital*. Boston: Houghton Mifflin, 1966. (Sickness & Health)

Rey, H. A. *Curious George Learns the Alphabet*. Boston: Houghton Mifflin, 1963. (Alphabet Books)

Rey, H. A. *Curious George Rides a Bike*. Boston: Houghton Mifflin, 1952. (Circus, Safety)

Rey, Margaret. *Curious George Flies a Kite*. Ills. by H. A. Rey. Boston: Houghton Mifflin, 1958. (Toys)

Reynolds, Marilynn. *Belle's Journey*. Ills. by Stephen McCallum. Victoria, BC: Orca Book Publishers, 1993. (Farms)

Riley, James Whitcomb. *The Gobble-Uns 'll Git You Ef You Don't Watch Out!* Ills. by Joel Schick. Philadelphia: Lippincott, 1975. (Halloween)

Rockwell, Anne. *Apples and Pumpkins*. Ills. by Lizzy Rockwell. New York: Macmillan, 1989. (Halloween, Seasons – Fall)

Rockwell, Anne. *First Comes Spring*. New York: T.Y. Crowell, 1985. (Seasons – Spring)

Rockwell, Anne. "The Gingerbread Man" in *The Three Bears & Other Stories*. New York: T.Y. Crowell, 1975. (Foxes & Wolves)

Ross, Dave. *Little Mouse's Valentine*. New York: W. Morrow, 1986. (Valentine's Day)

Rylant, Cynthia. *Henry and Mudge* (readers series). New York: Bradbury Press, 1987. (Dogs)

Rylant, Cynthia. *This Year's Garden*. Scarsdale, NY: Bradbury Press, 1984. (Gardening, Seasons – Spring)

Salus, Naomi Panush. *My Daddy's Mustache*. Ills. by Tomie de Paola. Garden City, NY: Doubleday, 1979. (Father's Day)

Sanderson, Esther. *Two Pairs of Shoes*. Ills. by David Beyer. Winnipeg, MB: Pemmican, 1990. (Clothing)

Sattler, Helen Roney. *Train Whistles*. Ills. by Tom Funk. New York: Lothrop, Lee & Shepard Co., 1977. (Transportation)

Scheffter, Unsel. *A Walk in the Rain*. Ills. by Ulises Wensell. New York: Putnam's, 1986. (Weather – Rainy Day)

Shulevitz, Uri . *Rain Rain Rivers*, New York: Farrar, Straus and Girous, 1969. (Weather – Rainy Day)

Schwartz, Amy. *Annabelle Swift, Kindergartner*. New York: Orchard Books, 1988. (School)

Scieszka, Jon. *The True Story of the Three Little Pigs*. Ills. by Lane Smith. New York: Viking Kestrel, 1989. (Foxes & Wolves, Pigs)

Sendak, Maurice. *Chicken Soup with Rice*. New York: Harper & Row, 1962. (Food, Seasons – Spring)

Sendak, Maurice. *One Was Johnny*. New York: Harper & Row, 1962. (Counting)

Sendak, Maurice. *Pierre*. New York: Harper & Row, 1962. (Cats, Emotions, Families)

Seuss, Dr. *Dr. Seuss's ABC*. New York: Beginner Books, 1963. (Alphabet Books)

Seuss, Dr. *Green Eggs and Ham*. New York: Random House, 1960. (Colour & Art, Food))

Seuss, Dr. *Happy Birthday to You!* New York: Random House 1959. (Birthdays)

Seuss, Dr. *How the Grinch Stole Christmas*. New York: Random House 1957. (Christmas)

Seuss, Dr. *If I Ran the Zoo*. New York: Random House 1978. (Zoos)

Seuss, Dr. *Yertle the Turtle and Other Stories*. New York: Random House, 1958. (Snakes, Turtles & Lizards)

Sharmat, Marjorie. *The Best Valentine in the World.* Ills. by Lilian Obligado. New York: Holiday House, 1982. (Valentine's Day)

Sheldon, Dyan. *The Whale's Song.* Ills. by Gary Blyth. New York: Dial Books for Young Readers, 1991. (Sea & Seashore)

Siebert, Diane. *Train Song.* Ills. by Mike Wimmer. New York: T.Y. Crowell, 1990. (Transportation)

Smith, Lane. *The Big Pets.* New York: Viking, 1991. (Pets)

Spier, Peter. *The Fox Went Out on a Chilly Night.* Garden City, NY: Doubleday, 1961. (Foxes & Wolves)

Spier, Peter. *London Bridge Is Falling Down.* Garden City, NY: Doubleday, 1967. (Houses)

Spier, Peter. *Peter Spier's Rain.* Garden City, NY: Doubleday, 1982. (Weather – Rainy Day)

Steig, William. *The Amazing Bone.* New York: Farrar, Straus & Giroux, 1976. (Foxes & Wolves, Pigs)

Steig, William. *Amos and Boris.* New York: Farrar, Straus, Giroux, 1971. (Sea & Seashore)

Steig, William. *Brave Irene.* New York: Farrar, Straus, Giroux, 1986. (Mother's Day, Weather – Windy Day, Weather – Snowy Day)

Steig, William. *Caleb and Kate.* New York: Farrar, Straus & Giroux, 1977. (Valentine's Day)

Steig, William. *Doctor De Soto.* New York: Farrar, Straus & Giroux, 1982. (Foxes & Wolves, Mice, Sickness & Health)

Steig, William. *Doctor De Soto Goes to Africa.* New York: Harper Collins, 1992. (Elephants, Sickness & Health)

Steig, William. *Farmer Palmer's Wagon Ride.* New York: Farrar, Straus, Giroux, 1974. (Farms)

Steig, William. *Roland, the Minstrel Pig.* New York: Harper Collins, 1968. (Music)

Steig, William. *Sylvester and the Magic Pebble* New York: Simon and Schuster, 1969. (Birthdays, Families)

Steig, William. *Tiffky Doofky.* New York: Farrar, Straus & Giroux, 1978. (Dogs, Valentine's Day)

Steig, William. *Zeke Pippin.* New York: HarperCollins, 1994. (Music)

Stevenson, James. *Happy Valentine's Day, Emma!.* New York: Greenwillow Books, 1987. (Valentine's Day)

Stock, Catherine. *Thanksgiving Treat.* New York: Bradbury Press, 1990. (Thanksgiving)

Stren, Patti. *Hug Me.* New York: Harper & Row, 1977. (Friends, Valentine's Day)

Sueyoshi, A. *Ladybird on a Bicycle.* Ills. by Viv Allbright. London: Faber and Faber, 1983. (Insects)

Taylor, Jane. *Twinkle, Twinkle, Little Star.* Ills. by Julia Noonan. New York: Cartwheel Books, 1992. (Christmas)

Tejima, Keizaburo. *The Bears' Autumn.* La Jolla, CA: Green Tiger Press, 1986. (Seasons – Fall)

Thaler, Mike. *The Clown's Smile.* Ills. by Tracey Cameron. New York: Harper & Row, 1986, c1962. (Circus)

This Old Man. Ills. by Carol Jones. Boston: Houghton Mifflin, 1990. (Father's Day)

Thornhill, Jan. *The Wildlife ABC.* Toronto: Greey de Pencier Books, 1988. (Alphabet Books)

Tibo, Giles. *Simon and the Wind.* Montreal: Tundra Books, 1989. (Weather – Windy Day)

Tibo, Giles. *Simon in Summer.* Montreal: Tundra, 1991. (Seasons – Summer)

Tibo, Giles. *Simon Welcomes Spring.* Montreal: Tundra, 1990. (Seasons – Spring)

Tolhurt, Marilyn. *Somebody and the Three Blairs.* New York: Orchard Books, 1991. (Bears)

Tresselt, Alvin. *Autumn Harvest.* Ills. by Roger Duvoisin. New York: Lothrop, Lee & Shepard, 1951. (Thanksgiving)

Tresselt, Alvin. *Rain Drop Splash.* Ills. by Leonard Weisgard. New York: Lothrop, Lee & Shepard, 1946. (Weather – Rainy Day)

Tresselt, Alvin. *World in the Candy Egg.* Ills. by Roger Duvoisin. New York: Lothrop, Lee & Shepard, 1967. (Easter)

Trivizas, Eugene. *The Three Little Wolves and the Big Bad Pig.* Ills. by Helen Oxenbury. New York: Margaret K. McElderry Books, 1993. (Foxes & Wolves, Pigs)

Truss, Jan. *Peter's Moccasins.* Ills. by Philip Spink. Edmonton, AB: Reidmore Books, 1987. (Clothing)

Tworkov, Jack. *The Camel Who Took a Walk.* Ills. by Roger Duvoisin. New York: E.P. Dutton, 1951. (Animals of the Wild)

Udry, Janice. *The Moon Jumpers.* Ills. by Maurice Sendak. New York: Harper, 1959. (Bedtime)

Utton, Peter. *The Witch's Hand.* New York: Farrar, Straus & Giroux, 1989. (Halloween)

Van Allsburg, Chris. *Polar Express.* Boston: Houghton Mifflin, 1985. (Christmas)

Van Allsburg, Chris. *Two Bad Ants.* Boston: Houghton Mifflin, 1988. (Insects)

Van Kampen, Vlasta. *Orchestranimals.* Ills. by Irene Eugen. Richmond Hill, ON: North Winds Press, 1989. (Music)

Van Leeuwen, Jean. *Tales of Amanda Pig.* Ills. by Ann Schweninger. New York: Dial Books for Young Readers, 1983. (Pigs)

Van Woerkom, Dorothy. *The Queen Who Couldn't Bake Gingerbread.* Ills. by Paul Galdone. New York: Knopf, 1975. (Royalty)

Vincent, Gabrielle. *Ernest and Celestine .* New York: Greenwillow Books, 1982. (Mice)

Vincent, Gabrielle. *Ernest and Celestine at the Circus.* New York: Greenwillow Books, 1989. (Circus)

Vincent, Gabrielle. *Ernest and Celestine's Picnic.* New York: Greenwillow Books, 1982. (Food)

Vincent, Gabrielle. *Feel Better, Ernest!* New York: Greenwillow Books, 1988. (Sickness & Health)

Vincent, Gabrielle. *Merry Christmas Ernest and Celestine.* New York: Greenwillow Books, 1984. (Christmas)

Waber, Bernard. *Snake: A Very Long Story.* Boston: Houghton Mifflin, 1978. (Snakes, Turtles & Lizards)

Wahl, Jan. *Doctor Rabbit's Foundling.* Ills. by Cyndy Szekeres. New York: Pantheon Books, 1977. (Rabbits)

Wallace, Ian. *Morgan the Magnificent.* Toronto: Groundwood Books, 1987. (Circus)

Wallis, Val. *The Secret in the Matchbox.* Ills. by John Shelley. New York: Farrar, Straus & Giroux, 1988. (Monsters)

Walsh, Ellen Stoll. *Mouse Paint.* San Diego: Harcourt Brace Jovanovich, 1989. (Colour & Art)

Walter, Mildred Pitts. *Ty's One-Man Band.* Ills. by Margot Tomes, New York: Four Winds, 1980. (Music)

Watanabe, Shigeo. *I Can Take a Bath!* Ills. by Yasuo Ohtomo. New York: Philomel Books, 1987. (Bathtime)

Watanabe, Shigeo. *Let's Go Swimming!* Ills. by Yasuo Ohtomo. New York: Philomel Books, 1990. (Bathtime)

Waterton, Betty. *Plain Noodles.* Ills. by Joanne Fitzgerald. Toronto: Groundwood Books, 1989. (Babies, Food)

Watson, Wendy. *Thanksgiving at Our House.* New York: Clarion Books, 1991. (Thanksgiving)

Wells, Rosemary. *Timothy Goes to School.* New York: Dial Press, 1981. (Clothing, School)

Wheeler, Bernelda. *I Can't Have Bannock but the Beaver has a Dam.* Ills. by Herman Bekkering. Winnipeg, MB: Pemmican, 1984. (Animals of the Wild, Food)

Wheeler, Bernelda. *Where Did You Get Your Moccasins?* Ills. by Herman Bekkering. Winnipeg, MB: Pemmican Publications, 1986. (Clothing)

Whitney, Alma. *Just Awful.* Ills. by Lillian Hoban. New York: Harper & Row, 1971. (Sickness & Health)

Wild, Jocelyn. *The Bears' Book of Colours.* London: Heinemann, 1989. (Colour & Art)

Wild, Margaret. *The Very Best of Friends.* Ills. by Julie Vivas. San Diego: Harcourt Brace Jovanovich, 1990. (Cats)

Wilde, Oscar. *The Selfish Giant.* Ills. by Lisbeth Zwerger. Natick, MA: Picture Book Studio: 1984. (Giants)

Wildsmith, Brian. *Brian Wildsmith's Circus.* Oxford: Oxford University Press, 1970. (Circus)

Wildsmith, Brian. *The Little Wood Duck.* London: Oxford University Press, 1972. (Ducks & Geese)

Williams, Barbara. *Albert's Toothache.* Ills. by Kay Chorao. New York: E.P. Dutton, 1974. (Sickness & Health; Snakes, Turtles & Lizards)

Williams, Barbara. *Chester Chipmunk's Thanksgiving.* Ills. by Kay Chorao. New York: E.P. Dutton, 1978. (Thanksgiving)

Williams, Vera. *A Chair for My Mother.* New York: Greenwillow Books, 1982. (Families, Mother's Day, Shopping))

Williams, Vera. *More, More, More, Said the Baby.* New York: Greenwillow Books, 1990. (Babies)

Williams, Vera. *Music, Music for Everyone.* New York: Greenwillow Books, 1984. (Music)

Williams, Vera. *Something Special for Me.* New York: Greenwillow Books, 1983. (Music)

Wiseman, Bernard. *Morris Goes to School.* New York: Harper & Row, 1970. (School)

Wolde , Gunilla Random House. *Betsy and the Chicken Pox.* New York: Random House, 1976. (Sickness & Health)

Wood, Audrey. *Twenty-Four Robbers.* New York: Child's Play, 1990, c1980. (Food)

Wynne-Jones, Tim. *I'll Make You Small.* Ills. by Maryann Kovalski. Toronto: Groundwood Books, 1986. (Giants)

Yashima, Taro. *Umbrella.* New York: Viking Press, 1958. (Weather – Rainy Day)

Yolen, Jane. *No Bath Tonight.* Ills. by Nancy Winslow Parker. New York: T. Y. Crowell, 1978. (Bathtime)

Young, James. *A Million Chameleons.* Boston: Little, Brown, 1990. (Colour & Art)

Zolotow, Charlotte. *But Not Billy.* Ills. by Kay Chorao. New York: Harper & Row, 1983. (Babies)

Zolotow, Charlotte. *Something Is Going to Happen.* Ills. by Catherine Stock. New York: Harper & Row, 1988. (Seasons – Winter, Weather – Snowy Day)

Zolotow, Charlotte. *The Bunny Who Found Easter.* Ills. by Betty Peterson. Berkeley, CA: Parnassus, 1959. (Easter)

Zolotow, Charlotte. *The Storm Book.* Ills. by Margaret Bloy Graham. New York: Harper & Row, 1952. (Weather – Rainy Day)

Zolotow, Charlotte. *William's Doll.* Ills. by William Pene du Bois. New York: Harper & Row, 1972. (Babies, Father's Day, Toys)

NONFICTION

Ahlberg, Janet & Allan. *The Baby's Catalogue.* Boston: Little, Brown, 1982. (Bedtime)

Aliki. *Feelings.* New York: Greenwillow Books, 1984. (Emotions)

Anholt, Laurence. *Going to Nursery School.* Richmond Hill, ON: Scholastic Canada, 1992. (School)

Anno, Mitsumasa. *Anno's Counting House.* New York: Philomel Books, 1982. (Counting)

Anno, Mitsumasa. *Anno's Mysterious Multiplying Jar.* New York: Philomel Books, 1983. (Counting)

Back, Christine. *Chicken and Egg.* London: A. and C. Black, 1984. (Farms)

Back, Christine. *Tadpole and Frog.* London: A. and C. Black, 1984. (Frogs)

Back, Christine. *Spider's Web.* London: A. and C. Black, 1984. (Insects)

Barth, Edna. *Turkeys, Pilgrims, and Indian Corn: The Story of the Thanksgiving Symbols.* New York: Clarion Books, 1975. (Thanksgiving) (adult)

Barton, Byron. *Airport.* New York: T.Y. Crowell, 1982. (Space, Transportation)

Barton, Byron. *Building a House.* New York: Greenwillow Books, 1981. (Houses)

Berger, Melvin. *Germs Make Me Sick.* New York: Crowell, 1985. (Sickness & Health)

Bailey, Jill . *The Life Cycle of a Duck.* Ills. by Jackie Harland. East Sussex: Wayland, 1988. (Ducks & Geese)

Boechler, Gwen. *A Piece of Cake: Fun and Easy Theme Parties for Children.* Toronto: McGraw Hill Ryerson, 1987. (Birthdays) (adult)

Boucher, Helene. *Make-Up Magic.* St-Lambert, Quebec: Heritage, 1989. (Circus)

Brown, Laurene Krasny. *Dinosaurs Alive and Well.* Boston: Little, Brown, 1990. (Safety, Sickness & Health)

Brown, Laurene Krasny. *Dinosaurs Divorce: A Guide for Changing Families.* Ills. by Marc Brown. Boston: Atlantic Monthly, 1986. (Families)

Brown, Laurene Krasny. *Dinosaurs Travel: A Guide for Families.* Boston: Little, Brown & Co., 1988. (Seasons – Summer, Transportation)

Brown, Laurene Krasny. *Visiting the Art Museum.* New York: E.P. Dutton, 1986. (Colour & Art)

Brown, Marc. *Dinosaurs, Beware!* Boston: Little, Brown, 1982. (Safety)

Brown, Marc. *Party Rhymes.* New York: Dutton, 1988. (Birthdays)

Brown, Marc. *Your First Garden Book.* Boston: Little, Brown, 1981. (Gardening)

Burton, Jane. *Foxes.* Richmond Hill, ON: Scholastic, 1992. (Foxes & Wolves)

Burton, Jane. *Kitten.* Richmond Hill, ON: Scholastic, 1992. (Cats, Pets)

Burton, Jane. *Puppy.* Richmond Hill, ON: Scholastic, 1992. (Dogs, Pets)

Buxbaum, Susan Kovaes. *Splash! All About Baths.* Boston: Little, Brown, 1987. (Bathtime)

Byron and His Balloon: An English-Chipewyan Counting Book. By the children of La Loche. Edmonton, AB: Tree Frog Press, 1983. (Counting)

Carle, Eric. *1, 2, 3 to the Zoo: A Counting Book.* London: H. Hamilton, 1987. (Counting, Zoos)

Carrick, Donald. *Milk.* New York: Greenwillow Books, 1985. (Farms)

Cauley, Lorinda Bryan. *Things to Make and Do for Thanksgiving.* New York: Franklin Watts, 1977. (Thanksgiving)

Chad, Dorothy. *Playing on the Playground.* Chicago: Children's Press, 1987. (series) (Safety)

Chad, Dorothy. *When I Cross the Street.* Chicago: Children's Press, 1982. (Safety)

Chorao, Kay. *The Baby's Bedtime Book.* New York: E.P. Dutton, 1984. (Bedtime)

Clayton, Gordon. *Calf.* Richmond Hill, ON: Scholastic, 1993. (Farms)

Clayton, Gordon. *Foal.* Richmond Hill, ON: Scholastic, 1992. (Farms)

Cole, Joanna. *A Frog's Body.* New York: Morrow, 1980. (Frogs)

Cole, Joanna. *Cars and How They Go.* New York: Crowell, 1983. (Transportation)

Cole, Joanna. *How You Were Born.* New York: Morrow, 1984. (Babies)

Cole, Marion. *Things to Make and Do for Easter.* New York: Watts, 1979. (Easter)

Coombs, Ernie, and Shelley Tanaka. *Mr. Dressup's 50 More Things to Make & Do.* Toronto: Stoddart, 1991. (Birthdays) (adult)

Cowcher. *Whistling Thorn.* New York: Scholastic, 1993. (Animals of the Wild)

Crews, Donald. *Carousel.* New York: Greenwillow, 1982. (Transportation)

Crews, Donald. *Flying.* New York: Greenwillow Books, 1986. (Space, Transportation)

Crews, Donald. *Freight Train.* New York: Greenwillow, 1978. (Transportation)

Crews, Donald. *Harbor.* New York: Greenwillow, 1982. (Transportation)

Crews, Donald. *Truck.* New York: Greenwillow, 1980. (Transportation)

De Paola, Tomie. *The Family Christmas Tree Book.* New York: Holiday House, 1980. (Christmas)

De Paola, Tomie. *The Popcorn Book.* New York: Holiday House, 1978. (Food, Halloween)

De Paola, Tomie. *Things to Make and Do for Valentine's Day.* New York: F. Watts, 1976. (Valentine's Day)

Dorros, Arthur. *Ant Cities.* New York: Crowell, 1987. (Insects)

Ehlert, Lois. *Color Farm.* New York: Lippincott, 1990. (Colour & Art)

Ehlert, Lois. *Color Zoo.* New York: Lippincott, 1989. (Colour & Art)

Ehlert, Lois. *Eating the Alphabet: Fruits and Vegetable from A to Z.* San Diego: Harcourt Brace Jovanovich, 1989. (Food)

Ehlert, Lois. *Fish Eyes: A Book You Can Count On.* San Diego: Harcourt Brace Jovanovich, 1990. (Sea & Seashore)

Ernst, Lisa Campbell. *Up to Ten and Down Again.* New York: Lothrop, Lee & Shepard Books, 1986. (Counting)

Face Painting. (by the editors of Klutz Press). Palo Alto, CA: Klutz Press, 1990. (Circus)

Farm Animals. (Eye Openers series) Toronto: Douglas & McIntyre, 1991. (Farms)

Feelings, Muriel. *Moja Means One: A Swahili Counting Book.* New York: Dial Press 1971. (Counting)

Fischer-Nagel, Andreas. *Birth of a Kitten.* London: J.M. Dent, 1982. (Cats)

Fischer-Nagel, Heiderose. *A Look Through a Mouse Hole.* Minneapolis : Carolrhoda Books, 1989. (Mice)

Fischer-Nagel, Heiderose. *A Puppy Is Born.* New York: Putnam, 1985. (Dogs)

Garne, S. T. *One White Sail: A Caribbean Counting Song.* Ills. by Lisa Etre. New York: Green Tiger Press, 1992. (Counting)

Getz, Susanna. *Teddy Bears One to Ten.* New York: Four Winds Press, 1986. (Counting)

Gibbons, Gail. *Christmas Time.* New York: Holiday House, 1982. (Christmas)

Gibbons, Gail. *Clocks and How They Go.* New York: Thomas Y. Crowell, 1979. (Time)

Gibbons, Gail. *Department Store.* New York: Crowell, 1984. (Shopping)

Gibbons, Gail. *Easter.* New York: Holiday House, 1989. (Easter)

Gibbons, Gail. *Farming.* New York: Holiday House, 1988. (Farms)

Gibbons, Gail. *Fill It Up!* New York: T.Y. Crowell, 1985. (Transportation)

Gibbons, Gail. *Fire! Fire!.* New York: Crowell, 1984. (Safety)

Gibbons, Gail. *Flying.* New York: Holiday House, 1986. (Space, Transportation)

Gibbons, Gail. *From Seed to Plant.* New York: Holiday House, 1991. (Gardening)

Gibbons, Gail. *Frogs.* New York: Holiday House, 1993. (Frogs)

Gibbons, Gail. *Halloween.* New York: Holiday House, 1984. (Halloween)

Gibbons, Gail. *How a House Is Built.* New York: Holiday House, 1990. (Houses)

Gibbons, Gail. *Milk Makers.* New York: Macmillan, 1985. (Farms)

Gibbons, Gail. *Monarch Butterfly.* New York: Holiday House, 1989. (Insects)

Gibbons, Gail. *New Road!* New York: T.Y. Crowell, 1983. (Transportation)

Gibbons, Gail. *Spiders.* New York: Holiday House, 1993. (Insects)

Gibbons, Gail. *Surrounded by the Sea: Life on a New England Fishing Island.* Boston: Little, Brown, 1991. (Sea & Seashore)

Gibbons, Gail. *Things to Make and Do for Halloween.* New York: F. Watts, 1976. (Halloween)

Gibbons, Gail. *Things to Make and Do for Your Birthday.* New York: F. Watts, 1978. (Birthdays)

Gibbons, Gail. *Trucks.* New York: Harper Collins, 1981. (Transportation)

Gibbons, Gail. *Valentine's Day.* New York: Holiday House, 1986. (Valentine's Day)

Gibbons, Gail. *Zoo.* New York: T.Y. Crowell, 1987. (Zoos)

Godkin, Celia. *Wolf Island.* Markham, On.: Fitzhenry & Whiteside, 1989. (Animals in the Wild, Foxes & Wolves)

Grosvenor, Donna. *Zoo Babies.* National Geographic Society, 1978. (Zoos)

Hague, Kathleen. *Alphabears: An ABC Book.* New York: Holt, Rinehart, and Winston, 1984. (Bears)

Haldane, Suzanne. *Painting Faces.* New York: Dutton, 1988. (Circus)

Haskins, Kim. *Count Your Way Through Japan.* (and other countries in this series) Minneapolis: Carolrhoda Books, 1987. (Counting)

Heller, Ruth. *Chickens Aren't the Only Ones.* New York: Grosset & Dunlap, 1981. (Birds, Farms)

Heller, Ruth. *The Reason for a Flower.* New York: Grosset & Dunlap, 1983. (Gardening)

Henwood, Chris. *Earthworms As Pets.* (Keeping Minibeasts series) New York: F. Watts, 1988. (Gardening)

Henwood, Chris. *Spiders.* (Keeping Minibeasts series) New York: F. Watts, 1988. (Pets)

Henwood, Chris. *Snails as Pets.* (Keeping Minibeasts series) New York: F. Watts, 1988. (Gardening)

Hirschi, Ron. *Spring.* New York: Cobblehill Books/Dutton, 1990. (Seasons – Spring)

Hirschi, Ron. *What Is a Horse?* New York: Walker, 1989. (Farms)

Hirschi, Ron. *Where Do Horses Live?* New York: Walker, 1989. (Farms)

Hirschi, Ron. *What Is a Bird?* New York: Walker, 1987. (Birds)

Hirschi, Ron. *Where Do Birds Live?* New York: Walker, 1987. (Birds)

Hoban, Tana. *26 Letters and 99 Centre.* New York: Greenwillow Books, 1987. (Alphabet Books, Counting)

Hoban, Tana. *Big Ones, Little Ones.* New York: Greenwillow Books, 1976. (Teeny Tiny Things)

Hoban, Tana. *A Children's Zoo.* New York: Greenwillow Books, 1985. (Animals of the Wild)

Hoban, Tana. *Count and See.* New York: Macmillan, 1972. (Counting)

Hoban, Tana. *I Read Signs.* New York: Greenwillow Books, 1983. (Safety)

Hoban, Tana. *I Read Symbols.* New York: Greenwillow Books, 1983. (Safety)

Hoban, Tana. *Is It Red? Is It Yellow? Is It Blue?.* New York: Greenwillow Books, 1978. (Colour & Art)

Hoffman, Mary. *Bear.* London: Belitha Press in association with Methuen Children's Books, 1986. (Bears)

Hoffman, Mary. *Elephant.* Milwaukee: Raintree Childrens Books, 1984. (Elephants)

Hoffman, Mary. *Zebra.* Milwaukee: Raintree Childrens Books, 1985 (See also Giraffe and Hippo, in *Animals in the Wild* series). (Animals of the Wild)

Hogan, Paula. *The Honeybee.* Milwaukee: Raintree Childrens Books, 1979. (Insects)

Hopkins, Lee Bennet. *Circus! Circus!* New York: Knopf, 1982. (Circus)

Hubbard, Woodleigh. *C Is for Curious: An ABC of Feelings.* San Francisco, CA: Chronicle Books, 1990. (Alphabet Books, Emotions)

Isenbart, Hans-Heinrich. *Baby Animals on the Farm.* New York: Putnam, 1981. (Farms)

Isenbart, Hans-Heinrich. *A Duckling Is Born.* New York: Putnam, 1981. (Ducks & Geese)

Johnson, Odette. *Apples, Alligators and Also Alphabets.* Don Mills, ON: Oxford University Press, 1990. (Alphabet Books)

Jonas, Ann. *Color Dance.* New York: Greenwillow Books, 1989. (Colour & Art)

Kaizuki, Kiyonori. *A Calf Is Born.* New York: Orchard Books, 1990. (Farms)

King, Elizabeth. *The Pumpkin Patch.* New York: Dutton Children's Books, 1990. (Seasons – Fall, Halloween)

Kitchen, Bert. *Animal Alphabet.* New York: Dial Books, 1984. (Alphabet Books)

Kitzinger, Sheila. *Being Born.* Photos by Lennart Nilsson. New York: Grosset & Dunlap, 1986. (Babies)

Krensky, Stephen. *Big Time Bears.* Boston: Little, Brown & Co., 1989. (Time)

Kuchalla, Susan. *All About Seeds.* Ills. by Jane McBee. Mahawah, NJ: Troll Associates, 1982. (Gardening)

Kuklin, Susan. *Going to My Nursery School.* New York: Bradbury Press, 1990. (School)

Kuklin, Susan. *Taking My Cat to the Vet.* New York: Bradbury Press, 1988. (Pets)

Kuklin, Susan. *When I See My Dentist.* New York: Bradbury Press, 1988. (Sickness & Health)

Kuklin, Susan. *When I See My Doctor.* New York: Bradbury Press, 1988. (Sickness & Health)

Larrick, Nancy, comp. *When the Dark Comes Dancing.* Ills. by John Wallner. New York: Philomel Books, 1983. (Bedtime)

Lauber, Patricia. *An Octopus Is Amazing.* Ills. by Holly Keller. New York: Crowell, 1990. (Sea & Seashore)

Leedy, Loreen. *The Dragon Thanksgiving Feast: Things to Make and Do.* New York: Holiday House, 1990. (Thanksgiving)

Lewin, Betsy. *Cat Count.* New York: Dodd, Mead, 1981. (Counting)

Lewis, Richard. *In a Spring Garden.* Ills. by Ezra Jack Keats. New York: Dial, 1965. (Seasons – Spring)

Ling, Bill. *Pig.* Richmond Hill, ON: Scholastic, 1993. (Pigs)

Lobel, Anita. *Alison's Zinnia.* New York: Greenwillow Books, 1990. (Alphabet Books, Gardening)

MacCarthy, Patricia. *Ocean Parade: A Counting Book.* New York: Dial, 1990. (Sea & Seashore)

Machotka, Hana. *What Do You Do at a Petting Zoo?* New York: Morrow Junior Books, 1990. (Farms, Zoos)

Maestro, Betsy. *Big City Port.* Ills. by Giulio Maestro. New York: Four Winds Press, 1983. (Sea & Seashore)

MacDonald, Suse. *Alphabatics.* New York: Bradbury Press, 1986. (Alphabet Books)

McMillan, Bruce. *Growing Colors.* New York: Lothrop, Lee & Shepard Books, 1988. (Colour & Art, Food)

McMillan, Bruce. *Time To . . .* New York: Lothrop, Lee & Shepard Books, 1989. (Time)

Miller, Margaret. *Whose Hat?* New York: Greenwillow Books, 1988. (Clothing)

Miller, Margaret. *Whose Shoes?* New York: Greenwillow, 1991. (Clothing)

Morgan, Nicola. *The Great B.C. Alphabet Book.* Markham, ON: Fitzhenry & Whiteside, 1985. (Alphabet Books)

Morozumi, Atsuko. *One Gorilla: A Counting Book.* New York: Farrar, Straus & Giroux, 1990. (Counting)

Morris, Ann. *Hats, Hats, Hats.* Photos. by Ken Heyman. New York: Lothrop, Lee & Shepard Books, 1989. (Clothing)

Morris, Mary. *Between the Tides.* Vancouver, BC: Pacific Educational Press, 1987. (Sea & Seashore)

My First Look at Time. New York: Random House, 1991. (Time)

Olesen, Jens. *Snail.* Morristown, NJ: Silver Burdett, 1986. (Gardening)

Ormerod, Jan. *When We Went to the Zoo.* New York: Lothrop, Lee & Shepard, 1990. (Zoos)

Oxford Scientific Films. *Bees and Honey.* New York: Putnam, 1977. (Insects)

Oxford Scientific Films. *The Butterfly Cycle.* New York: Putnam, 1977. (Insects)

Oxford Scientific Films. *The Chicken and the Egg.* New York: Putnam, 1979. (Farms)

Oxford Scientific Films. *The Common Frog.* New York: Putnam, 1979. (Frogs)

Oxford Scientific Films. *Dragon Flies.* New York: Putnam, 1980. (Insects)

Oxford Scientific Films. *Harvest Mouse.* New York: Putnam, 1982. (Mice)

Oxford Scientific Films. *House Mouse.* New York: Putnam, 1978. (Mice)

Oxford Scientific Films. *Jellyfish and Other Sea Creatures.* New York: Putnam, 1982. (Sea & Seashore)

Oxford Scientific Films. *Spider's Web.* New York: Putnam, 1978. (Insects)

Oxford Scientific Films. *The Wild Rabbit.* New York: Putnam, 1980. (Rabbits)

Pallotta, Jerry. *The Ocean Alphabet Book.* Chicago: Childrens Press, 1991. (Sea & Seashore)

Parnall, Peter. *Apple Tree.* New York: Macmillan, 1987. (Seasons – Fall, Gardening)

Pets. Toronto: Douglas & McIntyre, 1991. (Pets)

Petty, Kate. *Rabbits.* New York: Gloucester Press, 1989. (See also other titles in the First Pets series) (Pets, Rabbits)

Prelutsky, Jack. *It's Thanksgiving!* New York: Greenwillow, 1982. (Thanksgiving)

Reid, Barbara. *Two by Two.* Richmond Hill, ON: North Winds Press, 1992. (Animals in the Wild)

Reiss, John. *Colors.* Englewood Cliffs, NJ: Bradbury Press, 1969. (Colour & Art)

Robbins, Ken. *Boats.* New York: Scholastic, 1989. (Transportation)

Robbins, Ken. *Tools.* New York: Four Winds Press, 1983. (Houses)

Rockwell, Anne. *Boats.* New York: E.P. Dutton, 1982. (Transportation)

Rockwell, Anne. *Fire Engines.* New York: E.P. Dutton, 1986. (Safety)

Rockwell, Anne. *Planes.* New York: E.P. Dutton, 1985. (Space, Transportation)

Rockwell, Anne. *The Toolbox.* New York: Macmillan, 1971. (Houses)

Rockwell, Anne. *Things That Go.* New York: Dutton, 1986. (Transportation)

Rockwell, Harlow. *My Dentist.* New York: Greenwillow Books, 1975. (Sickness & Health)

Rockwell, Harlow. *My Doctor.* New York: Macmillan, 1973. (Sickness & Health)

Rockwell, Harlow. *My Nursery School.* New York: Greenwillow Books, 1976. (School)

Rogers, Fred. *Going on an Airplane.* New York: Putnam, 1989. (Space, Transportation)

Rogers, Fred. *Going to Daycare.* New York: Putnam, 1985. (School)

Rogers, Fred. *Going to the Dentist.* New York: Putnam, 1989. (Sickness & Health)

Rogers, Fred. *Going to the Doctor.* New York: Putnam, 1986. (Sickness & Health)

Rogers, Fred. *Going to the Hospital.* New York: Putnam, 1988. (Sickness & Health)

Rogers, Fred. *Making Friends.* New York: Putnam, 1987. (Friends)

Rogers, Fred. *Moving.* New York: Putnam, 1987. (Houses)

Rogers, Fred. *The New Baby.* Photos by Jim Judkis. New York: Putnam, 1985. (Babies)

Rogers, Fred. *When a Pet Dies.* New York: Putnam, 1988. (Pets)

Royston, Angela. *Cars.* New York: Aladdin Books, 1991. (Transportation)

Royston, Angela. *Chick.* Richmond Hill, ON: Scholastic, 1991. (Farms)

Royston, Angela. *Diggers and Dump Trucks.* Toronto: Douglas and McIntyre, 1991. (Transportation)

Royston, Angela. *Duck.* Photos by Barrie Watts. Richmond Hill, ON: Scholastic, 1991. (Ducks & Geese)

Royston, Angela. *Frog.* Richmond Hill, ON: Scholastic, 1991. (Frogs)

Royston, Angela. *Lamb.* Photos. by Gordon Clayton. Richmond Hill: Scholastic, 1992. (Sheep)

Royston, Angela. *The Penguin.* New York: Warwick Press, 1979. (Birds)

Royston, Angela. *The Sheep.* New York: Warwick Press, 1990. (Sheep)

Royston, Angela. *Shells.* Toronto : Grolier, c1991. (Sea & Seashore)

Royston, Angela. *Trains.* New York: Aladdin Books, 1991. (Transportation)

Ryden, Hope. *Joey: the Story of a Baby Kangaroo.* New York: Tambourine Books, 1994. (Animals of the Wild)

Schwartz, David. *How Much Is a Million?* Ills. by Steven Kellog. New York: Lothrop, Lee & Shepard Books, 1985. (Counting)

Sheffield, Margaret. *Before You Were Born*. New York: Knopf, 1984. (Babies)

Sobol, Harriet Langsam. *Clowns*. Photos by Patricia Agre. New York: Coward, McCann & Geoghen, 1982. (Circus)

Supraner, Robyn. *Happy Halloween! Things to Make and Do*. Mahwah, NJ: Troll Associates, 1981. (Halloween)

Supraner, Robyn. *Valentine's Day: Things to Make and Do*. Mahwah, NJ: Troll Associates, 1981. (Valentine's Day)

Tafuri, Nancy. *Who's Counting*. New York: Greenwillow Books, 1986. (Counting)

Tanaka, Shelley. *Mr. Dressup's Birthday Party Book*. Vancouver, BC: Douglas & McIntyre, 1988. (Birthdays) (adult)

Taylor, Kim. *Butterfly*. Richmond Hill, ON: Scholastic, 1992. (Insects)

Taylor, Kim. *Owl*. Richmond Hill, ON: Scholastic, 1992. (Birds)

Terry, Trevor. *The Life Cycle of a Butterfly*. New York: Bookwright Press, 1988. (Insects)

Terry, Trevor. *The Life Cycle of an Ant*. Hove, East Sussex: Wayland, 1987. (Insects)

Tester, Sylvia Root. *A Visit to the Zoo*. Chicago: Childrens Press, 1987. (Zoos)

Thompson, Carol. *Time*. New York: Delacorte, 1989. (Time)

Thornhill, Jan. *The Wildlife 123*. Toronto: Greey de Pencier, 1989. (Animals in the Wild, Counting)

Thornhill, Jan. *The Wildlife ABC*. Toronto: Greey de Pencier Books, 1988. (Animals in the Wild)

Trucks. Toronto: Douglas & McIntyre, 1991. (Transportation)

Watts, Barrie. *Butterfly and Caterpillar*. Morristown, NJ: Silver Burdett Co., 1986. (Insects)

Watts, Barrie. *Hamster*. Morristown, NJ: Silver Burdett Co., 1986. (Pets)

Watts, Barrie. *Ladybug*. Morristown, NJ: Silver Burdett Co., 1987. (Insects)

Watts, Barrie. *Mushroom*. Morristown, NJ: Silver Burdett Co., 1986. (Gardening)

Watts, Barrie. *Rabbit*. Richmond Hill, ON: Scholastic, 1991. (Rabbits)

Weihs, Erika. *Count the Cats*. Garden City, NY: Doubleday, 1976. (Cats)

Weiss, Ellen. *Things to Make and Do for Christmas*. New York: Watts, 1980. (Christmas)

West, Robin. *Paper Circus: How to Create You Own Circus*. Minneapolis: Carolrhoda Books, 1983. (Circus)

Wildsmith, Brian. *Brian Wildsmith's 1, 2, 3's*. New York: F. Watts, 1965. (Counting)

Williams, John. *The Life Cycle of a Frog*. New York: Bookwright Press, 1988. (Frogs)

Williams, John. *The Life Cycle of a Rabbit*. New York: Bookwright Press, 1988. (Rabbits)

Windsor, Merrill. *Baby Farm Animals*. Washington, DC: National Geographic Society, 1984. (Farms)

Wormell, Christopher. *An Alphabet of Animals*. New York: Dial Books, 1990. (Alphabet Books)

Wu, Norbert. *Fish Faces*. New York: Henry Holt, 1993. (Sea & Seashore)

Yenawine, Philip. *Colors*. New York: Museum of Modern Art: Delacorte Press, 1991. (Colour & Art)

Yenawine, Philip. *Shapes*. New York: Museum of Modern Art: Delacorte Press, 1991. (Colour & Art)

Yoshida, Toshi. *Elephant Crossing*. New York: Philomel, 1989. (Elephants)

Zoo Animals. Toronto: Douglas & McIntyre, 1991. (Zoos)

First Line Index

to Nursery Rhymes, Fingerplays, & Songs

F

Farmer Brown had five red apples, 110

Fee, fi, fo, fum, 114

Fiddle-dee-dee, 126, 196

First I loosen mud and dirt, 54

Five birthday candles, 36

Five brown teddies sitting on a wall, 24

Five eggs and five eggs, 74, 88

Five fat peas in a pea-pod pressed, 96, 111

Five fat sausages frying in a pan, 96

Five gay valentines from the ten-cent store, 194

Five gray elephants marching through a glade, 78

Five green and speckled frogs, 105

Five little bells hanging in a row, 46

Five little brownies standing in a row, 45

Five Little Chicks, 88

Five little children on Thanksgiving day, 182

Five little ducks went swimming one day, 70

Five little Easter eggs lovely colours wore, 74

Five little farmers, 88

Five little fishes were swimming near the shore, 157

Five little flowers, 109

Five little froggies sitting on a well, 106

Five little ghostesses sitting on postesses, 116

Five little goblins on a Hallowe'en night, 116

Five little jack-o-lanterns sitting on a gate, 116

Five little leprechauns dressed in green, 151

Five little leprechauns knocked at my door, 151

Five little mice came out to play, 128

Five little mice on the pantry floor, 128

Five little monkeys swinging from a tree, 16, 130

Five little monkeys walked along the shore, 132

Five little monkeys jumping on the bed, 62, 130

Five little monsters, 134

Five little piggies had my dad, 142

Five little pigs went out to play, 83, 88, 136, 142

Five little puppies were playing in the sun, 66

Five little puppy dogs sitting by the door, 66

Five little puppy dogs, 66

Five little rabbits under a log, 144

Five little snow men, 206

Five little snowmen happy and gay, 205

Five little snowmen made of snow, 205

Five little valentines were having a race, 194

Flop your arms, flop your feet, 186

Flying-man, Flying-man, 175, 190

Fox went out on a chilly night, 100

Fred had a fish bowl, 157

Frère Jacques, 29

Frog Went A-Courtin, 197

Frosty the Snowman, 206

Fuzzy little caterpillar, 124

Fuzzy wuzzy caterpillar, 125

G

Georgie Porgie, pudding and pie, 194

Go in and out the window, 122

Go round and round the village, 122

Go tell Aunt Rhody, 72

Goodbye, my friends, goodbye, 9

Gonna jump down, turn around, pick a bale of cotton, 111

Good morrow 'tis St. Valentine's Day, 195

Goosey, goosey gander, 69

Gotta shake, shake, shake my sillies out, 10, 80

Gray squirrel, gray squirrel, 16

Gregory Griggs, Gregory Griggs, 52

H

Ha Ha this a-way, 140

Hambone, Hambone, where you been, 187

Hark, hark, the dogs do bark 66

Hat on head, chin strap here, 53, 166

He's got the whole world in His hands, 84

Head and shoulders, 11

Head and shoulders, baby; one, two, three, 12

Hear the steeple clock go tick-tock, tick-tock, 184

Hector Protector was dressed all in green, 52, 58

He'll Be Comin' Down the Chimney, 48

Hello everybody, how d'ya do, 7

Hello, my friends, hello, 7

Here are the lady's knives and forks, 19

Here Comes Santa Claus, 48

Here comes Peter Cottontail, 76

Here is a beehive, 121, 125

Here is a bunny with ears so funny, 143

Here is a nest for a robin, 121

Here is a tree with leaves so green, 110, 164

Here is old Santa, 44

Here is the chimney, 44, 45

Here is the church, 121

Here is the ostrich straight and tall, 33

Here is the sea, the wavy sea, 156

Here sits the Lord Mayor, 148